# DAVE VS. THE MONSTERS

## RESISTANCE

# JOHN BIRMINGHAM

# DAVE vs. THE MONSTERS
## RESISTANCE

**TITAN** BOOKS

Dave vs. the Monsters: Resistance
Print edition ISBN: 9781781166239
E-book edition ISBN: 9781781166246

Published by Titan Books
A division of Titan Publishing Group Ltd
144 Southwark Street, London SE1 0UP

First edition: May 2015
2 4 6 8 10 9 7 5 3 1

A CIP catalogue record for this title is available from the British Library.

Printed and bound by CPI Group (UK) Ltd, Croydon, CR0 4YY

*For my dad, the old lion in winter.*

# PROLOGUE

On a warm evening of the second day of Autumn in the year of our Lord, 2015, Supervising Agent Donald Trinder, of the Office of Special Clearances and Records (OSCAR), went out to catch him a goddamned Russki.

Trinder's Russki was a colonel of the GRU no less; the *Glavnoye Razvedyvatel'noye Upravleniye* or Main Intelligence Directorate of the Russian Federation. Not just an agent, but an in-field controller of deep cover agents and a femme-most-fatale. Trinder insisted on belt and braces, and safety pins all around, to ensure it was not he who ended up pants down and red-faced at the end of the night. He didn't care that the FBI and local law enforcement assets under his control thought him a pompous ass. Neither the feebs nor local law enforcement had found this woman. OSCAR had.

He had.

And now she was his.

Right on the knocker at 1930 hours, nine government fleet vehicles rolled out of the underground car park at 26 Federal Plaza, bearing thirty-three special agents, including twelve heavy hitters from Manhattan's FBI SWAT team, all of them under the temporary authority of the Office of Special

Clearances and Records. Also known more simply as 'The Office', or even just 'Clearance'.

The convoy moved west on Chambers for five blocks, escorted by two police cruisers. By prior arrangement with Metro Transport their progress through the thick, early evening traffic was hastened by staging a pulse of green lights between Federal Plaza and the target address on W27th Street. The two cruisers did not power up their flashers. The long train of heavy black vehicles did draw the attention of some New Yorkers as it passed, some of whom used their phones to take photographs of the convoy, doubtless posting them immediately to Instagram or Twitter, and causing Trinder to wonder for the umpteenth time how anybody in his line of work was expected to get anything done in secret these days.

The soft warmth of the summer just gone still lingered in the evening air, and in the lead vehicle, a black Chevy Tahoe, Supervising Agent Trinder was sweating. He rode up front on the passenger side–the shotgun seat as he liked to call it–with the climate control pushed all the way down to Antarctic, but his bespoke three-button blue suit was a heavy wool blend that he had had tailored at a very reasonable price in Hong Kong. It looked smart, but did not breathe well. The heavy ballistic vest he wore over it did not breathe at all. Every special agent rolling in convoy toward the small art gallery in Chelsea was similarly attired and weighed down by armour. Boss's orders.

The twelve tactical operators riding in two anonymous commercial vans just behind Trinder's Chevy were kitted out in armour, helmets, combat goggles and tactical black. They too looked the part but Trinder still worried about their combat load-out and readiness. They were not the Hostage

Rescue Team (HRT), which he had requested. Twice. They were part-timers. Amateurs, really.

The FBI's New York office, like all regional offices, maintained a tac squad of part-time volunteers. Certainly, they received extra training, MP-5s, M4 carbines and specialised equipment. The very name of the squad–Special Weapons and Tactics–would otherwise be a misnomer. But Agent Trinder worried that his twelve borrowed operators were not quite special enough. OSCAR did not have its own strike team, in spite of Trinder's tireless bureaucratic scheming toward that end. OSCAR was a clearing house, not a barracks, as he had been told so many times. Reassurances from higher up that many of his operators this evening had military backgrounds, some within the United States Special Operations Command (SOCOM) community, did not allay his concerns. They weren't going after a bunch of broken down insurgents in some Afghan slum. This was one of the GRU's top field operatives. This lady had game, probably been to Afghanistan, or worse, Ukraine or Chechnya. She wouldn't just be familiar with the playbook. She'd have authored some of the best chapters.

Supervising Agent Donald Trinder had thus seen fit to remonstrate with the FBI's Assistant Special Agent in Charge Malcolm Preston, the part-time commander of New York's part-time SWAT team, that he was mistaken if he thought this would be some sort of cake run just because the target was a woman and her intention tonight was not to openly subvert the United States of America, but rather to launch an art exhibition. The art, after all, was part of her cover.

And anyway, were you to ask the opinion of Supervising Agent Donald Trinder, when he was off the clock and entitled to a private opinion, he would definitely tell you that as threats to the long-term survival of these United States went, artists and communists (all Russians being commies at heart) were not a thousand miles removed from each other, or Ay-rabs or gay marrieds or that damned Rachel Maddow woman.

As the police cruiser ahead of him swung off Chambers for the quick run up West Street, Trinder could only wish that his request for a full HRT squad had been approved. Or even his request for a couple of backup NYPD SWAT teams in BearCat armoured vehicles. Or a helicopter. Just one lousy helicopter.

It wasn't that he thought they couldn't execute the mission with the assets to hand. It was that he had been thwarted in his wishes and when the mission was done, he would be forced to plan a terrible ass-fucking on everyone who had so thwarted him.

He sighed and shook his head.

There just weren't enough hours in the day to get to everyone he needed to ass-fuck.

Special Agent Rudy Comeau needed to take a piss–badly needed to take a piss. The empty Big Gulp bucket of Fanta on the bare wooden floor of the small room hadn't helped. But maybe it could now. If Special Agent Dee Madigan didn't object to him pulling out his Johnson and relieving himself in front of her. Or even behind, in the corner, perhaps.

Of OSCAR's four stakeout teams on this job, Overwatch Three–Madigan and Comeau–had the prime location. They were comfortably seated on the top floor of a five-storey walk-up on W27th, with a God's eye view of the target address, a couple of surprisingly comfortable 1950s vintage office chairs from which to conduct their surveillance and, blessed be the Great Pumpkin, a thin trickle of sweet, sweet chilled air from a rumbling unit hanging precariously from one of the room's two sash windows. What they didn't have was a toilet. That was down on the next floor and with Trinder rolling on them Comeau didn't want to abandon his post just to take a leak.

Well, he did, but he wasn't going to, because that puckered asshole seemed to have eyes everywhere.

Rudy Comeau frowned. That hadn't come out right.

'What's up?' asked Madigan. Like him, she had decided to hazard the wrath of Trinder by removing her jacket to enjoy just a little bit more of the cool air leaking out of the old, groaning ventilator. Unlike him she wasn't full of fizzy orange soda. Special Agent Madigan kept her eyes on the prize, training a small pair of Zeiss binoculars on the entrance to the renovated warehouse across the street. Already 143 guests (she had counted them) had been ushered along the small red carpet by two dark-suited attendants.

'Four more,' she announced, without taking the binoculars from her eyes. 'You get that, Rudy? You sound like you're doing a riverdance back there.'

'I'm gonna be pissing a river in a minute,' he muttered.

'Oh for fuck's sake. I told you not to drink so much. Just go in the goddamn cup, will you. You got another ten minutes before Trinder turns up. Go on. Doesn't bother me. I got five brothers, you know. Grew up in a goddamn sausage factory.'

'Thanks, Dee,' he said, with relief. It was funny how you could hang on and on and on when you had to, but as soon as you were offered the prospect of deliverance it was like the floodgates had to open right the fuck then. He grabbed the oversized soda cup and hurried into the farthest corner to relieve himself, groaning with the pleasure of release as he let go.

'Holy shit, Rudy,' said Madigan. 'It sounds like you're hosing a kettle drum with a fucking firehose back there. Keep it down, would you?'

'Sorry,' he said even though he wasn't. But he did direct the stream down the deep, steep side of the Big Gulp container. That set up a whirlpool effect that he couldn't help but find a little bit fascinating.

'What's happening now?' he asked to draw attention away from his bathroom visit. 'Any sign of the target?'

'Clocked her twice through the windows on the second floor, workin' the room. She's really good. I don't know whether she takes her cover super serious, or whether she actually needs a second gig because the GRU pays like shit... Overwatch Three,' she confirmed, reaching up to thumb the button on her headset. 'Another four entrants, two Caucasian female, one Asian female, one African-American female. I make that 147 civilians. Over.'

Shosanna Nguyen was getting nervous. She had been a special agent of the Office of Special Clearances and Records for only two months and she didn't feel very special at all. Two months and one week ago she had been a brand spanking new agent trainee at OSCAR's small Boston campus. Truth be known, she still thought of herself as being on probation. They could put you in the field and they could call you special but nobody would believe it until you had proven yourself. Special Agent Shosanna Nguyen had been perfectly content with the idea of putting her hard-working ass to the grindstone for however many years it would take to prove to her more experienced colleagues that they could depend on her.

But all that went out the window the moment Donald Trinder laid eyes on her.

Oh, it wasn't like that. Trinder was a legendary asshole, but not in some busy-handed creepy uncle kind of way. No, the moment he'd seen her hurrying through the New York offices, carrying two fat folders full of complaints about hate speech on Facebook that absolutely nobody wanted to deal with, he had reached down from on high and plucked her from the obscurity of noob status to raise her to the exalted realms of Special Clearances.

Why? Because she was Blasian, the daughter of an African-American father and a Vietnamese mother, blessed with just the right mix of 'exotic' looks that Supervising Agent Donald Trinder deemed critical to 'infiltrate the target function' on the Varatchevsky case. Translation? Trinder thought a little Blasian girl would slip in sideways to an art gallery opening where a big dumb white bastard, like Donald Trinder for instance, would 'stand out like dogs' balls'.

'Although you might want to think about getting yourself a face tattoo,' he suggested. 'Just a temporary one. Your arty crowd, they go in for that sort of thing.'

And here she was, Special Agent Nguyen, way out of her depth, rocking a black leather pant suit and Maori design henna tattoo that obscured half of her face, trying not to be too obvious about not drinking the champagne she'd been nursing for twenty-five minutes, and trying even harder not to keep hitting up the waiter with the shrimp cocktails. Because they were delish, and she'd look mighty funny trying to waddle at high speed after an escaping Russian spy if this all went wrong.

She mingled with the crowd, avoided being drawn into

conversation with anyone, kept her distance from the target, and tried not to be too obvious about what she was doing. She wasn't there to take this Warat or Varatchevsky chick down. Trinder and her overwatch team leader had been red hot on that point. She was simply there as a pair of eyes to warn of any last-minute problems. She bobbed her head, pretending to listen to music which she could not hear in the Skullcandy earbuds she wore, the cord with an inline mic running down inside her jacket. Occasionally she would talk as if chatting to a friend at the other end of the call, just giving her the goss on the fabulous night she was having in the Big Apple.

'Yeah, it's pretty cool, there's lots of cool people, gotta be about 150 people here now, and man, you should see the security guys, they're as big as houses, they're cool but...'

In this way, keeping up an inane line of chatter, she fed details back to the overwatch team about what was happening inside the gallery, and received occasional terse updates on what was heading toward all of these beautiful, rich, fabulous Manhattanites. And she was not worried about the security guys, such as they were, given that her Glock 27 loaded with Hydra-Shok .40 S&W party favours was snugly tucked away in her Hello Kitty purse.

'Strike team, seven minutes out.'

To this information, she reacted in character.

'That's awesome, bitch.'

It was not hard to track the target. Karen Warat was a striking blonde woman. She would have drawn the eye in any room. But here, at her own event, everywhere that Karen Warat–or Colonel Ekaterina Varatchevsky–went, her presence was signalled by a discernible rise in delighted chatter and the click of phone cameras. Some people were even toting digital SLRs to capture the magic. Thankfully they were not photojournalists, as best Shosanna could tell. Not even freelancers. The reviewers had all been in for a pre-show earlier that afternoon. There were probably a dozen or more bloggers in the crowd, of course, but Trinder was not much fussed about them.

'They can be contained,' he'd said.

Special Agent Nguyen pretended to admire a pair of twelfth century fighting knives from what was now Vietnam. The long, curved daggers looked brutal, and not nearly as decorative as most of the other ancient weapons and armour on display. Keeping Warat on her radar, she glanced briefly at the small card explaining the provenance of the pieces. They had been captured by the forces of Kublai Khan when he invaded the northern reaches of Vietnam and were taken as booty by one of his soldiers, probably a Korean. The knives had disappeared for a few centuries after the collapse of the Mongol empire, before reappearing in a museum collection in the seventeen hundreds. Looted during the Boxer Rebellion, they had fallen into the hands of an American collector, who was showing them tonight as a personal favour to Ms Warat. She was, in addition to being a full-blood white Russian agent of the GRU, a successful dealer specialising in rare weaponry.

Recalling her briefing notes, Special Agent Nguyen could not help but wonder if Varatchevsky's early, and officially curtailed, career as a champion fencer might have had something to do with her obvious fascination for this sort of martial ephemera.

She realised with a start that while she had been wondering about her target's early teenage years, the Russian colonel had slipped out of sight.

And then the screaming started.

# 01

The Chairman's Suite at the Bellagio was a great place for a hangover, or it would be, if Dave had one, which he didn't. And that was just awesome. Sure as hell he'd made a champion effort to get himself a hangover, but despite his best efforts–or maybe his worst–here he was in this expensive hotel suite, on this enormous and bouncy bed, atop this small but even bouncier Saudi princess, while he chugged a super strong Belgian beer and scarfed down a really excellent breakfast burrito. The beer, his fourth, could probably fuel a ride-on lawn mower. But the princess, his first, was a much better ride and a helluva lot more fun than any goddamned lawn mower.

'America! Fuck yeah,' he roared for no particular reason beyond the dizzying joy of being alive, as he bucked away in time to AC/DC's 'Shoot to Thrill'. The music pounded from a massive TV that loomed over them like the screen of a drive-in movie theatre. The Chairman's Suite had two bedrooms, but one had been an early casualty of some super-powered romping. Kneeling on the second bed, the unbroken one in the other bedroom, Dave did his best to take a bit more care.

'I fucking love this show,' he yelled, after swallowing a mouthful of burrito, ordered by the suite's full-time, by now exhausted bartender who was herself a significant hottie and the reason the Bellagio was going to need to do some repairs to the sunken bar. Structural repairs.

'Fuck yeah! A classic of American cinema!'

Ostensibly he was commenting on the *Dukes of Hazzard* YouTube clip they were watching–or rather *he* was watching, the princess being indisposed and somewhat facedown at that moment–but Dave Hooper could just as easily have been making a larger comment on the strange turn his life had taken this past wild week.

To be sure, he was not a guy who was entirely unfamiliar with jungle sex in hotel rooms, and beer and burritos for breakfast. He was, however, more familiar with the kind of hookers you took to Motel 7, and six-packs of 7-Eleven Game Day Ice to wash away the sour taste afterward. Maybe, if he was really flush, he sprung for a Big Mac. But there had not been much to spring at his middling stage of life. Not until a few days ago. Now, he was permanently sprung.

'Sprung,' he chuckled through the mouthful of meat and cheese.

The burrito was a step up in quality too. Some kind of tasty Italian ham and bacon in there, they'd told him; *they* being the accommodating management and ever friendly staff of the Bellagio, who insisted on comping him into the Chairman's Suite lest he have to drag ass back to the budget dive the government had rented for him when he was stranded in Vegas at the last minute. Dave Hooper was a hero, a superhero even, and the Bellagio did not turn away genuine American superheroes just because Uncle Sugar was too fucking cheap to pony up for anything better than a three and a half star flop house, a couple of blocks beyond the frayed edge of downtown.

No, the Bellagio did not do that–not when genuine superheroes were so damned good for business, it didn't.

And there was no question that having Dave at your tables was good for business. Half the city had crowded in to get a little touch of him last night, once word got out he was there–and the Bellagio's hard-working PR flacks made damn sure that word got out fast. It seemed the other half of the city had dropped by to get a look at Lucille, currently resting on a hastily built display in the main entrance to the hotel. There was no chance of anyone stealing his enchanted splitting maul. Only Dave had been able to lift her up there on to the black satin cushions, and only Dave would ever be able to take her down. In his hands she seemed to weigh far less than the factory-specified twelve pounds of American steel. To anyone else, Lucille was heavier than the super dense mass at the core of a neutron star.

It bothered him only slightly that he seemed to be able to hear her whining to him about being abandoned. Stupid enchanted hammer was as bad as his ex-wife.

Thoughts of Annie were enough to wilt him slightly, forcing Dave to refocus on the princess. A few moments of concentrated effort and she started moaning all over again, causing him to harden, and a happy, mindless grin reappeared on his face.

'Sprung,' he giggled again. 'Totally sprung.'

This end of the world shit had all turned out so well. For him, at least.

Dave had rolled into Vegas, quietly, modestly, around chow time yesterday, a couple of hours after their flight to 51, or Nellis, or whatever the fuck they called it, had been forced down by the dragons…

Well, okay, back it up again, he conceded, while enjoying

the vision of Jessica Simpson backing it up toward the camera, and while Princess–er, Mulan?–backed it up toward Dave. Only he'd said they were flying to Area 51. Captain Heath and Ashbury and that puckered ass Compton just called it 'the base'. (Dead giveaway in Dave's opinion. Had to be a cover for something X-Filey with a name like that.) And no dragons–or Drakon, as Urgon, the daemon in his head, reminded him– had come anywhere near their slow-moving transport plane on the uncomfortable haul up from New Orleans. It was just that every flight all over the damned country was grounded now because a bunch of big-ass fire-breathing lizards had dropped out of the sky on top of half a dozen planes, some big, some small and one of them Air Force fucking Two, no less.

That particular dragon hadn't flame-grilled old Joe Biden. He'd been waiting to pick up his ride at the other end. But, long story short, millions of angry, frightened travellers were stuck wherever Homeland Security and their freaked-out air traffic controllers had ordered the planes to put down.

Hence the cheap hotel room. Las Vegas was full, according to Compton.

Everywhere was full.

Including, for once, Dave Hooper. He tossed the remains of the burrito aside and, as AC/DC gave way to Motörhead ('Fuck yeah!'), Dave Hooper turned his full attention back to Princess Mulan or Pocahontas or whatever her name was.

'Holy shit!' another voice cried out. 'What time is it?'

Dave ploughed on with just a bit too much enthusiasm, collapsing the bed frame. Wrapping his arms around the Saudi princess as they rolled out of bed in a hurricane of sheets and comforters, he found he could keep the beat going while getting to his feet.

'Damn,' he said happily, taking in yet another broken bed.

The voice was female, light, corn-fed. A blonde and breezy American voice. Midwestern charming despite the discernible edge of panic. The sort of voice Dave Hooper was familiar with from an unknowable number of titty bars. The anonymously pretty blonde girl emerging from beneath the rumpled sheets of Dave's ginormous bed could easily have been asking him if he wanted 'more Buffalo wings with the next jug, honey'. But instead she was cursing in a very focused and unfriendly fashion, putting up her little fists and punching him on the shoulder while the princess ignored them both, continuing to grind her ass back into him.

'You promised me. You promised that you'd give me an exclusive this morning. A live fucking cross. And I promised New York, Dave. I *promised* them.'

But Dave was laughing, Mulan was moaning, and Motörhead were not much interested in any live cross. He flipped over Mulan and started walking back to the bar and the snoring barmaid, carrying the princess in front of him. She laughed and gasped something in Arabic that Dave didn't understand, but that was *hawt* if you asked him. *Hawt* enough to make him want another beer and perhaps more if the full-time bartender was willing.

'Darlin',' he said, 'I dunno why our two cultures can't get on like this all the time.'

But Foxy–Dave had insisted on calling her 'Foxy' all night because she said she worked for Fox News–was not to be put off. She would be reporting, and America would be deciding, and there was no way known she was letting any reprobate fucking superhero ruin this chance for her.

'Come on, Dave! Hurry up.'

Dave just grinned at her as he woke up the lady bartender to ask for a beer. She smiled slowly and happily when she saw him.

He got his beer, winked, and turned around to head back to the bedroom, ignoring the shattered dining room table behind him. It lay under piles of sweet, sweet swag that had started showing up from folks wanting Dave to say a few nice things about their fine products.

'Can't hurry the superhero, darlin',' he said, still ploughing into the princess, her legs locked around his back while her long black hair thrashed back and forth. 'It wasn't just my ass kickin' skills got a power up in N'Orleans. They call me Captain Stamina now.'

He favoured Foxy with an exaggerated wink before making his point by ever so slightly hyper-accelerating while he held onto Mulan. Two seconds of Captain Stamina going at it like the Flash was enough to send Her Royal Hotness over the edge. Quite literally. When Dave let go on his final thrust she flew off him for a soft landing on the ruins of their bed, shrieking and laughing.

'Great, you're done. Think you can you get your pants on now, Captain?' said Foxy. More of an order than a question.

'Oh baby.' He chugged his beer while admiring her. There was something about frustrated, angry blondes that really excited him. 'You really aren't a morning person are you?

'No, damn it, I am a morning news producer. Now get your pants on, mister, you have a live cross to get to.'

'Can't I even have a shower?' he asked, pointing down at himself. 'A bit messy here. We could shower together. You could make sure I was scrubbed 'til my belly button shined.'

She marched through the ruins of the bedroom, past the shattered bed and ducked into a white tiled bathroom, also one of two in the enormous suite, this one still in usable condition. The water ran for a bit as Dave stood there pondering his situation, sipping the bottom half of his beer. When she emerged, she threw a wet towel across the room at him. He accelerated just a notch to catch it with his still erect penis, a feat he could not have managed even in his high school days.

'Ta-da!' he shouted until the icy cold moisture sank in. 'Wooo! Not fair! Come on, have that shower.'

'It's not smell-o-vision, Dave. No one's going to know. They just want to see your pretty face and hear about how you kicked monster butt. Especially after last night. People need a good news story. And this week, you're it.'

Dave scrubbed and massaged himself with the wet towel in one hand while making sure every last drop of beer was drained from the bottle. He set the empty down with some care and patted the princess on the ass as he passed her by. She panted something in her native language which he took to be contented congratulations. He was inclined to just stand there in all of his naked awesome—and damn if he wasn't all kinds of awesome these days—enjoying his beer and checking out his reflection in the full-length mirror at the end of the room. There wasn't an ounce of fat anywhere on him. A description of a young Schwarzenegger came back to him from somewhere. Like a ton of walnuts stuffed in a brown condom. Or something.

'Fuck yeah,' he grinned, narrowing his eyes just a little, and totally believing that his hairline, which had been creeping backward ever since he got married, was now beginning to inch forward in the right direction, chasing the grey away with it.

'Do you think my balls got bigger during the night?' he

asked. 'What do you think, Princess? I think they got bigger.'

Mulan merely mumbled into the mattress, sated and falling toward sleep.

But he didn't linger. Or not for long anyway. He had the excuse of a long walk toward the bathroom to enjoy the arresting vision of his ripped and naked body–was it possible his dick was getting bigger?–but he didn't want to piss off Foxy too much. He was fast recovering from his last orgasm and his thoughts were turning naturally toward where he might find his next one. And, to be honest, he did recall promising to do this cross thing for her. And then he'd done all those things *to* her... so, turnabout was fair play, he supposed.

Plus, he was still pissed at some of those first stories that'd come out blaming the explosion and the fire on the Longreach on 'human error'. Like it was his fault, him being the safety boss of the rig and everything.

Yeah, he could easily imagine some floor-walking asshole at Baron's Petrochemical in Houston briefing the press against him, just to give themselves some wriggle room.

'Well,' he imagined them saying, 'Hooper has always been a terrible fuck-up. We have files, detailed files...'

Yeah, fuck them, Dave thought.

Motörhead abruptly cut off, giving way to a rapid succession of infomercials, cartoons and talking heads until Foxy found what she was looking for–the vapid twitterings of some haircut and that chick from *Survivor*, the one where they dumped them in outback Australia. *Fox and Friends*, according to the scrolling news ticker. Yeah, now he remembered. He'd promised to give his first ever interview to those assholes, just because lil ol' Foxy here was a damn sight hotter than the old scrote who'd fronted him at the craps tables last night and said he was from *The New York Times* and most interested in recording an interview with 'Mr Hooper. For posterity'.

Dave had never been one for watching the news, unless it was sports. His ex-wife, on the other hand, was always obsessing about some bullshit story that meant nothing to anyone, but that was why she loved MSNBC. Annie'd go apeshit if he was in *The New York Times*. And a whole different kind of apeshit if he turned up on Fox.

He chose Fox, because a sexy producer plus pissed off ex-wife equalled all sorts of epic win.

He couldn't tell what the Haircut and *Survivor* hottie were talking about because Foxy was already yelling that they were late, they were late, they were very fucking late, to which Dave responded that her bosses looked cool with it. He waved one hand at the screen while climbing into the jeans he'd discarded just inside the door last night.

'That's because it's their job to look cool. But they are not cool, Dave. They are a thousand miles from cool. You think She-Ra managed to survive in the Outback because she's cool? No, she survived because she's a life-sucking hellspawn who uses kittens for sanitary pads. Can't you use some of your superhero speed to put your fucking pants on? I'm going to lose my job if we're not there five minutes ago.'

'Okay, okay,' he muttered, putting on a burst of speed which, far from helping, put them even further behind the clock when he tore the new pair of Levi's as though they were made from wet tissue paper.

'Shit,' said Dave. 'Tore my jeans.'

'It's a headshot,' Foxy fired back at him. 'We don't need the pants. Let's go. Get a bathrobe.'

'Mine's wet. In the hot tub.'

And that was how Dave Hooper, American superhero, found himself hurrying through the corridors of the Bellagio Hotel, without pants, but wearing a dry towel and the fetching black silk blouse of a sleeping Saudi princess as a concession to modesty.

They headed for the double doors leading into the hallway where he found Chief Petty Officers Zach Allen and Harley 'Igor' Gaddis. The Navy SEALs were dressed in dark polos and khaki cargo pants with pistols at their hips and Oakleys on their mugs. They were talking about firearms while sipping coffee. Seated in comfortable chairs they did not give the appearance of being on guard duty. Dave noticed for the first time that Igor sported a simple wedding band on one of the thick dowel rods the man called a finger. Or rather, it wasn't that he noticed the gold ring, but he attended to it for the first time as Igor lifted his coffee mug to drink. Dave rubbed at the smooth skin of his own ring finger. The imprint of his discarded wedding band was almost faded. Almost.

'I'm thinking an Alexander Arms fifty cal might do the job,' Igor said. 'Just swap out the upper receiver and away you go. Better than trying to haul a Barrett around.'

'Yeah,' Zach said, taking note of Dave and Foxy without making any comment. 'You'd lack the range of a Barrett and I don't know that I want a bunch of those monsters turning my legs into drumsticks while I'm changing mags. Mornin' Dave. Ma'am.'

'When did you guys come on shift?' Dave said, trying to act as though he emerged from luxury suites dressed like a transvestite every morning.

'Six,' said Zach. 'Busy night?'

'Up all night, am I right?' He winked at Foxy.

'Ma'am, I can shoot him, if you please?' Igor said to the producer, who just shook her head.

'After my live cross,' she said, taking Dave by the arm as she worked her cell phone, requesting the concierge deliver a light blue business shirt to the hotel's media centre ASAP.

'Thank you, thank you, thank you, Armando. I love you, babe. And I owe you. Big time. Yes, it's for Dave. Something stylish, but not too gay, no offence. No, I can't give you a size. You've seen him. Make your best guess. And bring a couple of sizes on either side of that. Big through the neck and chest, narrow at the waist. Yeah, your basic male stripper.'

'I was a stripper once,' Igor supplied, trying to be helpful and possibly make some ground. Foxy ignored the six foot four SEAL completely.

'Igor, one night drunk in a Manila strip club does not make you a Chippendale. It just makes you a little sad,' Zach said, tapping his mike. 'Asset mobile, overwatch in close order.'

Dave might have objected save for the fact he was hurrying down the hallway in his undies, a towel and a princess blouse, escorted by Igor and Zach, all of them whipped along by a small blonde hurricane, herself kitted out in nothing more than bed hair and the sole surviving waffle-weave bathrobe from Dave's suite. Always a leg man, Dave was enjoying the sight of her brown calves and dainty ankles as she hurried on ahead of him. The robe was short enough that the slight H-shaped folds of skin on the backs of her knees were visible. He had always found that sight powerfully arousing, and he glanced to either side of him at his military escort to see if either of those good old boys were enjoying the view.

Igor looked pained. So enticing, so close and yet so far away.

Zach, on the other hand, smiled for a ghost of a second.

'Dude, what would Sammy think?' Zach whispered.

'You know that's not me. And Sammy's cool,' Igor said, trying to sound unrepentant.

The married man, Dave thought. You could always tell them by the clinking of the ball and chain.

Foxy finished her call to Armando the concierge, decelerating to drop back beside Dave but only to take hold of his arm and speed up again, dragging him along. It was early enough that most of the hotel guests were either still in bed or hanging on grimly at the gaming tables. The breakfast traffic hadn't started up yet and Dave and his escort moved down the hallway toward the elevators without having to dodge around tourists or conventioneers.

'You need to get up on what's happened, Dave,' Foxy said. Dave was aware of the feel of her hip against his, and was way more interested in getting up on Foxy than the news. 'Normally this first interview would be all about you, but after last night they're going to want to ask you about the dragons, and the demons, especially if they're busting out all over, like the one in New York, and they're going to want to know what people can do to protect themselves.'

Dave almost stopped in his tracks and Igor had to swerve to avoid running into him.

'There were Horde in New York?' he asked as they got moving again with a few excuse-me's and apologies.

'Yes,' said Foxy. 'What, they didn't mention that on *The Dukes of Hazzard*?'

'Shit,' he said. 'I didn't know. That sucks. Anyone hurt?'

'It was only one of them, as best anybody knows. And it jumped into the middle of some FBI thing. Totally unrelated.

Got cut down pretty quick, but there were some people killed, some more injured.'

He hadn't seen or heard anything of New York, but then he had been distracted and there was more than enough monster news from New Orleans, and now with the dragons, that maybe a lone monster didn't rate the front page anymore.

'The Feds locked down the scene,' she said as they weaved through a couple of housekeeping carts. 'They blacked out all the surrounding phone calls going in, and put all the witnesses into protective custody. Or quarantine or some shit. Hardly matters. No visuals, no witnesses, no story. And we got plenty of orcs and dragons to go around. So, what you got for us on that?'

'But I don't know shit about *dar Drakon*,' Dave said, dropping into the old language without thinking about it.

'What's that?' Foxy asked, turning to him but not stopping. 'What did you call them?'

Dave had to think about it for a second. *'Dar Drakon,'* he repeated, a little slower and more thoughtful this time. 'That's what the Hunn call them.'

'Cool,' said Foxy. 'Right there, you can talk about that, everyone's calling these things dragons, except for the freaks who think they're like mystical visitors or some shit. You tell us that the real name is that Day-crone thing and right away we got a news lead. What else can you tell me about them? No. Hold that thought. You need to get across your brief.'

'My briefs?' Dave asked playfully as they pulled up in front of the elevator. She ignored him.

'What a dick,' Igor sighed.

'I know, right?' Foxy said, taking proper notice of Igor for the first time. 'And yet… you know.' She sighed, and shrugged. 'What a dick.'

Igor nodded.

'Come on, Dave,' Zach said, sounding peeved. 'Some of us didn't get to party in the Frank Sinatra suite. Which floor?'

'Down on five,' Foxy said. 'They've set aside a lounge for us.'

Long before the doors of the elevator opened on a large party of drunken frat boys, Dave could hear them coming. Or at least Dave took them to be drunken frat boys. Maybe they were drunken software millionaires. Who knew these days? They were already pretty rowdy but as soon as one of them laid eyes on Dave, they erupted.

'Holy shit! You're that guy. Super Dave. You kicked fuckin' monster *ass* down in N'Orleans, dude.'

'Don't encourage the egomaniac, please, sir,' Zach said.

'Why yes, son. Yes I did.' Dave grinned at the boys.

'DAVE!' they shouted at once, and it was much better than being blamed for an explosion and a fire that had nothing to do with him.

Foxy cursed under her breath, Zach and Igor both broke out of character to roll their eyes and the frat boys erupted in cheers and hoots. Mostly for Dave, but in one confusing case somebody let go with a loud, lingering shout-out for some guy called 'Leroy'. They poured out of the elevator in a sweaty, masculine wave punching Dave on the shoulder, slapping him on the back, trying to do the same with the SEALs who had kicked a lot of monster ass too. A couple of the boys finally paid some attention to Foxy, standing there in her little Bellagio signature waffle-weave bathrobe looking fit to blow steam from her ears.

'Autographs, man. We need autographs.'

'No. Beers. We need breakfast beers with Super Dave.'

'Soooooper Dave!'

'*Woot woot woot.*'

'Later, boys, later,' Foxy cried out over the uproar. 'You can have all the beers with Super Dave later. Right now he's got some very important TV to do.'

'Awesome,' one of the drunken frat boys said, 'What TV?'

'*Fox and Friends*, guys. He's going to be on *Fox and Friends* in just a few minutes. Get on Twitter or Facebook or whatever, tell everyone you met him and where he's gonna be. Then go back to your rooms, turn on your TV. *Fox and Friends*,' she repeated, slowly. 'Hashtag it. He'll do his bit to camera then I'm sure he'd *love* to have breakfast beers with all of you, isn't that right, Dave?'

In truth, all Dave wanted was to get Foxy back to his hotel suite so he could do this take-charge piece of ass like her old man owed him money.

All of his appetites were running hot; had been since he'd recovered from the first real fight with the Hunn, in New Orleans.

Foxy prevailed upon Zach and Igor to gently remove the drunks from the elevator door, which was madly pinging in protest at being held open so long. The SEALs tried to manoeuvre Dave inside, suffering a slight delay while he posed for a few selfies with the bros, which they promised to hashtag as #SuperDave.

'Breakfast beers later, fellas, for sure,' he promised, waving them off. They cheered and hooted him some more as the doors began to close on them, still calling out a few final questions.

'Dave, you eating downstairs? Don't go there, man. They ran out of waffles.'

'Dave, are you wearing that chick's nightie?'

'Dave, is that like a super boner?'

The doors of the elevator whispered shut on peals of

laughter and the four grown-ups all pretended not to notice the massive erection testing the structural integrity of Dave's Y-fronts.

Igor punched the button for the fifth floor and they rode down in awkward silence before Dave could stand it no more. 'So, I've never been on television before.'

'Don't worry,' said Foxy. 'The camera won't show anything below the waist.'

'Give me strength, Lord,' Zach muttered.

'We can totally shoot him,' Igor offered again. 'He'll probably get better.'

'No one is shooting anyone until I've had my live cross,' said Foxy, powering up the screen of her phone again and flipping through some sort of list on-screen.

'Right. Dave. We'll cover New Orleans after the first break, but there were six dragon attacks last night. And that's leading everything today. Two of these things were killed. The one that attacked Joe Biden's plane was shot down, I guess, by the escort.

'Another one seems to have ridden an American Airlines passenger jet all the way into the ground. As best we can tell the other four knocked their targets out of the sky and then disappeared. Where the fuck you hide a dragon these days, I have no idea. But they've gone to ground somewhere.'

Dave thought on this for a moment.

'Prey,' he said at last. 'They weren't targets. They were prey. You know, like an eagle or a hawk taking a big fat pigeon.'

They all stared at him as the elevator dropped through another six or seven floors.

Igor faced Dave. 'They were trying to eat Joe Biden's plane?'

'Probably hungry,' Dave said. 'Been a long time between feeds.'

'Okay, we can go with that,' said Foxy. 'But let's not get carried away with the Biden angle. We don't want to turn him into some kind of victim, or a hero for fuck's sake, not for just... not getting eaten. We got lots of good, innocent dead people on those other planes. Lots of dead dragon chunks too. We might push that. Anything you can tell us about that, Dave?'

'Tell you what? I don't even know where this happened. I was preoccupied.' He smiled, to no good effect. Foxy just stone-faced him. Damn, but this chick knew how to maintain focus. He was certain she still wanted him. And it wasn't just Bad Dave being bad. He could smell it coming off her. Same way he'd smelled it on Mulan and half the chicks in the casino last night. It was a musky, salty, meaty *animal* scent he could taste at the back of his throat.

He had to admit, he was sort of impressed she wasn't blowing him right now. But she stayed on mission.

'I'll be feeding them the questions, and they'll be asking you the questions. Don't worry, it won't be anything you can't answer. There's a seven second delay, so if you get nervous and swear, it'll just get beeped. Oh, and the American flight went down over Montana, by the way. If that makes any difference.'

'Not really.'

'Okay,' said Foxy. 'So, news of the day. We've got six aircraft down. Two... dragons down with them.' She shook her head, obviously tripping on the insanity of what she was saying, before gathering her wits together and pushing on. 'So all commercial and noncombat military flights are currently grounded throughout the continental United States. Canadian airspace has also shut down. The Europeans will be closing their airports as soon as those flights currently in transit have made their destination. You got all that?'

Dave nodded.

'Sure. That's why I'm stuck here. Fair enough too, unless you want more planes getting bit in the ass.'

'Yeah, whatever. Don't bother yourself with the policy questions,' Foxy told him. 'We'll have our own experts to do that. You just need to answer some basic questions about dragons. How dangerous are they? How do we kill them?'

'But you already know the answer to that,' said Dave. 'Really fucking dangerous, and you kill them by shooting, I dunno, missiles or something at them. Whatever those air force guys did last night.'

'AIM-9X Sidewinder,' said Igor. 'And twenty-millimetre cannon fire. Though I think an A-10 might be better.'

'What are you? An air force groupie now?' Zach asked.

His colleague gave him a surprised look, to which he replied with a shrug.

'It's all over the war blogs.'

'Thank you, soldier,' said Foxy, favouring him with the sort of grin Dave hadn't had out of her since she woke up. 'That's great detail. Our audience will love that sort of stuff.' Igor nodded and coughed to cover the blush that crept up from his neck as the elevator stopped and the doors whooshed open.

A small crowd was waiting for Dave.

# 02

They weren't as rowdy as the college boys, but there were more of them. Maybe a dozen in all. And they were way more determined. They started calling his name as soon as they saw him.

'Dave.'

'Dave.'

'Mr Hooper.'

Bellagio security–there were four of them, big slab-shouldered dudes in identical grey suits–seemed at a loss. One guy in a much nicer, more expensive-looking dark blue suit stepped forward with his hand out to shake.

'Ms Knox, Mr Hooper, if you'll come with me we have a media suite ready for you.'

'Thanks, Alec,' said Foxy.

Hey, thought Dave, I've been banging Foxy Knoxy. That's awesome.

He allowed himself to be carried along in a flying wedge of hotel security, reinforced by Zach and Igor. Behind them trailed the small crowd of hangers-on who'd been hanging on since he'd exited the elevator. Dave wondered why this Alec dude didn't just have his goons run them off. What was the point of having goons if they didn't run people off?

'Huh, yeah whatever,' said Dave in reply to something Alec had said. He wasn't sure what. He'd been distracted by the small crush of expensively dressed men and women trailing along behind him, calling out his name. They reminded him a bit of the photographers you saw at red carpet things like the Oscars, except that none of them were toting cameras. A few waved their phones at him, and one seemed to be gesturing to him with a large envelope of some sort, but he really had no idea who the fuck they were or what they wanted of him other than his undivided attention. He almost slowed down to ask them what business they had with him, but found himself carried along on a fast-running flood tide of hotel muscle.

'That's great, just great,' said Alec, obviously pleased with Dave's response, whatever it had been. 'Armando has some outfits ready. We took the liberty of providing a complete ensemble.'

'If we have time, Alec,' said Foxy. She made to look at a wristwatch that Dave recalled hanging from the taps in the hotel suite's spa. Instead she checked her phone, and swore under her breath again.

Dave was suddenly very aware of how he was dressed and how bizarre it must look and he was seized by the anxious certainty that somebody would take his photograph and his boys would see him splashed all over the web. But nobody else seemed to notice or care. The security detail merely hurried him along as efficiently as they could while manoeuvring to stop his well-dressed entourage getting too close. As they had done since leaving New Orleans, his SEAL escort merely tagged along, just making sure he didn't disappear on them. Foxy Knoxy kept up a steady barrage of news bites and factoids she thought he needed to know. Hospitals in New Orleans were over capacity. There had been such a run on guns and ammunition that even the biggest retailers were being forced to ration what they could sell to individual customers. Fourteen cities had imposed curfews. The Feds were denying a second outbreak in New York. The president was still hiding somewhere in a secure and secret location.

'Oh, and we're getting unconfirmed reports of someplace in Georgia…'

She frowned at her phone as though somebody had sent her a porn link.

'This can't be right,' she said. 'Look, Reuters has picked up some Internet chat, Facebook posts or something, out of someplace called… Buttecrack,' she frowned again. 'Something about them fighting off a demon horde on their own.'

Igor chuckled.

'I think it's pronounced beau-cray, ma'am.'

'Boo what now?' she asked.

'Beau-cray,' said Igor. 'But sure, yeah, everybody calls it "butt crack".'

The faces of Igor's companions obviously needed further particulars. He shrugged.

'Dumbass small town names is my party trick. I got one for every state. And yeah, Buttecrack–beau-cray–is in Georgia. Beat out some real competition from Beaver's Lick too.'

Foxy Knoxy shook her head as they arrived at the Bellagio's media suite, or some room they had set aside as a media suite. 'Just go with the French name if you have to,' she told Dave. 'It sounds like the sort of podunk shithole where Fox makes out like bandits.'

Then she stopped so quickly Dave almost tripped over her.

'Shit! The hammer! We forgot the big hammer.'

'Lucille? She's downstairs. Want me to get her? She'd love to be on TV.'

Foxy Knoxy gave him a sidelong glance that may have spoken to a lack of faith in his sanity. 'Damn it,' she said. 'They're gonna want to see the hammer.'

'It's a splitting maul, technically. Marty Grbac's–'

'Yeah, whatever. We don't have time for you to go get it. Alec, you got any... splitting mauls in-house?'

Alec, the hotel suit, stood by a double door, waiting to run a swipe card through the electronic lock.

'I can ask, Ms Knox. But I don't think so. There's probably a sledgehammer somewhere, or a fire axe.'

She frowned.

'Maybe not. Fucking Jon Stewart would probably find out and do us like a drunken frat girl. Okay. Forget the hammer. Let's just go with Dave.'

Alec shrugged and swiped open the doors. He ushered them into a lounge room where two technicians and another nattily dressed man were waiting for them. The man carried armfuls of clothing.

'Armando!' Foxy cried out. 'I love you. You are my new favourite.'

Armando, narrow of waist, thick of shoulder and long of ponytail, smiled and dipped into a strangely formal little bow. Could he have been any more gay? No, Dave thought. No he could not.

The room looked as though it was normally used as business lounge, but the techs–a camera guy and sound man to judge by their equipment–had pushed a lot of the furniture up against the walls to create a small, makeshift studio space.

The video camera wasn't a big studio unit, but it was a lot bigger and more expensive-looking than the camcorder Dave had used to capture his boys' Little League games in happier times. Cables snaked across the floor. Harsh white lights burned inside spindly looking silver umbrellas, illuminating a chair perched in front of a bookshelf where he presumed they wanted him to sit.

The Bellagio goons deployed across the entrance to the suite, and the SEALs took up position inside, blocking any chance of access for the trailing entourage. Their cries grew louder for a moment as Dave stepped inside, but were cut off abruptly as the doors closed behind him.

'So, who the hell were those guys?' he asked.

Alec looked uncomfortable.

'Yes, I am sorry about that,' he said. 'It is a difficult situation for the hotel.'

'They're scouts, headhunters,' said Knoxy. When Dave looked perplexed, she waved her fingers to bring Armando over with his clothes and explained as Dave dressed.

'Seriously, you don't need the pants. Just get the shirt on and let me put a bit of makeup–'

'Makeup? No way.'

'Yes way,' she said, 'unless you want to look like a toothless crack whore.'

She ripped the silken shift from his chest with one ferocious movement.

'Now that's more like it,' Dave said, but Armando was suddenly there slipping Dave's arms into a light blue business shirt, while Knoxy patted at his face with some kind of powder puff.

'The guys outside have been stalking you from the moment

word got out you were staying here,' she explained. 'Most of them probably drove overnight from LA to get here because of the no-fly rule. Nobody from the East Coast would've been able to make it in time. That fucker from the *Times* was here for a conference.'

'Hey, thanks Armando, but I can do my own buttons, dude,' said Dave brushing the man's flighty hands away from his abs. 'So, who are they?'

'One minute,' one of the technicians called out. 'Gonna have to go with a hand mic. No time for a lapel.'

He tossed Foxy a small black tube which she plucked out of the air with practised ease.

'I'll turn this on just before I hand it to you,' she said. 'Hold it about a hand span from your mouth, and don't wave it around when you talk. Don't touch the power button, just speak in to it normally.'

'Sure, got it,' said Dave. 'But my wolf pack outside, who are they?'

She hurried him across the room and pushed him down into the chair facing the camera. Dave felt her fiddling around with something in his ear. 'What the...'

'It's just an earbud so you can hear the questions coming from the studio,' she explained.

'But you said the questions were coming from you.'

'Yes,' she sighed. 'From me, to New York, and from New York back to you.'

He wanted to ask what was the point of all that fucking around, why didn't she just ask the questions of him directly, but a warning look made him back off. She rewarded that rare instance of common sense by answering his previous question.

'The people outside want you as a client, Dave. Some of

them will represent talent agencies, some of them the big PR firms, I think there was even somebody out there from *Next Top Model*. That's making it difficult for Alec. He can't fuck them off. They're repping for some powerful interests who already have a relationship with the resort. But he's running interference for me, aren't you, sweetie?'

She threw Alec a smile and he nodded.

'We do have relationships with these agencies,' he explained. 'Many of their clients are our clients too. I cannot just kick them to the curb. Only delay them for Ms Knox.'

'And we love you long time for it, Alec.'

'But of course.'

'Thirty seconds!'

'Now you will remember, won't you, Mr Hooper?' continued Alec, looking a little anxious in his expensive suit. 'You tell the people watching at home how much fun you're having at the Bellagio. How you really needed to unwind after New Orleans. How you can't think of anywhere better than here in Las Vegas to do just that. All good?'

'Err... Sure.' He looked at Foxy Knoxy, who somehow managed to be the most commanding person in the room while dressed in a too short bathrobe. 'Is that cool?'

'More than cool, Dave. It's a done deal. Alec has comped our suites and turned over the facilities of the hotel to the network while you're here. And he's made sure the other networks don't get a fucking look-in. This is an honest to fucking God exclusive, Dave. And Alec helped me get it. Just give him a decent reach around, would you?'

Igor chuffed with laughter just behind him. Alec smiled and made a gesture with his hand as though he was shooing away a butterfly. 'Georgia, it was nothing, really.' He turned back to Dave. 'I'm sure Mr Hooper will do fine.'

'Ten seconds.'

Georgia–her name is Georgia Knox, Dave said to himself. Georgia. Georgia. Georgia.

Georgia Knox flipped on the microphone, handed it to Dave, positioned it at just the right distance from his face and withdrew out of shot. Alec smiled, nodded eagerly, and gave Dave two thumbs-up. The technician with the headphones pointed at the screen in front of Dave, which suddenly came to life with the smiling faces of the two weekday *Fox and Friends* anchors–whose names Dave promptly forgot when he saw his own face on a smaller screen-in-screen display in the corner. He was sure the whole country was now looking right at his junk.

The screen exploded in a riot of bright primary colours and blaring, vaguely martial music before the studio camera swooped in on the frowning face of the Haircut who announced that later in the hour they'd be crossing to Washington to hear some bullshit from some other Haircut about how Obama was fucking it all up and surrendering to the monsters before the war had even begun.

Or something.

Dave had all the trouble in the world not looking down to where his bare legs poked out from under the hem of the natty blue dress shirt Armando had put him in. And then *Survivor* Chick was smiling and talking about Navy SEALs and American heroes and even American superheroes and he thought he heard his name and it was all going by in such a rush that he wasn't quite sure what *Survivor* Chick had asked him but Alec from the Bellagio was nodding and grinning and giving him another thumbs-up and that was enough of a cue for Dave to get rolling.

'Thanks… guys,' he said. 'Right now I'm at the Bellagio which is just fucking awesome. I mean it's… it's a really great joint… Oh… Sorry… Damn… Anyway, yeah the Bellagio rocks. You should all stay here next time you're in Vegas. I will be.'

He flashed a grin that he'd hoped might be endearing, but it came back at him on the monitor like Wile E. Coyote licking shit from a wire brush.

*Survivor* Chick didn't look at all put out and even managed a giggle which might've been partway toward genuine. He expected to see Foxy Knoxy face-palming over in the corner, but she had some sort of headset on and was busy staring off at a point a thousand miles away, talking into the attached microphone, but in a voice so low he could barely hear her. She stood with one foot on a low, heavy-looking marble coffee table piled high with tapes, cables and industrial-grade plastic carry-cases. He heard his own name again, and with an effort of will dragged his attention away from the fine brown curve of Foxy's thigh and back onto the TV panel where–

Elisabeth. That was her name.

–where *Elisabeth* seemed to be waiting for him to say something.

'I'm sorry, darlin',' Dave said, breaking out his best boyish grin. Or at least one that unpacked a helluva lot easier than that last shit-eating grimace. 'You'll have to ask me that again. I'm nervous as hell here. Happy to kick monster butt sun up 'til sundown. But I'm afraid talking to a pretty girl like you makes old Dave a bit anxious.'

He fluttered one hand over his heart to emphasise the point.

She laughed then, a real laugh he was sure of it.

'Oh you,' she mugged for the camera, 'I was just asking, Dave, if you had any advice for the people at home who are worried about their safety this morning.'

'Well it's probably best just to sit tight for the next little while,' he said, thinking properly of his own kids for the first time in at least a day. There's no way Annie would be watching Fox, but one of the neighbours or one of her friends was sure to nark him out. 'Lay in some supplies, same as you would for storm season.'

'What about ammo, Dave?' asked the Haircut. Dave still couldn't remember that guy's name. 'A lot of our viewers would like to know about home defence options.'

'Well, I'm not a gun owner...' he paused to see if he could jog the Haircut's name loose from his memory. Nope. 'But the Hunn down in N'Orleans, they lit up real good under tracer fire. And they got some thick demon-hide asses. So armour-piercing would be nice too. The bigger the bullet, the better.'

Igor nodded to Zach, mouthing, 'See, I told you so.'

Zach responded with a knife-hand slash in the air to shut it.

The Haircut seemed pleased with that. Knoxy mouthed something into her headset and Elisabeth reappeared on-screen.

'For those viewers who might have just joined us, we're talking exclusively to Dave Hooper, the hero of New Orleans. His first and only interview since saving the people of that city from the horrors of Hell. Dave, can you tell us how you killed the monsters on the Longreach? Is this something our viewers could try at home?'

Dave saw his eyes go wide on-screen.

'Whoa. Hell no, Lizzie! I got lucky. The monster I knocked on the head was drunker than a goddamn Astros fan. And the hammer I brained him with, it was an oversized splitting maul, not the sort of thing most folks are gonna have lying around. Seriously, don't even try.'

'He was drunk?'

'On blood, yeah. Sorry. Hot blood gets 'em shit-faced.'

They hadn't reacted to him swearing before, and he felt more comfortable speaking the way he normally would, so Dave gave up trying to edit and censor every word before it came out of his mouth. Seven second delay, he thought. They must have been bleeping him whenever he cut loose. They were probably loving it. It'd make a great YouTube vid.

Then he remembered Annie would be watching this, and bad-mouthing him to his boys, so he had to put the clamps on again. All this second-guessing made it hard to concentrate on what the talking heads were saying. He decided to do what politicians always seemed to do and answer the question he wanted to answer anyway.

'Thing is, Liz,' he said. 'These things are dangerous. Not like a meth-head or a grizzly bear. More like a whole army of grizzly bears on meth and packin' a whole heap o' big-ass battle-axes and swords. If you can run or hide, do that. If you can't, and you got a gun to hand, you need to start shooting and keep at it until you run out. Go for the face, the throat, and this area just under the arm if you get a clear shot. Bone cage is thinner there. With a big enough bullet you might not even need armour-piercing rounds. But really, call the cops or the army. Or the National Guard, or whatever. Let 'em do their job.'

'What about you, Dave?'

It was the Haircut, back again.

'Will you be going after these things? People are saying you saved New Orleans. There's photos and videos all over the Internet of you standing down the big bad all on your own. It's viral, Dave, all over the world now. People need a hero, and you're it, big guy. What you gonna do?'

Dave had the decency to blush and at that moment he remembered the Haircut's name.

'Steve,' he said quietly, leaning toward the camera a little. 'That's just not right. I did my bit in New Orleans, but plenty of others did plenty more. You're forgetting not everyone who fought those things got blessed with superpowers.'

Dave thought back to the marine who'd died saving him in the weed-choked lot where the small monster raiding party had emerged. So much blood and horror it undid him for a moment and he realised he had vagued out on national TV.

'Sorry,' he said.

'That's all right, Dave, we understand,' said *Survivor Chick*, doing a passable imitation of sincere concern. 'What can you tell us about the ones you fought in New Orleans? Are they connected to these... Drakon... which attacked six aircraft last night?'

She pronounced the word 'Draykon'.

'*Dar Drakon*,' he corrected. 'Dragons. That's some crazy shit right there, eh?'

He smiled weakly and shook his head, starting to relax into the interview.

He noticed Foxy–*Georgia. Her name is Georgia*–motioning at him to lift the mic a little closer to his mouth.

'I don't know so much about the dragons,' he said. 'But the Hunn? The Horde? Yeah I can tell y'all about them.'

And he did. At length. Until the screen turned to white noise.

## 03

Dave knew something was going down before the video link to New York dropped out. The disturbance in the hall outside would have set his Spidey senses tingling even earlier, had he not been so wrapped up in flirting with *Survivor* Chick. He was certain she was flirting with him. Right there on cable TV. Smiling and giggling, playing with a few strands of hair while alternately beaming, gasping and shaking her head in mock horror as Dave relayed some of the gnarlier moments from the Battle of New Orleans.

That's what they were calling it now, 'The Battle of New Orleans'. You could hear the capital letters in the way *Survivor* Chick said it. She was good at her job, getting him to talk, or maybe Georgia Knox was. The diminutive producer in the waffle-weave bathrobe never once looked at Dave while she channelled her questions through to the studio. But she led the two anchors and their guest–'the talent' he heard one of the techs call him–through the entire adventure from the moment he'd landed on the Longreach in J2's chopper, to Compton ordering the helicopter gunships to open up on the remnants of Urspite's revengers party. Dave was smart enough not to reveal his true feelings about that. Years of ass-covering practice in the vicious pig circus of Baron's Petrochemical's office politics had taught him some discretion. He might have thought that firing on the retreating Horde after he'd negotiated their withdrawal from the field had been an epically dumbass piece of douche-baggage, but he knew better than to hang that out in public. There would probably come a moment to tell the truth of it, or his version of the truth at any rate. But for now, sitting half naked on breakfast television, he didn't feel like that moment had arrived.

What had arrived were the Men in Black.

That was Hooper's first thought as two of them, then three, then four and then a small army, all wearing dark suits, crisp white shirts, and mostly blue or black ties, burst into the temporary media suite. He'd heard them coming. Or he'd heard the commotion outside the suite, but had just put it down to pushing and shoving between hotel security, and the small pack of would-be agents and reps and ten-percenters scratching at the doors outside. But then the signal to New York dropped out as he was explaining to Elisabeth Hasselbeck–Lizzie he called her now–how braining a shit-faced Urgon Htoth ur Hunn had been his personal *Biggest Loser* and Marvel Comics origin story moment all rolled into one. Lizzie had even talked him into standing up and taking off his shirt to show America his newfound six-pack. Perhaps she'd forgotten that he wore no pants, or perhaps she was very much aware of the fact. It didn't matter in the end because hissing white noise suddenly filled the screen.

He'd finally attended to the muffled shouts and protests outside then. Georgia Knox had started cursing up a storm, and the double doors of the suite had crashed open to admit a phalanx of gorillas in suits. All of them giving the impression they wanted to have a serious word with Mr David Hooper about his unfiled tax returns or unpaid parking fines, or some grim and difficult shit like that.

'Shut it down,' ordered one suit. Dave assumed he was the man in charge since he seemed pretty comfortable throwing orders around. And he wore a red and gold striped tie. The only splash of colour in the bunch.

'You two,' he barked at the cameraman and sound tech, 'power down the equipment and don't try any bullshit. Pull out the batteries, unplug everything, and get the fuck outside. You,' he stabbed a finger at Knoxy. 'You sit the fuck down, shut the fuck up, and start contemplating how your cooperation in the next five minutes is going to keep you out of federal prison for the next twenty years.'

There were a dozen suits in the room now, moving swiftly to take control of the space. Dave could see more outside, pushing back his newfound entourage, brushing off the Bellagio muscle, while those in the room tried stone-facing Zach and Igor, who took up the challenge but reacted each according to his disposition. Zach showed the suits his open palms and surfer dude mellow, while Igor looked ready to throw down and get bloody.

The agent in charge, or whatever he called himself, turned his attention to Dave. He was a middle-aged man, with a slight paunch, watery eyes and thick mousy brown hair, heavily lacquered with what looked like a couple of handfuls of styling gel. Except this guy was a relic from before the time of styling gel, so it had to be some sort of old-school pomade. Brylcreem Original, or something like that. Dude had Don Draper's suit, hair grease and cigarette habit, judging by the stink leaching out past his slightly yellowed teeth, but none of that *Mad Men* style.

'Who the hell are you?' Dave asked. It didn't come out quite as forcefully as intended, because of his crucial lack of pants.

With pants comes dignity and a certain moral authority, after all.

Georgia Knox spoke up before Dave could get an answer.

'You ever hear of the First Amendment, asshole?'

The producer was undeterred by her lack of appropriate day wear, nor by the threat of running the in-house breakfast TV show at some federal penitentiary.

'Patriot Act trumps the First every time, sweetheart.'

All the suits were beginning to notice Dave's half-naked state, but at least he wasn't wearing Mulan's sexy-time pyjama top or sporting any wood. He started to do up the buttons he'd previously undone for Lizzie.

'Mr Hooper, my name is Agent Donald Trinder and I am authorised to escort you to a secure and secret location under the–'

'Authorised by whom?' Georgia Knox demanded to know before turning and snapping at the camera crew. 'I didn't tell you to stop shooting.'

Her crew seemed to weigh up the various threats and decided they were more frightened of her than Trinder. But as the camera guy tried to turn his lens on the lead government man one of the agents kicked the legs out from under the tripod, toppling the equipment. The camera hit the corner of the marble coffee table and shattered into a dozen pieces with a loud crash and tinkle of breaking glass.

'Shit!' cried Knoxy. The cameraman also swore but for good measure he threw in a wild haymaker aimed at the agent, who blocked the punch without visible effort and jabbed his stiffened fingers into the man's armpit.

The cameraman toppled over, clutching his shoulder and crying out in pain as he landed on the table full of broadcast gear. The other techie tried to swing the sound boom like a club and found himself pinned up against the wall by two more agents. Bellagio Alec fell to his knees, running his fingers through his hair and crying out 'Noooo' in such a theatrical fashion that Dave couldn't help but laugh, while Armando surprised everyone by elbowing another agent in the face.

Dave saw a gun appear and he felt the *quickening* come on. One moment he was just a guy with no pants in a room where everything was spinning out of control, and then he was the calm centre of a world which had slowed down to the point of all but stopping. He didn't so much focus his hyper-accelerated, super-acute senses as he let them flow out into the world all at once, and let the world flow back in on him at the same time.

He took the time to count the number of agents. There were thirteen of them in the room, including Trinder, and more outside. Men and women. They weren't blank-faced automatons. One little cutie, some Asian chick, was rockin' a face tattoo. Trinder was caught mid-snarl, jabbing one pudgy finger at Armando who had his elbow buried deep in the face of the suit standing next to him, attempting to restrain him. Maybe Armando had had just about enough of being treated like a pussy, thought Dave. Because it looked like he was one of those gay guys who spent a lot of time doing karate or *krav maga* or something. He'd struck clean and hard, breaking the agent's nose and splitting his upper lip where it had been crushed against his teeth. Dave paused for a moment to appreciate the glistening arc of blood droplets and spittle blooming from the point of impact.

Nice work, Armando.

It was as though everybody in the room—everybody in the whole world, he presumed—was caught, suspended in a thick, invisible gel through which he alone could pass without hindrance. He smiled appreciatively at the muscles standing out on Georgia's legs as she launched herself toward her cameraman, whose face was a pale mask punctured by the rictus of his mouth as he cried out in pain. Turned out Foxy Knoxy was quite the hellcat out of bed as well as in it. He couldn't help giving her a playful squeeze on the rump as he moved past to disarm an agent who was pointing a pistol at Armando.

An older, redundant instinct almost tricked him into slapping the weapon out of the hand of the unmoving agent but he caught himself at the last second. If he chopped this guy's arm, he'd probably sever it at the point of impact, and not cleanly. And for sure the damned gun would have gone off anyway as the agent's fingers spasmed with the trauma.

Instead, Dave took a few seconds of his own time, long enough for him to detect the slightest incremental changes in everybody's positions, to place one hand over the top of the pistol, forcing the muzzle to point down at a large leather couch in one corner, and away from all of the people he had effectively paused mid-heartbeat. Only when he was sure an accidental discharge wouldn't blow a dirty great hole in anybody, including any of Trinder's people, did he give the agent a quick, light tap on the bicep. He had to wait a little while for the signals to travel slowly through the man's nervous system, into his brain and back down into the muscle, giving Dave another chance to take in the scene around him. He frowned at the deep, low frequency hum which he assumed to be the radically throttled down sounds of chaos. And he grinned at the ferocious, almost animalistic set of Igor's features compared to the goofy, disarming smile with which Chief Allen was responding to a couple of agents who were attempting to get them to back away from the door. He tried to make sense of the entourage–his entourage, he reminded himself–who were still trying to get to him in spite of this added complication. Some of them were waving papers at him. One had a fistful of hundred dollar bills.

Then he felt the agent's gun hand relax slowly, but appreciably. Just enough for him to twist the weapon out of the man's grip without breaking his fingers. He turned and walked back toward Trinder. He had to stop and take a few moments of his own accelerated time to locate the gun's safety and click it on, or what he hoped was on, before decelerating in front of the boss hog and slamming the solid lump of metal down on a small, nearby table like a judge's gavel. The report was almost as loud as a gunshot, and split the wooden tabletop with a terrible, secondary crack. But it had the desired effect as Dave yelled out, 'Enough!'

He had the weird, discontinuous experience of seeing everybody speed up and then stutter to a halt, but this time they froze not because he had accelerated beyond any human ability to perceive his movement, but merely out of shock. It was possible, he conceded that Georgia's little squeal was also a result of the gentle butt squeeze he'd given her. She did reach around and grab at her delightfully tight buns, as though goosed by a ghost travelling at warp speed.

The agent he'd disarmed cried out in surprise and probably some pain. The suit Armando elbowed in the face crashed into the wall. And then Georgia swore once, loudly, even as she jumped involuntarily away from the space where Dave appeared to simply pop into existence, after having disappeared in a blur of fluid movement.

'Stand down!' Trinder shouted. 'I said, stand down!' It was the first smart move he'd made since barging into the room. His face, which had been florid with excitement, now looked sallow and slack. A long, uncomfortable second or two of silence followed, broken only by the thump of the elbowed agent sliding to the floor, groaning and snuffling through his broken nose and bloody lips.

'Comeau,' said Trinder. 'See to Agent Bates.'

One of the Men in Black moved toward the injured agent.

'So, who'd you say you were?' Dave asked. 'I'm Dave, by the way. Or Super Dave if you like. That works for me too.'

'His name is Donald Trinder,' a deep, commanding voice announced from the back of the room.

Heath.

Dave Hooper didn't know whether to smile or flinch. Instead he settled, like everyone else, for turning toward the severe-looking black man who had just forced his way into the proceedings at exactly the right moment. Almost as though he had been waiting for it. A couple of inches over six foot, a long dark streak of corded muscle and deep disapproval with the world, Michael Heath, Captain, United States Navy, gave the impression of glaring at everyone all at once.

Agent Trinder, Dave noted, did not appear to be pleased by the arrival of his... What? His colleague? Dave had worn that same look on his own face many times at Baron's. Most recently when he thought they were hanging him out to dry for the fire on the Longreach. Before anyone knew what had actually happened.

Even the small pack of carnivorous management consultants, or talent handlers, or whatever they were, fell silent under the power of the glowering, dark-skinned officer in khaki trousers and a short-sleeved tan dress shirt.

Again with the confusing wardrobe choices, thought Dave. They were in the desert, why not wear the desert cammies? The mind boggled.

'Chief Allen?'

'Sir!' Zach dropped the surfer dude 'tude for pure military mode.

'Clear the room of civilians,' Heath barked, leading Trinder to issue a follow-up order to the agents he had out in the hallway to assist.

The protests, empty threats and cries of outrage faded away as the small crowd was forced out of earshot. Dave was sorry to see that fistful of Benjamins disappear.

'Them too,' said Heath, indicating the Fox News staffers.

'No way,' Georgia Knox said, folding her arms and jutting her chin at the naval officer. 'You're on private property, buddy. We're here as guests of the Bellagio, isn't that right, Alec?'

Alec looked as though he was in no shape for a fight with anyone, and simply muttered something unintelligible. Armando bristled in his place.

'She's right,' he said. 'Unless you want a civil rights suit from both the hotel and Fox News you can back the fuck up, Sinbad.'

All of the smooth polish and charm on display when Armando had been helping Dave get ready for the show, and possibly copping a bit of a feel, was gone. The fluttering tone of voice, the barely perceptible lisp, the lightness of touch, they had all been replaced by an aggressive brawler's demeanour.

Dave expected to find Armando with his fists bunched up in a challenge to Heath, but instead saw the man had shifted position only slightly into what looked like a combat-ready stance. He had turned himself forty-five degrees away from the nearest of Trinder's agents and was holding up both hands, almost as though he cradled an invisible baby in his arms. It wasn't an unnatural stance. He looked like a man having a perfectly reasonable discussion, the sort of man who liked to speak with his hands, perhaps. But with Dave's vision newly attuned to such things, and with one of Trinder's Men in Black holding his caved-in face between bloodied hands, it seemed quite obvious that the concierge was not the mincing ass-bandit Dave Hooper had taken him for.

Or maybe he was, but he just happened to be a really badass bandit. Dave suppressed a chortle at his private joke.

'Get rid of them,' said Trinder, pointing at the techs again. As if by peeling off a couple of them he'd somehow got his way, instead of being thwarted.

'I'll get the doctor,' Alec offered, hastening to exit the scene. A couple of Trinder's men helped the injured camera guy and his now subdued offsider out through the mess they had made of the room.

The injured agent made no move to leave with them. Instead he tried to staunch the flow of blood with a handkerchief which had been white but was now a red ruin. Alec paused at the door motioning back over his shoulder to his colleague.

'Armando, seriously, I think it's best we leave these gentlemen to their business.'

The concierge, or style maven, or whatever the hell he was, favoured Trinder and Heath with a cold glare. He held his position long enough to make sure everybody in the room knew he was only leaving because his boss had asked him to.

'Pussy,' he said to the man whose nose he had broken, before following Alec out the door. That left Georgia Knox as the only 'civilian' in the room. Dave had no illusions about his own status. Trinder had already given him the impression he was little more than government property. Heath might have dressed it up in some bullshit about him being 'part of the team' or something after New Orleans, but it hadn't escaped Dave's attention that he had not been without a military escort since waking up in the hospital three days earlier.

'I'm not leaving,' said Georgia, just in case anybody remained in doubt.

'That's fine,' said Heath, 'but we are.'

'Whoa,' said Trinder throwing up one hand like a traffic cop. 'I have travel orders for Mr Hooper alone. Not for you, Captain, or any of your merry men.'

Dave laughed. 'Are you trying to lure me into your van? Are we having a stranger danger moment here, Agent Trinder? Because my mother warned me about going off with odd men.'

Trinder did not even bother looking at him, keeping his eyes fixed on Heath.

'I have orders from the National Intelligence Assay Group to secure Mr Hooper and conduct him to a location I am not at liberty to disclose to you, where he will assist us with OSCAR's investigations into any and all hostile incursions into CONUS since the on-water incident at datum point Longreach ...'

'Did you say incursions? Plural?' Georgia demanded to know. 'Have there been more that you haven't told us about like New York, or...' She frowned for a moment and looked at Dave, pleading with her eyes.

He grinned. 'Buttecrack. Or, you know, beau-cray.'

Trinder spun on him, but seemed to catch himself at the last moment, perceptibly shifting his attention to the young female producer.

'I don't know what you think you've heard,' he said, 'but you won't be repeating any wild rumours and causing unnecessary panic on my watch.'

Dave's attention was split between Trinder and Heath, and he missed the slight movement of the agent behind Georgia until it was too late. He jabbed her in the neck with something that looked like a small squeeze tube and she yelped in surprise and pain before her eyes rolled back into her head and she started to slump to the ground. The agent was already there to catch her, but his body suddenly flew across the room, crashing into the wall which buckled under the impact.

Dave had accelerated from a standing start, shoulder-charging the man out of the way and scooping up Georgia as though she were a new bride he intended to carry across the threshold. The sudden blur of movement and the violent shock of seeing Trinder's man flung across the room as though hit by a car startled all of the other agents into defensive postures. Dave found himself targeted by a dozen firearms, some of them looking like serious pieces of handheld artillery, including a couple of machine guns with abnormally long hand grips from which he could see extended magazines protruding.

For an awful moment he was convinced they were going to shoot even though he held an innocent woman in front of him. As though she was some sort of human shield.

The thought of what someone like Trinder would do with that, the lies he would tell about what had happened, paralysed Dave for a moment.

'Okay, everyone just calm down.'

It was Heath, his voice strangely soothing. He spoke softly, but with enough projection to carry his words to everyone in the room.

'Dave, put down the young lady. Do it gently. Put her on that couch over there.'

Hooper did as he was told, aware of all the gun muzzles tracking him as he moved slowly across the room to deposit the unconscious young woman into the two-seater lounge her techs or Armando had pushed up against the wall. She looked much younger asleep in his arms, and he experienced an unfamiliar wash of hot emotion across his face.

It might have been shame.

'Agent Trinder,' Heath said then, 'it seems pretty obvious to me that Mr Hooper won't be going anywhere against his will. So unless you have an executive order I can lay eyes on right here and now, I'm afraid you're stuck with asking him nicely. And since you just knocked out his girlfriend...'

'Well, I don't know that I'd call her a girlfriend...' Dave said.

'Dave, not helping.'

'Shutting up now.'

Heath picked up the thread again.

'So, unless he is inexplicably enthused by the prospect of going on an adventure with you I would suggest,' and now his voice became hard, 'you're shit out of luck.'

This time Dave saw the agent tensing to move before he actually moved. To the men who were watching closely, Dave appeared to pop out of existence, before popping back in behind the suit who was suddenly gargling and waving his arms about while Dave stood close, restraining the man with what looked like a reasonably soft one-armed chokehold.

He grinned and held aloft the small gel packet containing whatever drug they had used to knock out Georgia.

He winked at Trinder.

'How's this work?'

And he jammed the small half-inch spike into his own neck before giving the gel sac a little squeeze. Trinder's eyes went wide, but Heath merely rolled his in exasperation. Dave grinned.

'Whoa. Donald, my man. You been holding out, dog. That is some sweet shit. You gotta hook me up with your dealer.'

Dave let go of the agent he held at the same time as he flicked the gel sac into Trinder's chest. The first man slumped to the floor, gagging. The second didn't move so much as a muscle.

'So, do you have an executive order?' Heath asked in a tired voice. When Trinder didn't reply the smallest hint of a smile played across Heath's otherwise stern-looking face. 'I didn't think so.'

'Not that it would make any difference,' Dave added. 'Just so you know.'

Trinder lowered his gun, a signal to all of the other agents to do the same. He regarded Hooper in silence for a moment before coming to a decision.

'Mr Hooper, I can see we got off on the wrong foot here.'

Dave burst out laughing, genuine laughter it was too, driven by the utter sincerity with which this asshole had just spoken. His reaction seemed to catch Trinder by surprise, and he gaped with his mouth open for a second before Dave got himself under control and motioned for the man to continue.

'No, please, go on. You just reminded me of everybody I ever worked with at head office.'

Trinder holstered his weapon, rolled his shoulders, and

fiddled with the button of his jacket.

'I'm glad you're amused, sir,' he said. 'But there is nothing funny about what is going on out there.' He waved one hand, gesturing vaguely behind him.

'What? In the corridor?'

Trinder controlled a flash of anger with an obvious effort of will.

'No. Not in the corridor, Mr Hooper. Not even back in New Orleans. And not out on your rig where all this started. I mean all over the country, because that's where we lost six aeroplanes and over 900 people last night. I mean in Mississippi, where I can confirm another ground incursion, with significant loss of life. I mean in New York, not a long way removed from where your wife and children reside, as I understand.'

'Ex-wife,' he corrected without thinking, before catching himself. 'But what… What happened in New York?'

Trinder slowly and deliberately turned to Heath when he answered.

'I'm not at liberty to discuss that until you have agreed to accompany me to a secure location for debriefing.'

Dave looked to Heath for an answer but got nothing except a shrug in return.

'My boys in any danger?' he asked, before adding, 'More than anybody else, I mean.'

Trinder didn't smirk, but you could hear it in his voice.

'I am not at liberty to–'

Dave cut him off.

'Fine, then you can fuck off.'

It wasn't the response the agent was expecting. He blinked once and his mouth opened a little ways, but nothing came out. Recovering quickly, Trinder pressed on.

'Mr Hooper, I would ask you to reconsider, sir. It is a matter of national security that–'

'A couple of seconds ago it was a matter of my boys being in danger.'

Trinder's anger got the better of him.

'Everybody is in danger, you idiot. And you're just lying around here in Vegas getting your dick sucked and enjoying the complimentary minibar.'

'But not at the same time,' Dave said.

'Dave, again, not helping.' It was Heath. He moved into the centre of the room, picking his way around the mess, giving no sign that he was hindered by his artificial leg.

'Agent Trinder, I'm not sure what your movement plans are, but ours are not a secret. We were on our way to Nellis and then on to the Office of Science and Technology Policy's West Coast office. As soon as we have clearance to fly we'll be moving again. We only set down here because it was the nearest strip when Washington cleared the sky yesterday. Mr Hooper has been liaising with OSTP and JSOC since the initial hostile contact in the gulf. I have had no orders to alter those arrangements.'

He paused for a moment to lower his hardest, most ill-favoured expression on Trinder.

'I have, however, had to fend off more or less aggressive headhunting parties from the CIA, NSA, Strategic Command, Homeland Security, the FBI and, as of 0700 this morning, a booking agent for *America's Next Top Model*. You want him? Get in line.'

Trinder made one last attempt at bagging his trophy.

'Assay Group and OSCAR have oversight and coordination responsibilities for all national level assets and programs.

Your friends in OSTP have none of the experience or expertise to handle this threat level. For God's sake, man, they're supposed to be stopping the Chinese from stealing our solar hot water systems or something.'

If he was trying to bait Heath it wasn't working. It did work with Compton, however. The bald and bearded academic pushed his way past the OSCAR muscle at the door, with some help from Chief Allen and Igor to clear a path.

'Great,' muttered Dave. 'I was getting worried that we didn't have nearly enough assholes here.'

Heath shot him a frown, but if Compton had heard anything he chose to ignore it. And as unimpressed as Dave was with the intrusion of Compton, his spirits lifted when he saw that Professor Ashbury had come in behind him.

'Hey prof,' he smiled. 'Heath says I'm gonna be on *Next Top Model*.

She didn't return the smile.

He wondered if his lack of pants, or the unconscious Fox News hottie curled up on the couch, might have something to do with that. Probably some combo of both, he thought.

'OSTP is more than capable of overseeing and coordinating any federal government response to this incursion,' said Compton. 'We dealt with these creatures down in New Orleans and we will deal with them wherever they manifest in future.'

'Yeah, if dealing with it means turning a shit sandwich into an all-you-can-eat buffet,' muttered Dave, careful to keep his voice low enough so that only Heath, and maybe Trinder, could hear. 'Fact is I'm not going anywhere for now,' he said in a louder voice. 'Not unless Heath came over to tell me we're cleared to fly again?'

The navy man shook his head.

'Nobody is cleared to fly anywhere,' he said. 'Only thing besides dragons in the sky at the moment are combat air patrols looking to shoot them down. Caught another one over Yellowstone an hour ago. But that's not public yet. You especially, Dave, are not to fly anywhere.'

'Suits me,' he said, finally pulling on the black trousers Armando had chosen for him. He did his best to look as though this was the most natural thing in the world, getting dressed in front of a roomful of armed Feds.

'Probably should have put them on before you went on national television,' said Professor Emmeline Ashbury. An expression of annoyance mingled with distaste on her face.

Trinder couldn't give it up.

'Mr Hooper, if you would please reconsider, I can get you on a plane to see your family again.'

'He's lying,' said Compton.

'I just told you that my orders specify he is not to fly anywhere until we have secured the airspace,' said Heath, finally losing patience.

Hooper threaded a nice leather belt through the black dress pants and tucked in his shirt. He felt better now he was dressed. More in control, especially given how he'd just rubbed Trinder's nose in the fact that he was the boss here.

'Here's what I'm going to do,' he said as he searched around for shoes and socks.

'For God's sake, you can't even dress yourself properly.' Ashbury marched across the room and plucked a pair of black lace-ups from under the lounge where Foxy Knoxy was sleeping off the drug they'd used on her. Dave hadn't injected the whole gel pack into his own neck, even though after last night he was pretty sure he could've handled it. But it had left him feeling lightheaded and buzzy, as though he'd slammed down a couple of full-strength beers on a hot afternoon.

He took the shoes and a pair of socks from Ashbury with a nod of thanks. Everyone waited for him to continue while he finished getting dressed.

'I'm going to go back to my room,' he said. 'Have me a shower. Then I'm going to hit the breakfast buffet.' He looked at Trinder, 'Thanks for the suggestion, by the way. I'm happy to roll with these guys for now,' he indicated Heath and Ashbury, but not Compton. 'And I'd appreciate it if you looked after Ms Knox. How long will she be out?'

Trinder tilted his head toward one of his men.

'About six to eight hours,' the agent replied.

'Okay, find her a room. Talk to that Alec guy. He seems to be the go-to guy around here. I'd say just put her back in my room but housekeeping is going to want to come through there today. We made kind of a mess last night. And you're going to want to keep an eye on her anyway. I'd hate to have to go back on TV to tell everyone about how you drugged and fucked up such a pretty girl.'

Trinder looked as though he was setting himself up to object, but Dave quietened him with one finger to his lips.

'No, seriously, I will. Those Fox guys are going to want to know what happened to their producer and their interview. And those guys, they never struck me as being well-disposed toward...' He paused for a moment searching for the right words. 'Civil servants.'

Nobody made any move to restrain him as he headed toward the door. That was a good thing, thought Dave, because the drug he'd injected in a show of stupid machismo was really starting to slow him down and dull his senses. He wanted to get back to his room, have a hot shower and maybe give Mulan a bit of a tumble to clear his head.

His SEAL detail fell in on either side of him as he left the room, walking with slow, stately care, exactly like a drunken teenager trying not to be found out.

'Nice work, Dave,' said Zach. 'I think you just pissed off the guys from *The Bourne Identity*.'

'Hey, Mr Hooper?'

Dave blinked away some of the fuzzy headedness from the drug and squinted to focus on a casually dressed man who had just emerged from a door to his left.

'Hey,' said Dave, expecting to be asked for an autograph, and kind of glad of it after the unpleasant confrontation with Trinder and Heath. It was nice to deal with somebody who just wanted to tell him what a great guy he was. Perhaps, if Mulan wasn't waiting for him back in his suite, he might even kick on and join those frat boys for a few breakfast beers like he'd promised. They could tell him whether they thought he had a chance with *Survivor* Chick.

'Yeah,' he said a little groggily, patting down his new shirt looking for a pen with which to sign his name.

But the man was already prepared and handed him an envelope.

'You're served, Super Dave.'

# 04

Lord Guyuk ur Grymm dipped one talon into the bubbling stew of the blood pot. The brew was near scalding hot, thickened with marrow and chunky with great cuts of rump and leg and sweetmeats. Guyuk's nostril slits flared as he sniffed at the rich human ichor coating his fore-claw, a reduction of the choicest offals and rendered fats. He suppressed a shudder of anticipation. There was so much fat.

The ancient records of the Consilium did not offer many recipes for cooking with a surfeit of human lard. It had been an uncommon delicacy in the oldest times, and completely unobtainable since then, of course. But this recent game taken from the Above, like so much else from there, had surprised. It appeared that in the long eons since the banishment, humanity had grown large in more than one way.

The Grymm lord breathed deeply of the aroma. Digestive acids squirted into his mouth and both stomachs rumbled as he further restrained himself. He was proud of his forbearance. A score of blood pots bubbled away over heaped and glowing coals, filling the chambers of the Inquisitors Grymm with a heady miasma of rich murder and fear. He could hear the moans and cries of the captive cattle drifting up from the pits, where they had soiled themselves with their own pastes and liquid excretions, adding a particular piquancy to the already sweetened humours of the dark, hot cavern. And just beneath the lowing of the cattle, the constant *scritch-scritch-scritch* of the Inquisitorial Factotae. Two recorders to a pit, each one taking down every word–or at least the sound of every word–spoken or cried out or screamed by the occupants. Scolari Grymm would do their best to translate the guttural nonsense later. Although Lord Guyuk was coming to doubt the efficacy of the procedure.

He peered into the nearest pot, troubled by his thoughts. Lord Guyuk ur Grymm had not tasted of the feast being prepared down here. He had not given into temptation, because weakness was not the way of the Grymm. But neither was waste, and the rigours of the inquisitorial process were proving so harmful to his captives that he had ordered royal cooks summoned lest the work of his scouts come to naught. He might not be able to present Her Majesty with any usable intelligence, but at least he might seek her indulgence if he was able to present a fine repast. It was more than that idiot Scaroth had been able to do after all.

Two full Talon of Hunn he had taken with him through the breach to the Above, with four Lieutenants Grymm and a clutch of Sliveen scouts into the bargain. And with what had he returned?

Nothing.

Indeed he had not returned at all.

Only the broken, humiliated remnants of his thrall had escaped with their worthless hides intact. BattleMaster Urspite Scaroth Ur Hunn, it seemed from the survivors' tales, had led his so-called Vengeance party into a human trap, where Scaroth himself had been challenged and humiliated by a champion.

The so-called Dave.

A human champion? Guyuk had trouble accepting the absurd myth, but he was Grymm and accepting hard truths was his reason to be.

He flicked the cooling stew from his talon and hawked a mouthful of acid into the nearest pit, where he heard it land with a satisfying splat and sizzle, followed by a terrified squeal of pain. He had not lost his appetite, but his determination not to be diverted by it was redoubled. The Hunn were fools. But that was less explanation than description. All Grymm knew the truth of it, from the newest hatchling to the old lord himself. Hunn charged into situations where finesse and nuance or even restraint should have been the watchword. They never prepared, apart from loading themselves down with mountainous piles of edged metal and thinning their own ranks with ridiculous Shurakh contests before they even took the field.

Just thinking on the dull-witted brutes and the iniquity of the high station they presumed in Her Majesty's regard was enough to turn his already foul mood into a dangerous, seething chancre of impacted rage.

'Inquisitor!' he roared. 'Have up another prisoner. And have a bit more care about it this time. The blood pots are full. We don't need more ingredients, we need answers.'

The Captain Inquisitor on duty grunted and mumbled and shuffled toward the edge of the nearest holding pit, peering over as he snarled and worried at the problem of how to extract one of the prisoners without killing it. Guyuk consoled himself with a lesson in patience. A stupid Hunn would probably have just harpooned another calfling and stood there scratching its nuts in confusion as the poor dead thing refused to yield any useful information. The human cows really had proven themselves to be fragile creatures, even more so than the old scrolls had implied. A goodly number of them had actually died in the process of simply being transported here. They were not even mistreated to any notable extent. Guyuk himself had insisted upon that cautionary measure. It was known the creatures became deranged with fear if handled too harshly, and indeed, it was considered great sport to do so under the right circumstances. But these were not the right circumstances. Even so, in spite of his instructions, it appeared one third of the number taken had simply passed away from fright.

He sighed in vexation.

The Diwan Sliveen's scouts had brought back three score captives from the Above. Not just from the unobserved fringes of the engagement between Scaroth's forces and the human host led by the Dave, but from sorties Guyuk had dispatched in great stealth as soon as it was known the breach to the Above was open. It had been eons, of course, since any from the UnderRealms had sallied up into the Above, and much had been forgotten about the lands of men, but the Grymm lord was satisfied that he had cast his net as wide as fortune would allow and hauled in such a catch as would enable him to judge the disposition of the human forces.

He snorted in disbelief at that.

Human forces. It was an affront to any right-thinking daemon to even say those words one after the other. And yet... The reports he had seen from Scaroth's remnants–reports compiled by his own Inquisitors within these very walls–left no other conclusion to be drawn. These were not men as the

Scrolls knew them and the Hunn were piling ignorance upon shame as they gave into their blood lust and clamoured for ever larger revenge raids.

The Captain Inquisitor of the Night squatted on his haunches at the edge of the pit, grunting with exertion as he leaned over with pole and hoop attempting to snag one of the prisoners. The Grymm Lord Guyuk allowed himself a moment's indulgence, closing his third eyelids, sucking in a deep draught of the blood-pot scent and enjoying the terrified shrieks of the cattle as the captain attempted to rope and haul one up for questioning. It made him almost dizzy with hunger, and beneath the base physical desire he could feel the terrible thirst of *gurikh*, his warrior spirit, for even a sip of the bloodwine.

But Lord Guyuk had not risen to command Her Majesty's Grymm by giving into desires. He examined the temptation, tasted it in the acid still squirting into his mouth, even imagined himself upending one of the blood pots and simply pouring the contents into his open maw. By allowing himself to consider exactly how he might succumb to his most basic lusts, how he might sink to the level of a Hunn, or even worse to one of their leashed Fangr, the Grymm lord was able to take the measure of his weaknesses and put them to one side.

The shrieking coming from the pits, for instance, as his Captain Inquisitor attempted to lasso another human, would normally have left him dizzy with hunger. Instead Guyuk concentrated on separating out the various cries and screams. There were, he determined, at least five of the creatures being held in this, the nearest pit. Two full-grown animals, and three much younger calflings. It was most likely, he deduced, that these were one of the nestling groups his scouts had brought back. The worst of the hysterical screeching almost certainly emanated from their egg-layer, while a sort of deeper barking noise he attributed to the nestling founder, the... he searched for the human term... the father of the nest. The sweetest, caterwauling shrieks and cries of terror must then have emanated from the tiny throats of the three hatchlings they were trying to protect.

Moving to the edge of the pits, on the far side from the Captain Inquisitor, Lord Guyuk peered over the edge to confirm his deductions. He grunted once in satisfaction. It was exactly as he had thought. One large male, one fully grown female, and three diminutive hatchlings squirming away from the Inquisitor's hoop, attempting to hide behind their progenitors.

'Take the large male,' Guyuk advised, although advice from the commander of Her Majesty's Grymm was as good as an order sealed in the blood royal. 'It keeps getting in the way. So get it out of the way. Are you some Tümorum half-breed that you cannot see that?'

'Yes, my Lord!'

'What?'

'I mean no, my Lord!'

Lord Guyuk exhaled slowly.

'Just get me the big one, and be careful about it.'

The Captain Inquisitor grunted his acknowledgement and assent before returning to his job. Guyuk would never admit it of course, but he had some little sympathy for the captain. The shrieking of the nestling group was most distracting, and the dominant male–the father–was proving difficult; not just placing himself in front of his nest mates but actively working to thwart the captain's attempts to corral and lasso any of them. Guyuk could see the creature's arms were bloody and bruised from batting away the pole again and again. He put aside his frustration to learn what he might from this. A Hunn Dominant would long ago have become enraged to the point of jumping into the pit and killing them all. That was why Her Majesty did not rely on the Hunn for much beyond the simple, brutal business of massing great forces before an enemy and crushing them with one great stomp.

He watched as the man foiled the captain's repeated attempts to slip the noose over his head. He was tiring, but remained surprisingly agile and determined, in spite of the fear which came off him in waves. This was all fascinating, and worthy of further study, but in the immediate moment it intrigued Guyuk because in no way did it accord with what he knew of the habits of cattle from his study of the scrolls. If the scrolls spoke true–and the scrolls were holy writ so how could they speak otherwise?–these creatures should simply have collapsed in abject submission before their daemon overlords. Instead, just as Scaroth had discovered, they resisted.

To be sure, the resistance of this lone male was not just frustrating but ultimately futile. And unlike the resistance Urspite Scaroth ur Hunn had encountered, it posed no threat.

But the very fact of resistance itself was the threat, thought Guyuk. There was so much they did not know about the world Above but one truth had always been known. Men did not resist. They might flee. They would certainly scream and soil themselves. But they could not and would not resist.

Yet here was one of them, an unremarkable specimen, pale of hide, fat and slow, leaking its vital bodily essences, and yet it resisted. It resisted even though that resistance was meaningless.

Fascinating, thought Guyuk.

'Think I got him, my Lord,' grunted the captain.

The Inquisitor distracted the male by jabbing the end of the pole into the face of its female nest mate, shattering a few bones and possibly destroying one of the eyes to judge by the damage Guyuk could see. The brood cow wailed in pain, which drew the attention of the male long enough for the captain to whip the noose around his head and jerk him up toward them. His body slammed into the side of the pit with a dull thud, which was almost drowned out by the cries and protests of the hysterical nestlings. The Grymm lord hadn't thought it possible they could screech any louder, but they proved him wrong.

'Daddee, daddee,' they cried. Guyuk noted the scratching of the Inquisitorial Factotae on their clay pads as they transcribed every word drifting up from the pits. Thorough but possibly as meaningless as all the thrashing-about goings-on beneath their very claws, he thought.

The Captain Inquisitor of the Night hauled steadily on his difficult load while the caterwauling grew worse. And still the Factotae scratched and scribbled away.

This was going nowhere, thought Guyuk, just as the captain proved him wrong by crying out aloud and tumbling over backward.

What now, thought the Grymm lord. But a quick look down into the pit told him everything he needed to know.

'Gah! You damned fool,' snapped Lord Guyuk ur Grymm at the sprawling Inquisitor. 'You've pulled his head off.'

# 05

Nothing shrivels a man's woody faster than a letter from his ex-wife's lawyer. Dave's hand was shaking as he read the court papers ordering him to appear somewhere to do... some legal thing... that he... Damn.

The drug was really kinda fucking with his ability to sort this shit out.

'Paternity test?'

It was Heath. Alone.

Whatever showdown he'd had with that Trinder asshole, it was over. Dave blinked very slowly and wondered where Em and Compton were because... well, drugs.

And then, because drugs, his wandering mind wandered back to the papers he was holding.

'No,' he said, trying to concentrate. 'My ex-wife, chasing me for money. I think. Well, she's not legally, you know, my ex, not yet. But... but soon. I think.' He frowned, trying to decipher the legal-speak on the summons, trying to remember whether he was in fact separated or divorced, or just on a break. 'She thinks I got these deals now. Ralph Lauren, the Bellagio, and shit... And...' He read slowly, quoting from the document with difficulty, '...Any and all such marketing, merchandising, promotional and/or sponsorship arrangements as heretofore indicated by the parties of the...'

He crumpled the paper in his hands.

'What the fuck does this even mean? I don't have any of these things.'

He trailed off.

'Your wife's got a good lawyer,' said Zach, shrugging. 'Must've seen you on TV this morning. Saw the shout-out you gave the hotel and picked it up from there. Man that's super fast work. They must have been on a hair trigger,' he said turning to Igor, 'if I ever get married, and then get divorced, I'm totally getting Dave's ex-wife's lawyer. Dude's a monster.'

'Gotta respect skills like that,' Igor said.

'No, no you do not!'

A man was coming at them down the hallway, a man too short to contain the surfeit of energy that seemed to be powering him down the ornately carpeted corridor. Dave thought he recognised him through the drug haze. Same guy who'd waved a bunch of hundred dollar bills at him earlier. His suit was crumpled, as though he had slept in it, or perhaps driven through the night to get here. What was left of his hair floated around his head in an unruly shock, creating a mad scientist halo that was hard to discredit once the thought had occurred. His bald head seemed to be... what?

Klingon.

He had a Klingon head, Dave decided. But he was a sort of pasty-faced, short-ass Klingon in a crumpled suit.

A few strides brought him directly to Dave and the SEALs where he held out his hand as if to take the papers from him.

Heath moved to put one arm out, blocking the man, but

Dave brushed it away. Like a drunk brushing away a friend who wanted to take his car keys.

'Let the dude… er. Let him…'

Man, Trinder had some good drugs.

'Do you mind?' asked the Klingon. 'Of course you mind. You have no idea who I am. Let me put your mind at ease on that if nothing else for the moment. Boylan is my name. Just Boylan will do, although I have other names, of course. My parents were hippies, and although they approached most social conventions with a deplorably relaxed attitude, they did think to smooth my path through the world by providing me with more than one name. Professor is my other name. And X. Professor X Boylan. An impressive moniker, yes? But of course single initial names are always striking, and there are few letters in the alphabet more striking than X. It is both mysterious and foreboding. X implies danger, don't you think? And promise too. X marks the spot, after all. And X crosses out all options.'

He speed-read the legal papers as he spoke, never once looking up from the document to gauge the reaction of his audience. Dave's reaction was mostly to be confused and very, very stoned.

'You look like a Klingon,' said Dave.

The man called Boylan did not look up.

'I have a prominent occipital crest,' he said. As if that explained anything. 'This!' he declared then. 'This is nothing!'

He threw the sheaf of papers over his shoulder and they came apart in midair as the paperclip holding them together failed. 'Pah! Don't worry about that. I just did that for effect. I will gather up those papers in a moment when you are gone and no longer looking and it won't be embarrassing for me to scramble around hunched over like some sort of helper chimp.'

'Dave, seriously,' said Heath. 'We need to get going.'

'No, what we need to do, sir, is crush M. Pearson Vietch like a bug. That is the plan, isn't it? Crushing the insectile lawyer of your soon-to-be former wife?'

'Dave,' Heath's voice sounded lower, and a little more dangerous.

'Wait, what?' said Dave, shaking his head as though to clear it of cobwebs, 'No, I need to hear about the crushing.'

'M. Person Bitch?' said Igor, out the side of his mouth.

'Lawyer,' said Dave. 'Annie's lawyer,' he added. 'Crush Annie's lawyer.'

'Yes, I'm all about the crushing,' said Boylan. 'I will sneak back now and get those papers I threw over my shoulder to demonstrate my contempt for the feeble efforts of M. Pearson Vietch Esquire to separate you from your newfound wealth.'

Boylan performed a little dance toward the scattered papers, almost curtseying as he bent down to gather them up. Heath gently took Dave by the elbow and started to move him toward the elevator.

'Come along, Dave.'

'But… but my newfound wealth?'

He was having terrible trouble holding any thought for more than a few seconds. He'd start to say something, but forget what halfway through.

'I have wealth?' he asked, focusing in as best he could on the most interesting thing the Klingon had said. 'I thought I…' He shook his head, squeezing his eyes shut, trying to force some sort of clarity.

Boylan laughed hugely and theatrically.

'Oh I am well aware of your disastrous financials, Mister

Hooper. I have done my due diligence and arrived fully informed of the daunting task ahead of us. But make no mistake, for once the appalling M. Pearson Veitch is correct and it is you, sir, who is misinformed, at least on this matter. Your newfound wealth remains illusory only because I have not yet brought to bear my nigh on magical skills. Allow me to deal with this Veitch, pro bono, sir, which is to say, at no cost to yourself whatsoever. I shall smite him with the full fury and force and majesty of the law not purely to insinuate myself into your affections, although that will surely be a corollary effect, but because it is the right thing to do, sir. I am, after all, an officer of the court and it behoves me when confronted with incompetence and effrontery and the sheer fucking cheek of one such as this Veitch to ruin him utterly for the sake of the very law, sir. *The sake of the very law.*'

'Really?' said Dave groggily, not at all sure where this was headed.

But he seemed to be headed to the elevator. With Heath. While Zach and Igor followed, blocking his view of Professor X, or whatever this free-roaming Klingon mental case called himself.

'Hey. That paper. I need… I think I need that,' he said.

'Concern yourself with this no more, sir. It is done, it is done,' the strange little man cried out as he seemed to disappear toward a vanishing point. 'Already the great iron wheel of the law grinds slowly to reduce M. Pearson Veitch to an unsightly and rather sticky professional pulp. Let us instead concern ourselves with more pressing matters.'

'Like what?' Dave asked as he walked backward, still being drawn along by Heath.

Boylan raised his voice as Dave drew further away.

'Why, breakfast of course. What could be more pressing than breaking our fast at this point? Unless it's breaking our fast with lobster hoagies.'

'Oh fuck yeah! Lobster hoagies!' Dave yelled, suddenly finding his focus again, shrugging off Heath and stumbling back toward his new best friend. 'Lobster hoagies for breakfast is gonna be awesome.'

He paused, thinking of something.

'You got this, right, Heath? Because I still haven't found my wallet. Reckon it's out on the Longreach or back at the hospital.'

'Do not worry about it,' Boylan answered, before Heath could speak. 'The house will comp us breakfast. And I'll get them to send a new wallet up to your room.'

'Awesome.'


But breakfast was far from awesome.

'Who is this wanker?' Emmeline asked as Boylan seated himself at the booth in the executive dining lounge.

'Where's my lobster?' groused Dave, by way of reply. His head was clearing, but that simply left him more disappointed when the duty manager of the private dining room stood before them wringing his hands, apologising for the unexpected and unavoidable and deeply, deeply disappointing absence of any lobsters which might contribute toward Dave finally getting that lobster hoagie which had been his life-long dream for at least a quarter hour now.

'I do have an omelette bar set up,' the manager said, gesturing to two chefs who had been spirited up to the lounge along with burners, pans and all of the fresh ingredients they had left.

'Eggs, toast and coffee will be fine,' said Heath, taking a seat while gesturing for everyone else to do so.

'No. It will not be fine,' Boylan protested, but before he could lean into another performance Heath cut him off with a hand chopping gesture and fixed the eyes of the floor manager like a snake with a baby rabbit. 'Eggs. Toast. Coffee.'

'Dave, your eggs, you have a preference?' Boylan asked.

'Dave will take his eggs in whichever form the chef decides best suits the egg,' Heath said in a voice that allowed for no further negotiations. 'With toast. And coffee. Now.'

'And I'll have tea,' Ashbury added. 'Made in a pot, with loose leaves. Not tea bags, which are an abomination in case you were wondering.'

The floor manager acknowledged the order with something that looked like relief. Toast and eggs they could do. Coffee wouldn't be a problem. Even loose leaf tea they could handle. As he hurried away from the table he began to orchestrate servers with the deft hand movements of a concert conductor.

'And ham!' Boylan called out after him. 'Some baked ham would be nice. To make up for the lobsters.'

'Who is this wanker, again?' Emmeline asked.

'My lawyer,' Dave said. 'And he's staying.'

Two servers, both young women, soon appeared with baskets of pastries, pots of black coffee and small jugs of milk, skinny milk and non-dairy creamer. The manager returned with Emmeline's pot of English breakfast tea and news that a platter of hot, freshly carved *jamon iberico* would be forthcoming.

'Excellent,' cried Boylan.

'What's this ham on berry thing?' asked Dave under

his breath. He didn't like fancy, stuck-up food that ruined a perfectly decent feed like ham by turning it onto berry-flavoured foam or something.

'The lobster of the Catalans,' Boylan assured him. 'Except made of ham.'

'Okay. Ham is good.'

The executive lounge floated high above the artificial lake and soaring fountains that were the resort's principal contribution to the street life of Las Vegas. Not as striking as the replica Eiffel Tower, Arc de Triomphe and gigantic novelty Montpelier balloon across the strip, but it was still cool to gaze through the high windows and down on the water feature. Or it would have been if their little breakfast club had not been so tense.

Professor Compton frowned across the table at Dave and Boylan. 'Is there any reason why the ambulance chaser needs to be here? If Hooper has personal business to attend to, I'm sure he'll have plenty of time to do so after we've discussed matters of national security, which Professor Boylan is not cleared for.'

He sneered the word 'professor'.

'Ha ha ha! National security? Oh Professor, puh-lease!' said Boylan, giving back as good he'd just got. 'You people have no idea! Let me introduce you to your new best friend, attorney–client privilege. Attorney–client privilege mocks the feeble attempts of national security to keep your secrets secret. Nothing is as secret as a secret secured within the chamber of secrets that is attorney–client privilege.'

'Seriously, who is this arse-clown again?' asked Ashbury, stirring her tea with delicate swirls of a silver spoon. 'I so do not care for him that I find myself agreeing with Professor

Compton. And nobody wants to do that.'

'Nonsense,' said Boylan, favouring her with a professionally polished smile. 'We shall be the best of friends before this day is done, Professor Ashbury. I shall make it my second priority; my primary responsibility being the sound management of Dave's interests. On which, I would appreciate knowing what further interference, if any, we might expect from the villainous Trinder. He has already done his best to sabotage one national television interview, which, granted, I did not organise, and rest assured if I had, Dave, your tête-à-tête with the charming Ms Hasselbeck would not have been–'

'Tête-à-tête,' Ashbury interrupted. 'Is that a French term for making a sex video?'

'Jealous?' Dave grinned.

'No,' Ashbury said. 'I'm just disappointed, Dave.'

'That's only because we've never made a sex video,' he grinned, instantly regretting it as her face grew darker.

'Too far?' he asked, his grin turning from boyish to sheepish.

'A little,' Boylan confirmed in a stage whisper. 'But it's in the past now. Let's move on.'

Emmeline was flanked right and left by Compton and Heath, neither of them looking very happy either, and not because Dave and Boylan had grabbed up the seats with the best view of the Bellagio's dancing fountains. The private lounge was full, with a couple of guests standing by the doors, looking unimpressed as they waited their turn. Zach and Igor had been left outside as well, but they were perfectly happy with the bottomless coffees and hot ham and egg rolls provided on Boylan's say-so.

'What? Are you guys pissed at me for doing that TV thing?' Dave asked. 'Because you told me I was cool to do that shit.'

'And it is totally cool,' Boylan assured him over the top of any possible objections. 'And you'll be doing many more, Dave. Many more. Once we've worked out a schedule of appearance fees.'

'It is not about you doing interviews,' said Heath as he slowly turned his coffee cup around on its saucer. Around and around went the coffee cup with a quiet scraping noise. 'We agreed back in New Orleans that there was no point in trying to keep a lid on this. You're not a prisoner and you're not a conscript. I can't order or compel you to do anything.'

You got that right, Dave thought.

'You have no legal obligations, only moral ones,' said Heath.

Dave found himself bristling at that too, but he said nothing. It was all just words. Orc motherfuckers had killed his friends and work mates. Made him look bad doing it too. For a while anyway. They'd be getting a full measure of payback, and moral obligations be damned. The Horde was gonna find out that Dave Hooper was a guy who paid his debts.

Well, okay. Maybe not all of them.

But…

Boylan raised one hand and opened his mouth as if to speak but also seemed to think the better of it as their servers returned with hot food. A large omelette, piled with cheese, made a soft landing in front of Dave. The waitress brushed against his arm as she laid the plate out, her cleavage in clear view. Dave's dark mood lightened and he winked, gratified to see her blush. Her friend laid a perfectly crispy side of hash browns next to the omelette.

'I don't think you appreciate the gravity of the situation,' said Compton when they had the table to themselves again. 'There's danger here, Hooper. Not just of going without your damn lobster sandwich because the delivery truck didn't make it through. I mean things could quickly fray to the point of falling apart.'

'What, in Vegas?'

'Don't be obtuse,' said Emmeline, who seemed in an especially poor mood. Dave was starting to be thankful he hadn't tried to fuck her when they were out on the rig. And then he wondered if that was why she was pissed at him. Even though she'd said she wasn't interested? Dave had many faults, but a lack of basic comprehension wasn't one of them. He knew no meant no. He'd sure as hell had enough women tell him 'No' over the years to take the lesson to heart.

'Do you know how many days it takes for a modern city to run out of food?' said Compton.

'The way you're inhaling those cheese crullers, I'd say by this afternoon,' Dave answered, smiling at his zinger. He began the process of systematically dismantling and devouring the omelette. He switched between scoops of egg, ham and cheese with crispy hash browns.

'Nine days, give or take,' said Boylan, surprising them all. He shrugged off their querying expressions. The lawyer's soft little hands whirled up by his head like hairy helicopters. 'I'm one quarter Greek. My grandparents were in Athens during the Second World War. What my family don't know about going hungry is not worth knowing.'

Dave nodded, while chewing. The fogginess of Trinder's drug was gone. Dave shovelled in the last calories from the first round of breakfast just as a large plate of bacon materialised courtesy of the waitress who brought along his second omelette. She placed her hand between Dave's shoulder blades and smiled.

'Doing all right?' she asked.

'Are pancakes possible?' he asked.

'Oh for pity's sake,' Compton muttered.

Heath's knuckles cracked from the clenched fist he formed three times to dissipate whatever urges he was experiencing.

'Yes, everything is possible here,' she said, dragging her fingers across Dave's back as she went off.

He turned his attention back to Boylan.

'Appreciate it, Professor,' Dave smiled. He was beginning to enjoy having the Energizer Bunny on his side. It had been so long since he'd had anyone in his corner he'd forgotten what it was like.

'Of course! Of course, you do, sir. As you will come to appreciate the many services I… Oh, dear. Just wait a second.' Boylan threw up his hands again, before shooting them into his jacket pocket to retrieve a ringing cell phone. He pulled two phones out, then a third, holding it up and signalling to the table that he had to take this call.

'It's Zack Snyder,' he mouthed. 'About Dave's film.'

And with that he was away, bouncing across the room.

'Zack, baby! I hope you have good news on Pitt and points on the front end for us…'

# 06

Compton frowned after the retreating figure.

'We cannot allow that man anywhere near the Office of Science and...'

'Why?' Dave interrupted, with a fistful of bacon just inches away from his mouth. 'You think he might pull a dick move like murdering a bunch of Hunn warriors after I negotiated a truce with them?'

Compton's face was partly hidden behind his ridiculous neckbeard, but you could see the flush of ire that coloured his cheeks and neck where the skin lay bare. His lips lost all of their colour as he pressed them tightly together. Heath looked as though he was about to issue another one of his traffic warnings to Dave, but Compton beat him to the punch.

'They were hardly warriors. I'm surprised you couldn't tell the difference. After all, dozens of real warriors had been fighting and dying around you for hours to give you a chance to do your little comic book hero act. As I recall, one of them had to sacrifice himself for you to unlock some mystery achievement that let you get off your ass before one of the orcs came by to chew it off.'

Dave stared at Compton with cold fire in his eyes. And

then the world was utterly still and midnight quiet as he alone moved through it. He launched himself across the table, grabbing the academic by his shirt front and hauling him out of the seat. Picking him up like a bag of garbage. Tossing him through the floor-to-ceiling windows which shattered without sound as Compton's body crashed through and arced out over downtown Las Vegas, tumbling and turning and dropping back toward the earth so very far below. But not moving as you'd imagine a man who'd just been thrown to his death would move. No spastic thrashing of arms or legs. No clawing at the building from which he'd just been launched. No...

The coffee cup Dave was holding shattered with a sound like a gunshot, causing everybody except Heath to jump. An uncomfortable silence fell across the room for a few seconds, before the buzz of conversation resumed. Dave shook off the homicidal daydream, pulled out of murderous reverie by the stinging pain in his hand. Luckily the cup hadn't held more than a few drops when he'd crushed it so there was little to wipe up other than a few bloodied shards of crockery.

'Sorry,' he muttered, staring at the tablecloth to avoid looking at Compton, and digging a few pieces of pottery out of his flesh. The wounds stung, but not that much, and he watched, fascinated, as the cuts in his flesh sealed themselves up again. Itching.

'I'm gonna need a pastry,' he said, wiping the blood off with a white linen serviette. 'Or some ham and eggs. And you're gonna need to watch your mouth, Professor,' he added quietly.

'No, I think you're going to need to watch your temper, Mister Hooper,' Compton replied, but his voice shook. 'And you need to start seeing the hard realities of this situation. Not the comic book version.'

It was Professor Ashbury who broke the tension between them, leaning over and using a menu to brush up the broken pieces of the coffee cup.

'Behave. The pair of you. You're as bad as each other,' she said.

Dave grabbed a croissant and started tearing it up, stuffing it into his mouth just to have something to do with his hands, because he felt a serious need to hit something and Compton's ugly head was looking mighty tempting. The little French pastry got smeared with some of his blood, but he didn't care. He chewed quickly and dry swallowed, calming just a little as the food went down. The other diners returned to their meals, but he could tell the attention of most of the room had turned decisively in their direction.

Heath stepped in before the confrontation could spool up again. He nodded over Dave's shoulder, where the waitresses were returning with plates of omelettes, scrambled eggs and toast, and a baking dish piled high with ham.

'Oh dear,' exclaimed one of them at the sight of the smashed cup. It was the little cutie who'd been flirting with Dave earlier. Or at least he thought she'd been flirting.

'Sorry, darlin'.' He smiled apologetically. 'Don't know my own strength.'

'Just eat your breakfast, Dave,' said Heath. 'And you, Professor,' he added, turning to Compton, 'you should say sorry.'

It was a suggestion, not an order, Compton being Heath's boss, Dave supposed.

'But–'

'No buts. You were out of line.'

Heath's tone was reasonable, not at all like the ass-chewing

Dave imagined he'd give a junior officer who fucked up. But neither did he look like he'd back down.

Compton appeared to think it over. He turned to Ashbury for support but all he found there was one raised eyebrow.

'Fine,' he said at last. 'I apologise.'

Dave was taken a little aback at how sincere he sounded.

'Okay, then, me too,' said Dave.

The waitresses, alive to the awkward vibe at the table, hurriedly served up the food and disappeared, promising to come back and clean up the mess Dave had left. He still felt the need to make his point, however. 'You shouldn't have done what you did back in New Orleans, Compton. Ordering those helicopters to fire on the Hunn,' Dave said in a low voice, when the waitresses were gone. 'I had a deal worked out. If there's gonna be trouble now, it's down to you.'

The professor narrowed his eyes just a little, but didn't bite back.

'I didn't order the gunships to do anything,' he said. 'Captain Heath can confirm that. I don't have that authority. The order came from Washington.'

Heath nodded, but didn't look as though he enjoyed it.

'But the suggestion came from you, Professor,' Heath said, 'and you didn't help matters by *suggesting* the ambush. You put that option on the table, pushed it up the chain of command. They were always going to take it.'

'And what option was that?' Compton asked, keeping any sarcastic edge off the question. 'Teaching a pack of dark age brutes they made a terrible mistake in attacking us? Because I think they learned the lesson.'

'And I think we got lucky,' Heath said. 'They happened to manifest in a time and place we could bring our resources to bear. Not every part of the country is going to be so fortunate. They could potentially boil up out of the ground anywhere.'

'And what they learned,' said Ashbury, 'is that we can't be trusted. Our word means nothing.'

Compton waved her off. 'They see us as food, not foes, Emmeline. A pact with… what do they call us… cows?'

'Cattle,' said Dave.

'Right. Whatever. It would mean nothing to them. It would be like Hooper negotiating a truce with his omelette.'

'Never gonna happen,' said Dave, shovelling a forkful into his mouthful.

'You seem very sure of yourself, Professor,' Ashbury said, pointedly using his academic title.

Compton put down his cutlery with a rattle. 'A lot of good people died in New Orleans, and in New York and on those planes. I think more, a *lot* more, are going to die before this is done, and this… fellow'—he flicked his hand at Dave again—'somehow fell ass backward into the role of our Chosen One. All you did in New Orleans,' he said, addressing Dave directly, 'was play a video game hacked to give you infinite life and ammunition while everyone else had to stumble through in hard-core mode. Get killed and stay dead.'

Dave felt the blush creeping up his cheeks, but it was shame not anger which turned his features red. Compton had just put into words something he'd been feeling since New Orleans, since he'd spectacularly failed to save those marines. He might even have been a big enough man to admit it aloud too, but Compton seemed to sense the ground shifting and pushed in harder.

'You set yourself up as the champion of humanity in New Orleans. But you need to understand you are not our champion.

You are not a superhero. Or even a hero. You got lucky on that rig, and I think you know it. That boy who bled out all over you, he has a claim to heroic status. The ordinary men and women who died with him to save a city full of other ordinary people, them too. But you don't, Hooper. And you should not have led the Horde into assuming you would be the one they were dealing with when it came time to negotiate terms with us. Because you won't be. Yes, turning the gunships on them certainly complicated *your* relationship with the Horde. But it clarified *ours*. A war between the realms means a war with us, the United States of America. Not some sort of wrestlemania smackdown with you.'

This time Dave was not seized of a vision in which he threw Compton out of a window. He was struck dumb by his inability to find any argument to throw back in the guy's face.

'Dave, just eat your breakfast,' said Heath. 'For the protein if not for my sanity. Put some more bacon in your mouth, keep your mouth closed while you're chewing, and listen up.'

Whatever Heath was about to say, he paused because the waitress had returned to clean up the broken coffee cup. She apologised for interrupting them and apologised for the mess, which Dave thought was a little strange since he'd made it.

'If they try to dock your pay for it, you tell me,' he said.

'Thanks,' she smiled, 'but that's all right. They wouldn't do that.' She said sorry again and left them in peace, blushing a little as Dave winked at her again. Ashbury was eating a single piece of toast and shaking her head, staring at him. Heath and Compton had taken the opportunity to serve themselves some eggs and ham. Boylan was still away from the table, working his phone.

'Trinder was right,' said Heath when they were alone

again. 'In one sense at least. We need to get you out of here, Dave, and into a facility where we can systematically work up the intelligence you have on the Horde. If we can't get a military flight out of here before this evening I'm going to request ground transport.'

'We could just rent a car now,' Dave suggested as Heath's phone started to ring.

'No, we can't,' said Compton. 'There are certain asset protection protocols in place around you now, Hooper. We can't just rent a Hertz. If we roll out of here it will be in armoured vehicles with air support and full spectrum command and communications.'

Dave stopped with his fork halfway to his mouth. A long piece of ham slid out of his omelette and dropped back onto the plate.

'I *think* I understood what you just said.'

'If we move, we go in convoy, with lots of guns,' Emmeline clarified. Dave was about to say something to Compton but Professor Neckbeard's phone also started to buzz. He turned back to Emmeline.

'Well that sounds cool. But not as cool as *that*,' Dave said, as Boylan came dancing back to their booth. Actually dancing, old black and white musical style. And not at all fussed by the attention he was drawing, nor by the increasingly anxious and even fearful expressions on the faces of Heath and Compton. Getting his excitement under control again, Boylan finally pulled up a chair at the table and poured himself a cup of plunger coffee. He was almost panting.

'Dave, we absolutely must speak about Mr Bradley Pitt and the frankly unspeakable amount of money he is offering to secure the rights to your story before Michael Bay gets hold of them. Did I mention we have a conference call with Michael Bay in half an hour?'

'The *Transformers* guy?' Dave said, noting Emmeline's baleful eye turning back toward him. Heath had his hand over the phone and was talking in a low voice that Dave had no hope of hearing. Compton was arguing with somebody on his phone too, but it was all in jargon that made no sense to Dave.

'The one and only,' Boylan confirmed, as he grimaced at the coffee. 'This is cold, too cold, and that's not at all acceptable.' He turned in his seat looking for a waiter to refill the coffee pot. The private lounge was even busier than before, with at least another dozen guests lined up at the door waiting to get in. The attention of the room, or at least of the tables not immediately surrounding theirs, had slipped away from their party again, with many people, as was so common these days, not talking to their families or friends or fellow guests dining with them, but rather yapping into cell phones, or reading the little screens, or even working on laptops. It was then, when Dave noticed the number of phones in the room, that they all started ringing within a few seconds of each other. Even Boylan's incessant chatter was muted by the shrill beeping and pinging and ringtones of maybe two hundred electronic devices.

'We're out of here, now,' said Heath, who had terminated his own call.

'Problem?' Dave said when Compton hung up as well.

'Yes,' Heath replied, 'you might say that. Especially if you lived in Omaha and you just woke up to find a demon army camped next to the highway out of town.'

Compton smiled. 'You're going to have to postpone Michael Bay.'

# 07

Thresh squatted at the bottom of the pit, occasionally shifting its weight from one haunch to the other in a vain attempt to get at least partly away from the burning heat of the iron trapdoor on which it rested. Although, thought thresh, it was not so much resting as squirming and scraping and moving constantly to keep as small an area of its hide in contact with the hot metal grate as possible. It could endure the discomfort only so long before it had to move again, but moving was not easy in the cramped confines of the pit. Indeed, its mostly futile attempts to avoid the slow building agony of roasting in its own skin entailed almost as much pain from scraping its raw and bloodied flanks against jagged spikes of rusting spearheads and shattered Tümor bones set into the rock wall. Not a lovely, smooth rock wall of river stones and mortared pebble of the like enjoyed by the human captives in the larger, more commodious pits which commanded the better part of the Inquisitor Grymm's principal chamber either. No. Those urmin squirts were held in luxury while thresh was jammed into a tube of volcanic spikestone which tore and dragged at its wounded hide almost as often as the barbs buried in the wall.

Oh woe was thresh.

Its many eyestalks lifted up as it contemplated this wretched situation. There was no climbing out of the pit. Even if it could, even if it were possible to scale the narrow volcanic funnel without being torn to shreds, to haul itself over the fixed circle of sharpened wulfin teeth which ringed the open mouth of the pit so far above, to crawl broken and bleeding onto the stone floor of the main chamber and evade the blades and slings and arrakh-mi bolts of the guards, the snapping, drooling jaws of the Fangr, and to somehow escape into the wider Realm... even if all those things were possible, they were not conceivable.

Thresh had failed. Thresh was disgrace. Thresh was shame upon unutterable shame.

Its place was down here in the worst of the pits, waiting for the trap to open, for the long drop into the feeding fires of *dar Drakon*. Or its place was dangling and shrieking at the end of hook and chain as the Inquisitor Grymm, or more likely one of his underlings, dragged thresh up out of confinement and threw it into the blood pot to bulk out the rations for the guards and their Fangr. Already thresh had heard many of the remnants of Urspite's command go this way. Some willingly, almost enthusiastically, as if to purge the scrolls of their nest from the failure they'd dragged back from Above. And, shamefully... oh so shamefully... some had gone to their fate fighting and cursing and struggling against what would be. What could only be, for creatures which had so signally failed She of the Horde.

Thresh grimaced and bit down on a snarl as it heaved itself into a slightly more comfortable position by way of tearing two great gouges out of its backside on the vicious prongs of a pair of Tümor bones. They seemed to have been fixed into the mortar with just such a purpose in mind. Thresh squeezed all of its eyes closed at the end of its stalks and tried to settle its deeply unsettled thinkings on a more agreeable think. It recalled the taste and texture of the man meat it had enjoyed in the Above. So much stronger and yet so much more delicate than even the ancient legends hinted at. Thresh recalled its summons to the receiving chamber of Her Majesty and the audience it had enjoyed there; honour enough for any creature of the Horde to be satisfied. Even to remember its thinkings when it led the Queen's Vengeance through the break in the capstone–the rift that it, thresh, had discovered–even those thinkings came tinted with just enough remembrance of how significant, how very, very important thresh had felt itself.

Until it all turned to urmin squirt, of course.

Even now thresh did not know what went wrong. Oh, it certainly recalled all the terrible and humiliating details. The confusing lines of the human settlement, the way the village they thought they were to overrun went on and on appearing to grow ever larger the further it was from the eyestalk. The vexing way in which the calflings themselves did not immediately flee in the face of their natural predators. The deeply disturbing and impenetrable magicks they appeared to wield, not just their wizards, but all of them. Glowing amulets, beastless chariots, Drakon of steel that seemed to be leashed to their warriors... To *human* warriors. The very memory was an abomination of such mesmerising power that thresh remained too long hunched down in one spot, suddenly yelping when it realised that the pain it felt was not a memory of human fire scorching its ass, but the glowing iron grate burning a cross weave pattern into its ass right then and there.

Thresh squealed in a most undignified fashion and

gouged a couple more furrows in its hide as it struggled to quickly change position.

Oh yes, it remembered the details. It remembered the pain and confusion and fear. Most of all it remembered the Dave. The human champion who had challenged and humiliated Urspite Scaroth ur Hunn before his thrall. There was as little explanation for the mystery of the Dave as there was for any of the many, many myriad mysteries and embarrassments of their failed sortie into the human realm.

Thresh could recall every detail, every slight, every insult offered by the calflings, and of course thresh well remembered their treachery when the Dave had challenged Scaroth and bested him in single combat. Safe passage they had been promised back to the UnderRealms. Treachery and ambush were all the Dave delivered.

None of it made any sense.

Except the treachery, perhaps. You had to give the Dave some credit for the treachery. As treacherous as it had been, it was a stroke worthy of a BattleMaster. Not at all the sort of thing one would expect from a calfling.

Thresh grunted and shifted again, wondering when its moment would come, when the trap door would drop away beneath it, or one of the Inquisitors Grymm would appear far above to shoot a snatching hook down to drag Thresh up for dinner.

'Thresh, attend.'

The latter, it seemed.

Thresh lowered its eyestalks and bared its neck for the hook. It tried to clear its tiny mind of all thinkings and feelings as it waited for the end. Best not to go dwelling on its many failures and fathomless disgrace lest it be taunted by the spirits of the nest forever in the AfterRealm.

'Thresh, ATTEND!'

The stentorian roar echoing down the volcanic throat in which Thresh lay like an undigested lump of calfling meat was loud enough and fierce enough to jolt thresh from its morbid revelry. Slowly, fearfully thresh turned its eyestalks upward. Expecting to find an Inquisitor guard and leashed Fangr, all rational thinkings deserted it upon discovering the squat and massive form of Lord Guyuk ur Grymm himself.

'My... My Lord... thresh... thresh...'

'Yes, yes, thresh has no idea of what is happening or what to do. Nor does the Lord Commander of Her Majesty's Grymm, thresh. None of us do. But you are going to help me change all that.'

'Be careful, Captain,' growled Guyuk. 'We don't want it coming apart like the last one.'

The Captain Inquisitor of the Night had the good sense to look abashed at the rebuke, but relieved as well. It was not so long ago that the Grymm lord's predecessor would have thrown the clumsy oaf down into the pits for his incompetence in killing a captive before they had extracted any useful confessions. The irony of wasting a perfectly good Inquisitor for wasting a perfectly good prisoner had not been lost on Lord Guyuk, however, and under his enlightened rule summary executions had largely been replaced with vicious floggings and the threat of vicious floggings, with the occasional execution thrown in to keep everyone up on their claws.

Having pulled the head off the last prisoner he'd

attempted to haul up, the good captain made a studied effort to be more careful, even gentle in presenting this one to his lordship. He didn't even use a hook, instead lowering down a knotted rope after removing the guard ring of wulfin fangs from the pit mouth.

'He might be a bit messy, my Lord,' the captain said by way of apology. 'I'll do my best but this is one of our pointier sinkholes. Tenderises the prisoners, you know. For the pot.'

'Well he's not going into the pot, Captain. The pot is full. They all are full, thanks to your efforts.'

Guyuk allowed enough displeasure to creep into his voice to imply that more pots could be dragged down here if he found it necessary to put a certain captain on the menu for the barracks.

'Take care, thresh,' the captain called down the hole. 'Watch out for that next pointy bit.'

Slowly, by degrees and by inches the tiny empath-daemon was drawn out of the hole. It emerged torn and oozing, with great flaps of its hide hanging loose and one eyestalk completely broken. Pus and blood dripped from fresh ruptures while older bruises and scars were still livid and green. The Captain Inquisitor stood full three times its height and had to crouch at the knees to gather up the tiny thresh and carry it to a waiting litter.

'Here, give it this,' said Guyuk, passing across a goblet of bloodwine. The captain held the cup to its lips and let the creature sip. The effect was not immediate, but it was soon noticeable. The thresh struggled to rise so that it might prostrate itself before its betters.

'Save your strength, thresh,' said the Grymm lord. 'You will need it.'

The commander of Her Majesty's elite forces indicated to the Captain Inquisitor of the Night that he should not spare the bloodwine.

'Nothing better for an injured warrior,' said Guyuk. That brought a response from the thresh, all of its functioning eyestalks turned on him. 'Oh yes, you are a warrior, thresh. And a valued one. We Grymm are of the Horde but don't imagine that I share the prejudices of those fool Hunn. You didn't lead Her Majesty's Vengeance into ignominy and shame. You did all that was asked of you, all that could be expected of one so puny. And more.'

The Lord Commander of the Grymm patted the coarse scaled armour of the creature's neck ridges.

'You brought us an account of the rout that was admirable in its honesty. You did not try to dissemble or distract, to apportion or even to lay blame. Nor can we overlook your original discovery of the breach in the capstone. As much trouble as it has brought upon certain individuals within the Horde, it remains of epochal importance.'

Guyuk leaned in close and held the goblet up to the creature's lips again.

'You have ended eons of banishment, thresh. But your work is not done.'

The creature's eyestalks quivered.

'I… I… thresh…'

'We understand,' said Guyuk. 'This has all been very unsettling for all of us. Would that this affair had been left to the Grymm alone. There need have been no embarrassment to Her Majesty, to the Horde. Alas, it was not. And even now, thresh, I struggle to restrain the stupidity of the Hunn. I wonder if I might call on you to assist me…'

He regarded the empath as one would a new tool of doubtful provenance and utility.

'...or whether I should just toss you back in the hole.'

'Thresh can assist! Thresh can always... always assist my Lord.'

'Excellent,' said Guyuk. 'Come, hobble with me, if you will.'

It rolled off the litter, licking the last of the bloodwine from the goblet and shambling along after him.

'Can you sense them, thresh? The calflings?'

The empath stopped and sniffed the thick, sulphurous air. Its sensory stalks, the ones that still worked anyway, seemed to test some humour that floated on the air but which the Grymm lord could not see.

'There are many of them, my Lord,' it croaked, still weak. 'Two, three score.'

'Indeed,' said Guyuk.

'I feel their fear and their pain and... a great confusion and... mourning. A sort of mourning. But mostly pain and fear.'

The creature seemed to grow a little in strength as it fed on whatever it could taste in the air.

'Would my Lord have me encourage their terrors?' it asked.

'Not yet. I have something else I want of you. Something the Scolari Grymm have advised might be possible.'

Thresh looked from the Grymm lord to the captain with no great certainty.

'The Scolari, my Lord. But I... I am merely thresh. I...'

'We know what you are, thresh. And the Scolari insist you try.'

Guyuk leaned forward as if to impart a great secret, or some terrible blasphemy. The latter, as it happened.

'They believe they know the seat of the human thinkings.'

'The cattle, my Lord? But... but... they are cattle. They do not...'

'Thresh!' he barked. 'You are no longer under Scaroth's yoke here. You serve the Grymm now and we do not hold with the *wilful* ignorance of the Hunn. If the Scolari Grymm tell me they have located the seat of human thinkings, then I do not rage and rake against the profane. I simply do as I will to fight the greater profanity it promises. As must you.'

The creature dipped its stalks in a show of obeisance.

'Come, Thresh,' rumbled Lord Guyuk, inflecting the tone in which he addressed the creature with a slight, but noticeable guttural emphasis that raised it in his consideration from object to subject.

'Of course, of course, my Lord,' babbled the creature, all but undone by the recognition it had just been paid.

Guyuk was not being generous or indulgent. He needed this creature at its best. Of all the *Hordem* who had so far ventured to the surface only this creature had done so twice and survived. The confessions of the remnants of Scaroth's thrall also spoke of the Thresh endeavouring to advise the disgraced BattleMaster more than once that caution should be his watchword. Advice the wretched brute had ignored at great cost to Her Majesty. Already the Grymm lord's spies across the realms whispered of her rivals making due preparations not just to swarm their own forces Above, but to press on the borders of his monarch, who had lost standing as word of Scaroth's incompetence spread.

The three daemonum approached the edge of the largest pit, a great open-throated maw, large enough for a circular staircase to have been carved out of the walls of the volcanic flume. The rough-hewn steps were not quite wide enough for the two Grymm to walk down abreast of each other, but more than adequate for the Grymm lord to descend with Thresh at his side while the captain led the way. A guard with leashed Fangr waited a few strides from the bottom. He roared acknowledgement of their approach, smashing his mailed fist into an iron breastplate as he stood aside to allow them access to the prisoner.

It was a pitiable thing, and not for the first time did Lord Guyuk question whether he actually stood here or whether he'd wandered through some strangely coherent delirium brought on by sucking addled Drakon eggs. This was a human as he had learned of them from the old scrolls. Thin and stringy prey, so undone by the terror of proximity to even daemon minorae such as the Thresh that it was crippled by deep body tremors, basted in its own pastes and juices and unable to communicate in anything other than garbled babbling, shuddering moans and the occasional scream. Again, Lord Guyuk had to struggle against his appetites as the rank, delicious odour of the calfling reached his nostrils. It was particularly strong down here. Strong enough that the lord commander wondered if the Captain Inquisitor of the Night had seen to the feeding of the guards before they came on duty. It would be a powerful temptation, even to a Grymm, to take just a little bite.

He noted with some satisfaction that the Thresh, although likewise affected, was making an obvious effort to restrain itself. In its weakened state it must have been a terrible provocation, having prey so near and so helpless. Perhaps there was something more to this minor daemon than the dumb luck of having been one of the first through the breach in the capstone. It turned to him now, all eyestalks and anticipation. When it spoke it did so in a noticeably stronger voice, undoubtedly revived by the bloodwine, and perhaps by some empathetic nourishment taken from the calfling, which had tried to back itself into a corner to get away from them.

Stupid calflings. There are no corners in circular cells.

Guyuk grunted in fatigue and exasperation. He had not rested since receiving first word of the breach into the Above. Had not been able to rest because of the way the Hunn had turned what should have been a triumph into a septic wound. As was their way.

'What would you have me do, my Lord?' asked the Thresh.

'I would know its thinkings, Thresh,' replied Guyuk, holding up a claw to forestall any objection or demurral. 'I understand it is not within your ken to know such things in the particular. And I do not need an empath to tell me that this animal is terrified and confused to the point of disorder. What I would know are its most intimate thinkings, Thresh, and these, my Scolari Grymm imagine, are to be found in the creature's tiny head. In the sweetmeats contained therein.'

Both the Thresh and the Captain Inquisitor of the Night could not contain their surprise.

The captain bared his canines involuntarily, before quickly snapping closed his jaw and fixing the prisoner with a blank stare. Lord Guyuk was bemused and even encouraged to see the little Thresh, on the other claw, give free rein to its surprise. This was what the Grymm lord needed. Allies, or at the very least vassals, who could see a threat for what it was and not some arcane blasphemy.

'But my Lord, it is only… as you say… an animal…'

Guyuk leaned down until his maw was so close to the empath that the little daemon was forced to retract its eyestalks.

'These animals,' he growled, 'destroyed two Talon of the Horde. Their champion, the Dave, not only challenged a BattleMaster of the Legion but put down two of my Lieutenants Grymm. You have confessed yourself to the unexpected extent of the human village you entered and to the unanticipated depth of craft displayed by their smiths and armourers. These would be surprise enough for anyone, but surprise me one last time, Thresh, and tell me of this creature's thinkings.'

The creature itself seemed to understand it was the object of their exchange, but unlike the Dave, which had not just spoken in the Olde Tongue but done so with the distinctive nasal drone of a Hunn superior raised from hatching within the nest of the Fourth Legion, their captive was all but deaf and mute. Save for its miserable whining, naturally. Also obvious was the confusion and indecisiveness of the Thresh as to how it might proceed. Guyuk was not asking it to merely listen to and amplify the waves of *zhi* humming off the human cow; he was asking what had always been assumed to be impossible: to read and express the very thinkings of a creature without such things. Cows did not think. They felt, but they did not think.

The captain and the pit guard were doubtless as nonplussed as the inferior daemon, and both had retreated into stone-faced silence to mask their curiosity. And probably their outrage. For what the Grymm lord suggested, whether on the advice of the Scolari or not, was the very definition of an outrage.

'The sweetmeats?' asked the Thresh.

Guyuk squatted down on his haunches so that he merely towered over the empath by a measure of twice its height.

'In the skull. The Scolari Grymm are not settled on this question, but a consensus has emerged that it is a question worth asking. They entertain a presumption that should the creature be possessed of thinkings, and should these thinkings be contained within the soft grey meat housed within the bowl of the skull, that a suitable empath daemon might consume the lot, sweetmeat and the thinkings within, were it able to ingest both within a reasonable period.'

The Thresh turned its eyestalks on the prisoner, back to the Lord Grymm Commander, and then to the calfling again.

'Do the Scolari Grymm entertain conjecture of how...'

'With all dispatch,' Guyuk said softly, with one great armoured limb around the tiny daemon as though it were his own nestling. 'They advise that we puncture the bowl of the skull front and rear at exactly the same moment and draw the soft contents out as swiftly as prudence allows.'

'Suck them out? All at once?'

'Indeed.'

The Thresh, which had recovered much of its composure, if not its shredded hide, took one last look at the cowering human.

'It shall be done, my Lord.'

Lord Guyuk ur Grymm had not even climbed back to his full height before the Thresh had sped across the width of the cell, caught the prisoner's head in its talons and punched two neat holes fore and aft through the thin mantle of bone which was somehow supposed to protect the animal's sentience. The captive creature had but a fraction of a moment to react. It stiffened in shock and drew in barely half a breath before two solid wet crunching sounds signalled the penetration of its skull. Guyuk heard a slight sucking sound and a large pop. The Thresh stood quite still for so long that the pit guard took one step down in anticipation of trouble.

Thresh shuddered violently. The tremors passed quickly enough but when the empath daemon turned around it was observably changed. Not in appearance, but in attitude, in posture, in the way its eyestalks moved about the cell examining every surface, every detail before settling back on the figures of the guard, his captain, and their Lord Grymm Commander.

'Whoa, dude,' said the Thresh in a most unusual intonation to carry the most unusual of words. 'This totally sucks ass.'

## 08

They tried to get rid of Boylan. Heath in particular tried very hard, which surprised Dave. He'd have thought Compton might take the lead on that.

'Dave, I have no idea what we're flying into,' Heath said as they hurried out of the lounge, where the background mutter of conversation was growing louder and getting a jagged edge to it. 'But it is going to be a gigantic shit show compared with New Orleans. I really don't think it's a good idea for you to be taking your damned attorney.'

'Hunter S. Thompson would disagree,' said Dave, refusing to take the issue seriously. Because if he did, he might have to concede they had a point, and he was kinda digging having Boylan in his corner.

'And Dr Thompson would be right, God rest his soul,' said the lawyer, hurrying to keep up with the small group, his little legs taking two strides for every one the crippled Heath required.

'Dave,' said Heath, practising his Very Patient Voice, 'I'm sure Professor Boylan would best be able to advance your interests if he remained here at the hotel, or even at his own office, where, presumably, Brad Pitt and Michael Bay and

*America's Next Top Model* know to find him.'

Boylan, unsurprisingly, was not to be bumped off the A-List so easily.

'Oh fear not, Captain,' he said. 'I am the cavalry, sir. I do not sit idly by and wait for opportunity to seek me out. Rather, sir, I seek it, which is to say I hunt it, without relent or remorse. Wherever my client goes, so do I, even if that means following him into the Gates of Hell.'

He turned slightly and took Dave by the elbow as they continued toward the elevators, led by Chief Allen and Igor.

'Dave, I hope you realise,' Boylan said in a stage whisper, 'that by the Gates of Hell I'm speaking metaphorically, implying that I will accompany you into quite difficult situations, up to and including the mildly hazardous, but I'm afraid I will not literally be able to follow you through the Gates of Hell, should they have opened in Omaha. I'm a lawyer, Dave, and it's probably best I don't get anywhere near the Gates of Hell.'

The elevator doors hummed open and Emmeline stepped in, holding a hand up to hold them off.

'Somebody has to go down and let the hotel know that show-and-tell is over. Hooper will be needing his mighty hammer of smashening. Igor?'

Her unusually expressive cocked eyebrow was enough to let the giant SEAL know she'd be wanting an escort. Dave wondered if she practised in the mirror when nobody was watching.

'On it,' said Igor. He followed her out.

Compton finally spoke up when the door shushed closed on them.

'I flatly refuse to countenance him travelling anywhere with us,' he said.

'Oh my. How rude,' said Boylan. 'I'm standing right here you know.'

'S'cool,' Dave shrugged. 'You can stay if you want. Compton, X is coming with me.'

'The protocols simply don't allow for it,' said Compton, stabbing at the button to summon another elevator car.

But Dave wasn't having any of that shit.

'You got your protocols, and I got mine, buddy,' he said as the next car arrived and they stepped in. 'And I say X comes with us. Not sure if you noticed, but your pal Trinder isn't the only asshole wants a piece of old Dave here, and I don't see you doing much to help on that score. Sure, you'll fend off guys like Trinder because they're pissing on your turf. But guys like Trinder aren't my problem, they're yours. My problem is a soon-to-be ex-wife and her vengeful fucking lawyer. My problem is a bunch of carnivorous fucking credit card companies and their debt collectors and their vengeful lawyers. *My* problem is the Internal Goddamned Revenue Service and *their* vengeful fucking lawyers, and I know for a stone fact you're not going to do diddly fucking squat about them, because any pressure they can put on me is going to make it easier for you to pressure me as well. *Ooh Dave just come with us to our secret underground military base and we'll put in a good word for you.* So I'm taking my lawyer with me. I will protect him from the Horde and he will protect me from you, and Trinder and Annie and anybody who wants to get between me and my lunch with Brad Pitt. And Angelina,' he added, muttering to Boylan, 'Angelina's going to be there, right?'

Boylan looked doubtful for the first time that morning.

'I would never lie to you, Dave.' He frowned. 'Never. That's why I told you, quite honestly, I cannot possibly follow you to the Gates of Hell. Because I cannot tell a lie, Dave. Not about this.' He took a deep breath, as though to pronounce a death sentence. 'No, I don't think Angelina will be there. I'm pretty sure she's gone shopping for more orphans in Africa. But if you like, we can get somebody else along. Anybody, really. Except Jennifer Aniston.'

The lawyer seemed impervious to the ugly glare he was still getting from Compton.

'That's too bad,' said Dave. 'Jennifer Aniston's hot.'

'And she's not dating at the moment either,' declared Boylan, brightening up. 'Would you like me to set something up while we're in LA?'

Dave would very much have liked that, but Compton cut them off with a single word, loud enough to make everyone jump.

'No!'

The elevator stopped at that moment, the doors hummed open and they poured out onto the little balcony which led to the suspended bridge to the Chairman's Suite. Dave and Boylan stepped out, and for a second the others remained behind, as if refusing to follow them.

'You are not going to LA,' Compton said again.

'Whatever,' said Dave.

And he punched on the warp drive, leaving the others behind him.

He stopped. Everything had stopped, of course.

But that was the first time he recalled flicking the switch on his personal warp core just because he felt like it, and not because of some imminent danger.

Did that mean something?

*Meh.*

Dave shrugged and got moving. Until he got his Nobel Prize in monster physics, he'd never know.

For now, he figured he'd pick up his stuff, and sure, he'd get on the damn plane for Omaha. But because of Heath, not Compton. Heath could be a pain–the way that a four foot rod of hardened tungsten could be a pain if it was jammed up your ass–but he hadn't done Dave wrong yet. He had to admit that. So he'd go to Omaha, kick some ass for Heath. But then, by God, he was having lunch in LA with Brad Pitt.

First though, he knew he had to give a little something with these guys, even Compton. Not because Heath could stop him doing anything, of course, not if Dave *really* wanted to do it. But because fuck knows where he'd be a week from now if he threw in his lot with some asshole like Trinder. Not having lunch with Brad Pitt and trying his luck with Jennifer Aniston, that's for sure. He'd probably end up strapped on a gurney in some Gitmo dungeon with dozens of tubes stuck in his ass. He'd been in the shit with the one-legged spec ops guy since the start of this thing, and he just had a feeling he could probably get away with a bit more if he stuck with him. After all, unlike his wife, Heath seemed to understand Dave was a man who needed his freedom.

All these thoughts Dave had in the microseconds it took him to cover the distance between the elevator and his suite. He used the key card to gain entrance to the penthouse, closing the door behind him but staying in warp, so he didn't have to put up with anyone's shit. Cleaners had been through in the short time he'd been away. A whole team of them, judging by the immaculate state of the apartment. The broken beds and the busted dining table had been replaced.

Obviously not their first rodeo, Dave thought.

All of the clothes he and girls had tossed on the floor, over the furniture, hanging from light fittings, had been neatly folded and stowed away. Somewhere. That was okay. He was cool with the outfit Armando had chosen for him. Looked kind of boss in it, actually, now that he had Captain America's body. He headed straight for the larger of the two bathrooms, stripping as he went. What he wanted most in the world right now was a quick hot shower and somebody to make his problems go away so he could enjoy being a superhero, which, on the evidence so far, mostly consisted of living in hotels for free and getting lots of pussy.

Problem number one was Annie's lawyer.

Annie's lawyer would definitely interfere with Dave having nice things and getting lots of pussy. In that way he was the perfect expression of Annie's will. If dealing with them meant taking on this guy Boylan, then so be it. He'd never had a decent lawyer before, and this guy seemed to know his stuff. Or at least he knew enough to be persistent, which was more than Dave could say for the useless softcock he'd hired to shepherd him through the separation and on into the promised land of divorce. That ass-clown had basically taken a huge fee for separating Dave from way more than half of everything he owned and earned, before passing it on to Annie wrapped up in a big red bow.

He turned on the faucet and frowned. After a few coughing spurts of warm water, nothing came out. For a second he was about to curse out the front desk, then he remembered he was in warp. The water would be moving very, very slowly through the pipe.

He popped back into real time for a few moments, just long enough to get wet and lather up.

He didn't want Compton or Heath interrupting his shower.

The more he thought about Annie and the papers she served on him, the angrier he got. A couple of days ago, when he spoke to her on the phone after getting out of hospital, she'd at least pretended to be concerned about him, even if that concern manifested itself in Annie's usual manner: judgmental sniping. It wasn't fair, he thought, as he scrubbed away at his scalp under the steaming hot shower. He'd done the right thing in New Orleans. Been the guy everyone wanted him to be. And now she was going to make him pay for it? Literally?

He paused in his lathering. Was 'literally' right in that context? Yes, he decided, yes it was. She was literally going to fuck him for everything, and not in a good way. He dropped out of warp long enough to rinse off the shampoo, keeping his eyes squeezed tight, and then reached for the small bottle of conditioner before he stopped, suddenly aware of what he was doing. He hadn't used conditioner in years. Hadn't needed to. He didn't have that much hair left. Its 'condition' was 'gone'. But he'd been so pissed off about getting served by Vietch that he hadn't really noticed while he was washing his hair that he was actually *washing his goddamn hair,* not just running fingertips across stubble.

'Damn,' he said to himself. 'I got hair now.'

That had been another casualty of his marriage, of course. He'd gone from merely thinning out a little to full-blown chrome dome those last couple of years with Annie. And since the hair had retreated from his scalp of course it'd started growing like pubic kudzu everywhere else, including out of his ears.

Forgetting the conditioner, he finished rinsing off before

stepping out of the marble and glass shower stall. He checked himself out in the bathroom mirror, using his towel to wipe away the steam. Hell, yes. He had a full head of hair on the top while his body hair faded off into nothing. Before long he'd look like one of those guys who were on the covers of the trashy romance novels Annie liked to read when the boys were asleep.

Dave grinned and knocked on the side of his head with a fist.

'Hey. Urgon? You still in there, buddy? Thanks for the fucking do, man. Owe you a solid, orc brother.'

Urgon did not reply.

His thoughts slipped back to Annie, however, and the smile faded.

He wondered if he should call her. Try to calm her down. Or maybe just call the boys and ask them whether Mom had been acting kind of nutty the last couple of days. You know, like extra nutty. He hadn't spoken to them since kickin' ass in N'Orleans, a happy parental memory for once. Toby and Jack had climbed over each other to get to the phone when he'd called.

'You're all over the net, Dad,' they'd cried, and for once he didn't have to worry about whether that meant they'd found his hairy ass hanging out of some chick's Facebook timeline.

Dave was a hero, a genuine hero, not just on the news but to his boys and that had been such an unusual and pleasing moment that afterward he had gone right out to a titty bar to celebrate. The Penthouse Club in the French Quarter. The whole bar had stood him drink after drink, the management threw him a complimentary lap dance and a couple of the girls got him up onto the actual forbidden zone of the runway to re-enact his showdown with Urspite, one of them donning a gorilla mask to play the role of the BattleMaster while her colleague worked the pole because... well, because it was there.

Of course, he hadn't ridden Urspite like a mechanical bull, or playfully smacked his fine tattooed ass while hundreds of cheering drunks roared encouragement, but there had to be room for artistic licence.

The club had been relatively quiet when he'd arrived, but it was roaring when he finally left, escorted off the premises by an unamused Compton flanked by Zach and Igor.

'Yeah, good times,' he said in the mirror, his reflection obscured by the steam again. The lights flickered for a second as he was wiping the steam off the glass to get a better look at his new hairline, but they came back on and stayed on, so he could admire himself a little longer.

'Hello Dave.'

'Holy shit,' he squawked, jumping at the unexpected voice. For the briefest moment he wondered what'd happened to his time warp. But he'd turned it off. The woman at the bathroom door was about thirty years old, blonde, good-looking and...

'Samantha McIntosh.' She smiled. 'But my friends call me Smack.'

'Oh. Hi, Smack,' said Dave still off balance. She seemed to have snuck into the room under his radar. He had radar now. He didn't think much about it, but when he did, he could close his eyes and tell where everybody in a room was standing. He didn't know whether it was some weird monster skill he'd inherited from Urgon, or just the natural amplification of his own senses; in the same way that his strength and speed had been amplified, he supposed.

'Sorry to break in,' she said with a slow smile that seemed to imply she wasn't sorry at all. 'But it's what I do.'

'What? You're like a cat burglar or something?'

'Something,' she said. 'I work for the Central Intelligence Agency, Dave. Perhaps you've heard of us.'

She advanced on him slowly, placing her feet one in front of the other as carefully as any catwalk model. Perhaps she had been a model at some point. She had the looks for it. Her head was tilted slightly toward one shoulder and a few strands of long hair had come loose of her carefully arranged coif. Come loose on purpose, he thought, as she twirled them around one finger. He felt his dick stirring as she drew closer and he couldn't help imagining doing to her just a little of what he'd done with Knoxy and Mulan last night.

Oh man, he thought. Think with your head, not your dick, just for once.

The CIA played a large part in sending his brother to Iraq.

The CIA was no friend of his.

No matter how much he might be inclined to tumble one of their representatives into bed and grudge-fuck her.

He did give it a moment's thought. He was Dave, after all. But the memory of his mother falling to the kitchen floor when the death notice came to the door, splitting her head on the corner of the table as she fainted, was enough to shrivel his cock.

'Sorry, Smack,' he said, leaving her caught in the gel-like embrace of normal time while he warped through the suite, grabbing up his bag. He stayed in the fast-track as he dressed again. He had no idea how much energy he used doing this stuff, as opposed to, say, leaping tall buildings in a single bound. It occurred to him that maybe it might be an idea to sit down with the pointy heads and get some tests done to find his limits and how much fuel he needed to reach them and stay there.

But for now he was content to avoid any entanglement with the CIA and their sexy messenger, goosing her gently as he passed by. He slipped back outside and rejoined the others. He had to stifle a snort of amusement when he heard the spook cry out in surprise behind him.

Nobody else seemed to hear it.

'Let's go,' he said, holding up the bag for Heath to see.

The door of the Chairman's Suite opened and red-faced Agent McIntosh appeared.

'Who's that?' asked Heath.

'The hoagie delivery woman,' said Dave. 'She came about my foot-long.'

He stepped past Compton and Heath, heading for the elevator which would take him down to the main foyer to grab Lucille.

**09**

Their ride through the sky looked like every other commercial jet liner Dave had flown on, more than big enough for the two SEAL teams stomping up the stairs with all their carry-on gear.

'Air Force was sending a C-40 but that had to get in from the 201st Airlift over in Washington,' Heath said as they waited on the tarmac at Northtown. Smaller than the big international field at McCarran, it was also a handy three klicks from downtown. Dave could see the airfield was crowded because of the flight ban, but most of the craft were twin prop and lesser commercial jets. The fat boys were all over at LV's main airport. Jumbos. 767s. Airbuses from all over the world. Piled up around the tarmac like cars at a weekend swap meet. When the last of the commandos was aboard Heath gestured for the civilians to climb the stairs into the plane.

'So what, you guys leased this bird?' Dave asked.

'After New Orleans, OSTP received an emergency funding line,' said Compton, who seemed to have accepted the presence of Boylan when he was made to understand he had no goddamned choice about it. And after Boylan had signed a stack of non-disclosure agreements in his own blood.

'So yes, we leased it. And no, I won't be covering your bar bills at Hooters. Now get in.'

Climbing up the stairs Dave muttered to himself, 'They must have given you one of them plutonium Amex cards.'

He felt surprisingly comfortable in the luxurious surrounds of the airplane which, Boylan informed him, was a Boeing Business Jet 737–700. Unlike most jets, which felt like being jammed into a tin can, this bad boy was outfitted with a conference table, flat-screen televisions, a lounge area and a full service wet bar.

'Fuck me,' Igor breathed. 'Bond never had it this good.'

'Connery would definitely approve,' Zach said.

'Nah, this feels more like Craig,' Igor replied.

'Craig's pretty badass.'

Igor nodded; it was a slow, measured movement which took in Dave's entire frame.

'Mister Hooper, we are very happy to have you onboard,' a hostess said with a noticeable moistening of her lips. 'Your seat is over here.'

Maybe it was the natty outfit Armando had dressed him in. Maybe it was the hostess telling him, yes, she could totally make him a martini as soon as they were in level flight. But most likely it was the enormous and obscenely comfortable leather chair he sank into as though returning home after a long absence. It all made him feel as though every path he had walked had led him right here. The plane even boasted a humidor. He had a smoking buddy from Georgia who would die to be with him right now.

'Oh man, I was meant to live like this, not work for assholes who live like this,' he said, as Igor and Zach Allen stowed their baggage up front.

'And never forget that, Dave,' said Boylan, who was about to take the seat opposite until shooed away by Emmeline.

'Why don't you work your phone?' she suggested. 'Aren't you supposed to be pimping out Jennifer Aniston?'

'Oh you,' Boylan mugged back at her.

He held up his briefcase for Dave to see. 'We have a four or five hour flight in front of us,' he said. 'I'm going to get on top of this problem with your wife. Unless of course you want me pimping out Jennifer Aniston. In which case…'

'It's okay,' Dave said, throwing up his hands. 'If you can get Annie off my back as a starter, that'd be awesome. I'll go kick some monster butt. You deal with this Vietch asshole, and then we can go have some D-time in LA.'

'D-time?' Emmeline said. 'Please don't tell me that means Dave Time.'

'Then I can tell you nothing.' He grinned.

Emmeline muttered something under her breath, and he was pretty sure it was uncomplimentary to the concept of Dave Time, but unlike Compton there never seemed to be any personal malice in Emmeline. It must just be that she was British, he thought, or retarded with her autism and stuff.

Without hundreds of other passengers to board carrying tons of hand luggage to avoid excess baggage fees, the small group was seated and ready for takeoff within minutes. The Boeing had been fitted out with eight extra-large recliners staggered in sets of two through the first third of the compartment. The hostess made her way around to ensure everyone was strapped in, and Dave was certain she paid particular attention to his harness.

'Thanks darlin',' he said. 'How long until I can get that drink?'

'Couple of minutes, hon.' She smiled. 'After wheels up. Stay frosty.'

'Oh for the love of God,' Ashbury muttered.

Dave felt the same stirring in his groin occasioned by Agent McIntosh back at the Bellagio, but a sharp kick to his shin by Professor Ashbury shut that shit right down.

'Ouch!'

'Oh don't be a baby. You're supposed to be indestructible.'

She returned to stowing her gear and ignoring him. There was none of the usual delay with taxiing and waiting for takeoff. Maybe because they had priority, but probably because there were no other flights coming into or out of the airfield.

'What if we do meet *dar Drakon*? Sorry, dragon,' Dave asked. 'You ain't figuring on me going out there on the wings to punch it in the snout are you?'

Heath spoke up from across the aisle and down a few feet, where he was deeply recessed in the buttery leather of a comfy Blofeld chair, facing Compton. 'We have an escort out of Nellis. Four Air Force Warthogs and our own Super Hornets. They should be airborne now, providing combat air patrol. Tankers will meet them along the way to top them up. We'll be fine, as long as your fire-breathing pterodactyl friends don't travel in packs. And even then we'll probably be fine. The Hornets can take on multiple hostiles at once while the Warthogs can mix it up close.'

'Super Hornets are probably too fast,' Igor said. 'The dragons fly pretty slow I heard. The Red Baron could probably take one in a drag race.'

'Okay,' said Dave, having to raise his voice over the engine whine as the jet's acceleration pressed him back into his seat. The same G forces, he noticed, pulled Emmeline a little way forward out of hers and he wondered whether there was any difference in safety between having a forward-facing or rear-facing seat. Probably none that made a difference in the end.

The high-pitched scream of the engines became a deeper roar as they poured on power. The nose of the jet lifted up, and soon they seemed to be climbing much more steeply than he'd ever done before. Dave waited for the usual in-flight announcements from the captain, but there were none. Presumably Compton, having chartered the flight, was across all that shit.

Only the briefest interlude passed between the plane levelling off and the hostess reappearing with Dave's drink.

'I hope you don't mind, sir. I took the liberty of making you a dirty martini. I took you for a dirty boy.'

'Oh for fuck's sake,' said Emmeline.

'You can take me anytime, sweetheart.' Dave grinned. 'And keep these bad boys comin'. I got me a powerful thirst these days and it needs a whole heap of tending to if I'm even gonna–'

'Hooper,' said Emmeline in a voice that could crack ice. 'Do you think we could have a word.'

The look she fixed him with was significantly scarier than anything Urgon or Scaroth had ever managed.

'Sorry, Prof. Am I hogging the waitress? Would you like a frosty beverage?'

She glowered at him.

'No, I would like a word. Now.'

'Maybe I'll wait a few minutes on that second martini,' he told the attendant, and she nodded in a way that acknowledged the sudden tension and somehow made her Dave's accomplice in it.

When she was gone, Emmeline undid her seatbelt and leaned forward, beckoning Dave to do the same. He complied, not sure what was going on. But he really hoped she wasn't about to give him a lecture on sexual harassment. He risked a quick glance back and across the aisle at Heath and Compton, but they seemed to be ignoring him with studied intensity, pouring over documents and maps as though they hadn't heard any of the exchange that had just taken place.

'You have to stop doing this,' said Professor Ashbury.

'Doing what?'

'Trying to fuck every trolley dolly and chippy and Saudi Arabian princess you meet. It's not fair to them and it's going to get you into the sort of trouble that even Rumpole of the Bailey back there can't get you out of.'

Dave took a long pull on his martini. It was excellent, one of the best he'd ever had, but he was drinking it as a prop. Just something to put in front of his face to protect him from the anger of this strangely intense Englishwoman. Hard to believe he'd been attracted to her during the brief quiet time they'd spent out on the Longreach, because he was feeling the opposite of attraction now. He was feeling a serious need to get the hell away from her.

'What is your problem?' he asked, genuinely confused. He hadn't put the moves on her. In fact she'd told him in no uncertain terms that she wasn't interested in him, and he was enough of a grown-up for that to be the end of it.

The Boeing was remarkably quiet compared to all of the budget flights he'd endured over the years, but he didn't think of that as an advantage at the moment. Would've been good, in fact, if there were some kids screaming nearby, and some idiot teen sitting next to him leaking thrash metal from a pair of poorly insulated Beats.

Might have helped ease the feeling that he was standing naked in a spotlight.

'I don't have a problem,' said Emmeline in her clipped English tones. 'You do. You have a problem with women and I don't think you're even aware of it.'

He laughed and leaned back, taking the opportunity to finish off his drink. He didn't feel even the slightest buzz from it yet and part of him wondered how many he'd have to down before he got a decent drunk on.

'Oh hell, people been telling me I got a problem with women all my life. My wife, my girlfriends, the sensitivity trainers at Baron's.'

Emmeline squeezed her eyes shut and shook her head as if trying to fight through a migraine.

'That's not what I mean. Actually, that's exactly what I mean, but it's not all I mean. You have a problem, Dave. You've had it since New Orleans. Or rather, since the Longreach. And it's not just a matter of you being a tosser. Although that's a very large part of it.'

He made a conscious effort not to let Resentful Dave get in on this conversation. Resentful Dave was an old master at working his magic in these sorts of exchanges. But Resentful Dave, in the long, weary experience of Core Dave, rarely added anything useful.

'I don't know what you're talking about,' he said in as reasonable a voice as he could manage. 'Well, I suppose I do. But it's really none of your business, Emmeline. You're not my wife. You're not my boss. I'm not even sure what the hell you are to me other than some woman who's…'

Resentful Dave was about to say 'busting my balls'. Luckily, he shut the fuck up before he could toss that turd on the table.

'Okay. Look. Sorry. I shouldn't have said that. Yes, I know I can be an asshole, but...'

Emmeline rubbed at her temples. She stared at her knees. It was like trying to have a conversation with an angry fortune teller.

'That's not what I'm talking about, Hooper.'

He noted the use of his last name, and even felt a little stung by it. But he kept his mouth shut and waited for her to go on. She seemed to be struggling to find whatever words she needed. And then she looked up at him.

'I want to fuck you so much right now.'

A heartbeat. Two heartbeats.

'What the... er...'

He wasn't sure he'd heard her correctly.

The English professor, the rather good-looking English lady professor with the dark hair and the peaches and cream complexion, and the bodacious ta-ta's rolling around inside her shirt, she leaned forward and looked into his eyes with a cold detachment completely at odds with the words she'd just said to him. Or he thought she'd just said to him.

And then she confused him even further by repeating it, enunciating each word.

'I want to fuck you so much right now.'

Dave had to suppress a laugh at the idea of the word 'SPROING!' suddenly appearing over his crotch in large cartoon letters and explosion lines. What she said next helped him with that.

'But I'm not going to. I'm never going to do that. Because I don't really like you very much. You are quite an awful man with very few redeeming qualities beyond an ability to bash monsters to death. You are crude, unsophisticated, a vulgarian of the worst sort. I would sooner pull barbed wire out of my arse than allow you to lay a hand on me.'

Dave hardly knew what to say, so he kept it simple. 'Okay then.' The moment seemed to require that he say something more but all he had were gobbling noises at the back of his throat. They eventually formed themselves into something like, 'Jeez, Prof,' before she started up and rolled over the top of him again.

'And yet, I want to fuck you so much right now. Do you understand where this is going? Can you guess what I mean?'

He was blushing again. He'd done a lot of that lately, perhaps catching up on a lifetime's worth of it he seemed to have missed. He was also certain that everybody in the jet was studiously avoiding looking in his direction or giving the impression they'd heard a word of what Emmeline had just said.

'Well, I, er... I guess it's like hate-fucking someone you don't like. We've all done that.'

'No. No, we haven't. You may have extensive experience in the area, but normal people don't, Dave.'

She leaned back in the chair and released a shuddering breath as though she had just performed some difficult physical task like lifting a heavy weight.

'The women you had sex with at the hotel? The hostie you were just flirting with? The honey trap the CIA laid for you back at the hotel? Yes, Heath told me. Pretty much every woman who has brushed up against you since the Longreach? Then started rubbing up hard against you for no apparent reason? Other than you being awesome? Every single one of them was drugged.'

Anger flared inside Dave and he couldn't help himself. 'Bullshit,' he snapped back. But before he could get rolling Emmeline cut him off again.

'I didn't say you drugged them, although you did, even though you weren't aware of it.' She made an effort to sound conciliatory. 'Dave, from the moment I met you, and I suspect from the moment you killed the BattleMaster out on the rig, you have been...'

He watched her struggle for the words, and her struggle seemed so genuine that he kept his anger in check. He had no fucking idea what she was talking about, but it was costing her to do it.

'You have been... Exuding something. A pheromone, perhaps. Some sort of subliminal mating signal, below the level of hearing, unseen...' She reached into thin air with her hands as if trying to wrestle the idea out of nothing. 'I don't know what,' she said at last. 'But there is something coming off you, Dave. Something very strong, and for those who are unprepared, it is...'

The professor's inability to express herself was almost painful to watch.

'Are you saying it's like I'm wearing some kind of monster cologne?' Dave asked. 'Like Old Spice from Hell, or something? And the ladies just can't resist?'

She nodded, looking relieved, almost as though he had lifted the great weight from her.

And then her nodding turned into a shake of the head.

'No, or... almost. I can resist. I'm sure even you, Dave, have had the experience of being attracted to someone but deciding not to follow through. Perhaps someone who was so drunk that even you could not bring yourself to take advantage of her, no matter how much you liked her boobies.'

He snorted laughter at that.

'I think I should be insulted, but I'm gonna take it as one of your strange English compliments, all back-assward and up-fucked.'

'I'm sorry,' Emmeline said. 'This is very difficult. I think I'll take that drink now, actually. Do you think you could order it? I believe that if I have to speak to that hostess it will be the end of me.'

'Sure,' Dave said, surprised by the tenderness in his voice. 'Just gimme a second while I do my Speedy Gonzales thing.'

He popped down the back of the aircraft–quite literally. The hole in the cabin's atmosphere where he had been sitting made a small popping noise when he exited the chair at warp speed and flashed down to the galley where the flight attendant was busying herself preparing meals to distribute. She jumped a little when he appeared out of nowhere, and then smiled.

'Hello Mr Hooper,' she said, leaning back against the bulkhead in a way which let her breasts say hello too.

'Just call me Dave,' he said pleasantly, examining her to see whether or not she looked like she'd just taken a big hit off Dave's patented sex bong. Her cheeks were a little flushed, and her eyes very sparkly, but what the hell did that mean? She might have just taken a really good dump.

'Do you think I could get another martini now, and a gin and tonic for my friend? That's what English chicks drink, isn't it?'

'I make a lovely gin and tonic, Dave. Everyone drinks it.'

'Outstanding,' he said and winked before returning to his seat at a normal walking pace.

Emmeline raised one eyebrow at him. 'And?'

'Maybe,' he shrugged. 'But maybe I'm just awesome. Or maybe this is my fifteen minutes. D'you ever watch *Batman*, you know, the old TV show?'

'Sure. But why?'

'Well I read Robin's autobiography once.' When Dave saw the sceptical look on her face he protested. 'Hey, I read books.'

She rolled her eyes. 'Oh I do not doubt you read the autobiography of Batman's little friend. Go on.'

'Okay, I read it in Macy's, while Annie was shopping for shoes. I was desperate. You wouldn't think a woman could spend so many fucking hours confused about what to put on her feet.'

He saw The Look on her face, again.

'Or maybe you could. Anyway, I picked this thing off the shelf and read most of it standing there in the store. Let me tell you, Professor, Robin might've been a little guy, but he was a giant of the game when it came to chasing pussy. Whole damn book was about how much pussy he got. Except for the last chapter, which was this weird thing about how he found God or something. But anyway, a little bit of celebrity was all it took. You don't think that's what's happening here?'

She shook her head and smiled, almost sadly.

'I almost admire you for thinking that, Dave. But no. I am immune to celebrity. I don't even own a television these days.'

She paused when the flight attendant reappeared with their drinks. Two martinis for Dave, one dirty and one with a twist. And a sparkling cut-crystal tumbler, clinking with ice and fizzing with gin and tonic for Emmeline.

'Thought maybe you'd go for a twist, too,' she said to Dave.

'It's like you can read my mind.' He smiled.

This time, Professor Ashbury didn't react, or at least she didn't scold him. She just took half of the drink in one long gulp.

'Thank God for the British Raj,' she said.

'The what?'

She held up her drink and tinkled the ice cubes from side to side, a dainty movement, lest any of the contents slosh over the side.

'An artifact of Britain's colonial expansion,' she explained. 'Serving G and T's in the mess was the most effective and efficient way of administering quinine to Her Majesty's Indian regiments. To protect them from malaria.'

That was the sort of factoid that could win you an easy bar bet, Dave thought, filing it away. But before he could speak, Emmeline went on.

'No, Dave. It's not celebrity. I can tell you from unsettling personal experience that you have some kind of aura, I suppose, which affects me, affects all women, when they get to within about a cricket pitch's length of you. Twenty yards or so. It turns on like a light. I don't know what it is. I don't know what function it serves. Maybe it's some evolutionary trick, to ensure the bloody Chosen One's DNA gets handed on or some such rot. I have no idea. But I do know it's real and you need to be aware of it. You need to stop acting like a complete tosser.'

'A what?'

Dave sounded unsure, not because he didn't understand what she meant by the weird English expression, but because he was suddenly seeing the last few days through a radically different lens. Never shy about pursuing sex, he was also experienced in absorbing rejection, disinterest and even the occasional incident of physical revulsion at the very suggestion a woman might want to take a ride on the Dave Train. All of the interest in him since New Orleans, he'd put down to his new status. He was not just a hero, but a superhero, no matter what Compton said. He was buff. He was on TV. Everywhere they'd been in the last few days, every airport lounge, every bar, every fast food joint and hotel lobby. There he was, again and again, saving the world.

Who, besides the hardest of hard-core lesbians and his ex-wife, wouldn't want a piece of that? And what man wouldn't take advantage of it?

'A tosser, Dave. You've been a bit of a tosser. A wanker. I believe the delightful American colloquialism appropriate to your circumstances is douche bag.'

The sharp, serrated edge was gone from her voice, even as the words became crueller and more accusatory.

'So, on the rig. When we were alone and talking…' He trailed off. He had quite pleasant memories of that night, or at least those few minutes he spent talking with Emmeline. He'd thought she liked him.

'I wanted to climb you like a stairmaster. It was very confusing. I'm sorry if I gave you the impression that…'

She shrugged.

'That you wanted to climb me like a stairmaster?' Dave asked and she nodded.

'Yes. Sorry. I was undone, unbalanced. I had no idea where the sudden, quite unhinged erotic feelings I had for you had come from. But I'm an intelligent woman, Dave. Quite a bit smarter than you, and you're an intelligent man. In spite of your best efforts to pretend otherwise. I knew that whatever was happening had to be related to whatever had happened to you and so I put it aside. I've been doing that ever since.'

It was his turn to apologise but she brushed off his attempt before the word 'sorry' was fully out of his mouth.

'Don't be silly. We're grown-ups. And grown-ups put aside ridiculous infatuations all the time, for all sorts of reasons. Because they're inappropriate. Because they're impossible. Because they are dangerous. The question for you, Dave, is whether you will be able to put aside the effect you now seem to have on any woman who wanders within a stone's throw of you.'

It was as though the plane had dropped out from underneath him and he was free falling. It hadn't bothered him at all when he thought Georgia Knox had gone to bed with him because she wanted to get an exclusive TV interview out of him. And it had bothered him even less when that Saudi princess, who spoke about half a dozen words of English, used those half-dozen words to talk her way into his bedroom as well. Why the fuck would that bother any man? But he wasn't so sure he felt as good about the deal if it turned out they had been knocked sideways by some weird-ass mojo from the UnderRealms.

Or, maybe he was cool with it. What's the difference between some chick grabbing his joint because he'd been on TV, or doing the same thing because he was—what? Just more magnetic?

'Well I can see you're at least thinking about it,' Emmeline said before finishing off the last of her drink. Dave leaned forward again, keeping his voice down. He didn't need to look around the aircraft to know where everybody was, or that they had their heads down in whatever business they could find. Boylan working on his court documents. Heath and even Compton picking over binders full of documents, checking them against laptop and iPad screens. Igor and Chief Allen pestering the attendant for beers. Joy was her name, he knew, having noted her name badge without even being aware he'd done so. Was that more monster magic, or just him being a bit of an asshole again? The rest of the SEAL team were spread throughout the rear of the plane, checking gear, enjoying the comforts or catching some z's.

'So what, you got deputised to talk to me about this?' he asked in a low voice.

Emmeline leaned forward and whispered, 'You'd prefer to talk to Compton about it? He's really pissed off, by the way. I don't think he's been laid since his freshman year.'

Dave resisted the urge to look across at the academic.

'Figured,' he said conspiratorially, before leaning back. 'So, you know, what do I do about all the ladies wanting a taste of Super Dave's Special Sauce?'

Emmeline shrugged.

'Maybe you could ask Brad Pitt about it.'

# 10

Dave held Lucille in his hands as they passed over the Rocky Mountains. It was a clear day, affording a grand view of the western part of the continent's dark, broken spine, capped here and there on the highest peaks with thin dustings of ice and snow. Emmeline was asleep, knocked out by her gin and tonic on top of an exhausting week. He reached over and pulled down the shade on her window to spare her the late afternoon sun. None of them had enjoyed a full night's sleep since the Horde had emerged, and being on the road didn't help. It was less of a problem for Dave. When he did sleep, he slept heavily, almost too heavily, but any sort of rest, even a nap, seemed to recharge his batteries.

He left the softly snoring lady professor in her seat and carried Lucille down to hang out with Zach and Igor. He felt more comfortable with them, perhaps because they were the working stiffs of this outfit, not the bosses like Heath and Compton.

'You lay that thing down, it's not gonna punch a hole through the floor is it?' asked Igor as he approached.

'It's a *she*, and no. Just because she weighs a ton to a small boy like you, doesn't mean she weighs an actual ton to a real man.'

Igor snorted and gave him the finger.

'Ol' Luce here sat real happy on the display case those Bellagio guys knocked up in Vegas,' Dave said. 'And underneath all the silk and cushions, that was just plywood. Probably would've collapsed if Compton dropped his fat ass on it.'

He took a seat across the aisle from them, placing the weapon with its heavy steel head on the carpeted floor, the handle leaned up against his armrest. And there it would stay, as though welded in place. Heath insisted Dave carry Lucille with him whenever they were in transit because, not knowing anything about the physical properties of an enchanted splitting maul, they couldn't be certain that if it fell out of an overhead luggage bin it wouldn't crush or even messily cut in half anyone it landed on. The fact Lucille never moved an inch unless Dave laid hands on her meant nothing to the cautious officer.

'It's your responsibility,' said Heath. 'You carry it and you treat it like a suitcase nuke.'

Warm to the touch, Lucille reminded him of a dog he'd once had, way back during those long childhood summers when he liked to get in trouble with brother Andy and their cousin Darryl. Dave suspected she would not care at all for the comparison were she aware of it.

And he couldn't be entirely sure that she wasn't aware. The living weapon—that's how he thought of her, she was no longer a dumb tool—could sense his moods. He was sure of that, but she could not read his mind. Just like most women he knew.

'You hear any of that thing with Emmeline before?' he asked them, quietly.

'Some,' said Zach, suppressing a grin. 'She give you a schoolin' in modern gender etiquette, did she?'

'Yeah, some of that. So Heath or Compton didn't say anything to you guys?'

Zach Allen snorted this time.

'In the food chain of this operation, they're beef bourguignon and we're chicken-in-a-can.'

There was some relief in that for Dave. He didn't give a shit what Compton thought of him, and he was still sorting through how he felt about Heath and Emmeline. But the young chief petty officer with the weirdly Christian surfer dude charm, and even Igor, the grim-faced giant, their good opinion he found he did care about.

He peered out of a window where one of their escort planes, an ugly grey thing with a big honkin' cannon in the nose, kept station with a much sleeker, deadlier-looking jet fighter a few hundred yards away. He assumed he'd find a matching pair on the other side if he could be bothered to wander across the aisle and take a look. He didn't bother. He was just glad to have them along, riding shotgun.

*Dar Drakon*, he knew, were drawn to strange sounds. Intelligent and curious, but cruel as cats, they could not resist investigating anything that might prove to be a tasty treat, or provide a few moments of distraction by screaming or burning or coming apart in their claws in some new and exciting fashion. Dave suspected *dar Drakon* would find the sound of modern jet engines plenty strange, and way too fascinating a distraction to ignore.

Zach raised a cup of coffee and took a bite out of what looked like a freshly made Reuben sandwich. When he was done chewing and swallowing he said, 'This is pretty sweet, dude. We don't normally fly like this. Usually we're on C-130s. Prop jobs, noisy and cold. Mondo uncomfortable.'

'Like riding in the back of a pick-up?' Dave offered.

'Yeah, but without the complimentary keg or a mattress.'

Igor stared off out of his window, an empty plate smeared with gravy trails on the tray table in front of him.

'Cold down there in winter,' he said to no one in particular, already on the way to growing back his beard a day after he had clipped it all off. 'Worse than the Hindu Kush I reckon.' He rearranged himself, getting more comfortable, throwing one booted foot over his leg like a man settling in to watch a long football match, or a streaming binge on Netflix. Gone were the polo shirts and cargo pants of Las Vegas, replaced by green camo fatigues for both men. Compared to some of the other military types Dave had now met, the SEALs were more apt to look like they'd climbed out of bed in an Army Surplus store and thrown on whatever they picked up off the floor. He supposed they had to do the spit and polish thing at some time, but he had yet to see it. Another thing that endeared them to him.

'So you know what we're flying into?' Dave asked. 'You know, besides the shit?'

Zach took another sip of coffee and shrugged.

'Chicken-in-a-can here, Dave. When they want me to know, they'll update my Facebook page.'

Igor turned from the window. 'I read online that 0600 this morning, some fucking emissary of the Horde presented himself to the local notables at a Cracker Barrel outside of Omaha. Before one of the customers put five shells from a Remington autoloader into his ugly face, those patrons who didn't shit their pants and pass out straight away swore it was grunting something like "Pay tribute and respect to us and your village will be spared".'

'Really?' Dave said. 'So, what'd the folks in Cracker Barrel say about that?'

'They paid 'em some tribute.' Igor laughed. 'Five rounds of solid slug. Right in the fuckin' kisser.'

'That's a money shot,' Zach nodded. 'May the Lord forgive me.'

'It's gotta be bullshit,' said Dave. 'You read this online?'

'Strange Thingies dot com,' Igor said, without the hint of a smile.

'Seriously?'

A pause.

'Nah, io9. Why bullshit?'

'Because how could anyone but me understand what they were saying? Google Translate?'

'Ah, Dave, what's-a matter? You not feeling so special now?' Igor teased.

'No, he's right,' said Zach. 'Probably just a cool story. Net's full of them. News too. Even *New York Times* is running something about a bunch of rednecks fighting off a pack of Hunn last night, some place where cousins get married and play banjo with their toes. Heard it on the radio riding over to the airport.'

'Whatever,' Igor said. 'Cap'n tells me there's a concentration of 'em southwest of Omaha. Ten thousand or more. Says we don't have much time.'

'Outside?' Dave asked. 'Like in a field or something?'

'Yeah, near the SAC museum.'

'Wait? What?' Dave said. 'Nebraska has a sack museum? Like?' He grabbed his crotch and gave it squeeze.

'Missiles,' Zach said, rolling his eyes. 'Strategic Air Command.'

'Oh, right, okay. Because they shouldn't be outside in the day. These things hate sunburn like a Baptist hates disco. It's like their kryptonite.'

Zach's patience faded just a notch. 'Dude, this Baptist happens to like disco.'

'It's true.' Igor grinned. 'Sad but true. You should see his iPod.'

'It's sadder that he still has an iPod,' Dave said.

He consulted his monsterpedia but couldn't dig up anything. As far as Urgon was concerned a walk in the sun was just an ugly, painful death, and not a quick one either. When Dave closed his eyes and let the BattleMaster imagine a day at the beach he saw blistering tumours boiling up on the surface of his hide, suppurating lesions and ulcers exploding into fiery, pustulant life on every exposed inch of skin. It wasn't like a vampire in the movies or on *True Blood*. They didn't just burn up or disappear in a puff of dust. They sort of boiled down, over a couple of hours, as though consumed by a cancer even more hideous than they were.

'Dude, you okay?'

It was Zach, shaking his arm. The CPO had unstrapped himself and leaned across the aisle to pull Dave out of the movie running inside his head.

'I'm cool,' he said, although he sounded like he was a long way from it. He had no idea, really, what killing Urgon and stealing his strength or his magic, his mojo or whatever, had really done to him. Would there come a day when he'd have to stay in the shadows, never show his face in daylight again, for fear of melting into a puddle of toxic offal?

'You should eat,' said Igor. 'Fuel up.'

'Yeah,' Dave grunted. 'Might have another drink first.'

He ordered a triple bourbon from Joy, who was pleased to serve him with a tumbler of 25-year-old Pappy Van Winkle. Pappy helped some, and Dave asked her if he could also get a couple of steaks.

'Sure sweetie.' She beamed.

'Dave, you got any idea what your basal metabolic rate is?' Chief Allen asked when Joy left them to fill Dave's order.

'My what?'

'How much energy you burn, every day, without even trying,' he explained. 'We've been watching you put away a trailer park full of trailer trash food for the better part of a week, and you've lost weight. Packed on muscle mass. But you haven't completely broken the laws of physics. If you don't fuel up, you power down. We've seen that too.'

Dave nodded absently, and his gaze drifted through the window again. He'd never been one for listening to lectures by the company medics, or the gym rats on the rig. He'd always believed in the basic math. Energy in versus energy out. If you ate too much and you didn't exercise you got fat. That was why he'd been a little porky until recently. Just a little, you understand. He was a big guy. He could carry some extra weight on him without anyone noticing.

'Yeah, Zach said you were a bit of fat fuck first time he saw you,' Igor said.

Dave gave Allen an offended look. 'Hey.'

'Come on, Dave,' Zach said. 'You know it's true.'

'I been working out,' Dave protested.

'Just sayin',' Igor replied, unrepentant. 'If I ate like you, I'd look like Jabba the fucking Hutt too.'

The plane banked to the left, and silvery light streamed in through the windows on that side. Far below them Dave could see thick green forests covering the lower slopes of the mountains, thinning out at the tree line where they gave way to hard granite.

'So, Dave? You have any idea?' Chief Allen said. 'You look to me like you can get down all the calories for eight or nine men every day. But then I'm not with you all the time. You might be snacking.'

'Might be you're right,' he conceded as Joy returned with a couple of porterhouse steaks smothered in mushroom sauce. He supposed they'd been mostly cooked pre-flight, then snap frozen or chilled to be nuked as they were needed. Still looked pretty damn good, though.

'Do you want a glass of wine with that, honey? Or a beer. Got plenty of both.'

'A beer thanks, Joy. You can choose. Make me happy.'

'Always.' She smiled, holding his gaze.

As she returned to the galley he turned back to the SEALs to find them lost in the first moments of a quiet argument.

'Zach, tell me you are not even a little bothered by the fact that she doesn't notice you,' Igor said.

Zach shrugged. 'When the time is right, the Lord will provide.'

'You always were a sanctimonious prick,' Igor muttered.

'Dude, that's a lot of syllables for you to pack so tight into one sentence,' Zach said.

'Uh, guys?' Dave waved at the two SEALs. 'What's it matter about the food? As long as I keep topped up, and I got a supply of energy bars for emergencies, I don't see the problem. Figure my calorie counting days are behind me.'

Not that his calorie math had ever been particularly good, or his study of it especially diligent.

In reply, Zach took a knife from the scabbard he wore on his hip. The Boeing's recliners were ample enough to let him do so without having to contort himself. He held it up for Dave to see.

'This is a weapon, Dave. A pretty simple one, probably as old as mankind itself. And yet, not simple at all. Thousands of years of metallurgy, hundreds of years of materials science and developments in mass production, all of them led to this.' He held the knife up. 'It's a simple weapon, especially compared to any of my firearms. And next to one of those Super Hornets or Warthogs out there, it's like a Zen koan.'

A shaft of sunlight caught the blade's sharp edge and flashed around the interior of the cabin. Joy was coming back at that moment and gave a little gasp of alarm when she saw the naked blade.

'Sorry, ma'am, just making a point, if you'll excuse me,' said Zach. 'Thing is, Dave. As simple as this knife is,' he put it back in its protective sheath, 'it still requires attention, care and maintenance. I have to oil it, sharpen it. I had to be trained to use it, and I have to keep up that training if I want to maintain the skill set.'

The flight attendant carefully placed Dave's beer, a bottle of Barley John's strong porter, and hurried off to see if anybody else needed anything. Anybody who wasn't waving an edged weapon around. Dave had no idea where Zach was going with the metaphor, so he tucked into his steak, which was delicious, microwaved or not, and let the chief get on with going there.

'You are a weapon, Dave. And we know nothing about you. You know nothing about you.'

'You know nothing, Dave Hooper!' Igor chortled.

Zach pointedly ignored him.

'Sometimes, it's like you are no more self-aware than a knife or a bullet. Knives can break and bullets can misfire and I'm pretty sure you can be killed. Chances are the 10,000 orcs camped outside Omaha came here to do just that.'

'Well, duh,' Dave said, instantly regretting it and hurrying on to an apology. 'Sorry, Zach. I was being a dick. Go on. I think I'm getting your point.'

'Point is, asshole,' Igor growled, 'we can't trust you, because we can't rely on you.'

Zach frowned at him.

'Too harsh, man. But not wrong. Dave, you have any idea of how much weight you could lift? Your one rep max? If a Hummer rolled on top of Emmeline, say, and we had to get her out in a hurry, could you do that?'

Dave stopped chewing on his steak to ponder the question. He had no idea, but he thought it might be possible. Zach had more questions for him, however. None of them he could answer.

'We know you can run pretty fast. Maybe even win a bet with the Flash. But how fast exactly can you travel, and how long can you move at speed? If you were ten miles from Emmeline when the Hummer rolled would you run out of fuel before you covered that distance? How many calories would you burn fighting a dude like Scaroth for ten minutes? We all know what happens when it's Red Bull time. If you don't get your little pick-me-up, you're pretty much sunk. And if we are relying on you, that means we're sunk as well. I think that was Igor's point.'

'Yeah, but I was more fucking succinct,' said the big SEAL.

'So, what, you need me to go and do another physical?' Dave asked, looking down at his plate, not liking the judgment he could read in the eyes of the other men. He was surprised to see he had almost finished the second porterhouse. He'd inhaled more than five pounds of prime beef in a couple of minutes without even taking the top off his beer.

'No time for that now,' said Zach. 'But yeah, assuming we don't get eaten in Nebraska, you should totally make some time to get that done. Captain Heath could set that up, no problemo. A couple of days of your time and, frankly, a load off all of our minds.'

Dave took a moment to contemplate his bottle of beer. He didn't even know the growlers were allowed to sell bottled beer under Minnesota licensing laws. Maybe it was some special interstate, airline variety. He shrugged before necking at least half of it. He burped. He supposed Zach had a point. Be cool to know what he was capable of, and what he wasn't. But he wondered when they might find time. He had no idea how long this Omaha bullshit would take, and then it was a laydown certainty that Boylan was going to need him to do stuff, not even cool stuff like having lunch with Brad Pitt, or trying out his newly found charms on Jennifer Aniston.

Oh yeah, he was totally doing that, no matter what Emmeline thought. But as a concession, he had determined he would not be fucking the defenceless flight attendant.

Boylan was working away a few seats up from him, his attention split between two laptops and a blizzard of paper. In contrast with his behaviour in Vegas, he had been almost entirely silent since boarding the plane. Apart from a couple of words with Emmeline when she shooed him out of his preferred seat near Dave and an order for a sandwich and a club soda, Boylan kept to himself. Dave was going to check in with the lawyer, to see about scheduling some tests, when the intercom chimed and a pleasant female voice filled the cabin.

'Good morning, this is your captain, Claire Harvey. I have just been informed by our escort that they have detected an anomaly ahead. Two of the planes are investigating, and we will remain in a holding pattern with the other escort craft until they return. I'm sure you're all familiar with the routine. Please do up your safety belts, return your tray tables to the upright position, and the attendant will be through to collect any glassware, utensils and so on. As soon as I have more information I will pass it on.'

Another chime and Dave felt the plane tilt to the left as the muted roar of nearby warplanes kicking it up to full power reached him. Having been told to strap in, he did exactly the opposite and unbuckled his harness.

'Mr Hooper, sir. Dave, please, you need to sit down,' said Joy as she moved through the cabin, gathering up anything that could become a missile in flight. 'Professor Boylan, sir, if you could please close your laptops and stow them away, sir. Just for a short while, for safety.'

Boylan, who looked as though he was coming out of a trance, shook his head, but not in refusal. He looked a little like someone who'd just walked into a spider nest and was trying to shake himself free of the cobwebs. 'What's that? Oh, sorry, yes, of course, yes.'

'Sit down, Dave,' barked Heath, who compromised the authority of the command by unbuckling his own seatbelt and following Dave to a free window to see what was happening.

'What is it?' asked Boylan, finally becoming animated as he synced back to reality. 'Is it dragons, Dave, is that what it is? Because I'm not ready for dragons. I prepared myself for giant pig demons and carnivorous monster ghouls. Not dragons.

Not on a plane. I can't do dragons on a plane, Dave.'

'I think it's dragons,' Dave confirmed. 'Look.'

And soon almost everyone was pressed up against the windows on that side of the plane, either shielding their eyes from the sun and staring out of the window next to their seat, or moving seats to do so. Everyone except Emmeline, who remained asleep, and Compton who had followed the instructions to strap himself in and was now craning around, looking very unhappy with his travelling companions.

It took a few seconds to find the aircraft against the background of the mountain range.

'Over there, near those lakes,' said Igor, and then Dave had them. Two bright geometric shapes, metallic flashes picked out in the morning sun, moving impossibly fast and straight amidst the visual clutter and chaos of forest and rock.

The Super Hornet, an arrowhead of the Gods, left the Warthog behind. Dave tracked its flight path for a moment then extended ahead a few miles, squinting with the effort to pick out whatever they were chasing. It didn't take long; a plume of bright orange fire lit up the tree line well ahead of the fighter.

*Dar Drakon.*

From this distance the torrents of beast-fire looked a trifling thing, like a barbecue flaring up in someone's backyard. And yet he knew that the arc of super-heated bile could reach out the length of a city block and was hot enough to crack rocks and melt sand into glass. Trees would be exploding down there, their sap flash-boiling to vapour, detonating like a string of bombs dropped on the side of the mountain.

The Boeing turned in its holding position and they lost sight of the creature. Everyone hurried to the other side of the plane.

'Oh come on now,' shouted Compton, still firmly strapped

in, but nobody was paying attention. Even Joy had found herself a spot to view the battle from down near her station at the rear of the plane. Dave ended up crouched next to Heath who didn't need any superpowers to find the creature again, or the two human aircraft screaming toward it.

'At ten o'clock,' he said, pointing into the middle distance, where Dave saw the flying tank they called the Warthog and, by extending its flight path, the Super Hornet. It seemed that the moment he locked eyes on the jet fighter, twin puffs of smoke appeared under her wings, as two small points of light appeared to detach themselves and speed away.

'AMRAAMs?' said Dave. He'd read that in a Tom Clancy book.

Heath didn't turn away from the window and neither did Dave, but he sensed the officer nodding. 'Heat seekers,' he said. 'Air-to-air. Pilot must've got tone. We'll see soon enough.'

It did not take long. To Dave's untutored eyes, as quick as the jet was travelling, the missiles seemed to move away at two or three times its speed. He followed the burn trail all the way down to the slowly circling figure of the dragon. It must've been miles away, but he was certain he could see the great leathery wings as they flapped slowly, carrying the monster across the forest canopy. It was possible, he thought, that he could even make out the great tail, although he had no hope of picking out details like the giant spikes at the end, with which a dragon could impale up to two or three Hunn with one vicious swipe. His eyesight had improved as radically as his physique and he wondered how much detail the others could make out. None of them were complaining.

'Praise God and pass the ammunition,' said Zach, just before twin explosions bloomed silently around the dragon.

Dave flinched, expecting to hear its death shriek, but of course he never would. It was miles away and they were safely enclosed within the insulating steel and glass tube of the Boeing. When the fire died away there was nothing to see. It was gone, but the A-10 Warthog pressed on anyway, and after a moment Dave saw long, fluorescent strands of light reach out from the tip of the plane to rake at the mountainside where, he presumed, the dragon had fallen. The pilot poured on the heat for at least ten seconds, and fired rockets that followed the line of tracer fire into the burning forest.

'Nothing left of that sucker but loose meat,' said Igor, standing up and returning to his original seat. And indeed there seemed to be little left to see. The two aircraft were returning, and Dave lost sight of them as the Boeing resumed its original heading.

The intercom chimed and Captain Harvey thanked them for their patience, telling her passengers that they anticipated no more than a ten-minute delay. She kept her voice calm, but Dave thought he could hear the anxiety and wonder beneath that professional mask.

'Is that it?' Boylan said. 'There are no more? We're sure there are no more, Dave? I mean, that was quite spectacular, and reassuring too, but I would like to get back to my work, and I don't think I can do that unless someone can assure me this isn't going to be like that scene in *Jurassic Park* when the raptors tag-teamed poor Bob Peck. That's not about to happen to us, do you think, Dave? Because it will be quite difficult for me to provide the full suite of services you need if some airborne fire-breathing raptor is about to bite through the fuselage and turn us into human kebabs.'

'I think that's it, X.' Dave turned away from the window at

last and found Heath waiting for him.

'Dislodge any memories?' he asked.

'I don't think they had jet fighters back in the golden age of the Horde. What about you? You learn anything?'

Heath stretched and turned his neck from side to side. Dave could hear the bones clicking and he wondered how the guy's artificial leg handled long-haul flights. Probably quite well on a plane like this, not so well in economy.

'I'll make sure we get the After Action Report,' he said. 'Is that likely to be it? Mr Boylan won't have to worry about getting blindsided?'

'Professor Boylan,' said Dave, 'And no. I'm pretty sure they don't travel in packs.'

Everyone slowly resumed their seats, with Dave headed back toward the ass end of the plane to resume his conversation with Zach and Igor, wondering if he might be able to talk them into splitting a few beers. Maybe a couple of lights. They were on duty he supposed, but…

The intercom chimed again, sending a jolt through everyone's nerves.

'Dave?' Boylan squeaked. 'Dave, you said there'd be no more dragons. And I have a considerable amount of work to get through.'

'Thank you, everyone. This is Captain Harvey again. We have an incoming call for Mr Hooper on the air phone at the front of the cabin.'

Heath shot him a look somewhere between confusion and irritation.

'Did you tell anybody you'd be on this flight?' he asked, getting to the phone a few steps ahead of Dave. 'Your bookie? Some girlfriend?'

'Nobody,' Dave protested.

Compton, up out of his seat now, picked up the phone.

'Compton. OSTP.'

He paused and confusion won out over irritation. But only for a moment. 'If this is your idea of a joke…'

Emmeline, finally woken by all the excitement, blinked at Dave through bleary, bloodshot eyes.

'What's going on?'

'Yes. Yes, okay,' said Compton, his voice irritated. He passed the handset to Dave.

'It's for you. Routed here via the Pentagon. A Lord Guyuk of the Grymm.'

Lord Guyuk ur Grymm lurked back in the shadows, away from the mouth of the limestone cave. Forced to crouch under the low ceiling he still dwarfed the terrified calfling. The creature appeared to be babbling, and it had certainly soiled itself, but Thresh-Trev'r assured him that the calfling was doing as ordered. Lord Guyuk did not consider himself a conservative. In the long and ancient history of Her Majesty's Grymm, few commanders could claim to be as open to new ideas as he, and surely none had braved the sort of risk he did when he placed his faith in Thresh-Trev'r.

But he was not at all sure about this plan. The captive human was not entirely insensible with terror, and for that he paid the lesser daemon due tribute. Conversing with the creature in its own language, using the intonations and accents of the calfling that called itself 'Trevor' had been... Well, not a stroke of genius. The Thresh was still just a Thresh after all. But it had cracked *dar Drakon* egg. Now Guyuk wondered what they would taste inside.

Thresh-Trev'r sat on the floor, hunched right down next to the calfling, babbling in the strangely liquid and glottal tongue of the cattle. Thresh had said there would be a deal of difficulty and unavoidable frustration in trying to find and talk to the human champion, the Dave, by stroking the small magick amulet many of the human captives carried with them.

The lord commander let them get on with it. Guards in heavy war cloaks to protect them from daylight stood across the mouth of the cave, acting as a shield. They did not block the view of the outside world entirely, however, and Guyuk could not help but be drawn to the sight. So alien, so wrong. He had not even words to describe any of the colours and images he caught sight of over their shoulders. But the strangeness of it burned his eyes until they watered and he blinked.

The senior Scolari Grymm, a Master of the Ways, who had travelled with them Above, who had indeed navigated them to this very point, assured Lord Guyuk that they were nowhere near the Dave. The Way Master lived to study the perverse geography of the passages between the UnderRealms and the world of men, but it was entirely beyond the lord commander. There had been no need to ponder such things in the long eons since the capstone had trapped their kind so far beneath the hairless little feet of men that men had forgotten entirely about their rightful lords. The calflings had multiplied and spread across the world Above with such fervour that it seemed their hairless little feet ran everywhere. The Master of the Ways had attempted to explain to Lord Guyuk how they effected their passage from the realms of the Horde to a place far removed from the spot at which the Thresh had first emerged, but he had grown impatient with arcane theories and exposition, finally roaring at them to simply take him where he needed to go.

The small party had stepped through a breach in the barrier between the worlds a good few leagues from the rift discovered by the Thresh. They emerged into this cave system, bringing their captive with them. The human's whining and mewling had started soon afterward and at one point it had asked to be allowed out of the cave. It was only because Thresh-Trev'r assured them that such an exigency was necessary to facilitate the magick of the amulet that Guyuk allowed it. The amulet probably drew its power from the cursed sun. Truth be known, Lord Guyuk could only understand one in every three or four words of the Thresh when it spoke in the voice of Thresh-Trev'r, but having come this far there seemed no alternative. None that would deliver the victory toward which all of his efforts were now bent.

'My Lord, we have him. We have the voice of the Dave conjured within the amulet,' cried the Thresh.

Guyuk turned around as quickly as the confines of the cave would allow. Some undignified shuffling was involved.

'And he will parlay with us?'

'His warlords insist on it,' said the Thresh.

'But how do any insist the Dave do anything he would not wish of his own will? These cattle vex me more every night. Gah! Never mind. Are you ready to translate, Thresh?'

'Thresh-Trev'r stands ready, my Lord.'

And thus began the strangest, most perverse negotiation with which the Lord Commander of the Grymm had ever been involved.


Thresh-Trev'r tried to encourage the calfling not to fear for its life; an admittedly difficult thing to ask since the natural reaction of a calfling to a daemon was mortal fear.

'Dude, just chill, we're almost there and then you are on

the down low, my friend. Free to roam.'

The argot of the calfling, which once knew itself as Trevor, still felt strange in the mouth of Thresh, but the Scolari Grymm had been correct when they surmised the little daemon might consume all the creature's thinkings in one gulp by the simple method of sucking the sweetmeats from its head. As unnatural as the sounds felt in its mouth– and Thresh's mouth was not at all well suited to making them anyway–as strange as those sounds were, it understood them. It understood much now. Or rather, the part of its mind that had become Thresh-Trev'r understood.

The prisoner called itself Darryl and Thresh-Trev'r understood that this Darryl was a merchant of 'doughnuts'. Or at least he had been until captured by a Sliveen scout on the edge of the battle in New Orleans.

Thresh-Trev'r also understood now that the little village they had thought they were raiding was in fact a great metropolis. Blasphemy to say it, but a metropolis far grander in scale than even the inner *and* outer palace grounds of Her Majesty.

Thresh-Trev'r knew much indeed. He knew the iron Drakon which spat fire and death upon the Vengeance led by Urspite Scaroth ur Hunn were in fact 'helicopters', or 'choppers', or 'Apaches'. Thresh-Trev'r seemed to have many names for the flying creatures, which he now understood were not creatures at all, but some sort of manufactured tool of great complexity. Just like this Darryl's magick amulet, which he called a 'cell phone'.

'R-r-really,' Darryl stammered. It took him a few tries to say the word. Indeed, more than it would've taken Thresh-Trev'r. 'You'll really luh-let m-me go?'

'Duuude,' Thresh-Trev'r assured him. 'You do a solid for the Horde and you will be our made man. You be kickin' it, Darryl.'

The calfling still shook as he attempted to manipulate the jewels on the front of the amulet...

*On the phone*, Thresh understood via a strange double-thinking exchange with himself in the form of Thresh-Trev'r.

But Darryl, the provider of the delicacy known to Thresh-Trev'r as doughnuts, persevered. It seemed as though Darryl believed Thresh-Trev'r when he said he could go free after performing this one act for the Grymm. Thresh did not know why Darryl would place his faith in such a promise, since it was so very obviously a lie and they were going to tear him apart as soon as they were done with him, but Thresh-Trev'r knew it to be, if not a gambit sure of success, then certainly one worth trying. Although that's not how Thresh-Trev'r expressed himself.

*Dude*, Thresh-Trev'r thought when Thresh examined his thinkings, *dude, this Darryl asshole is a fucking nimrod. I'm telling you, he is totally going to suck this dick.*

Thresh was still not used to composing his thinkings in the mind of Thresh-Trev'r, and when he did so, he was not entirely convinced that the thinkings he had extracted from the head of Trevor were the finest thinkings the calflings had to offer. This Trevor, he was beginning to suspect, might well have been the human equivalent of a very slow, very stupid minion. His thinkings were not deep, and frequently veered away from those things Thresh needed him to think about, and onto other things. Like doughnuts.

But Thresh-Trev'r was all they had and he could communicate with Darryl, and through him to the human world of the Dave, where Thresh, Lord Guyuk and even

Her Majesty were utterly incapable of making themselves understood.

'Dude, come on. You gotta try harder. Guyuk's getting pissed, and when he be pissed, he be eating his motherfuckin' feelings. Which means you, dog.'

'I'm trying! I'm trying,' cried Darryl, 'but it's not easy. The reception is t-terrible. And they won't *buh-buhlieeeve* me.'

Thresh was beginning to think that maybe they should just eat Darryl and send some scouts out to find another doughnut merchant who could manipulate the amulet.

*Use the cell.*

It was maddening that he couldn't just use the thing himself. Thresh-Trev'r knew how. But talons were not suited to the task. They needed Darryl, or another calfling if they ate Darryl, to manipulate the amulet and talk to the cattle who would help them reach out across the unseen leagues so that they might actually parley with the Dave. Even as Thresh-Trev'r encouraged Darryl to persist in his attempts, Thresh marvelled at the magick these humans had harnessed. As dismal a figure as the wretched Darryl cut, Thresh could not help feel a creeping admiration, tantamount to heresy, for its kind. He wondered how a mere seller of doughnuts might come to wield such an instrument, for as much as Thresh-Trev'r recalled a great love of doughnuts, the memory was not accompanied with any great reverence for doughnut keepers.

Suddenly the calfling's face brightened. It was almost shiny with relief. Perhaps even ecstasy.

'I got 'em,' cried Darryl. I got 'em. Someone just cut in on my call. Said they were from the national security agency and they'd redirect me to Hooper.'

Hooper. Another name for the Dave, Thresh-Trev'r knew.

Some sort of clan designation.

'Awesome, Darryl. So you know what to do, right? You don't say shit, or we gots to bite you fuckin' head off. You put me on speaker as soon as you gets the Dave, and I'll hook him up to my man Guyuk. Then they're like, chewing on it, they be fuckin' Avon and Stringer Bell, you feel me? And we be sweet, Darryl! We be sooo fuckin' sweet!'

Darryl stared at him as though he'd slipped into the Olde Tongue.

'Just put him on speaker,' said Thresh-Trev'r.


Dave recognised the guttural accent of the creature at the other end of the line. It hailed from the same Sect as Urgon and Scaroth. *The Horde.* Dave's own Sect, he thought, with a shudder at the bottom of his soul. And yet it spoke to him, or tried to, in English. Or some approximation of English. Something like American mall-rat dialect. He assumed he was talking to a lowly Hunn warrior, rather than a BattleMaster, who would have announced himself, his title, his glorious history of slaying this and destroying that, wasting the better part of the day before getting down to business. But this thing on the phone, which the Pentagon apparently insisted he talk to, and which insisted on calling itself 'Trevor', was all about the business, which it pronounced 'bidness' with a slight lisp that Dave put down to having too many fangs.

'You do the bidneth with my homie Guyuk now, the Dave? Aight? Thith niggah be lord commander oth the muthafuckin' Grymm, yo?'

Dave put his hand over the receiver and shook his head at Heath and the others who gathered closely around him.

'I can't be sure,' he said, unable to keep the utter bafflement out of his voice, 'but I think the Grymm have got some moron to translate for them. That, or I'm getting punk'd by some really fucking sad try-hard white rapper with a speech impediment.'

'National Security Agency says to just take the damn call,' said Compton.

'Aight,' Dave sighed in imitation of 'Trevor', before taking his hand from the receiver.

'Er, yo. Trevor. Yeah. It's me again. The, er, Dave. We're good, I guess. Put your man Guyuk on.'

Having played his role, the prisoner placed the amulet on a large rock, where Guyuk might hail it without leaning over the calfling.

'Champion, you address Lord Guyuk ur Grymm. Lord Commander of Her Majesty's Grymm, dread bane of all her foe, inquisitor extremis, master of her holy terror, wielder of the great blade named–'

'Yeah yeah, got it,' said the Dave in the Olde Tongue, interrupting Guyuk before he'd even begun the roll of his many honours and offices. 'I'm Dave, swinger of the maul that, you know, mauls. You're really like the maximum Nazi?'

Guyuk found himself at a loss, and looked to the Thresh who indicated that he should just agree and carry on.

'I am... that, yes, Champion.'

No sound came from the amulet for a moment and he wondered if the magick might have failed, or whether the Dave had abandoned their dialogue. But then the human spoke again.

'Okay,' he said. 'That's cool. I guess. So. What's up?'

Guyuk forced himself to believe, to put aside all the voices that whispered to him, all the ancestors of his nest, every lord commander who had worn his chain of office, all of them insisting this could not be so. He closed his mind to the whispers and forced himself to believe that this was indeed possible, that he was conversing with the Dave by the magick of this glowing trinket. It was the purest madness.

'Champion, my heralds have sought you out for one purpose. To warn you.'

'Is that right?' the Dave said over the top of him. 'Well, thanks to your heralds and everything but...'

Guyuk's thoughts buzzed through his head like a swarm of enraged stingers. He was finding deep wells of unexpected sympathy for Scaroth. If the Dave was as difficult and unpredictable in combat as he was in conversation, Guyuk may have been too harsh in his judgment of the BattleMaster.

'Champion, do not doubt me. We are foe, yes. But you are not my only foe. You are not even my greatest. You are an embarrassment to one disgraced officer of the Horde and an inconvenience to me because of that. Have no doubt that we are enemies and that I will destroy you. But that shall be my privilege not mine enemies'.'

The human captive which had used the amulet to summon the Dave climbed unsteadily to its feet, brushing at itself as though the limestone dust on its coverings might be the worst of its problems. Guyuk gestured to Thresh to sit the creature down again, and the lesser daemon did so, forcing the calfling back to the floor of the cave with one claw.

'Okay, got it,' said the Dave, apparently having thought the matter over. 'You're a bad motherfucker. I'm toast. So, are we done with the mutual dick measuring now?'

'No!' Guyuk snarled. He took a deep breath to find his calm. 'We are not done with the mutual measuring of these dicks. Champion, a regiment of Djinn has invested one of your settlements, yes?'

The voice of the Dave crackled out of the human artifact.

'A regiment of what? If you mean a bunch of your buddies are camped outside of Omaha working on some bitchin' sunburn? Yeah, I knew that.'

'And at this very moment you speed toward them to give battle, would I be correct in that too, Champion?'

'Well that would be for me to know and you to find out when I speed toward you and kick your scaly ass,' said the Dave. 'What, you think I've never played *Gears of War*? Like I'm gonna tell you where my space marines are?'

Guyuk pondered this phrase, the 'gears of war'. Was the Dave not just a champion, one chosen by fate to carry all his people's hopes, but a marshal of armies too? Guyuk was reminded again of how little they knew of this enemy, and how dangerous he could be because of that.

'I neither know nor care where these puny space marines of which you boast might be. Come the time and I will destroy them too. But, Champion, and please do not interrupt me now, I seek to counsel you against precipitate action.'

'Hey, if I want to precipitate some action, action is gonna get fucking precipitated and—'

'It is a trap, you idiot! You are marching into a trap!'

All patience exhausted, Guyuk roared at the man.

That shut him up for a moment. The lord commander felt irrationally pleased with himself, at least until the Dave spoke again.

'Well of course it's a trap. Duh. But why tell me? Isn't it your trap?'

'No, it is not,' said Guyuk, gesturing at the Thresh to control its prisoner, which was squirming about with increasing vigour, whining like a skinned urmin.

'Wait,' came the Dave's voice. 'Who's that you got there? What're you doing to them?'

Without being ordered to, the Thresh quickly punched a hole in the prisoner's head and sucked out its brains. The whining stopped and Guyuk signalled his satisfaction to the underling.

'Nobody,' he said. 'There is nobody here. Let us discuss this trap, Champion.'

'Your trap?'

'No! I just told you that!'

The Dave made a sound the lord commander could only interpret as mocking laughter. 'Just fuckin' with you,' he said, causing Guyuk even more confusion. Why the human champion would want to couple with him he did not know. But the thought did not please him.

'I have many enemies, Champion. You are just the latest, and to be honest, the least of them. Encamped within a trebuchet arc of your settlement you will find the First Regiment of the Djinn. Not the Hunn. Their legions manoeuvre near my monarch's borders. The Djinn were emboldened by your humiliation of Scaroth and so now they seek to test our resolve. This is why I tell you that you face a trap, Champion. Because I have no desire to see my enemies further emboldened by killing or capturing you. The worthless scum stay their claws only out of fearful caution. They do not know what happened at the village you call New Orleans; only that cattle rose against their *superiorae* and threw them down. So they come upon you with the full power of a regiment and seek to entrap you, further humiliate my queen, and still the quavering in their cowards' hearts that has ever kept them in the second rank of all the Sects.'

The Dave did not speak immediately, leaving Guyuk to endure the stab of hunger pangs at the smell of the bloodwine jetting from the corpse the Thresh had made of their captive human. Guyuk turned away from the sight, the better to resist the temptation, staring instead out of the cave mouth across the emerald lands of the Above.

'So, let me get this straight,' the human champion finally replied. 'Scaroth getting his ass kicked made you guys look weak, and now all the other gang lords are moving in on your turf, but some of them want to throw down with me just to prove the point that you guys are even bigger pussies than they've been saying?'

Somewhat confused by the Dave's reply, Guyuk shuffled around as hurriedly as he could in the confined space to fix the Thresh, or rather Thresh-Trev'r, with an imploring look. What was he supposed to say? The human had spoken in the Olde Tongue, with almost perfect enunciation, but the words did not entirely make sense. They did, however, remind Lord Guyuk of the unusual rhythms of speech and choices of phrase the Thresh employed whenever he spoke as Thresh-Trev'r. The Master Scolari gave the little daemon a brief jab with his staff to draw his attention away from the corpse.

'Well, Thresh? Does this human have the truth of it? I know not his strange use of the dialect.'

'Oh yeah, Boss. 'Zactly.'

The Thresh shook its head as though emerging from a slime bath and gathered his wits from wherever they had fled, presumably following the thinkings of Thresh-Trev'r.

'My apologies, Lord Commander. The Dave puts it crudely, of course, as is his nature, but he is essentially correct. You may agree with him.'

The voice of the human shouted from the amulet.

'I heard that!'

Lord Guyuk felt his shoulders slump. If this was what dealing with the Dave entailed, he really was beginning to think Scaroth may have got the best of *dar Drakon's* egg.

'Yes, Champion,' he hissed in exasperation. 'You heard me. Excellent. Might we now move on?'

'Sure, buddy. What's next?'

Was it this easy? Was the Dave proposing that they intrigue together against the Djinn? He had all but destroyed the survivors of Scaroth's detachment with admirable treachery. The stroke of a master tactician, to accept the surrender, to promise safe passage, and to slaughter them all as they slunk from the field. Did he intend to lure Guyuk into such an arrangement? The lord commander wanted to ask Thresh-Trev'r all of these things, but the power of the amulet was such that he feared his words would fly to the Dave as though the champion stood before him in this cavern.

'What is next, Champion, is you hopefully surviving your encounter with the Djinn so that they might not aspire to greatness far above their station. Tell me, do you intend to take the field with your lieutenants as you did in New Orleans?'

Again the mocking laughter brayed out of the amulet.

'Why don't you give me your email address and I'll send you a dot point rundown of exactly everything we're planning to do. Even better why don't I come over and give you a PowerPoint presentation?'

Guyuk looked to Thresh-Trev'r again, imploring him to translate in some way that the Dave would not overhear. The Thresh made a face that told its commander he should pay no heed to what was obviously an empty taunt.

'This PowerPoint of which you speak will not be necessary, Champion. I understand if you do not wish to discuss your battle plans, but I will tell you for my own sake that whatever snare the Djinn have laid in your path will prove hazardous to yourself, and certainly lethal to your inferiorae.'

The Dave spoke in his native tongue, not to Guyuk obviously, but rather to someone standing nearby the human champion, wherever that might be.

'Ha ha. He called you my inferiors.'

The lord commander summoned the Thresh, and bade him attend closely so that he might translate any such exchanges. Other human voices seemed to leak from the amulet, but they were not loud enough for Guyuk to make out individual sounds or words. Not that he would have understood them, of course. But Thresh-Trev'r might overhear some background exchange of tactical or even strategic import, especially if the Dave was even now conferring with his lieutenants. The Thresh scurried over and listened attentively, but it was quite obviously distracted by the scent of carnage.

'Okay, I'm back,' announced the Dave. 'Sorry about that. Ran out of beer. So, yeah, okay. Omaha is a trap. Got it. Anything else? Like, you guys, your sect or clan or whatever, er, Guyuk, you planning on coming back at all? Like, swarming over the surface of the Earth, taking, you know, dominion or anything like that? I'm asking for a friend.'

Lord Guyuk ur Grymm and Thresh-Trev'r traded a silent and brief but significant communication. Thresh-Trev'r had suggested the humans would seek this assurance, and that they would not believe the lord commander if he promised peace.

Another sign the human cattle were not as stupid as they once were.

'Champion, a reckoning will come between us, be assured. But the world is not as we left it. Man is not as we once knew him. I will study your world, Champion, and I will take it from you and reduce your people to feedstock. But I am patient, and I am not foolish. I am not Urspite Scaroth ur Hunn. If an eon should pass while I study the problem of man and another eon while I determine a final solution, I am, as you say, Champion, cool with that. It is my judgment that your kind are as like to destroy yourselves for me.'

A pause and then, 'So, you'll be back, but not until you invent gunpowder and the wheel, is that it?'

'If it pleases you, Champion. And while I wait and ponder these matters, should mankind spend himself contending with my real foe, my rivals across all the Sects, perhaps reducing them as you did Scaroth, that will not displease me.'

'That's awesome, because keeping you happy is what I'm all about,' said the Dave.

Guyuk's nostrils wrinkled as he tried to interpret that statement. It was as though the Dave said one thing but meant another, but also as though he meant Guyuk to understand that he meant something other than that which he had stated, perhaps even its opposite. Which would be that the Dave was not at all about keeping the lord commander happy. Oh, this was a confusing human. It lied, certainly, but did so honestly.

'So, Guyuk,' the Dave continued, 'my friends were wondering where you were hanging out at the moment. Because cell reception in the UnderRealms sucks. Unless you're with AT&T I guess, 'cause they got that whole deal with Satan going.'

The lord commander bared his fangs at the Thresh, which was jumping from one talon to another now, even daring to tug lightly at Guyuk's fighting dagger. He gestured at the tiny imp to remain still and quiet but that only inflamed the Thresh's anxieties.

'Boss, we gotta split, like now,' hissed Thresh-Trev'r. 'This asshole is stringing us along.'

'Be still, Thresh-Trev'r,' the lord commander rumbled in as low a voice as he could. 'I parley with the champion.'


Thresh-Trev'r had remembered something. Something very important. A whole bunch of things actually. Stories and legends of other human champions. The Bourne. The Bond. The Terminator, although that last was a very confusing legend. A golden thread ran through these stories however, ran through them and across the leagues and into this very cave where Thresh-Trev'r could all but see it leading across the dusty white floor, through the spreading pool of cooling bloodwine and up onto the chalky white rock where Darryl's Razr2 sat channelling the presence of the Dave into their midst.

The humans could trace the filaments of magick that animated the Razr2 amulet–*the cell phone*, Thresh reminded itself–and if there was one thing the champions of human legend knew not to do, it was to spend too long talking with their mortal foe on an open amulet.

Generous pots of bloodwine and trenchers filled to overflowing with hot human offal had restored Thresh to its former self. Apart from a few larger scars and deeper furrows on its hide it no longer showed any sign of the injuries done it in the Above or down in the volcanic flumes of the Inquisitor Grymm's dungeons. Thresh was not disordered in its thinkings. Not fuckin' crazy, as Thresh-Trev'r would say. Thresh knew with the certainty of a war hammer coming down on its neck that they were in terrible danger and the Dave was conniving to keep them there.

'My Lord,' it hissed as urgently as it dared. 'The human Drakonen... the, the... the fire that disassembles as it burns... the...'

It was hopeless. Thresh had no words for what he needed to say. He shifted uneasily, all of his scales itching with the need to get out of this cavern. The green and soft brown fields of the human world seemed peaceful enough outside, but he knew that meant nothing. Even lesser humans, with none of the Dave's enchanted powers, could send flaming javelins straight in through the mouth of their hiding place from many, many leagues away. Thresh-Trev'r knew. Thresh-Trev'r could imagine the fucking cruise missiles screaming toward them right now. Or Blackhawks full of spec ops dudes loaded for orc.

'Boss! It's a trap,' cried Thresh-Trev'r, curling his claws into a hammer fist and smashing it down on top of the cell phone which shattered with the sound of a poorly forged dagger breaking on armour. 'We have to get the fuck out of here now, man. Er, I mean *el Jefe del Horday*. They know where we are. They're coming. The Dave's lieutenants riding in iron Drakon, spitting fucking lances of fire or some shit. Whatever the fuck. That old scrote...' Thresh-Trev'r jabbed a claw in the direction of the Way Master who navigated them here, 'he's gotta beam us off this planet, because any fucking second now it is gonna suck like a toothless crackwhore.'

The shock of the elder Scolari was total.

Not at the revelation that they were all about to get blown into finger food, but at the fucking cheek of a minor Thresh daemon daring to do as Thresh-Trev'r just had.

The two guards were the first to react, lowering spears and advancing on him.

'Wait,' Lord Guyuk roared. 'What sort of a trap, Thresh?'

'Omigod! The sort that fucking traps you!' Thresh-Trev'r wailed. 'Come on. We've gotta move now. You, old dude,' Thresh-Trev'r yelled at the aged Scolari Grymm, 'spool up your fucking walking frame and open the portal or beam us out of here or whatever you do. But now!'

The Master Scolari, utterly taken aback, looked to Lord Guyuk for instructions. The lord commander seemed at a complete loss too, but he raised his giant talons in a show of acceptance. All of his instincts were singing a high hymn to murder. His ichor burned with the need to put down the impudent Thresh. But his intellect bade him to listen to the creature who knew more of human trickery and magick than the entire Consilium of Scolari Grymm.

'Best heed the Thresh, Scolari.'


'Well that was weird,' said Dave, hanging up the air phone. 'Fun, but weird. You think the air strike got them? I think one of 'em seemed to tumble to your cunning plan right there at the end, Compton.'

The crush around the phone broke up as everyone headed back to their seats. Compton hung on with Heath, as ever looking underwhelmed by Dave's performance.

'You could have led them on more,' he said. 'I can't

imagine we got much intelligence from them in the short time you spoke to their commander. And we couldn't understand a damned word of it. We'll have to rely on you to recall and translate accurately.'

Compton's expression left Dave in no doubts about the odds he put on that.

'May have been enough to get a strike on to them, though,' said Heath. 'You can't put your head out of the window at the moment without getting a buzzcut by a passing combat air patrol.'

'I'm afraid you're going to have to put down your beer, Hooper,' Compton continued as though Heath had not spoken. 'I need to transcribe as much of that exchange as possible. I just hope you can remember it all.'

Dave stepped around the professor and picked up his half drunk bottle of premium suds. Didn't even have a decent headspin yet. No way was he going to sit through a Q and A with Compton stone cold sober. He caught the flight attendant's eye and waved the bottle at her in the internationally recognised signal for 'more beer please'. As ever, Joy was happy to help.

'Look, he said a lot of things,' Dave threw back at Compton. 'But mostly what he wanted to do was warn us we're flying into a trap.'

Heath's face, normally an obsidian mask, blank and unreadable, fell apart for just a moment in surprise. His eyebrows shot up, widening his eyes to comical effect.

'He did what?'

'Like I said, man, weird.'

\* \* \*

The Master of the Ways hurried them toward the rear of the cave. Thresh perceived the floor of the tunnel bending downward toward the Earth's core, just enough to notice. The hateful sting of daylight–Thresh found that even indirect daylight prickled unpleasantly at his hide–fell away, eventually giving onto the full, comforting darkness of the UnderRealms. And then the dim red-yellow glow and the sulphurous stink of home. The nest of his Horde.

The small party came to a halt on a black basalt outcrop overlooking a pleasingly barren waste studded here and there with sharp outcroppings of rock looking like giant fangs, or maybe Drakon spikes, had erupted from below. Massed formations drilled on the plane below. Legions and even full regiments of warrior Grymm. They had to be Grymm, Thresh knew, because only the Grymm trained that obsessively. A great weight descended on its shoulder plates and squeezed, subtly, but just enough to send a jag of white-hot pain shooting down that side.

'Explain yourself, Thresh. And I do not wish to hear the babbling of Thresh-Trev'r on this.'

The lord commander turned Thresh around with careful but irresistible force. The training field of the Grymm fell behind, and Thresh craned upward at its superiors. The Commander of Her Majesty's Grymm, the Master Scolari, and two heavily armed Lieutenants Grymm.

Thresh bowed its head, presenting its neck for the killing in a gesture of submission. The pressure from the lord commander's talons sharpened, as did the pain. The tip of one claw suddenly punctured hide and a thin trickle of ichor began to flow.

'Enough of this foolishness, Thresh. I do not need your

life. I simply need to know why we had to flee. Although, of course, if we did not have to flee, I shall have your life.'

Thresh shivered with fear. Much greater fear than it had ever experienced in the face of death, which was a constant in the UnderRealms. Thresh knew this down in its meat and bones. Why then this sudden, fearful clutching of its hearts?

'My Lord Commander, I apologise, but the Dave meant to strike at us as you parlayed with him.'

The Master Scolari spoke up before Lord Guyuk had a chance.

'But this is rank foolishness, even cowardice,' he growled. 'The Consilium has studied closely the reports of the encounter with the human champion. Including yours, thresh.' The Scolari, Thresh noted, did not deign to address him with the same tonal inflection conferred upon the minor daemon by the lord commander himself, a telling insult. 'The Dave, while proving himself to be a formidable combatant, fought in the manner of the ancients, drawing on the lore of battle as it ever was and will ever be. He did not ride the iron Drakon. He did not summon nor project the magick fire. He carried a maul into battle and when he was done it was honourably bathed in ichor. He is their champion. He has no need of their magicks.'

Before Thresh could respond, Lord Guyuk withdrew his painful grip, one long claw sliding out of the wound it had made and causing Thresh to stagger with dizziness. Guyuk spoke directly to the senior Scolari Grymm.

'All true, Master Scolari, and yet the Dave need not have visited treachery upon the remnants of Scaroth's revengers band and where are they now? What power did he call upon to make their humiliation complete? Certainly not his own strength. We had no reports of him fighting in that final encounter. He called down the talons of the iron Drakon to rake at Scaroth's thrall.'

'It is not settled that the Dave did any such thing,' the Master Scolari retorted. 'His lieutenants, none of them even remotely possessed of the Dave's inherent power, are much more likely to have summoned the iron Drakon.'

'And it is his lieutenants against whom we shall move first. But, Thresh, tell me now how you know of the Dave's treachery while I entreated with him.'

Desperately wanting to nurse its latest wound, Thresh nonetheless put aside its discomfort. Thresh-Trev'r would have little problem explaining how the government could track a cell phone. Indeed, Thresh-Trev'r had a great many thinkings and conjectures on the subject of exactly how much effort the government spent doing nothing but tracking him, listening to his phone calls, reading his emails, making a long list of every website he had ever visited including the gay ones which he only went to by accident. Thresh was not sure why Thresh-Trev'r was so convinced that his superiors were spying on him; as best Thresh could tell, the calfling had not been a particularly important or impressive member of the human Horde and yet he seemed utterly convinced that his accidental visits to websites where humans coupled in all manner of unusual arrangements was of interest to the human equivalents of Lord Guyuk and the Master Scolari. Probably best Thresh did not draw on the theories of Thresh-Trev'r then.

'The magick that allows us to converse with the Dave also allows the magicians who made the amulet to locate it,' explained Thresh. 'And when located, they can rain down fires. Knowledge of these human magicks only became known to me thanks to the thinkings of the calfling sweetmeats I consumed.'

What a lot of shit, thought Thresh-Trev'r, but Thresh wisely kept that thinking to itself. The Master Scolari's eyes were almost lost in the deep folds of the sceptical squint with which he received that explanation. But, much to the relief of Thresh, the master did not further question him. Lord Guyuk raised his chin a little to look down his nasal cleft at Thresh.

'If I understand you, Thresh, you speak of something like a great ballista firing a war shot into the camp of *dar ienamic* because...' And Thresh could see the lord commander forcing himself, step-by-step, through the thinkings necessary to understand what Thresh was saying. '...because... the artillery master has spied the signal flags of his foe and determined from that where to range his shot?'

It was passing strange, but Thresh felt as though it were the teacher, it was the superior, and Lord Guyuk ur Grymm the nestling with a mouthful of egg fangs.

'In essence, yes, you have the truth of it, my Lord.'

The Master Scolari who had leaned forward to hear Thresh explain himself now stood to his full height, towering far above the little daemon.

'I do not like this at all, my Lord Commander, not at all.' He slammed the ironshod butt of his staff on the fused glass ground, where it struck sparks, three times as if for emphasis as he growled, 'These are matters requiring too much thinking to be entrusted to the likes of daemonum inferiorae such as this creature.'

Thresh bristled, a reaction as alien, unwanted and dangerous as its earlier fear of extinction at the claws of Lord Guyuk. Nothing but a trip to the blood pot could result from challenging even a minor Scolari on a point of learning or interpretation. It was not that Thresh would never have done such a thing in the past, more that such a reaction would simply not have been possible. No more possible than imagining that Thresh could walk under the high sun Above without cloak or cover and hope to survive. What under the earth was happening to Thresh? Was this indignation that burned in Thresh some echo of Thresh-Trev'r's thinkings? Thresh knew not, but it also knew that to reveal its fears or resentments would mean torture and death. And for some reason, the prospect of torture and death bothered Thresh somewhat more than it had in the past.

'I propose,' said the Master of the Ways, who had continued talking while Thresh had allowed its thinkings to wander into dangerous realms, 'that we test this theory of Thresh by returning to the cave to examine it for any sign of attack by human magicks.'

'Knock yourself out,' said Thresh-Trev'r before Thresh could restrain him.

Instantly Thresh found itself knocked to the ground with the master's staff pressed so deeply into its throat that breathing became all but impossible.

'You dare snivel defiance at me?' roared the Master Scolari. He had moved so quickly, in such a disorienting blur of speed and precisely honed violence that Thresh was reminded of the Dave slaughtering the Lieutenants Grymm. It was possible to forget, especially when one's thickened cranium was not so large to begin with, that all the senior Scolari had once been BattleMarshals of the Grymm. You did not ascend to the rank of marshal, and you did not long survive there, through brute force. But, thought Thresh-Trev'r, you didn't even get to first base if brute force wasn't your thing. The Grymm might be the elite of the six Horde clans, but within those legions the warrior Grymm who graduated from battle armour to Scolari robes and staff lived on another, even more rarefied, plane.

'Forgive me, Master!' Thresh choked out. 'It is not the way of Thresh to defy any *superiorae*. It is the thinking of the cattle, inside my own thinkings.' Thresh moaned. 'It is like a sunspot canker in my skull, Master Scolari. It makes...'

The pressure on its throat was suddenly relieved as the figure of Lord Guyuk loomed into view and gently rested one claw on the bone plates of the master's chest, pushing him back just enough to allow Thresh to breathe again.

'Master Scolari,' Guyuk began, in surprisingly measured tones, 'you will recall that this was the very consequence you presumed to exploit by suggesting we have the empath daemon consume that skull meat wherein the Scolari theorised the seat of human thinkings might be found.'

Another gentle push and suddenly the staff was gone and the Master Scolari no longer towered over Thresh, but stood back, looking even more aggrieved, but less likely to do something about it.

'Your offence is well taken, Master, but ill timed,' Guyuk continued. 'Do not take umbrage, take satisfaction, for your theorems have proved out.'

Thresh found itself lifted to its hind-claws once more, where it lowered its head and bared the back of its neck once more. But the Master Scolari offered no further admonition.

'You are correct, Lord Commander,' conceded the master grudgingly. 'I apologise for striking your underling. But I would still test the judgment of this thresh by reconnaissance of the cave.'

'And it shall be done,' Guyuk assured him. 'If only to measure the treachery of the Dave and the power of his armoury. But Thresh convinces me of the urgency of pressing ahead with our own treachery. We must use the cover of the Djinn to thrust deep our hidden blades.'

# 12

Great titty bars, crude oil and good times were disgracefully thin on the ground in Nebraska. Hence, Dave Hooper had never set foot there. What little he knew of the place he'd taken from the cover of the old Springsteen album. It was like to be cloudy, flat and grey. Life was lived hard there, in a sort of watery, washed-out black and white that reached right back beyond dust bowl images of the Depression and landed on the bones of its ass somewhere around the Civil War. He knew a lot of frackers had moved into the Niobrara play in the west of the state, but that wasn't Dave's idea of oil work and, anyway, they were a long way east of that, circling the besieged city of Omaha, flying into a trap.

He turned those ideas over as the Boeing dropped toward the tarmac at Offutt Air Force Base. How long had it been since any American city had been under siege from an enemy force? He couldn't recall. The Brits had burned Washington in 1812, or something. And he supposed lots of cities were taken under siege in the Civil War, but he'd never been much of a history buff and as he stared out of his window over cultivated fields to the city's southeast (all the shades of green, and a few brown, freshly harvested) he saw no obvious evidence of siege works or even the enemy force.

*Dar ienamic.*

Yeah them.

The hour and a half after the dragon... had dragged on. He snorted at his own wit as he felt the undercarriage deploy. Heath confirmed the air force or NSA or someone had pinned a tail on the donkeys who'd called him on the air phone, and goddamn if they hadn't put a couple of bunker busters into the side of the hill where the call was coming from. A limestone cavern complex in lower Missouri, deep in some national park. His head spun with wonder at the bureaucratic fire hoops the air force must have jumped through to pull that off. But then, he had to concede as the wheels smoked and screeched on the tarmac, maybe bureaucracy just melted away when you found a regiment of Hunn on your doorstep.

Not Hunn, he had to remind himself. Djinn. Dave, it turned out, knew all about the Djinn, because Urgon did too. To Urgon they were shur-Hunn. Loosely translated, mud people, or subhuman, but only the way Nazis would have called Africans that. To Dave, when he closed his eyes and examined his race memory of the Djinn, they looked pretty much like Hunn to him. Maybe a bit redder of hide, with even flatter, more apelike faces. But Hunn.

Not to Urgon, though. Not to any member of the vast monster clan... No the monster *sect* he thought of as the Horde. The Hunn, he understood as soon as thought on it, were just a part of the Horde. One of the six clans. To Urgon, and presumably this Guyuk clown, the Djinn were *dar ienamic*. The Djinn and the Morphum and the Horum and Shakur and Krevish. Just more fucking orcs, all of them. Twelve sects as best he could count. All with their own constituent clans, bloody histories, mythology, feuds and hatreds and internecine bullshit. They reminded him of a bunch of squabbling former Soviet republics. The Chechnyas of Middle Earth.

The captain's voice came over the PA as they taxied toward the terminal, or whatever the air force had instead of terminals. Big fucking sheds, maybe.

'Ladies and gentlemen, welcome to Offutt Air Force Base, where local time is 2.40 pm. Air temperature is a very pleasant seventy-nine degrees, humidity is thirty-eight percent. Weather service predicts a low chance of rain later this evening.'

As Dave wondered what the UV rating was and when sunset would be, the captain thanked them for chartering Studio Air and wished them well.

'Go kick some monster ass, people,' she signed off.

'Dave?' It was Boylan, come back to life after burying himself in work for that part of the flight when they weren't in danger of being eaten by dragons which, thankfully, was most of it. He had his laptops slung across opposite shoulders, the straps creating a bandolier effect, and he carried a briefcase as well as an overnight bag. 'Dave,' he said. 'I have made excellent progress on three fronts. Your tax affairs, your credit card debt and your soon-to-be ex-wife. Considerably more on the first two than the last for the moment, but now we are back on solid ground, and failing a catastrophic fall of the city and scenes of chaotic bloodshed downtown, I mean to advance on that as well, just as soon as I secure a serviced office.'

'That's cool, X,' he said, carefully hoisting Lucille onto his shoulder. It was more than cool. His tax and the black hole of his credit card debt had been festering like an untreated wound for years, forcing him to rely on the mattress and mason jar method of fiscal management. It had been much easier when Baron's still used paper cheques but ever since they switched to direct deposit it all went to shit. Boylan took him by the elbow, guiding him around the SEALs, who were gathering up black bags and cases full of clanking metal.

'But Dave,' he continued. 'I want you to pause for a moment and imagine what your life would be like without Amex, MasterCard and Visa all chasing you, because my friend, they have abandoned the chase! And not only that, they are competing with each other to place within your possession debit cards to a combined value of more than four million dollars, in return for the usual industry standard endorsement and promo arrangements, which you can leave to me,' he hurried to add, before slowing again. 'It won't be possible to work with all three providers, naturally, but we'll choose the offer that best amplifies our other market partnerships and, I must reiterate, Dave, it's important you understand this, that as of right now, you have no credit card debt, no matter which company we go with. They have all wiped all of your liabilities as a gesture of good faith for the coming negotiations and, of course, because to not do so would leave them at a crippling disadvantage...'

The entire monologue was delivered on one gulping breath of air. Boylan sucked in another and was about to resume–'As for the IRS, they won't be bothering us either,'–when Heath forcefully interrupted him.

'Time to move, gentlemen.'

They emerged into a warm, cloudy afternoon and a large, busy military base. Combat aircraft patrolled high above while other planes were armed and refuelled on the concrete apron. Fat, double-bladed helicopters hammered at the air, waiting for their turn to disgorge soldiers gathered from who knew where. The men assembled in the big sheds, checking over gear while their bosses, sergeants he figured, oversaw it all. Others unloaded crate after crate of ammunition, distributing it among the soldiers who busied themselves loading magazines. Gunships like the ones he saw down in New Orleans plus heavier helicopters with two pilots were arrayed in a line down at the far end where their crews received a briefing.

'Our ride is over here,' Heath said, pointing to a couple of black Ford Expeditions, a cell phone to his ear as they left the Boeing.

'Carry a lady's bag, strong man,' said Emmeline, passing Dave a dark blue canvas shoulder tote which seemed to contain more laptops than Boylan was carrying.

'No problemo,' he said. And it wasn't, except for feeling a bit awkward knowing that part of her wanted to fuck him, but most of her was revolted by the idea.

Compton signed for the vehicles and they piled in. Dave rode in the first SUV with Heath, Emmeline and Zach. Boylan was content to be relegated to the chase car so he could work his cell phones and initiate hostilities against M. Pearson Vietch, attorney at law. Compton had notes to pore over from his debrief of Dave after the conversation with Guyuk and each man maintained an icy silence with the other.

It was still warm for September with green on the trees as they motored down Looking Glass Avenue toward the main gate. With Lucille sat between his legs, Dave took it all in as they sped past a Second World War bomber display and merged into highway traffic headed north.

'Yes, sir,' Heath said. 'We'll be there, ETA eighteen minutes and yes, we have the asset here with us.' He put the phone away. 'Okay, we're headed to the D-Tac.'

Zach, in the passenger seat up front, held his hand up. 'Sorry, sir. D-Tac?'

'An army advanced command post from the Big Red One, their show for the most part. They are set up at a Cracker Barrel just on the southwestern edge of town. First, we'll feed Dave, make sure he's up to full strength. The other task will be to meet with this Hunn emissary, or Djinn, or whatever he's calling himself and see what he wants.'

'Simple,' Dave said. 'He'll want a quarter to half the population to march into the blood pots. And in return, he'll let the other half live until he feels like a snack.'

'What about challenging their leader to single combat?' Emmeline asked from the back where she sat next to Dave. 'Worked well last time.'

'I got a better idea,' Dave said, leaning forward to poke his head between the two front seats. 'If they're sitting out there, doing nothing but keeping the sun off, why not just bomb them?'

Heath frowned, as if the idea had already occurred to him.

'A kill box has been designated,' he said, 'and the air force has strategic assets in theatre ready to service the target.'

'Translated, that means?'

'B-52's,' Emmeline explained. 'Loaded with bombs, Dave. Lots and lots of bombs. Some of them smarter than the bloody things they're aimed at, I'd hazard.'

'Well that's good,' said Dave, sounding hopeful. 'So, shouldn't they all be dead now?'

Heath answered as he turned left on to Harland Drive, which became the Strategic Air Command Museum Highway after a minute's rolling through open fields that gave way to standard issue American suburban housing on Dave's side of the car. 'Their emissary–and in case you were wondering, that is what he calls himself–wants to talk to you. About New Orleans.'

'Well maybe I don't want to talk to him. Did nobody hear the bit back on the jet where I explained that Guyuk said this was a trap? I'm not a military guy, but doesn't this sound very fucking trappy to you?'

'Little bit,' Zach agreed.

'You could take your lawyer,' said Emmeline.

Dave ignored that. 'So is there some good reason the air force hasn't reduced the lot of them to monster mist yet? I mean, you know, since you got them in your handy kill box already. Like, seriously, I vote we go with the kill box thing.'

'Not until we know their intentions,' Heath said. 'Especially not after what Guyuk said. If this is all just some underworld war spilling out into our world, Washington feels there's an advantage to be had from talking to this emissary. Maybe he wants an alliance against the Hunn? Maybe he's just staging out of our field, same way we do out of little countries who can't really stop us.'

'But we can totally stop these guys,' Dave protested.

'And we will, with the press of a button. I promise you, Dave, there is more than enough high explosive targeted on that field to kill everything there many times over. But the fact they're not moving to attack makes Washington think they are serious about negotiating.'

'They're serious about avoiding a bitchin' case of sunburn…'

And then he thought of something.

'You keep saying Washington, but aren't you the guys advising Washington?'

'We're not the only ones, Dave,' Emmeline said. 'And even our advice isn't necessarily as consistent as it could be.'

He leaped on that.

'Wait. Is Compton advising them that I have to talk to this emissary? Did that cock chafer sell the Pentagon a line about allies and staging posts and shit? Fuck!'

No wonder the little weasel had hopped into the other car with such enthusiasm.

'Dave.' It was Heath. 'I will be coming with you when you meet the Djinn emissary. We will be covered, don't worry.'

'You're the one who should be worried,' Dave said. 'And Compton should be the one coming with me if he thinks it's such a great idea.'

While he'd never been to Omaha, Dave had eaten at Cracker Barrel before. This one, on the edge of a business park overlooking a large swathe of undeveloped prairie at the southern limits of the city, was surrounded by soldiers in Hummers and armoured vehicles. Salted in amongst the olive drab and tan-painted military vehicles were half a dozen police cruisers. Some state cops, some Omaha PD. At a desert tan tent next to the entrance local emergency service personnel stood around drinking coffee out of paper cups and picking at a box of doughnuts that stood open on a folding table. The second SUV, carrying the rest of Heath's team was forced to park a few hundred yards down the road, delaying the reckoning with Compton. Emmeline volunteered to go fetch them while Heath stopped at the tent entrance and pondered the options for a moment.

'Come on in with me, Dave,' he said. 'We can eat in a minute. Something better than this, I would hope.'

'I'll hunt up some lean protein,' Zach Allen offered. 'And leafy carbs for a change, Dave. Let's get to work on the new you.'

Dave snatched a doughnut so quickly as he passed that it disappeared from the box in less than the blink of an eye. Inside the tent a dozen men and women worked at cheap trestle tables that bowed under the weight of the computers and other equipment piled high on them. Two men, one white and one black, leaned over an old-fashioned paper map on a large, low table with fixed bench seating. Dave thought it looked like a barbecue setting pressed into service. They both stood up as the newcomers pushed through the tent flap. The slightly shorter man nodded to Heath. 'Mr Hooper. Clayton Salas, Nebraska National Guard.' He extended his hand to Dave, who was forced to switch his doughnut over at hyperspeed and shake the general's with great care. He assumed Salas was a general from the single star at the centre of his grey, digital-funky looking uniform. 'We're glad to have you here, sir. This is General Vincent De Brito from the 1st Infantry Division. He'll be the combatant commander.'

Dave shook the tall, black general's hand as well. He counted two stars on De Brito which meant he outranked the other guy, the Salas adjutant dude. They both sported the same weird grey-tan pixelated uniforms. Dave was starting to straighten out this army shit.

'Clayton, Vince. How you doin'?'

'Fine. Is he cleared?' General De Brito asked Heath directly.

Heath shook his head. 'He hasn't been vetted by CIA or DISCO, no. We haven't had time for that. But he is reliable with secure information. I'll vouchsafe him, General.'

'Disco?' Dave asked.

'Not now,' Heath said.

Dave didn't know whether to feel insulted or not. 'Well, disco balls or the crystal sort, doesn't matter. I can be counted on to keep my word, generals. Baron's has a few secrets, you know. So, what's been happening here? Got yourselves a monster problem I hear.'

'I presume you were briefed in flight,' De Brito said, and Heath nodded. 'The enemy was detected encamped off the I-80, in a field thirteen miles southwest of here at 0433 hours local, by a unit of local law enforcement responding to reports of...' De Brito looked to his local colleague for help.

'A possible cow-tipping incident,' said Salas with just the hint of a smile.

'The officers did not approach the encampment but called in a report which was picked up by NSA. Clayton's people,' he nodded at the Nebraskan National Guard commander, 'were already on alert, having been mobilised after New Orleans. They scouted the position and fell back here to establish a forward post.'

Dave wondered if that was how Igor picked up his rumour about a Hunn wandering into the Cracker Barrel and getting both barrels in the kisser.

'We estimate the Hunn have close to 10,000 effectives, perhaps as high as 12,000. Our UAV and sat intel shows them hunkered down under camouflage cloaks and netting of some sort on the southwest side of the Platte River. They are arrayed in a line extending from the SAC museum to the northwest of their position.'

'Hides,' Dave put in. 'They'll be under thick, big-ass hides stitched together from dead Drakon, urmin queens, that sort of thing.'

'Yeah,' deadpanned Salas, 'that sort of thing. We've lost communication with anyone caught inside that engagement box. The phones and radios work fine but no one is answering.'

'Anyone they find will be dead by now,' said Dave. 'Eaten or worse so you don't have to worry about civilian casualties. And they're Djinn, not Hunn. Although, you know, same difference. They'll all die the same, and since you got 'em in your kill box and everything...'

'Their camp is surrounded by basic earth works and trenches with overhead protection,' De Brito cut in, before frowning down at the tabletop, 'and siege engines. Or what look like siege engines. Catapults. Towers. Trebuchet. We've got them sandwiched between our positions here in Omaha and heavy forces down in Lincoln to the southwest.'

'Hammer and anvil,' Heath said, nodding to himself, satisfied.

Dave gave up. These guys had obviously talked to Heath, or Compton, or some jerk in Washington who was red hot on the idea of him walking out into a perfectly good kill box for high tea and chit-chat.

'They'll have brought a couple of companies of Gnarrl to work them, the siege engines and stuff,' he said, resigning himself to having no control over how things turned out, even though he was technically the superhero. 'Gnarrl are just Hunn too, but they're like combat engineers. Maybe a foot shorter, two feet thicker through the chest,' he paused and looked off into the distance, as though peering through the tent across to where 10,000 orcs had set up camp south of Omaha. 'Although these guys don't call them Gnarrl. Djinn's engineers are called

Jorrn. They must be pretty good, or have some fat fucking pipes to the UnderRealms to have got so much of their shit in place.'

'Do you know much military history?' Salas asked.

'Apparently, I learned a shitload,' Dave said, knocking his fist against his head. 'But all of it about giant horror monkeys. And I did take a class on the basics of siege warfare but only in relation to it being an engineering problem.'

De Brito looked him up and down, as if deciding whether to trust him.

'Do we need to worry about an attack?' the tall, black general asked.

'Once the sun goes down?' Dave said. 'Shit, yeah. Whole city's spread out before them like a buffet dinner. They'll rip through it. And they'll be hungry.'

De Brito shook his head. 'I'd rather that not happen, but I'm still getting my heavy units into position down in Lincoln.'

'Refugees?' Heath asked. 'Highway to the southwest looked busy but not jammed when we flew in.'

Clayton Salas nodded. 'It's much worse on the northern exits. About half the city have battened down and the other half is on the fly. All north and east, away from the Hunn.'

'The Djinn,' Dave corrected him, without thinking.

'The Djinn,' Salas conceded. 'My soldiers are doing the best they can to keep the roads clear but there have been incidents. Too bad the *Djinn*,' he emphasised the word this time, 'don't seem inclined to advance south toward Lincoln.'

Dave raised his hand. 'Why?'

'Nebraska National Guard has significant assets down there. General De Brito is staging his own forces there from Fort Riley as well. Our biggest headache has been bringing in blocking forces to actually protect Omaha,' Salas said.

De Brito spread his hands over the map. 'I'm supposed to get a brigade of the 82nd in here within the hour. Still, it'll take time to get them out of Offutt airbase and on the road toward the Platte River.'

Dave tried to relate it to what he'd seen coming in on the plane. Omaha lay between two major water courses, the Platte and Missouri rivers, but sat much closer to the latter, straddling it at one point. The Platte, which looked much wider on De Brito's map, crooked around like an elbow southwest of the city, leaving a good wide swathe of farmland between the fields where the Djinn had dug in to wait out the day, and the dormitory suburbs in that quarter of the city. The burbs and light commercial area where Dave stood right now, in fact. He wondered why the orcs had hunkered down all the way over there, but figured they'd might have just dug in as soon as they'd breached the surface. Maybe there was another portal out there in some field on the far side of the Platte. He hoped these guys didn't expect him to lead anyone down there if so.

'Most of the OPFOR is on the other side,' said De Brito, pointing to a spot on the map just over the blue line of river which wriggled and curved around the paper, appearing to cup a bunch of letters and numbers inked in black felt pen at the edge of the grey city area. Dave assumed those were unit designations for De Brito and Salas's force. They were written over that part of southwest Omaha where the I-80 emerged from the city's road net to cut through the green open fields. Well, green on the map. Half of them had been brown when he'd flown in earlier.

'They're just clear of the flood plain,' De Brito said. 'I have assets from SOCOM out there now, feeling them out. They've had a few run-ins with creatures armed with large bows and arrows.'

'Sliveen scouts,' said Heath. 'But belonging to the Djinn. What'd you call them, Dave?'

'Sumateem.'

'Yeah. Them. Those arrows they're toting will punch right through body armour, I'd bet. And their effective range is greater than a human bow and arrow because the Sliveen or Sumateem or whatever are pulling a much heavier draw.'

De Brito nodded, 'Yes, we've found that out already.'

'So, what do you want me to do?' Dave asked, trying not to sound pissed off.

'We want you to go out to the Djinn camp and negotiate with them,' said a new voice.

Compton.

Dave turned toward a flare of light where the tent had just been pulled back. The bearded academic had stepped through with Emmeline but Boylan was not with them.

'You wanna tag along?' Dave asked. 'After all, you seem so fucking fired up for this idea I'd hate for you to have to rely on my untutored recollection. I might forget something real important. Some crucial detail of Djinn potty training, perhaps. You could take notes for a pop quiz later.'

'You would need remedial training before I could give you an open book exam,' Compton retorted.

'Is there a problem here?'

It was De Brito, his voice an octave deeper and carrying an edge of menace which hadn't been there before. Not that he'd been all that friendly either.

'No, General,' said Heath through a tightly clenched jaw, while he laid the stone face on Dave and Compton.

The professor rolled over to the map table with Emmeline one step behind, looking like a married couple who were trying to put aside a quarrel as they arrived at drinks.

'You are the only human being who can speak directly to these creatures, Dave,' Compton said, loading up Hooper's name with a big creamy dollop of false chumminess. 'We've only just begun to study them and their culture, and that only through what you can tell us, when you have the time of course.' He smiled again with more unconvincing sincerity. 'These creatures are not behaving in the same fashion as their cohort in New Orleans which simply boiled up out of the earth and began eating people. And, most particularly, they're asking for you. And just you.'

'There's always room for one more,' Dave replied. 'I could piggyback you there if you'd like.'

'Won't be necessary,' Compton said, as though he quite regretted being unable to accompany Dave into the midst of 10,000 monsters. 'We have full spectrum drone coverage. It behoves us to determine what they want. If we just unload on them we might be opening up a second front in a war with the UnderRealms and missing a golden opportunity to turn one monster sect against another.'

Emmeline, who looked as though she'd been forced to sit through someone else's bowel movement, dropped her heaviest laptop satchel on the map table as if banging a gavel to bring order to a court room.

'I disagree.'

Heath squeezed his eyes shut.

'With respect, Emmeline, you're not even qualified to agree or disagree. You're an exobiologist for pity's sake. Maybe if you'd studied Tolkien rather than Asimov...' Compton smiled.

'And you are making the basic mistake of attempting to impose your understanding of Iraqi and Pashtun tribal groups on creatures which aren't even human,' Emmeline said. 'I'd like to think it is a deliberate error designed for an unspoken goal.'

'Nah,' Dave chipped in. 'Compton's just being a dick. It's his natural state of being.'

'You guys are the experts, right?' Clayton Salas asked, not looking at all sure he hadn't just let a couple of crackheads into his tent.

'My record in Iraq and Afghanistan speaks for itself,' said Compton.

'No, it doesn't,' Emmeline shot back, 'because with you around even your bloody record can't get a word in edgeways. General?'

Both Salas and De Brito answered 'yes', creating the slightest echo effect. Emmeline addressed both of them.

'Professor Compton is basing his advice on what he knows about barbarian culture and war rites, which is a considerable amount. But we have no idea whether the Hunn or the Djinn or any of the demon clans are even remotely anthropomorphic in their practices and beliefs. They are by definition, sirs, alien. And the only alien intelligence we have any access to is the one that apparently jacked into Hooper's skull back on the Longreach. If he has misgivings about this plan I'd suggest we should at least listen to them and not the long, drawn-out brain fart of a tweed-jacketed neckbeard.'

A full second's silence followed her tirade, as though nobody dared speak lest she turned on them too. Dave finally broke the silence.

'Whoa, Compton. Sucks to be you.'

Before the academic could answer him, De Brito spoke again, sounding less baleful but more resolved.

'I am afraid, Mr Hooper, we need you to go out there, if only to buy us a few more hours to get our blocking forces in place.'

'Again with the goddamned blocking forces,' said Dave. 'What's there gonna to be to block once you light up the kill box? Excuse a dumb rig monkey for not understanding this shit but on one hand you're assuring me you can absolutely, positively kill every motherfucker in the house, but on the other hand you got like half the army rolling in here as insurance. So which is it? You can send these guys to monster heaven or not?'

De Brito did not look happy to be talked to in such a fashion and for a moment he reminded Dave of Heath, who so often looked as though he desperately wanted to turn into Hell's own drill sergeant and start roaring at Dave in a manner that would make the average deckhand on an oil rig go quite pale with the vapours.

But he didn't.

'Mr Hooper,' he ground out between his teeth. 'Everything Professor Compton says has some validity. And it may be that Professor Ashbury's countervailing point is well made too. But for now, the Djinn regiment is holding in place, while their leadership waits to confer with you. This gives us a chance to get our forces in place, and if you recall the carnage that a lesser unit of these things did in New Orleans, you'll appreciate how little enthusiasm there is for allowing even one of them over the city line in Omaha. Before night falls and they think about moving I would like two things. My blocking forces in place and some indication from you as to whether we'll have to engage with these bastards. And rest assured, sir, if we do,

I will absolutely, positively kill every motherfucking one of them, long before they get anywhere near anyone's house.'

'The other thing, Dave?'

It was Heath.

'If you don't go out and parlay with them, I will. I have to.'

Dave looked from Heath to De Brito to Compton. None of them spoke, but their expressions confirmed the truth of what Heath had just told him. Compton even had the hide to look sympathetic for once.

'They'll turn you into finger food!' Dave protested.

'That's irrelevant,' said Heath.

'I really don't think it's a good idea,' Dave said, sounding weak and hating himself for it. 'It's a trap. We know it's a trap. An ambush!' he said suddenly, leaping on the military term, hoping it might help. 'You wouldn't run into an ambush, would you?'

Nobody said anything. Not until Heath nodded.

'Sometimes you do, yes. Sometimes it's the only way.'

The silence in the tent stretched out uncomfortably. Dave could hear the shouts of military personnel outside, the grumble and grunt of heavy engines, but they didn't sound nearly as loud to him as the ticking stillness around the map table.

'Okay,' he said, after a moment, his resistance deflating. 'Just askin' is all.'

The tension which had been building dissipated some. He heard Emmeline breathe out loudly, but whether in relief or frustration he couldn't say.

'Could I ask one thing, sir?' said Captain Heath, addressing General Salas. 'My briefing wasn't clear about how the Djinn had made contact and asked for Dave in person. I was hoping you could clear that up. It might be important.'

Salas looked embarrassed and De Brito's frown grew even deeper.

'Well, I'm not sure how to put this, Captain, Mr Hooper. But I guess you'd call them the talking dead.'

# 13

'Oh Hell no,' said Zach Allen. 'Zombies? No way. I hate those guys!'

'Talking zombies,' said Dave, shaking his head, almost grinning at the madness of it all. 'I forgot about them, or, you know, Urgon never had reason to think of 'em.'

'Tell me this isn't going to get any weirder,' said Igor as he spooned up a plate of meatloaf with mac and cheese. It was splattered with red tabasco sauce which he'd produced from one of his pockets.

'This could work for us, Dave,' said Boylan. 'Zombies are hot right now. The project Brad Pitt is putting on hold to do your film? Unless we give it to Bay, of course, it's his zombie sequel! Coincidence? I think not. *Walking Dead* is still coining it for AMC. Again, zombies! I'm excited by this, Dave. Very excited. Numb with terror and horrified too, naturally, but very excited.'

Dave pushed away the empty platter that had held his Cracker Barrel sampler, a generous pile-up of chicken-n-dumplings, meatloaf, and sugar-cured ham. He pulled the plate of chicken-fried chicken toward him, much to Zach Allen's disgust.

'Couldn't you at least try a salad?' Zach asked, working on his own chef's salad and pinto beans.

'And they're not really zombies,' said Dave, ignoring the chief petty officer's dietary advice. 'More like meat puppets. Tümorum on the other hand…'

'Meat puppets?' asked Emmeline.

'Yeah, that works,' said Dave as he loaded up on fat and protein, feeling strangely content. Even Lucille was humming softly as though she'd eaten her fill of Cracker Barrel's 'fancy fixin's'. Cracker Barrel was Dave's sort of place. Partly because Annie hated everything about it. Half of the building was set up like a general store which sold bric-a-brac, trinkets and souvenirs, the sort of crap that caused children to howl if they didn't get their way. Annie resented the temptation of soda pops and candy, preferring the boys to snack on a wholesome avocado half or an apple, but even more than that she resented Dave undermining her, getting the boys a chocolate bar for the road or a Coke to 'top up the ol' tank'. He supposed he'd been a bit of a jerk, but on the other hand… avocado? Seriously?

The reduced Super Friends team–both SEALs, Emmeline and Boylan–sat in the dining hall, which could easily have done duty as a medieval dining hall. Behind them a stone fireplace lay unlit and cold due to the late September warmth. Dead fireplaces always struck Dave as looking colder than they actually were. Heath had remained in the tent to talk to the generals about important soldier stuff, with some important neckbeard input from Compton. Emmeline had stalked out with Dave, who'd announced he needed to do some important superhero stuff because he was hungry. He found he could get out of anything by saying he was hungry.

'You said something about meat puppets,' Emmeline

reminded him, 'before you put half a chicken in your face. What did you mean?'

He swallowed the food and took a mouthful of black coffee with it. He had no idea if the caffeine would help supercharge him like food seemed to, but he'd grown so used to drinking black, sugarless coffee with his meals out on the rigs that it had become a habit as unconscious as scratching his ass with his right hand instead of the left. Not doing it felt wrong.

'They aren't real zombies,' he said, searching out his knowledge of the... well, Urgon had no name for them. 'They're most likely just some poor folk the Djinn had killed that were raised or reanimated by a...' he paused to make sure he was translating the term correctly from the Olde Tongue. 'By a Revenant Master.'

'Ah, come on! What the fuck is that?' asked Igor. He'd moved to three pancakes, drowning them with the contents of half a dozen mini bottles of syrup. Dave had to pay the guy's appetite. He knew his way around a plate.

'Nothing like a Hunn,' Dave said. 'You don't normally find them working with the clans. In the ancient times...' He shook his head at his choice of words, which sounded as though he was reading from a scroll. 'Back when daemons and such were livin' large on our scrawny asses, the Revs were, uhm...'

Dave searched his inherited memories again.

'They were like wild catters. Sole operators. Might sometimes align themselves with a clan or sect in return for tribute...'

'What sort of tribute?' asked Emmeline, who was spooning small serves from a bowl of natural yoghurt with honey and berries.

'Dunno,' said Dave. 'Just tribute.' He thought about it

some more. 'I think if someone acknowledged they were the baddest motherfucker in the valley of the shadow of death that was good tribute. Or something. Anyways, they raise the dead, control them like Muppets.'

Zach bowed his head and clasped his hands together to say grace. Or at least Dave assumed he was giving thanks for his chef salad with a side of pinto beans. Then again, maybe not. Unlike Marty Grbac, Chief Allen kept his religion close.

'So, when you shoot 'em, the meaty puppets, are you going for centre mass?' asked Igor. 'Or is it like with zombies? A head shot?'

'Head shot'll do it,' Dave confirmed. 'But Urgon seemed to think chopping them up worked just as well. Maybe it gets harder to control them the more they come to pieces. Or maybe there's less reason to bother. Dunno. As I said, old Urgon seemed to know of them more as a legend. Might be more of a Djinn thing, too, of course. The different sects, they do have their ways. But as to killing them, best way is to put down the master pulling the strings. You drop him, you'll drop all of them. That's why you don't see Revenant Masters very often. They're sneaky fuckers.'

Igor nodded, 'Be bringing the nine iron then.'

Zach raised his head from his contemplations and unfolded his napkin. 'I still say a Beowulf and a Barrett is a little much.'

'Eat yer greens,' Igor said.

'And they're dead, right?' asked Emmeline. 'The people, the meat puppets,' she added with evident distaste.

'Deader than Elvis,' said Dave.

'Won't be an issue for you anyway, ma'am,' said Zach. 'You'll be chilling here with Professor Compton at D-Tac.

We're taking Dave and the captain for their meet-up with the big bad.'

'And I'll stay here too, Dave,' said Boylan. 'As per my previously stated preference for not approaching too closely the Gates of Hell. I had intended to seek out a serviced office in the downtown area, but the city seems to be in turmoil with a large number of businesses simply shut down, which I find remarkable given my need to rent a serviced office and the presence of so many of our fine military personnel and their massively destructive weaponry between the monster encampment and the central business district. Have people no faith?'

Dave thought about ordering up some of Igor's pancakes for himself but he was actually feeling a little bloated and sick from everything he'd eaten. He knew that'd pass quickly, but it was probably better he didn't waddle into any conference with the BattleMarshal of the Djinn Regiment drumming a march on his distended belly with greasy, maple-syrup-covered fingers.

'S'cool, X,' he said. 'You need anything here? Desk space or something? I could ask the management.'

'Already taken care of, my friend. You just need to pose for an Instagram with the manager before you go.'


Driving southwest down I-80, Dave and Heath were sandwiched between four Hummers commandeered from the Nebraska National Guard. The roads were clear of civilian vehicles, to Dave's initial surprise. But when he thought about it, who but an idiot would drive toward the daemons? That question was answered when they passed a state patrol/

military police checkpoint where officers were busy detaining a couple of men with video rigs and sound-recording equipment, which looked a little like Knoxy's crew had used back in Vegas. These guys weren't Fox News though. Their van was pimped out with some sort of storm-chaser artwork he couldn't quite make out as the Hummers roared past.

Something was bothering Dave. He didn't understand the military's plan and he said as much.

'What don't you understand?' Zach asked.

'All of it.'

'Ever make a sandwich?'

'Well duh.'

'Same thing,' Zach said. 'These guys are the meat and cheese in the middle. One slice of bread is the heavy armour guys from Fort Riley. They're setting up down in Lincoln, which is on the other side of the Djinn. That's mainly because they are closer to Lincoln and they can't get around all of the traffic, obstructions and what not to get to Omaha.'

'This an open-faced sandwich?' Dave asked. 'Where's the other slice of bread?'

'That's us,' Zach said. 'Plus the police, what national guard units there are and those airborne guys if they get into position. But the main barrier is the Platte River. If we can't work out a deal we'll blow the bridge and crush them between the two ground elements.'

'Plus air power,' Igor said. 'Lots of air power. Think of that as the gravy.'

'Make sense now?' Zach asked.

'Maybe.'

As they got closer to the river, they encountered lone figures who seemed to point at them, or reach for them, watching the vehicles roll past, stumbling awkwardly to follow them for a few steps. Some were still flush with signs of their recent departure from the land of the living while others had turned grey and flyblown.

Tümorum.

'Fuck!' spat Dave. 'There's your zombies, Igor,' he said when they'd passed the third shambling husk in a row.

'One of those Revenant asshole things?'

'No,' said Dave. 'Worse.'

He leaned forward and tapped Heath on the shoulder.

'You got a radio, or a cell or something? You want to get on to your general buddies and tell them anybody sees one of those shambling fuckers, they need to put them down, hard. Right away.'

Heath looked slightly confused.

'But didn't you say the Revenant Masters are the target?'

Dave scrubbed his hands over his face in frustration. It was tough being the one guy who knew any of this stuff, and not even knowing what he knew really. He hadn't shaved in Vegas and stubble was coming in hard on his cheeks.

'Sorry,' he said, breathing out in exasperation. 'My fault. Look, the shamblers who carried the message to your guys that the Djinn wanted to see me? They were controlled by a Revenant. That's why they could moan a few words. Not many, and don't ask me how. It's probably a question for Ashbury. Some muscle memory thing, or residual brain function or something. Seriously the Horde don't go in for deep academic papers on this shit.'

Their Hummer rolled past a nameless overpass after the speed limit sign advised them that they could go seventy-five miles per hour, although the armoured Hummers struggled to do better than fifty. Dave felt his balls crawl up into his body as a whole family of grey-faced ghouls reached for them from the ditch by the side of the road. Their pallid skin was painted with slashes of dark, dried blood and, looking more closely this time, he could see the telltale signs of Tümor infection. Jagged yellow spurs of bone erupted through the skin at seemingly random places all over the body. Festering pustules boiled up and broke like giant blisters pouring bad blood and toxic discharge from the wounds.

These ones would have no words. They would answer to no master. They were just a shuffling set of teeth and bone-knives. A transmission vector.

'Stop the car,' he demanded.

Heath was genuinely surprised. 'What? Why? We're on a schedule here, Dave.'

'Stop the fucking car or I'm just gonna warp out of here anyway.'

Zach looked to his officer who nodded. They pulled over to the side of the road, the Hummer behind them crunching off the tarmac too. The lead vehicle took a little longer to realise it had lost its companions, but eventually slowed and stopped a hundred yards or so further on.

'Don't get anywhere near them,' said Dave. 'Igor, Zach, you think you can put a clean round through their heads from here?'

Igor snorted at the idea that he might not be able to.

'Just wait a damned minute,' said Heath.

'Hey! You! Soldier!' Dave yelled at the man from the vehicle behind who had started to move toward the creatures. They in turn had locked on to him. Their arms, mutated with eruptions of mutant bone spur and dripping pus from the weeping lesions, lifted as if drawn up by a puppeteer. 'Get the fuck away from them. They're infectious. Move!'

The man did not need telling twice. He jogged up to where Dave and the SEALs stood on the highway.

'We can't go shooting civilians,' Heath protested.

'They're dead,' said Dave. 'Have been for hours. And now they're looking to share the love.'

He could hear their footsteps, or the dragging and slapping of their dead flesh on the hard concrete. A mother, a father, two kids.

'Look, I don't have time for a history lesson,' Dave said, as the first Hummer in the little convoy reversed toward them. 'I'm still unpacking most of this shit myself. But those things coming down the road? They're worse than zombies. They don't need to bite you. Just a poke with one of those bone shards you can see sticking out of them, or a juicy dollop of zombie custard from one of the boils will do it if it gets in your eye or mouth or up your nose or in a cut. I'm telling you, Captain, you got to put them down now, from here. Honestly. Just shoot them in the head now. They're not people. They're *Tümorum*.'

The soldier who'd joined them looked sick and horrified. He was staring at Dave as if he were the abomination, not the shamblers.

'Captain? I...?' said Zach.

Whatever Zach wanted to say, he couldn't find the words for it. The Tümorum were only a hundred yards away now. Close enough to hear the low animal noise they made. A predator's growl. The two smallest, the kids, even appeared to pick up a little speed. The girl–Dave assumed she was a girl because of the length of her hair, which still caught the afternoon light and threw off a few golden highlights–caught her foot on something, a break in the tarmac perhaps, and pitched forward. They all heard the hard-soft thud and crack of her face hitting the road surface. None of the others slowed or even moved to avoid her. Zombie Mom actually got her legs entangled with the kid's and went down too. The bone spurs on their lower limbs locked them together like fighting elk, leaving only the grown male and younger boy.

'I'll do it,' Igor said to Heath, his face a blank mask as he moved toward the Hummer to retrieve a weapon.

'If he doesn't, I'll have to,' said Dave. His heart was hammering hard enough that he thought everyone could hear it. 'And I don't know if I'm immune to their shit. So make a call, Heath. But do it now.'

No emotions played out across the man's dark features. His expression was as stony as Igor's. The mother and girl child had given up on trying to stand and disentangle themselves and were crawling toward the men like some sort of mutant crab.

'Do it,' said Heath.

Igor had his rifle out. In the giant's hands the gun looked small, but Dave could tell it was not the sort of compact firearm he'd seen the spec ops guys take into New Orleans. Igor pulled his weapon apart, setting the upper half on the hood while reaching into a bag. He pulled out something which looked like the piece he had just popped off his rifle, except the barrel was thicker. Not for the first time in his redneck life did Dave feel his lack of interest in guns left him at a disadvantage. Igor popped the two pieces together and went through a complex series of movements that Dave could not decipher. Once satisfied, Igor unfolded the bipod on the barrel and rested it on the front hood of the Hummer.

'Did you really need to fit that with a bipod?' Zach said. 'Clock's ticking, dude.'

'At close quarters I didn't want there to be a doubt,' Igor replied.

He took aim over iron sights.

The Tümorum were getting uncomfortably close now. You could see details of who they had once been in the wreckage of their faces. A middle-aged man, probably a white-collar worker, his small paunch split open, entrails and long scraps of flesh swinging low. The boy had light sandy-coloured hair like his sister, before the blood and crusted yellow mess got into it.

Igor fired.

The sound was enormous. A trip hammer, super-compressed into a fraction of a second. He squeezed off two bursts, traversing the muzzle just an inch or so to target the larger Tümor and then its smaller companion.

Better if you didn't think of them as father and son.

The first one came apart in three distinct pieces; a red blowhole erupting from the chest, a pot roast worth of meat and bone disappearing from the torso at shoulder level, and the head disintegrating. The effect on the smaller one was even more spectacular, leaving little behind save for twitching limbs, disfigured with toxic bone spurs, and a gaudy spray of offal that painted the road surface in a great fan behind them. Heath's stone face never slipped, and he never looked away. Zach grimaced and the grimace turned into a wince. The other soldier swore softly.

Igor changed magazines, adjusted something on the rifle, carefully took aim again and squeezed off two discrete rounds, taking the heads off the crawling horror which was still dragging itself toward them. They were close enough for Dave to throw a football at. The old Dave.

The SEAL kept his weapon fixed on the Tümorum, but nothing moved. Finally he dropped the muzzle and flicked another switch, presumably the safety.

'Beowulf fifties,' he announced as if at a tutorial. His voice was flat and strained. 'Go through an engine block. Dum dums every third round. Been meaning to try it out after New Orleans but...'

He trailed off.

Heath put a hand on the man's shoulder. 'My order.'

The look he turned on Dave was not so understanding.

'What the hell was that? You didn't say anything about tumours. Not ever.'

'Hey,' Dave shot back at him. 'You know the fucking deal. I don't know most of what's in here now.' He knocked on the side of his head with a fist. 'And it's Tümorum. Urgon had never seen one because there hasn't been a fucking Tümor to be seen since they all got jammed under the capstone.'

Heath's eyes were blazing. Chief Allen's were wounded and wet with emotion.

'Why, Dave?' he asked.

'Because you need *people* to make Tümorum. And the Hunn don't even use them. Spoils the meat,' he added with a bitter, nasty edge to his tone that he regretted.

Heath looked at the ruination of a Nebraskan family splattered all over I-80. He breathed out, a ragged-sounding release.

'And the Djinn?'

'Dunno,' said Dave. 'I got nothing. Maybe they use them like the Crusaders used plague victims in catapults, just throwing 'em out there to fuck up the enemy? But the Djinn are just the Hunn with different tattoos and slightly flatter faces. They can't eat Tümor flesh either.'

'Opportunistic infection,' Zach said. His head was turned away from the carnage, but his eyes kept slipping back there. 'Must be a pretty big gate, or portal, or whatever these things are coming through to put a whole regiment in the field. Maybe one snuck through at the edges?'

Dave wiped the sweat from his brow. The sun was lowering in the big Midwestern sky, dropping slowly toward the endless horizon. But it was still plenty hot enough. His hand was slicked with perspiration and his hair thick with it.

His hair.

Didn't seem like such a good deal now, did it?

'Maybe, Zach. I dunno,' he said, around a shuddering breath he hadn't realised he'd been holding.

'Dave?' said Heath, who was staring at him coolly. 'When we are done here you are going to sit down with Professor Compton and tell him everything you know. From Anubis to Zombie and all points in between. You are not going to lunch with Brad Pitt, or waving your dick at Jennifer Aniston until Compton is satisfied we have everything we need to know about what's coming down the turnpike at us.' He spoke with rising anger, and jabbed a finger at the dead Tümorum. 'Do I make myself clear, mister?'

'As mud,' said Dave, reining in his resentment at being told what to do.

'Right,' said the navy captain, pulling an iPhone in a ruggedised case from his body armour. 'Igor, you secure the area with your team. Do not approach the remains which I'm classifying as an extreme biohazard. I'll inform De Brito and

Salas of the new threat, call this into Atlanta as a quarantine situation and make sure we have new and robust rules of engagement for dealing with it.'

Igor's small group of SEALs acknowledged the order, but without enthusiasm.

'Sir, what do we do if more of them come?' asked one of the men.

'You saw what Igor did?' said Dave. 'That's a start. And the further away you get 'em, the better.'

'Just don't go shooting the town drunk,' said Igor, who had recovered at least some of his balance. He detailed his men off to set up a series of roadblocks before turning to Heath.

'Sir, I'd...' he seemed to think the better of whatever he was going to say, and then went ahead regardless. 'I know we've gone dark now, but I'd like to call Sammy, soon as you say I can.'

Igor surprised Dave with his tone. Apologetic, deferential, and not at all hopeful. Heath surprised him with the softness of his voice in reply.

'We're not in Helmand or the Sunni Triangle here, Chief Gaddis. Get set up, make a call if you can get any bars out here. I trust you. You're not going to give it away. And I know Sammy's cool too. He'll understand.'

'Thanks,' said Igor. 'Good luck.'

They climbed back in their Humvee and Zach turned over the engine again. The two Hummers staying with Igor took up blocking positions on I-80 facing toward Omaha. His men had their weapons out. Within moments one of them fired a shot. Dave could see another poor bastard out in the cornfield drop, finished permanently.

Something was bothering Dave, but it took him a while to

pin down the source of his anxiety. Throughout the encounter with the Tümorum, Lucille had remained utterly silent. In fact, thinking back on it, she hadn't hummed so much as a single note as they'd passed any of the shambling corpses. A hell of a change for her. She was a fucking Valkyrie when the Hunn were around. But the Tümorum?

It was like even she was frightened of the fucking things.

There was something else nagging at him, too. But he couldn't figure out what.

# 14

'I thought all the roads were jammed with refugees,' Dave said, not knowing what else to say as they left behind the edge of settlement in the late afternoon light. The westering sun picked out hundreds of solar panels, throwing a star field of sunbursts back at them. And then the burbs were gone, cut off as if by a guillotine and they rolled through pasture land and tilled fields, blemished here and there by small patches of forest.

Heath was on his phone, scrolling through texts and emails. He'd just spent a tense ten minutes trying to explain to General De Brito that they now had to defend themselves against undead members of the local populace who might come looking for a bite to eat. For a small mercy they hadn't seen any more on the road but Dave thought he spotted one on a low hill. When he craned his head to look up out of the window he could see the contrails of jets high above them. Lower down, helicopters swept over those patches of forest or circled what he assumed were entrenched positions of the national guard and De Brito's army units. Once or twice he caught sight of thirty or forty men in camouflage gear digging holes into a slope and he wondered how much use they would be when 10,000 daemons came thundering up on them. As they approached their destination—'Five minutes out,' Zach announced—he saw the first evidence of real defensive positions. Or what he thought of as real defensive positions. Bradley fighting vehicles ranged in a long, shallow half moon behind maybe a hundred men frantically preparing fighting pits and setting up mortars and heavy machine guns. He looked to the other side of the highway and saw a similar arrangement, all of the guns pointing toward the Djinn.

The light was leaking out of the day.

'Is that it?' he asked.

'No,' Heath said. 'These are just light blocking forces. The stuff they had available to throw into the breach. We're here to buy some time for De Brito to get his big dogs in place... If they're needed,' he added.

A few clouds were drifting in from the west, scattered and scrappy, but throwing shadows over the gently rolling plains, making it just that little bit less dangerous for Hunn and Fangr and Djinn and Gnarrl and Sumateem and whatever to be about their business. Dave wondered what the Djinn called their own Fangr leashes, the 'leashed' daemon inferiorae that every Hunn warrior learned to control.

Thinking on it, he was pretty sure they just called them Fangr, too.

Through the gathering gloom a collection of Hummers, five ton trucks and Nebraska state patrol cars appeared around a long, looping bend in the road. Hidden by a low hill they apparently marked the forward line. Zach slowed the Humvee to a stop.

'Hey! Wait,' said Dave. 'Sammy's a he?'

* * *

A tall soldier in a helmet and body armour walked up to the driver's window as Dave looked at more men, working away at positions on the hill he'd just driven around. These positions looked much better prepared, some of them actual bunkers with logs and sandbags for roofing. It'd help against an arrow storm, he supposed. And the many, many long barrels poking out of the firing slits promised to rake the riverbank in front of them with deadly waves of fire.

'Is there a Captain Heath present?' the soldier asked.

'That would be me, soldier,' Heath said. 'And you are?'

'Sergeant Ryan Mecum, 1-75th Rangers,' he said as he turned and pointed down the road. 'Your rendezvous is to take place in the southwest bound lane of I-80 on a bridge over the Platte River. We'll have eyes on you if anything goes wrong. Is this Mr Hooper?'

'That'd be me,' Dave said, but his attention was on the Djinn. Or rather, his attention was divided between the Djinn and the bewildering revelation that Igor's Sammy was Samuel, not Samantha. Assuming he'd heard right, of course. Assuming he'd heard Heath say *'Sammy's cool too. He'll understand.'*

'No fucking way,' he whispered to Zach as Heath spoke to the ranger. 'Igor bites the pillow?'

The look CPO Allen gave him could have curdled fresh milk.

'Okay,' said Dave, quickly putting up his hands. 'Not asking. Don't tell.'

He went back to watching the Djinn camp about two or three miles away over the river. There was no missing it. Even if he'd mistaken the dark hide tents, hundreds of yards to a side, for tilled fields, the eye could not slip over the giant siege towers arrayed behind them. They stood four or five storeys high, the tallest point on the plain for miles around. War banners flapped from them and inside, he knew, whole companies of Jorrn awaited the order to assault the human city.

His first thought was, 'Fucking idiots'. They had no idea. But then he wondered just how big the rip between the realms would have to be to march all those bastards and their toys through.

He realised Mecum was trying to tell him something. The soldier didn't look impressed to be meeting the hero of New Orleans, not like the lovely ladies at the Bellagio last night; a thousand years ago.

'They asked for you specifically.'

'Who? How?' said Dave.

Mecum's cheeks blew out.

'Best I show you, if you want to come along. They're on the way.'

The three men climbed out of the Hummer.

'Dave,' said Zach, his voice still a little clipped and cold. 'You're not really dressed for this party.'

And he wasn't, still wearing the outfit Armando had put him in for *Fox and Friends* that morning. Another thousand years ago.

'Here, take this,' Zach said, removing some sort of camouflage vest from the rear of the Hummer. Dave was about to say no, to explain that even Kevlar wouldn't stop a Sliveen arrow or the blade of a monstrous battle-axe swung by a nine foot tall daemon with shoulders as big as watermelons, but he held his tongue. These guys didn't need to hear that, and as he examined the vest he realised it was less about armour than it was all the pockets and loops to carry energy gels, snack bars and other high calorie treats.

'Gatorade in the CamelBak,' said Zach. 'Igor rigged this up for you with four combat knives, in safety sheaths. Figure with the arm you got on you now, you could probably throw them right through a Hunn.'

'Igor did this for me?' Dave asked, his cheeks warming a little.

Zach nodded. 'Yeah. Gonna be a problem now?'

'No! No, not at all,' said Dave. 'No problem. Just not really a knife guy,' Dave said but he thought he could feel Urgon in the back of his head, nodding with approval. The more sharp, pointy, stabby things, the better.

'Okay, and the best part,' said Zach, sounding a little wary, but wanting to move on, 'we got a couple of reinforced loops for you to slip Lucille through. Way more convenient than hauling her around everywhere, possibly dropping her on the toes of a passing chief petty officer.'

He helped Dave into the vest, just like Armando had that morning.

Big gay Armando.

'Thanks, Zach. I'll be sure to thank Igor too when we see him again,' said Dave. He was touched by the gesture, even if he was still reeling at the idea of being touched by Igor. Not that Dave was prejudiced against gays, you understand. It was that he was... that Igor was...

Hell, it was just that Igor was so fucking manly.

*No. Not manly*, he thought quickly. *Just...*

Fuck.

'I didn't get you guys anything,' he said, weakly.

He snapped on the clasps and tested the seating for Lucille.

She slid in and drew out in a nice fluid motion. He had to change his grip to take a fighting hold. It wasn't like drawing a samurai sword in the movies, ready to cut. But it did mean he could forget about her while he walked around. As long as she wasn't humming to him. And she was right now, a soulful sub-aural hymn to the slaying they would do here.

The crazy bitch.

They hurried a few paces to catch up with Heath and Sergeant Mecum who hadn't waited for them. They were striding down the slope toward…

Dave wasn't sure. It looked a bit like the Octagon on Ultimate Fighting Championship, but fashioned out of crash barriers, razor wire and scaffolding.

'What kind of overwatch can you provide, Sergeant?' Heath asked, as Dave and Zach caught up with them.

'Patchy, sir, to be honest with you. We're on a flood plain here and while I can get men close to the bridge, they won't have a good line of sight on the deck itself from down there,' Mecum said. 'There are no real high points of terrain which dominate the area, so there is no way for me to provide any high cover. But we do have some good snipers I've put up on top of the bigger vehicles. Any word on additional forces?'

Heath shook his head, 'What we have now is what we go with, if we go. We're not looking for a stand-up fight, Sergeant. I hope this will be a negotiated withdrawal. For them. We'll talk it out. Buy time for more of the heavy metal to get in here, but you can look to the heavens for deliverance if the shit kicks off. The air force has them in the box and they are weapons hot already.'

Dave didn't like the sound of any of that. Sounded to him like all those fine words about covering his ass weren't worth hen shit on a pump handle. Heath didn't seem much fazed by it, however, and he'd be coming down with Dave to talk to the orcs, so maybe this was one of those things it was best to let the professionals worry about.

Besides, they'd reached the Octagon and he had other things to worry about. Specifically, half a dozen reanimated corpses, all pressing themselves up against the razor wire, trying to reach through for him. It certainly put his discomfort with the idea of Igor reaching for his Johnson into perspective.

Unlike the Tümorum back on the highway these shamblers were talking, after a fashion. Or rather, moaning. His name, over and over.

'Daaaaave.'

'You got groupies,' Mecum explained, his features twisting into a mask lost somewhere between revulsion and unease. 'Been like this all day. Just kept coming in one after another.' He turned around to Dave. 'Calling your name, Mr Hooper. Calling out "Daaave" and what sounded like "Come". Afraid we put a couple of them down before we realised they weren't like zombies on TV or at the movies. They didn't seem to want to eat anyone. They're more like…' He shrugged.

'Ushers,' Dave supplied. 'To lead us to the meeting.'

He squinted into the setting sun, looking out across the plains. The squares of the Djinn regiment were dark blocks, as neatly arranged on the far side of the river as the chequerboard pattern of the fields from under which they'd emerged.

'Somewhere out there, or maybe even behind us,' he said, waving at the landscape, 'but somewhere within a mile or two, you'll find a seven foot tall, creepy-looking fucker, looking like he could turn to mist and vanish into a crack in the earth if you gave him even half a side-eye. And he could. But then he'd lose his hold over these poor bastards.'

'Daaaaaave... coooome...'

There was nothing ghostly about the voices. They rasped out of dry mouths with swollen tongues.

'Are they alive?' asked Mecum, staring at a stringy blonde teenager whose face was half eaten by maggots that dribbled out of her sinuses and dropped to the ground.

'No. They can't be. But the Revenant Master had to raise them when they were fresh. Chances are he had someone kill them for him. If you see him, put him down.'

Mecum pushed his helmet back and gave Heath a pained look.

'What the hell we dealing with here, sir? I just got home from Uruzgan. But I'm thinking I might like to go back there now.'

Heath smiled, the same humane smile Dave had seen on him when he assured Igor that shooting that family of Tümorum was his responsibility because he gave the order.

'We're all just doing our jobs, Sergeant. And speaking of mine, I should check in with your CO. It's almost game time.'

'He's up slope a little, sir. Checking on the firing positions.'

As Dave followed them up the gentle rise he was followed in turn by the moans of the dead.

# 15

Captain Heath checked his gear over one more time as Dave stood by chewing joylessly on a choc-nut Atkins Endulge bar. Zach scoped out the bridge over the Platte River as the sun made its final dip toward the horizon. Dave could hear a deep throbbing bass beat coming from the Djinn camp, the drums of the legions, muffled by the enormous tarpaulins of cured Drakon-hide under which the regiment still sheltered. Loud enough that it drowned out the choppers flying overhead.

'We should go with you,' Zach said. 'A close protection detail at least.'

Dave shook his head. 'Nah, it's a trap for sure. Fucking Djinn. Now we're here, I'd rather go by myself.'

'That isn't happening,' Heath said, finished with his checks. 'We need to buy another twenty minutes.'

He had more to say, but an Apache roared over, heading for the bridge like a dark bolt thrown by a minor god.

'Two things,' Dave shouted.

'Yes?' said Heath.

Dave dropped his voice as the uproar of the chopper died away. 'One, the orcs are familiar with the whole death from above thing because of the Drakonen, who love a barbecued orc. You'll need to tell your folks to be careful about flying too low near them. Remember that helicopter that got taken down in New Orleans?'

'Anything in particular they should watch for?' Heath asked.

'Big-ass crossbow thing,' Dave said. 'That gladiator movie with Russell Crowe? I think they had them in that.'

'Ballistas, I'll pass it on,' Heath said. 'And your other point?'

'We really should have done this at high noon.'

Heath gave him a little touch of his rare smile.

'We were in transit. As I recall you were drinking expensive bourbon like you were possessed of a thirst that could cast a shadow.'

Dave enjoyed the memory for a quiet moment.

'You get even a little drunk?' asked Heath.

'A little. Not for long.'

They stepped off, the two men starting the long walk down toward the bridge without either of them saying anything about it. Heath took out his phone and relayed the warning about big-ass crossbows back up his chain of command.

'*Vaya con dios, mis amigos,*' Zach called after them.

'*Hasta la vista,*' Heath replied with a wave back over his shoulder, a surprisingly non-military gesture. More like a man setting off on a pleasant walk to his favourite bar. Behind them Dave could hear Zach turning to his men, speaking low and calm, giving them orders to cover the two of them as they made their way over the bridge. They might not rate Hooper, but they had his back. He felt pretty good about that, for what it was worth.

Not much in a few minutes, he guessed.

'Other thing is, Dave,' Heath said. 'De Brito wasn't putting us anywhere near these things until he had his armour and airborne in place. Half an hour, they will be. If the air force has to start bombing, we want to make sure nothing gets away. Especially not those tumour creatures.'

'Tümorum,' Dave corrected, feeling silly now in his expensive casuals and tactical vest full of chocolate bars. Maybe he should have changed into something more kick-ass. Ahead of them the Platte River was broad, shallow and looked somewhat muddy, although it caught the dying light and threw off a few golden flares as they approached. It was a bit on the low side, Dave thought, not even suitable for canoeing. On the other hand, when it rained he suspected it would flood easily, the water running over the riverbanks and into the adjacent fields. Might explain the thick tree and foliage cover, where it hadn't been cleared for farming.

'Heath?'

'Yes, Dave.'

'You scared?'

Heath actually stopped to laugh at that. Only for a second, before resuming his steady, slightly lopsided gait toward the bridge. But it was a genuine laugh, surprised out of him, Dave supposed.

'Hell yes. Of course I am. You?'

'A bit, I suppose. Like I was a bit drunk. But only a bit. I think it's part of my superhero menopause. You know, the change.'

'Nothing wrong with being scared, Dave. Or admitting it. All you have to do is put one foot in front of the other. That's ninety percent of the game, right there.'

The drums grew louder again, perhaps because the choppers that had been circling had backed off a ways after Heath had warned them. Dave casually hauled Lucille out of her scabbard and hefted the weapon in his hands. She felt good and made him feel good, humming an unknown song in his head, in his hands, growing warm and yearning to have at the enemy.

'Can you hear that at all?' he asked Heath.

'Hear what? The drums?'

'No. Lucille.'

Heath looked at Dave as though he thought he was being kidded. 'The hammer?'

'Splitting maul. Yeah.' He sighed, as though confessing to something. 'She sings to me. Couple of days ago I wouldn't have told you that because I'd'a worried you thought I was good for the fucking nut hatch. Now, here we are strolling down for cocktail hour with 10,000 daemon assholes who probably just called us here to use our testicles as fucking olives in their martinis. So, yeah. I thought you should know. She's singing a sweet tune right now. I just wondered if only I could hear it.'

'Only you, Dave. Do you know what she's singing?'

'I think she's practising the epic ballad, that'll be sung around campfires for a thousand years, of the night Super Dave and his one-legged captain died glorious but ultimately stupid deaths after walking into a daemonic cocktail party they probably should have just skipped.'

'Catchy,' said Heath.

His limp, Dave thought, was a little more pronounced than usual. He'd have worn the nub of his half-leg raw in New Orleans. And he'd barely stopped moving since.

'I know some lyrics for her,' said the black officer and he actually addressed the hammer formally. 'Lucille. Ma'am, see what you can do with this…

*Then out spake brave Horatius*
*The captain of the gate*
*To every man upon this Earth,*
*Death cometh soon or late,*
*And how can man die better*
*Than facing fearful odds*
*For the ashes of his fathers*
*And the temples of his Gods?'*

It was Dave's turn to stop in his tracks. A shiver had run up his arms and into his shoulders, spreading out through his torso. The closest thing he could compare it to was the feeling of having a goose walk over your grave. But it wasn't creepy or unsettling, and it was definitely coming from Lucille. If he had to describe what she was doing then it would be 'purring'.

'Whoa! Heath! She likes you.'

'Really? Then she likes Macaulay.'

They crossed from the field they'd been walking down onto the hard surface of the highway, stepping over a length of guard rail.

'You seem okay with the idea of a singing war hammer,' Dave said.

'I've had to get used to more challenging ideas the last few days.'

'Fair enough.'

Dave looked quickly behind them. The thin lines of the army units seemed a long way off now. Captain Heath looked like the rest of his SEALs, geared up in body armour, a radio headset and fatigues. However, with each step, his gait grew a little more pronounced and laboured. Beads of sweat broke out across his forehead.

'One foot in front of the other,' he muttered.

Lucille positively thrummed in Dave's hands with murderous intent. The Champion of New Orleans and the navy SEAL captain walked on in silence, lost in their own thoughts.

The sun sank behind the western horizon.

'So. Igor's gay married then?'

The war drums stopped.

Heath stopped too. His face was carved from teak.

'Chief Gaddis is one of the finest men I have ever served with.'

'Hey! I'm not a guy to be judging. I think we both know that by now. Just asking. Nobody ever tells me anything. And I wouldn't want to, you know, say something dumb.'

'No,' said Heath. 'You wouldn't.'

'Oh look,' said Dave. 'Our new friends.'

On the southwest end of the bridge a party of the Djinn appeared from within a yurt carrying their battle standards, lengths of bone festooned with the skulls and hides of those who had fallen before the Djinn in battle. A single warrior held an improvised white flag, perhaps a bed sheet, which was weird. None of the Sects went in for that sort of shit. They were a fight to the last orc kind of deal.

'Shouldn't we have brought a flag of our own?' Dave asked as they stepped onto the bridge proper.

Heath tapped a finger against the American flag patch on his shoulder. 'I got your back.'

Now that they were off the sloping, uneven ground, Heath's ease of movement improved, but Dave understood why the captain had been forced out of the field. He also concluded the story he'd first given him in New Orleans was a cover. He hadn't flown out to the Longreach with the marines and the SEAL teams because they'd just been 'passing through' on some training exercise. Or maybe they had, maybe he could give him that much. But it was pretty obvious now, after a couple of days hanging out with them that Heath and the professors had worked together for a long time.

'Can I ask you something?' he said, as they slowly made their way along the span.

'Chief Gaddis has never broken out into a show tune in the field, no.'

'Yeah, okay, you got me. I deserve that. But that's not it. Well, not really. It is sort of about you guys not trusting me or telling me stuff. You knew Compton and Emmeline way before New Orleans, didn't you?'

Heath kept his eyes on the party of monsters moving toward them. Dave knew without looking again that there were eight of them. The BattleMarshal of the Regiment, perhaps, and if not him the BattleMaster of the Senior Legion, a couple of Lieutenants Grymm or the Djinn version of the SS anyway–the Kravakh–and some bodyguards, which would be a joke under normal circumstances because the most feeble daemon would have no trouble dismembering a grown man.

'Compton's work with the anthropology teams in Afghanistan and Iraq is legendary, Dave. He didn't invent the Human Terrain System but he refined it, and he saved a lot of American ass when he did that.'

Dave snorted. It hadn't saved his brother.

'Compton is a legend in his own lunch box, and you just avoided the question. You might have worked with him in Iraq or Afghanistan, but I meant whether you'd worked with

OSTP before this. See, I got this theory that just as they call in people like Emmeline for particular jobs, like if you got an alien you need autopsied, when they need some ass-kickin' done on the quiet, you get a call, captain, my captain. You and your boys Zach and Igor and SEAL Team 007 or whatever.'

'Ask me again, if we live though this,' said Heath.

'For reals?'

'For reals. If we survive. And when you've completed your S.H.I.E.L.D. security clearance.'

A pause.

'Hey! Did you just make a funny, Heath?'

The blank expression on Captain Michael Heath's face said that he had done no such thing, but a twinkle in his eyes said otherwise.

'Time to get back into character, Dave. We're good to go.'

'Pfft. I'm always in character.'

The Djinn had stopped in the middle of the bridge over the Platte River. With longer strides they'd easily reached the mid-point ahead of the two, smaller, humans. Dave looked up as he and Heath trudged the last few yards. Far overhead he could see war planes loitering, looping around like commuter jets in a holding pattern. If any had been flying.

He had a sudden urge to call his boys.

They pulled up about ten metres short of the Djinn.

The largest of the monsters took one step forward. He held a cleaver that could have split a whole steer nose-to-tail with one swing. His face was a misshapen ruin of broken teeth, a giant hole where his nose should have been and a puckered scar running from one milky eye down to his jawline. A freshly harvested, copper-green Drakon-hide cloak draped from the creature's shoulders to the ground. Human scalps sewn together in a necklace had dribbled clotted blood over rusted iron plate and chain mail. Around the monster's waist were a number of heads, some recent human decapitations mingled with Hunn, Grymm and Sliveen, their mouths still locked in a permanent state of shock. Each had a sigil carved into its forehead which told the story of the kill. At nine feet the creature had to weigh close to half a ton, an armoured nightmare festooned with spikes.

'Which of you is the Dave?' it hissed in the Olde Tongue. The accent was different. Dave heard that immediately, and his flesh crawled into hackles at the sound of it.

'You got me,' said Dave.

'A bold insult, to come upon us with only one lieutenant, calfling,' the Djinn said.

Dave jerked a thumb at Heath, who could understand none of the exchange, and replied, 'He's a captain, and that beats two lieutenants. And I'm the Dave, and that's all you need to know, monkey-boy.'

The Djinn bared its fangs and snarled, a guttural, animal noise, like something from a zoo—a private zoo, owned by a drug lord, where all the animals were mistreated. One of the Kravakh lieutenants lunged forward, drawing its blade, baring fangs, and hissing at Dave. He felt Heath flinch beside him, and sensed that flinch turning into a move to draw his sidearm. But before Heath could put a bullet into the meeting, and their chances of walking away from it, the leader of the Djinn swung a back-fist into the face of the Kravakh. The creature's forward momentum crashed into the unstoppable barrier of the Djinn leader's forearm and its legs shot out from underneath it as its face caved in with the sound of a rottweiler destroying a chicken carcass. Dave put his hand on

Heath's arm, catching his quick draw while the pistol was still mostly inside the holster.

'Easy there, Wild Bill. You plug one of these assholes and they'll demand I put you down, for honour's sake. Of course, I won't do that, but that'll just raise a whole heap of other problems.'

All of the Djinn, he noticed, were looking closely at the weapon Heath had tried to pull out. All of them except *el Jefe* who was still locked in on Dave.

'Dave, there are a dozen snipers training their sights on these fools. One of the orcs pulls another move like that and you and I are going to be covered in blowback.'

Heath's voice wasn't shaking, but it sounded so tightly coiled that Dave was certain it would be shaking if the guy were not holding it steady by sheer force of will.

'So,' he continued in the Olde Tongue to the spokesmonster, 'this is going well. But I don't think I caught your name, big fella.'

There was no direct translation for 'big fella'. What Dave actually said was much closer to 'unusually large member of your nest'. The Olde Tongue was not what an engineer or an English literature professor would call elegant.

It did the job, though.

'You have the honour and privilege of trembling before BattleMarshal Gurj im Sh'Kur ir Djinn, commander of Her Majesty's 1st Regiment.'

The rumbling growl of the BattleMarshal had a calming effect on his subordinates, as though they could relax now the boss was taking names and kicking ass. Or chewing ass, as the case may be.

'Well, not so much with the trembling,' said Dave, 'but

pleased to meet you.' He took a moment to look over Sh'Kur's host. 'So, you boys planning on hanging around long?'

The BattleMarshal growled back, 'You talk with the urmin squeak of the Hunn clan, calfling. Perhaps you are their pet.'

Dave smiled.

'No, I'm just the guy who comes in and kicks their asses for them.'

'So you have contended with my old foe?'

Dave could hear the quiet, slightly tinny sound of electronic chatter leaking out of Heath's headset. He was also aware of the officer muttering clipped phrases into his mic, although since Heath couldn't understand anything passing between Dave and the BattleMarshal he wasn't quite sure what sort of information the captain was sending back up the line. It was frustrating, but Dave found it almost impossible to talk with Sh'Kur in the Olde Tongue and still follow what Heath was saying. He didn't know what that meant, and the talk he'd had with Zach on the plane, about needing to understand his new powers and, more important, their limits came back to him with an unpleasant feeling. Dusk was thickening around them and he became aware of how few lights burned in the countryside. The land hereabouts, beyond the edge of the city, was sparsely settled, but he should have been able to pick out a couple of points of light here and there. A farmhouse, a gas station, even the trailer of a determined loner in the gentle folds of the hills or parked near a bend in the river. But there was nothing, just the gathering dark.

He turned his attention back to Sh'Kur, who seemed content to wait for a reply.

'Down in New Orleans, you mean? You heard about that?

Nah, that was nothing. Just a little thing with some cocksucker called Scaroth.'

The BattleMarshal seemed to cough and wheeze and when the wheezing went on for a while, Dave realised he was laughing.

'So this Scaroth gums his food like a nestling, does he?'

Dave frowned, wondering if he'd somehow mistranslated what the Djinn had said. And then he realised Sh'Kur was laughing because he'd called Urspite Scaroth ur Hunn a cocksucker. Given permission to laugh by the wheezing, hacking sighs of their leader, most of the Djinn officers did too. All of them, in fact, but the Kravakh. The one on the ground with inky dark daemon ichor leaking out of his shattered face. He probably wouldn't have been in a laughing mood anyway. But nor were his two comrades. If they were anything like their aptly named Grymm counterparts, the Djinn clan's fun police could probably only get the jollies from thinking up new ways to pull extra-long strips of flesh off prisoners in their dungeons.

'What's happening, Dave?' asked Heath.

'We're telling the most awful homophobic jokes,' said Dave out the corner of his mouth. 'And I don't mind telling you, Captain, I am appalled.'

'Just get on with it. De Brito and Salas are locked and loaded. Let's find out whether we have to pull the trigger.'

Dave listened to Lucille while he waited for the Djinn to stop wheezing. He'd never been one for listening to much besides rock music and maybe a little rap or hip hop when he was drunk. He liked the rhythm. One of his earliest dates with Annie, when he was still trying, he fell asleep in an opera. Or at least he thought it was an opera. They had a band there too, but in the larger scheme of things, the shrieking and caterwauling fatties on stage seemed more important. So that had to be opera, then.

Lucille wasn't singing opera, thank God. But she'd opened her pipes and was kicking out the jams. It reminded him, when he listened close, of an Irish rock band Annie also liked. Hot bitches with nice voices, but really troubling lyrics. All about slaughter and mayhem and dark times. Lucille's singing was just like that and she was doing her best to get Dave to sing along.

He had to pull himself out of the reverie with a physical effort.

The Djinn had finally had enough of the dicksucking jokes. Dave addressed BattleMarshal Gurj im Sh'Kur ir Djinn, commander of Her Majesty's 1st Regiment.

'So, Shakey, I don't suppose you came to Omaha to check out their world-famous Reuben sandwich? It was invented here, you know. No? Is there something else we could help you with? Before you turn around and go back down where you came from without causing any trouble at all?'

'I summoned you here that you might submit to the fearful power of the Djinn and negotiate terms for the surrender of this town and all the towns under your protection, lest we reduce them.'

'I see,' said Dave, slowly. 'Let me just have a word with my captain, here.'

Sh'Kur's lips drew back from the junkyard of his slitted mouth, but he did not object. He was probably used to having to consult with the Kravakh. A breeze blew, a warm breeze at the end of a hot day, but it chilled the sweat Dave could feel leaking through his shirt and he shivered.

'Okay,' he said, turning to Heath. 'They didn't come for Reubens. They're not here for stock tips from Warren Buffett and I don't think we can tempt them with a tour of the zoo either. They pretty much want me to turn over the keys to the city so they can roll in and get some dinner.'

Heath didn't reply immediately, instead hitting the push-to-talk button on his headset and murmuring into the mouthpiece, 'Arc Light this is June Bug. Confirm hostile intent. Repeat, confirm hostile intent. Stand by.'

Heath released the talk button and said to Dave, 'You sure these things can't understand what I'm saying?'

'Let's find out,' said Dave, before turning back to Sh'Kur and asking loudly, in good plain American English, 'Hey, Shaky, is the reason you guys wear pants because your nuts are so much smaller than the Hunn? Because my man, Scaroth, he had an impressive set of melons swinging on him and I can't help noticing that you don't.'

All eight of the Djinn warriors, including the injured Kravakh lieutenant, stared at him with blank, uncomprehending expressions. Some tipped their heads to one side, some furrowed the ugly knobs of weeping scar tissue they had instead of eyebrows, but none appeared to take offence. And taking offence was a natural state of being for these assholes.

'I think we're good,' said Dave. 'Want me to keep talking while we slowly back away and you launch the nukes?'

Heath did not.

'Keep them talking, find out as much as you can. I'd like to know how they got an army into that field.'

Dave returned to the Olde Tongue.

'Okaaay, Shaky, we're having a little trouble with the whole submission thing, right now.' Dave put up one hand to forestall any violence. 'Now don't go getting snippy on me, because I'd hate to have to kick your ass, seeing as how we have so much in common, you know, with you hating the Hunn, and me hating the Hunn. Perhaps it would help if you could explain exactly what submitting to you would mean. I'm just curious is all.'

He could see the giant claws of the BattleMarshal tightening around the shaft of the even gianter cleaver he was holding. Lucille's song seemed to deepen inside him, to pulsate more powerfully through his body. Dave prepared himself to go to warp speed. But Gurj im Sh'Kur ir Djinn did not bellow a war shout and start throwing the cutlery around. If anything, he reminded Dave for just a second of Heath, having one of those Heath moments when the need to get something out of Dave overrode his desperate need to choke the living shit out of Dave.

'When you submit to the Djinn,' growled the BattleMarshal, 'your lands and cattle become our lands and cattle. With your submission comes the protection of our majesty and, of course, a role of honour within her court for the Dave who would govern this realm in her stead.'

'Okay. That sounds cool,' said Dave. 'You're just going to have to give me a second to tell my friend here about it. He's like my scribe. Or my Scolari,' he added quickly with a flash of inspired bullshitting. 'He might need to jot down a few details.'

Dusk had darkened to full night and they were illuminated by the sickly yellow glow of the overhead lights of the bridge, the only points of brightness in the world. Dave could not even make out where the army had dug in back up on the hill, although that could be because he was looking from light into dark.

'You got like a notebook or something, Heath?'

'Sure,' he said slowly taking a small camo-fabric-covered pad from a pocket. He unzipped it to reveal a perfectly ordinary notepad. 'You need it? Why?'

Dave waved away the offer of the pad.

'No, I just need you to look like you're writing down what I'm about to say to you. Hell, why don't you write it down? Maybe someone can pull it off what's left of our bodies later on.'

Heath's expression told him he thought Dave's schtick was less important than taking care of business. He held a pencil over a new page.

'Okay. The deal is if I submit to them they get everything, and I get to be the royal buttboy at the palace. I'd rule over all the Earth, probably select who went into the blood pots–I can't help thinking of Compton for some reason–and the Djinn will "protect" us from nasty accidents. Like going into the Hunn's blood pots, I guess. It's your basic shakedown racket.'

'Very feudal,' Heath muttered. 'Figures.'

The pencil scratched across the page but Dave wasn't sure if Heath was writing it all down or just pretending. Dave was peripherally aware of drones circling hundreds of feet above them, probably recording everything. He wondered if they were armed.

'Why offer it, though?' said the SEAL.

'Word gets around, I suppose. They heard about New Orleans. Might have even had a couple of Sumateem scouts spooking about to report on it. I dunno. Lemme see if I can find a few things out.'

The BattleMarshal waited for Dave to finish consulting with Heath.

'Well, Champion?'

It was the first time he had called Dave that, but it came freighted with a heavy load of irony. Monsters do irony? Who knew?

'Shaky, we're making progress. I can feel the chances of an ass kicking receding with every moment. And I'm excited by your offer of selling out my fellow cattle, of condemning them to perdition and slavery and the occasional all-you-can-eat buffet for your homeboys there.'

The other Djinn snarled and growled. The Kravakh merely glowered at him.

'Still, coupla details I'd like to nail down about this protection you'd be offering. Because, you know, New Orleans was a hell of a close-run thing. Old Scaroth really had us by the nuts there. Just good luck really that we beat him. So yeah, protection is good.'

'The Hunn will not walk my fields or take my livestock, be assured of that,' Sh'Kur rumbled, his voice sounding like an idling bulldozer. 'Nor will any others.'

'None shall pass, eh? That's awesome. But, how you gonna do that? What if we wake up one day and there's half a dozen Hunn legions knocking on my door. I mean, how'd you get the regiment here? Scaroth only took a talon.'

One of the Kravakh stepped forward to try to whisper something to Sh'Kur but the BattleMarshal drove an elbow into its eye. The elbow was armoured and spiked. The creature dropped twitching and dead at the Djinn leader's feet. Or his hind-claws, to be anatomically correct.

'When you broke the capstone separating the UnderRealms from the Above it was but a small crack at first. But now that fissure widens and spreads. More fractures open. Other realms press against the barrier. Soon now, calfling, we shall take dominion over all your world. I offer life. Others will not be so generous.'

'Yikes,' Dave deadpanned.

'But now it is time for the Dave to kneel and submit.'

# 16

The BattleMarshal hefted his cleaver in a way that made Dave suspect that if he knelt down, he wouldn't be getting back up. He almost laughed. How big a chump did this tool think he was?

'Haters be hatin', Old Navy,' he said out the side of his mouth. 'And any second now, we be rollin'. Get ready.'

Heath started murmuring into his headset again but Dave was already back with Sh'Kur and couldn't spare him the attention. Lucille was no longer singing. But her silence was voluminous. It was the pause that swells and swells in that forever moment as the conductor holds aloft his baton. She was waiting for the symphony to commence.

'Kneel, human,' the BattleMarshal ordered.

Dave gently placed the back of his hand on Heath's chest and pushed, just enough to get him moving away from the immediate danger of that enormous, glinting blade. Heath did not resist, taking one, then two steps in reverse.

'The thing is, Shaky, it's my knees,' Dave explained. 'They're not what they were. And I don't like to kneel.'

The Djinn leaned forward slowly and said, 'Then you shall die.'

'Go!' Dave yelled at Heath, as he got ready to stomp on the accelerator and sidestep the carving blow from Sh'Kur. But it never came. Two things happened, one of which he understood, one of which he didn't, not at first.

He heard the crack of a rifle shot passing close by his ear and saw the head of one of the lesser Djinn commanders disintegrate in an explosion of bone and brain.

The snipers.

That he understood. More rounds came cracking in, but only one scored another headshot, one of the Kravakh taking a round in its nasal cavity that blew it shattered head over horned heels, and sent it toppling off the side of the bridge. The other Djinn were moving so quickly that glancing rounds sparked off heavy plate armour, or missed entirely. The daemons weren't ducking for cover from the human fire, however. They were diving and rolling left and right for no reason Dave could understand until he finally punched warp and found himself in that strange, suspended state where everything moved with glacial slowness. Everything but him, and the flight of harpoons whistling down the bridge toward him.

He stood, stupid, flat-footed and confused as dozens of Sumateem arrows came at him and Heath.

'What the fuck?' he mouthed, and in the time it took to do that, the war shots had advanced another two car lengths along the bridge toward him. And toward Heath, who was currently suspended in magical gelatine, and not likely to move much faster given the handicap of trying to do so on one leg. Dave doubted he'd been fitted with one of those blade runners the Paralympic guys used.

The need to start swinging Lucille with psychotic abandon, to smash her deep into the ugly skull of Gurj im Sh'Kur ir

Djinn, was a deep-body lust, but if he did that he would die. The volley was only a hundred yards away now and moving as quickly as a speeding car. Ignoring the song of murder in his head, in his limbs, down in his meat, Dave pushed off and away from the Djinn who were finally dying under a second burst of sniper fire. The bullets, which he saw as bright super-heated blurs of movement, punched into the creatures as they lay prone on the road surface to let the arrows pass safely over them. Some rounds spanged off armour with great slow showers of red and white sparks, but most hit the Djinn straight on and in, blowing huge gouts of monster meat out the other side.

Dave caught up with Heath just as the first of the arrows, as long as a javelin, shot past. As quickly but as gently as he could, he wrapped his arms around the SEAL officer and dragged him down out of the flight path, taking the impact on his own back as they hit the road surface. He felt the CamelBak full of Gatorade burst apart and his brand new tactical vest shred itself on the bitumen. Mass and speed, he thought, uselessly. The centrifugal force of the slow motion/hyper-accelerated tackle threw Heath's legs up in the air and Dave winced as he heard an arrow smash into the artificial limb, utterly destroying it, tearing it off at the knee and carrying the wreckage away. It did not take long for the arrows to pass over, however, and within a few seconds of his own subjective time he was up and running with Lucille gripped tightly in one hand and Heath thrown across his shoulder like a bag of garden mulch.

He could hear a high, keening sound and all of the muscles in his back tensed up waiting for the tearing pain of an arrowhead driving in deep between his shoulder blades, or into the back of his neck, or skewering the two men together in a shish kebab for the Djinn to eat at their leisure. But it was not another spear-sized arrow splitting the air as it raced toward his spine. It was just Heath, starting to scream in super slo-mo. The individual thunder cracks of large calibre sniper rounds disappeared under a deeper, rolling thunder that washed over them as Dave raced for the comparative safety of the dark hills where the army was dug in. The uproar grew into a slow, thumping storm of concussive detonations and impossibly slow strobing lights that flashed in the night but took long, long seconds of stretched time to fade.

Dave risked a glance over his shoulder and saw massive blossoms of fire blooming little by little, but unstoppably, amongst the Sumateem archers who had been hidden in Sh'Kur's yurt. The daemons came apart, gracefully, like ballet dancers; or the disarticulated limbs and torsos of ballet dancers, seen though a veil of acid. A few, just a few more arrows flew out in a second volley, some of them released when the creature holding the bow was blown apart. Most flew extravagantly high and wide but Dave dodged to the right of the bridge to get out of the way of one that seemed well aimed at him. The thunder rolled on and on, the bridge vibrating under his feet in a strangely measured, unhurried cadence.

He decided to field test his limits, rather than waiting for the chance to sit down with a bunch of clipboards and white coats as Zach had suggested. He felt, rather than knew that his control of the warp thing was improving, even though he had no idea how. Or even what it was, yet. He'd felt that way since Vegas. Dave sucked air deep into his lungs. He didn't just run harder, but *concentrated* for all he was worth on pouring more and more of his strength into speed. It worked. He passed through the world as pure acceleration, holding onto Heath just a little more firmly, lest the rough passage break every bone in the poor bastard's body. Rifle fire started to crackle past, sounding more like the long tearing of a great carpet or curtain than the crisp snap of a gunshot. Dave flew off the end of the bridge and down the road, covering half the distance back to their lines before he dialled it down. As he slowed and threw another look over his shoulder he saw the bridge swallowed by fire. Human fire, chemistry and physics, not magic; high explosives and hundreds, maybe thousands of rounds of small arms fire, long ropey arcs of green and yellow tracer. The whole world seemed aflame and he realised that nothing could have followed him off that bridge. The narrow structure served to channel any pursuers into the confines of a killing field. Calflings may have been puny to the swaggering giants of the Daemonum, but they had been busy this last eon or so. They knew a lot about killing.

He heard a scream as he dropped out of warp, and realised it was Heath. The cry was strangled as the SEAL gasped into his headset. 'Danger close. Danger close.'

'Copy. Rolling in,' a voice said.

'You okay?' Dave asked, feeling like a fool. 'Your leg's busted.'

He started to put the captain down then realised Heath would probably just fall over.

'Get to cover, Dave,' Heath grunted, as though somebody had just gut-punched him.

Dave could hear the shriek of jet turbines in the distance, getting closer, fast. At the very edge of perception he sensed something falling through the sky, put his head down, took a deep breath and started running again. Moving fast this time, but without slipping into the otherworld where he was the shadow that flickered between the statues he made of normal men. He was worried he'd damaged Heath with that last jump to warp.

A double crescendo erupted behind them with a muffled, slightly delayed one-two punch that blasted the Platte River Bridge out of existence. Tight formations of aircraft howled in from the northeast, passing over him on their way across the river, to drop their bombs on the other side. He felt the heat roll over him as an unexpectedly strong pressure wave, like a giant hand. When he thought they were well beyond any chance of being bombed by accident, he slowed and put the captain down. It took a moment for him to comprehend they were standing a few metres from the Octagon, where the soldiers had penned in the talking dead.

They weren't talking anymore.

Sergeant Ryan Mecum came running down toward them, with Zach and Igor not far behind. Zach called out for a medic, but needn't have bothered. Two teams bearing stretchers appeared out of the dark.

'Whoa, Mr Hooper,' said the ranger, now visibly impressed. 'That was awesome.'

'You get used to it,' Igor said as he dropped to one knee next to Heath. 'Hazmat team took over the site, thought we'd come see if we could get in on the party. Glad we made it in time.'

Heath nodded and clapped his hand to Igor's arm.

Dave wisely did not enquire after Igor's significant other.

Zach stood over them, scanning the night, his weapon ready, his boyish features decorated with the dancing light of high explosives and tracer fire. Bright flashes followed by concussive waves blasted apart the tree line on the southwest side of the Platte River. Helicopter gunships were hovering over the riverbank, hammering away at targets on the other side with chain-gun and rocket fire. They piled it on until Dave couldn't believe there was anything alive on the far bank, and sure enough the choppers soon peeled away. But not because the violence was done.

A blade ripped through heavy cloth, a small sound in the crashing din of battle. Igor cutting away Heath's trouser leg. The stump of his amputated limb was bloody and raw, but no bones showed through, and although he gritted his teeth and the muscles in his jawline writhed in the orange-yellow glow of the fires, Heath did not scream or pass out. He hauled himself up into a sitting position, his hands clawing up Igor's thick arms until the giant commando relented and helped him up.

'I want to see this,' said the officer. Their officer. The one Dave had walked with into harm's way and brought out less than the man he'd taken in. He followed Heath's gaze across the river into the inky blackness where he knew the 1st Regiment of the Djinn would be moving, charging toward battle. It was all they knew. The loss of BattleMarshal Gurj im Sh'Kur ir Djinn would not deter them, it would only enrage them. The fire would not stop them. They knew *dar Drakon* and many would even have battled the dragons. To them, helicopters were just another foe, or prey.

'Pick me up,' Heath said through his teeth, which were stained with blood that looked blacker than his skin in the night. 'I want to see this.'

Igor and Zach helped him to his feet.

*His foot*, Dave thought, and had to suppress the most

inappropriate snort of laughter of his adult life.

High in the sky, Dave could see them, outlined by blinking wing lights. Attended by smaller escorts, a quartet of B-52s passed overhead with a lack of hurry or bluster that was positively regal. He wondered how high they were. What the pilots could see. The burning ruins of the bridge, certainly. Perhaps the army units' positions, outlined in some sort of heads-up display. They probably had all sorts of Star Wars shit up there. Would the Djinn show up on infrared or some sort of low-light vision system? If so they'd present as a great mass of tightly packed iron and flesh, lumbering forward, gathering speed and energy like a stampede. They would charge the enemy, the human ranks, holding their formations as best they could. Four bands to a talon. Eight talons to a legion. Four legions to a regiment. Ten thousand stampeding raptor-orcs, clad in chain mail and boiled leather, in heavy steel plate that could probably turn a light rifle-round, all of them thundering toward the thin line of men and a few women, Dave supposed, spread out on the gentle hill overlooking the river.

The river.

It hadn't looked especially deep to him when he'd walked down there with Heath. He didn't suppose it was tidal, this far inland, but it was low. Low enough that the 10,000 sentient beasts screaming toward him would probably just splash across.

And then the very earth cracked open and the Apocalypse exploded out and up as thousands of tons of high explosive ordnance dropped into a precisely defined and moving kill box. The ground jumped beneath their feet, and the two SEALs were forced to brace themselves while they held their commander, lest all three be thrown to the ground.

'Holy shit,' said Dave, as a new day dawned over eastern Nebraska. A day of fire and death and utter negation. In less than a second the wave of destruction swept away from him at insensate velocities, atomising all of those war bands and talons and legions and the 1st Regiment late under the command of the great BattleMarshal Gurj im Sh'Kur ir Djinn.

'Fuck me,' Dave breathed out.

'Maybe in your dreams,' said Igor. 'Not mine.'

'Squirters,' said Zach, pointing at the edge of the vast area that had just been transformed into an infernal maelstrom.

'What?' said Dave, who thought the CPO might be hazing him, like Igor, but no. In spite of the seemingly inescapable scale of the violence a handful of men had visited upon the Djinn and their bonded clans, some still lived at the very edge of the slaughter. Some dozens, maybe even hundreds of surviving Djinn warriors tried for the river, some of them burning, diving in, trying to swim across. Still heading toward the thin line of soldiers between them and a city they could not yet see. Rifle and machine-gun fire raked at them and Dave heard the familiar shoop-chunk of mortar rounds going down range. Familiar from the movies, anyway.

'Looks like some of them are trying to exfil to the southwest,' Sergeant Mecum told them. 'Heh. Those teddy bears are going to be in for a big surprise if they go down to the woods tonight.'

Hooper stood there, taking it all in, feeling a bit useless and even duped. Southwest? He had to think about it. Survivors headed for the river and more going southwest *away* from it. The regiment had come apart. He shook his head and took a couple of Hershey bars from his ruined jacket, peeling them and eating the sweet familiar chocolate just as though he was watching this in a multiplex with the kids.

With the B-52s gone, the helicopter gunships returned and pressed their way into the smoke and ruin, releasing a storm of rockets as they passed over the river. Dave could hear something else. A high machine whine interspersed with deep bass booms mingled with the war shouts and cries of dying monsters. In his hands, Lucille purred and approved, although possibly saddened because she had not partaken herself.

The first tank emerged from the smoke and fire. An engineering marvel crafted of hard angles and set upon heavy treads. The human war machine pressed forward. It swivelled its main gun onto a point of interest, belched fire and turned to pursue. The first steel behemoth was followed by a second and a third. On the plains across the river the dying creatures faded against the armoured might of America.

'Might have gone quicker if the mech boys from Fort Riley had gotten up here a little sooner,' Sergeant Mecum said. 'Not easy moving a whole brigade of badass armour on short notice. Still, I think we can stick a fork in this one, boys, it's done.'

'What?' said Heath, but he wasn't talking to Sergeant Mecum. He had that abstracted look you see on folk deep in a conversation with someone on their cell phones.

'When?' he asked, as the mortar rounds landed amongst the remnants of the Djinn, picking them off one by one, which seemed an extravagance.

'Yes, sir. I'm… we'll get on it, sir…'

Everyone in the little group had turned to him now. Whatever was going on with the captain seemed more important than the mopping up ops over the water.

'It's the D-Tac,' he said, sounding shocked for the first time all day. 'They hit the D-Tac.'

'The who hit what?' asked Dave.

'The Cracker Barrel, Dave,' Zach said gently. 'Back on the edge of town. Where Emmeline and Compton were.'

'And your fucking lawyer,' Igor added.

'The Hunn, Dave,' said Heath. 'They're in Omaha, and they got our people. Hit them hard at De Brito's HQ and went through them.'

# 17

'Oh man, those dudes came to chew gum and kick ass and they kicked so much fuckin' ass they didn't even open their fuckin' Bubble Yum. This is like game over, man! Game over!'

Guyuk, who was becoming used to the bizarre extempore outbursts of Thresh-Trev'r, caught the looks exchanged between the BattleMarshals of the three Regiments Select ur Grymm. A wrinkling of the nasal cavities, a barely perceptible flicker of the eye slits away from the Sliveen priestess and onto the small, alien presence. An ever so subtle baring of yellow fangs.

The ill-regard of the Master of the Ways also shifted from the carved granite altar decorated with carefully crafted Seer Stone pieces. But unlike the sulphurous resentment seeping off the BattleMarshals, the palpable hostility of the Master Scolari was as frigid as the killing-breath of the great white Drakonen; the Way Master's pride still wounded by the discovery of the smoking crater and rockfall that had replaced the cavern in which they had spoken with the Dave. Prideful he may have been; stupid he was not. Guyuk could almost feel the Scolari straining to translate the meaning and import of Thresh-Trev'r's peculiar pronouncement.

'Control your thinkings, Thresh,' Guyuk warned. 'And stay your tongue lest I cut it out.'

'Staying my tongue, boss. Got it. But damn. Did you hear what happen–'

'Thressshhh!'

'D'oh! My bad!'

And the ridiculous creature actually held its tongue out, pinched between two fore-claws.

'Resume the telling of it, Worship,' muttered Lord Guyuk.

The Diwan to all the Sliveen who served Lord Guyuk regarded the tiny empath daemon with a flat curiosity, before she returned to moving the dormant Seer Stones around the smooth surface of the altar.

'I shall do more than tell, my Lord Commander. I will show.'

Satisfied with their alignment, she grasped the amulet that hung on a thin belt of braided wulfin-hide around her long neck. The Grymm closed their eyes and bowed their enormous heads as she began to pray. The marshals three, Master Scolari, and the lord commander himself.

'Thresh-Trev'r. Respect for the Diwan,' said Guyuk in a warning tone. He did not even need to break his own submission to know the wretched thing was gawking, eyestalks everywhere, at the ceremony.

'Got it. No peeking.'

The prayer became a chant and Guyuk felt the magicks of the Diwan Sliveen gathering in the chamber.

'Lord Guyuk ur Grymm,' the Diwan recited formally. 'Nine of my finest did I consume that you might know their seeing of *dar ienamic*.'

Still speaking into the dark, his eyes closed and head bowed, Guyuk went down on one knee, the ageing joints creaking and popping with the great mass they had to lower to the stone floor.

'Diwan dar Sliveen ur Grymm, their sacrifice will be written in the scrolls, with the blood of *dar ienamic*.'

'Then rise and behold what you would, my Lord, that the nine finest would not tender themselves to the Seer Stones in vain.'

'Whoa!' breathed Thresh-Trev'r before Guyuk had even climbed back to his hind-claws. 'Check it out, bro.'

'Quiet, Thresh.'

The chamber was darker than it had been, the red glow of coals in the rough-hewn wall sconces smothered by an icy blackness that seemed to press in close around the altar. But within the glow cast by the Seer Stones the altar was almost painfully illuminated. Guyuk and the other Grymm all squinted into the magick. The lord commander had an extraordinary view of the field on which the Djinn and the humans met, almost as though he rode the spine of a Drakon.

A river curved across the altar. Forests grew there. And the forces of *dar ienamic* faced each other across the fields. Men were digging into the hillsides down the end of the stone table by the Diwan. The 1st Regiment of BattleMarshal Gurj im Sh'Kur ir Djinn were sheltering under their field hides just in front of Guyuk at the opposite end.

'See that the water course over which the Dave and Sh'Kur meet is bounded on both sides by the tilled fields and woodland hunting reserves of the humans,' Guyuk said, meaning to make a lesson of the topography, but again his marshals bristled at calling this new foe anything other than 'cattle'. BattleMarshal Urddun Guyur of the 1st Grymm Regiment even dared spit a thin stream of hot bile onto the cavern floor at mention of the word.

'My apologies, Diwan,' said Guyuk before back-fisting Urddun with an open talon blow. The BattleMarshal staggered backward but appeared to rebound off the enclosing darkness as though it were a shield.

'Attend me, all,' snarled Guyuk. 'These are not the cattle of the scrolls. Make the mistake of thinking them so and you would soon join Sh'Kur in the blood pots of the human queen and the dire annals of–'

'Bossman,' said Thresh-Trev'r. 'Sorry. No queens up topside. Or not for the Dave anyway. And no blood pot for Sh'Kur either. The peeps'd be like, eww, gross.'

Guyuk controlled the curse that wanted to escape his maw. After all, it was he who had ordered the Thresh-Trev'r to attend this council, unencumbered by the constraints of deference that would be natural to a Thresh, that Guyuk might better know the thinkings of his enemy and correct the failings of his own understanding. And had he not just failed to understand something of the humans? And had not the most-knowing Trev'r corrected him?

Yes. Yes, he had.

'My thanks for your wisdom, Thresh-Trev'r,' said Guyuk, each word a slow, thrusting bone knife. 'Master Scolari, I would know the order of battle of the human host. Make it thus when we are done here. You will confer with Thresh-Trev'r. If the humans serve no queen, I would know to what final authority the Dave and his legions will admit.'

'It will be done,' the master agreed, with a stiff bow.

'Cram session? All right! Gourd of bloodwine, some urmin giblets, I'm there,' said Thresh-Trev'r with nestling enthusiasm.

'Diwan dar Sliveen, continue,' said Guyuk, 'and

Thresh-Trev'r, you would best serve me with silence now, that I might have the seeings of the Diwan.'

'Five by five, boss.'

The chastened BattleMarshal Urddun resumed his place at the altar as the Diwan swept her long, pale hands across the living world. As she reached into the scenery, the tattoos under the coarse black hair on her forearms curled as sinuously as vipuren and the gnarled ridges of ceremonial scar tissue puckered and knotted as though the dead flesh lived again.

'The Djinn emerged from the mouth of a great rupture less than a league from this water crossing,' she said. 'The passage remains open to the Djinn realms, for the Dave and his minions seem not to perceive the way between the worlds as even a lowly Thresh might,' she said, regarding Guyuk's pet daemon inferiorae with distant interest.

'Or the... human champion has not yet scouted the passage,' Urddun offered in the silence, perhaps to make redress for speaking out of place earlier.

'Perhaps,' said Guyuk, still annoyed with the BattleMarshal, and now irked by this interruption. 'But let us see and know what we can, rather than guess at what we do not. Way Master, what say you?'

The old Scolari navigator bowed to the Diwan, rather than to Guyuk who had questioned him.

'We do not perceive the Dave or any of his legions upon the ways between the realms. They seem not to have the knowing of it, Diwan, my Lord.'

The Sliveen priestess inclined her long head toward Guyuk. 'My Lord. If you wish it, I will detail more scouts to observe the human host as it seeks the point at which the Djinn entered their fields.'

'In time, Diwan. Thresh-Trev'r, do you think it likely the Dave or his lieutenants will seek out the portal between their realm and that of Djinn?'

'Are you fucking kidding me? Man, they're gonna be all over that like big-ass on Beyoncé.'

'That is a yes?'

'Totes. I mean yes.'

The longer Thresh allowed Thresh-Trev'r to leash him like a subject Fangr, the harder the empath daemon found it to throw off the leash. It was as though Thresh-Trev'r was the real daemon, and poor Thresh the thin vessel in which this new, alien intelligence was bottled. Thresh did not much like it. One bump, one stumble and what was to stop the vessel shattering, freeing Thresh-Trev'r to run amok? The memories of the doughnut merchant also lay somewhere deep inside the thinkings of Thresh. But it seemed that Thresh-Trev'r, the first human mind he had consumed, had somehow taken dominion.

And as soon as the lord commander understood that Thresh-Trev'r knew best the thinkings of the cattle–the *humans*–the matter was settled.

'As difficult and distasteful as it will be, Thresh, I need the thinkings of Thresh-Trev'r, not your translations of the same.'

And so, Thresh found itself fading and fading, as the vulgar, ungovernable mind of the animal it had consumed turned around and all but devoured poor Thresh like a tasty doughnut of Darryl the doughnut merchant.

'Totes, I mean yeah,' said Thresh-Trev'r, who was diggin' on this. Once upon a time, the feeble thing that had been known as Trevor Candly might have cowered before the likes of the BattleMarshals and that puckered ass the Master of the Ways, unless he was totally smiting them on Xbox or something. But Thresh-Trev'r was no Trevor Candly. Thresh-Trev'r was a badass motherfuckin' daemon and a genius level brainiac into the fuckin' deal. At least on matters human… you know, compared to these nimrods. Thresh-Trev'r wasn't even freaked by all the bugshit crazy monster magick these guys were laying on him. Of course they had some kick-ass magick monster chops. They were fuckin' monsters!

And this bitch they were all bending over to booty-kiss? This ugly-ass Sliveen priestess? Fuck her, too. Thought she was so fucking cool with her Seer Stone bullshit.

The orcs might lose their shit over that. Not Thresh-Trev'r. Just a monster magick holodeck trick is all that was.

Still, cool trick.

Thresh-Trev'r swivelled all of his many eyestalks to take in as much of the display as he could. It was some sweet hi-def shit too, like 1080p *and* 3D. Not that he was gonna try to explain that to ol' Guyuk. Dumb motherfucker had enough trouble using a cell phone with Monster Trev doing all the work for him.

On the tabletop display, which reminded him of a really badass Warhammer set-up, most of the Djinn losers were just standing around under their tarps and hoodies, holdin' their dicks and doin' sweet fuck all else while the bossman and his top faggots had their meet-up with this Champion Dave motherfucker.

'Hark. The human champion and his lieutenant approach Sh'Kur.'

'Only the one lieutenant, my Lord?' queried Myrthr Sepcis ur Grymm, BattleMarshal of the 2nd Regiment Select.

'As I planned.'

*As you and I planned you fucking mean, homie*, thought Trev. *But we'll let it slide for now.*

They watched without comment as the Dave and the Djinn had their meet-up, a passage of profound dullness for Thresh-Trev'r until he realised that the depth of field on the Seer Stones was amazeballz! All he had to do was focus in on a detail and it was just like the holodeck zoomed out toward him.

Okay, he'd pay the ugly-ass bitch that one. That was an impressive demo. Trev wondered how she did it, but Sliveen Diwanae weren't in the habit of explaining themselves to mere Thresh, let alone half-breed mutants like he was now.

Thresh-Trev'r wondered if he leaped down the length of the altar and punched a hole in her stupid head to suck out all the sweetmeats inside whether he'd be able to work the bitch's Seer Stone mojo himself.

Maybe.

Maybe the Diwan would give up her tricks as easily as Trevor Candly had his.

Still, no doubt old Guyuk would stomp him if he tried.

Thresh, the real Thresh–or 'beta' Thresh, as Thresh-Trev'r sneeringly called him inside his own mind–recoiled in horror at these thinkings.

What was this monster inside his head? What had the Scolari set loose in there when they bade him to feed on the hot grey skull meats of the calfling that knew itself as Trevor Candly. What did–

*Hey, why don't you just shut the fuck up*, snapped Thresh-Trev'r. And Thresh's thinkings fell silent.

'See how the champion moves with the swiftness of an arrowhead,' Guyuk was saying.

Shit was getting real on the holodeck. Besides a flight of war shots from a dozen or more Sumateem archers the Dave was the only thing moving. Thresh-Trev'r knew he wasn't called the Dave in real life, of course. That was just a mistake these ignorant assholes had made. Dude was just Dave. Dave Cooper or something. But what the fuck? It gave him a laugh whenever they said that.

'See how the champion gives precedence to preserving the life of his minion,' said Guyuk. 'This weakness did we exploit while crippling our ageless foe, the Djinn.'

'A masterful plan, my Lord,' put in BattleMarshal Vorpukh Khutr ur Grymm of the 3rd Regiment Select.

'Masterful,' agreed the other two, hurrying to beat each other to the ass-kissing.

'The advice of the empath played some small role,' Guyuk conceded, and Thresh-Trev'r bowed his head lest the others should see him smirk. Daemon smirks were nasty. 'Note that, Master Scolari,' Guyuk continued, 'when you and the Consilium have recourse to its understanding of the human ways.'

'Of course, my Lord Commander.'

The old cunt looked to Trev as though he'd rather feed his nuts to a wulfin pack.

'Attend now, Grymm,' ordered Lord Guyuk. 'For this is why I have summonsed thee.'

The Diwan did something with her magick necklace, muttered some words of power or some shit, and the close-up Thresh-Trev'r been enjoying of a Kravakh lieutenant getting its melon popped by a sniper round suddenly pulled back to display the entire field of battle again. Enough to see the lines of human soldiers dug into the small rise a short distance across the mud flats from the bridge, the great squares of the

Djinn legions beginning to move as one, and the cascade of human fire which destroyed them. Thresh-Trev'r was even able to follow the line of the highway back up the ten miles or so through the countryside to the southwestern corner of the city.

'Whoa,' Thresh-Trev'r drawled, unable to help himself. 'Awesome.'

The three Regimental commanders actually reared back from the altar, the fuckin' pussies, but Thresh-Trev'r leaned in close to get a better look now the Diwan had turned off the zoom function. He knew exactly what he was seeing. A B-52 or even a couple of stealth bombers lighting up a kill box. Thresh-Trev'r had fond memories of spending untold hours in *Call of Duty* and *Battlefield* on this sort of thing.

'What sorcery is this?' Myrthr demanded to know.

'Big ugly fat fuckers,' said Trev, with not a little smugness at knowing what was happening while these three muppets were shitting themselves.

'Explain, Thresh-Trev'r,' said Guyuk. 'As simply as you might.'

'Giant iron Drakon,' he said. 'So fucking high in the sky even your Sliveen couldn't spot them. They shat lots and lots of Drakon turds down on Sh'Kur's regiment. You know, the fresh laid turds that explode when they hit you. And there you go,' he said, gesturing at the hologram with one sweep of his fore-claw. 'Barbecued Djinn with all the fixin's.'

Silence fell over the cavern and Guyuk motioned to the Diwan to bring her display to an end. She merely touched one of the Seer Stones and the world Above went away, the inky curtain of blackness surrounding them receded and they stood where they had been a few minutes earlier, in the lord commander's war chamber.

'But… how…' said Urddun of the 1st Regiment. 'How are we to bring battle to… to…'

'Magickal cows?' asked Thresh-Trev'r, peeling his lips back from his upper fang tracks.

'Enough,' said Lord Guyuk, sounding tired. 'As Thresh-Trev'r well knows, this is not magick,' he said, pointing at the granite altar top which was now just lifeless rock. 'It is what the humans call their… technology.'

'Magick by another name,' cried Sepcis. 'How are we to defeat such as these?'

'By learning the ways of men and turning the knowing of it against them. As I have just done. The Dave knew he was being drawn into a trap, but he did not know that trap was not for him, but for his minions.'

# 18

Captain Heath settled the argument over whether Dave would fly to the ambush in a helicopter with the SEALs.

'You go ahead, Dave. You get there as fast as you can, and do what you can,' Heath grimaced as a medic quickly strapped up his damaged half-leg. 'We won't be more than a few minutes behind.'

Dave could hear the chopper approaching, even over the uproar on the far side of the river. Half a dozen tanks and armoured fighting vehicles ploughed up the scorched earth over there to run down small war bands of Djinn foolish enough to regroup and attempt a counter-attack with bows and arrows or sword and shield against chain guns, high explosives and flechette rounds.

'And you're sure it's Hunn? The Horde?' said Dave. 'Not Djinn?'

'The attackers were identified as the same hostiles we met in New Orleans,' Heath confirmed. 'And then we lost contact with the headquarters group.'

'Got a Blackhawk, one minute out, sir,' said Zach.

'We got played,' said Dave, hot shame colouring his face, with real anger rushing in behind it. 'That Guyuk bastard.

The Grymm, he...'

Heath cut him off. 'It doesn't matter now. Moving fast, striking back. That's what counts.'

'I can probably get there in less than a minute,' said Dave, viciously twisting the tops off a couple of energy gel tubes that had survived the shredding of his vest. His Armando-approved silk blend dress pants weren't looking so flash anymore either. The world seemed to hiccup as he accelerated while he ingested the gel shots, tore the wrapper from a protein bar, and ate that too. He felt like he was still running on an almost full tank, courtesy of all the fine eating he'd done the last twelve hours. But the conversation he'd had with Zach on the plane was haunting him. He was pretty sure he could cover the distance back to the Cracker Barrel before these guys even got airborne, but he had no idea what shape he'd be in when he got there. Or what he'd find. He dropped back into real time after topping up his tanks, and saw a couple of the soldiers who weren't used to him suddenly disappearing into a high speed blur jump back a little in surprise.

The night was alive and glowed with the golden red lustre of war. Gunfire still cracked and clattered from the gentle wooded slopes behind them.

'I'll see you there,' said Dave. Lucille's improvised scabbard was too badly torn to use, so he took as comfortable a grip as he could, with his right hand up near the heavy steel head, and his left about three quarters of the way down the hardwood shaft. He didn't like the idea of running through the dark without a weapon to hand, no matter how good his night vision was now, or how quickly he was moving. There were no guarantees he wouldn't run headlong into a nasty surprise.

But he didn't. And he was wrong about beating them there in a minute.

Dave covered the distance between the bridge over the River Platte and the parking lot of the Cracker Barrel on the edge of Omaha in just under a minute and a half. Twelve and a half miles through open country. If the physics of the real world had applied to him he would have been travelling at a very large fraction of the speed of sound. He was able to make the calculation as he flickered up I-80, past the frozen tableau of Hazmat teams cleaning up the mess Igor had made of the Tümorum. At that speed the wind in his passage should have ripped every stitch of clothing from his body and started to pull the flesh from his bones. But he was beginning to understand that he was not so much moving through space as through time. Somehow passing between moments, rather than through the landscape across which he travelled. Or some shit like that. Not like losing control of a car at high speed, when everything seemed to slow down. Not like that time he'd come off the trampoline as a kid and broken his arm, when for long, stretched-taffy seconds, he hung in midair wondering what would happen when he finally did hit the ground.

He had never moved this fast, for this long. He had no sense of physically exerting himself. Instead he simply willed himself to move through space. He chanced a look up toward the stars, hoping to find a jet plane against which he might pace himself. But the skies were empty and he had a feeling that no aircraft, even a Super Hornet, could have kept up with him.

Except of course, those Sumateem arrows had moved at a fair rate, hadn't they?

What was that about?

And when he thought on it further, the bullets hitting the

Djinn had kept hitting them, even when he was in warp.

He let go of the paradox, vowing to return to it later, when people weren't depending on him. People he'd probably left to their doom.

In his hands Lucille felt lighter than usual, but yet as substantial as ever. She was somehow lending her power to him. Or maybe adding to it? He had no idea. He literally had no fucking idea. And everything that Zach had said to him on the plane hit home. He had no fucking idea what he was doing, or what he could do. As he blinked up the last 200 yards of interstate freeway, slow fire lit his passage; burning vehicles and the pulse of the flashing lights on the roof of a police cruiser, the impossibly slow red throb like the last beats of a giant's dying heart. Dave decelerated at the edge of the pavement outside the Cracker Barrel, hefting Lucille, ready to hit pause on the world again so he could lay waste to any monsters dumb enough to challenge him. But none did. None lay in wait.

A pit seemed to open in his stomach as Dave encountered his first body, porcupined with war-shafts almost as long as the man they had killed. They pinned him to the ground, his weapon still gripped in his hands. Under the helmet the sightless eyes of a boy stared at the night. Blood clotted around the body, spreading out with syrupy slowness. Dave put one hand over his mouth, an unconscious move that was more about giving him time to think than holding back a rising gorge of Cracker Barrel's finest. He wasn't nauseous. If anything, he was thinking he could go for one of those hams which were hanging in a bag by the hostess station inside, maybe two or three of them along with a dozen jars of cherry cobbler mix. That hunger pang made him feel a bit nauseous—about himself.

His shoes crunched across shattered asphalt and the brass shell casings which lay everywhere. Above the burning army command tent the American flag flickered and disintegrated, caught in the flames. Below it the flag of the army unit was already gone. The radios were silent and the computer screens dead. Cops and soldiers were piled like cordwood behind police cruisers and Hummers, many of which were also burning, adding to the collective funeral pyre, but no daemons.

He knew without counting that twenty-three dead men and women lay outside the restaurant. Some had been pierced through by war-shafts or the smaller, but just as deadly, iron bolts. Sliveen darts, fired from a comparatively small, handheld weapon, something akin to the bolt of a crossbow.

One dead Sliveen lay in a gory heap of parts, like an enormous insect squashed under foot. He hadn't seen it at first because of the burning Hummer lying on top of it. Dave knelt down and examined the body. The tattoos, he knew—thanks to Urgon—marked this one as something special. A seer-scout for the Diwan of the Sliveen.

For just a second the old Dave, with the paunch and the problems and the job with the petrol company, stood over the huge insectile corpse and shook his balding head. A little 'what the fuck' moment. A man was entitled to one every now and then. But then the new Dave, with the enchanted and homicidal splitting maul, a full head of thick hair, and six-packs on his six-pack, processed it all. The Diwan of the Sliveen had dispatched her elite warrior scouts, probably to scope out the destruction of the Djinn, but also to effect the trap Guyuk had actually been talking about when he warned Dave he was flying into Sh'Kur's ambush.

Because he wanted Dave on that bridge by himself, and he

wanted Dave's lieutenants, his 'minions', tucked out of harm's way, where the Djinn could not reach them, but Guyuk could.

Dave Hooper roared a curse at the sky as he understood just how he'd been bent over the barrel and corn-holed by the lord high bastard of the Grymm. He stomped down on what was left of the daemon's head, crushing bone and brains under the heel of his expensive Italian loafers, spraying his ruined pants with wet chunks of sickly-looking grey and green matter. It was only the muffled thumping of helicopter blades coming in from the south that gave him pause enough to regain control of his rage.

He stood, smeared and spotted with gore, breathing heavily and taking in the scene again. There were no other Sliveen corpses, no Grymm casualties at all that he could see. He noted another couple of human dead, a male and female cop cut to actual pieces around the side of the building. He recognised the slaughter as professional. Or maybe Urgon did. The cops had been cleaved apart by one murderous blow of an edged weapon, but their killer had not stopped to celebrate by feasting on the fresh meat or drinking deep of *dar ienamic's* bloodwine, as a Hunn or Fangr warrior would almost certainly have done. They had been taken by stealth, cut down and left behind as the killers moved on looking for… what?

He already knew, but didn't want to face the truth of it.

*Tell me*, Guyuk had said, *do you intend to take the field with your lieutenants as you did in New Orleans? For whatever snare the Djinn have laid in your path will prove hazardous to yourself, and certainly lethal to your inferiorae.*

His inferiors. Heath, Emmeline. Zach and Igor. Boylan. And Compton, of course. Compton was definitely his inferior. Guyuk couldn't strike at Dave, not yet apparently, so he'd done the next best thing. An even better, smarter thing, really, if he was looking to damage the human cause. He'd reached out for the people around Dave.

For a moment his nuts tried to crawl up into his body as he recalled another threat to those around him. Trinder implying his boys were in danger.

But Trinder was not Guyuk, and Guyuk had said nothing of Dave's family. Still, he thought, stepping away from the ugly mess he'd made of the Sliveen, it might be an idea to get Boylan to call...

He caught himself, just the same way he had caught himself again and again in those first weeks after Annie had left him, thinking that things were one way, when in fact they were another.

Boylan.

He was nowhere among the dead out here. None of his guys were. When he gave himself permission to think about it now, he recognised nobody lying among the corpses strewn about the car lot. His stomach, feeling suddenly empty, seemed to contract as he stared at the burning wreckage of the big tent that had served as the operations centre for the two generals he'd met, and he knew he ought to search through the torn and bloodied canvas to see if Emmeline was in there. Or Compton, he supposed. It seemed more likely he would have been caught ass-kissing the big dogs when the Sliveen attacked. The last he'd seen of Emmeline she was inside the Cracker Barrel with Boylan, both of them working on their laptops. His skin tingled, feeling alternately hot then cold as he stepped over the lower half of a severed human torso, grimacing at the long ropey strands of entrails. He moved toward the restaurant, peering through the vast hole smashed in the facade and into an interior lit by fire.

Nothing but the flames seemed to move in there. No sentry challenged him, no survivors rushed out. Stuffed animals for the road danced in the firelight, wilting under the heat as their innards, made in China, caught flame and filled the air with a black toxic smoke. He stepped over piles of broken crockery and shattered displays, moving toward the long wooden counter to his left where a cashier lay sprawled out over the bar, head on the floor, arms reaching as if to put it back on. Blood tainted the stacks of Tootsie Roll logs. A good ol' boy in flannel and Carhartt still gripped a cast-iron frying pan looking as if this were the perfect place to lay down for a nap. The ragged slice from crown to jaw meant he would never wake up again. Dave pressed on into the interior of flickering lights and flame.

Lucille approved.

The prospect of imminent combat set her humming with satisfaction, a tonal shift in his weird link to her that annoyed him at first, but quickly served to soothe his frayed nerves and to steady his breathing and rapidly beating heart. Dave's stomach rumbled and he took the cap off another energy gel before sucking it down, preoccupied by the scene before him. There were bullet holes in the ceiling and the counter. Vivid slashes of drying blood painted a couple of heavy tables in a corner that had been turned over, perhaps as a barricade, but no bodies or torn limbs or cooling piles of human meat were in evidence. In contrast to the butchery outside, it appeared as though the Sliveen and the Grymm had forced their way in here not to kill everybody but to… To take them?

The thump of rotor blades from the helicopter grew thunderous as the aircraft landed outside on the street. Dave could hear voices, men shouting orders and acknowledgements at each other, the crunch of heavy boots on the tarmac. The fire, which must have been contained by the building's automatic safety systems burned feebly here and there, throwing a shifting, yellow light out across the dining hall. Dave stood, feeling utterly useless. He could take a guess at what had happened here, but being honest with himself, again, he had no fucking idea. Lifting Lucille into a better position to swing the cutting edge of her heavy steel head into any threat, he ignored the navy commandos calling his name outside. He accelerated over the counter, landing on the balls of his feet outside the kitchen, ready to split the skull of anything that might be lying in wait for him. But there was nothing, and he dropped back into the normal flow of time.

The kitchen seemed less shambolic than the rest of the Cracker Barrel, apart from the small fire burning on the stovetop. He took the fire blankets and doused the flames, regretting it for a moment as the dark of night closed in around him, but only until his own much-improved night vision adapted. A large bag of frozen potato wedges was thawing into a puddle and a giant pool of light-coloured waffle or pancake batter covered the floor near the grill top. His stomach rumbled.

Dave was about to abandon his search when he heard a squeak, an almost familiar squeak, coming from the far corner where a heavy stainless steel door stood slightly ajar. The meat locker?

'Who's there? It's me, Dave Hooper,' he called out, reasoning that a survivor would answer and a daemon would not, unless answering meant exploding out of the freezer in a storm of talons and teeth. He was getting ready to speed up when a voice answered him.

'Dave? Oh my God, is that you, Dave?'

Boylan.

'Oh my God, oh my God,' the lawyer kept repeating from inside the darkness and comparative safety of the Cracker Barrel's freezer. 'I did not sign on for this. I did not sign on for this. Oh my God, I did not...'

Dave heaved open the heavy door and Boylan squeaked again in fearful surprise. Dave's eyes were fully adapted now and he had no trouble making out the hunched and terrified figure of the attorney bundled up in a camouflaged parka and shivering as he cowered behind a tall box of the same potato wedges Dave had seen just a moment ago. His temper flared, but he suppressed it. Or maybe it was Lucille's temper? The anger seemed to come from outside him. But that was a thought too bizarre to deal with, so he put it aside along with the strange feeling of being annoyed with Boylan for... What? Not being Emmeline?

'You all right, X?' he said. 'Come on, it's over now, they've gone.'

Boylan slowly pushed himself up off the floor and crept out from behind the big box of potato wedges, moving on painfully stiffened joints.

'I know, I know,' he said. 'They killed everyone, Dave, everyone, well everyone except the professors and a couple of waitresses from the Cracker Barrel, and a soldier, there was a soldier in here too.'

'Come on,' said Dave, using a tone of voice he might have employed once upon a time with his boys if they had got themselves into some sort of trouble that might not have been entirely their fault. Dave Hooper had a deep wellspring of sympathy for people who got in trouble for reasons that were not entirely their fault; it was the recurring theme of his adult life, his childhood too, when he thought about it. 'So they took them? They didn't kill them? They took Emmeline?'

'And Professor Compton and the others. I only got away because I was in the kitchen when they came. I've been working, Dave, working on your family law matter. Working so hard in fact that the time had slipped away from me and I had completely forgotten to eat because that's how hard I was working, Dave, and I was hungry and I don't know about you, Dave, but I am not entirely familiar with the offerings of the Cracker Barrel chain of restaurants but I thought perhaps if I spent just a few minutes in the kitchen I might whip myself up something that was not without nutritional merit.' He was babbling, talking about twice as fast as he normally did, which was about twice as fast as anyone but a horse race caller, leaving Dave to wonder whether he might need to step on the accelerator to keep up with what Boylan was saying.

'Okay, okay, just calm down,' he said in a low, soothing voice. 'So you're in the kitchen, and the shooting starts or whatever, and you do the smart thing which is to take cover, and that's how you end up in the meat locker and alive. Let's concentrate on that, X. You're alive, and that's a good thing. Now I need you to help me find Emmeline and the others.'

Boylan was shuddering. Deep-body tremors that looked powerful enough to eventually shake him apart. Dave heard the SEALs enter the building, shouting 'clear left' and 'clear right'.

'I'm in the kitchen with Boylan,' he called out, not wanting to get shot in the back of the head. 'Whole place is clear, no critters.'

He heard them dialling it down as he returned his attention to Boylan, who was slumping toward the floor in a dead faint. Dave threw him over one shoulder like a bag of frozen wedges and carried him out into the dining room. Heath was limping in through the gaping hole where the front door used to be, leaning on one of his men. Zach and Igor jogged over as smartly as they could, taking care not to trip over all the debris on the floor. They took Boylan and sat him down at the one table and chair which remained undisturbed. Still set with napkins, cutlery and a kerosene lantern.

'Just give me a second,' said Dave, before leaving them all in suspended animation as he searched for and found a bottle of bourbon from the deserted gas station a block away.

'Not a problem,' Zach Allen started to say, but Dave was already back and pouring the lawyer a solid shot before the chief got the third word out.

'Here you go, X, get this into you. It's just Jim Beam, I'm afraid, none of that top-shelf stuff we had on the plane, but it's good for what ails you.'

Boylan took the triple shot in one long gulp, his Adam's apple bobbing up and down as he drained the glass. He paled, turned his head to the side, and vomited it all back up.

'Hit me again, just as hard,' he gurgled, tapping three fingers on the tabletop.

Zach Allen made a face at Dave as if to warn him off, but Dave shrugged and poured again. He'd seen some interesting drinking styles in his long and illustrious career at the bar. Boylan took this one a little slower, but only a little. His hands shook violently as they raised the glass but had steadied some when he put it down.

Captain Heath's human walking frame deposited him gently in the chair across from Boylan.

'Professor,' he said, his voice a little strained, probably

with pain. 'This is very important. We need you to focus, to tell us anything you can that might help us find the others.'

Boylan nodded, partly in answer to Heath but also to encourage Dave to pour him another bourbon.

'I know they went in different directions,' he said unsteadily, raising the second drink, but only sipping at it this time. 'I'm sorry, I don't know who went which way. I couldn't see much from where I was hiding. I hope you don't think the less of me for hiding, Dave. It's pretty much all I had to offer in the circumstances, hiding and spying on them. Spying is good, though, isn't it?'

'Spying is excellent,' said Heath, cutting across Dave, forcing Boylan's attention back onto him. 'It means you can tell us something. So what did you see, Professor, when you were spying on the monsters?'

Boylan raised a hand, the one holding the whiskey glass and a few drops splashed out over the side as he pointed through the destruction at the front of the restaurant.

'Some of them went that way and the others took off in the opposite direction,' he said. 'I... I don't know why they did that, or who they took with them. I heard your lady friend screaming.'

At this, they all stiffened.

'I think... I think she might have been with the group that was heading back toward wherever you came from, back up I-80, or in that direction anyway. But I don't know, I'm sorry I just don't...'

Heath laid one dark hand on the top of Boylan's arm. 'It's enough. Or I hope it's enough. Thank you, Professor Boylan.'

He turned to Zach Allen and said, 'Chief, I need an air controller five minutes ago, or at least a working link to one.'

'I'm on it, sir,' said Zach, hurrying outside.

'What are you going to do?' asked Dave. 'And what can I do?'

He didn't like the panicky edge to his voice. His job was to deal with the shit when it blew up in everyone's faces. He wasn't supposed to panic. Never had before. But he knew every second that Emmeline was with the Sliveen or the Grymm or whatever had grabbed her up, she was a whole hell of a lot closer to dying horribly.

'You can help, Dave,' said Heath. 'We're going to need your help. But first I need a couple of aircraft with some sort of night-vision system. Anything that could help to pick the orcs out of the dark. You have any sense of where they might go?'

'Back where they came from,' said Dave. 'The UnderRealms. And I guess the holdings of the Grymm if it was Guyuk who put this together. If they didn't kill them on the spot, they got a reason for wanting them alive, for taking them. We really need to get her before that happens.'

Zach Allen ran back in, dragging another soldier, or maybe an airman, behind him. The new guy was wearing tan military coveralls that looked like a flight suit. Heath levered himself up from the table and put one arm around the shoulders of the SEAL who stepped forward and bent low to offer himself as a walking aid.

'Son, I'm going to need a couple of eyes in the sky,' he said to the airman in the coveralls.

'Won't be a problem, Captain,' the pilot shot back. 'There's an E-8 Joint STARS providing recon cover over the area of operations. We've also got an AC-130 plus other army assets en route from the river.'

Dave wondered how all those bright and shiny assets would do down in the UnderRealms.

# 19

They fitted Dave up with new clothes, which he was relieved to discover hadn't come off a dead man. Boots and thick socks better suited to stomping through the countryside, a pair of navy-grey camouflage pants which seemed to be mostly pockets, a black T-shirt and a dark hoodie. Dave transferred a couple of gel packs and protein bars from his vest into the voluminous pockets of his new pants, but then thought what-the-hell and ate them anyway. He could tell he'd burned up a lot of his fuel reserves warping over to the Cracker Barrel from the Platte River Bridge.

He stood slightly apart from a larger group of SEALs gathered in the parking lot of the Countryside Suites, which had the misfortune to be situated next door to the Cracker Barrel. The other SEALs had circled around Lucille, trying to lift her from the ground. Heath said the motel had been evacuated when the army set up its command post, but there were still a few civilian vehicles parked out front and the lights were on in a few of the rooms.

'Put this on,' said Zach Allen, helping him fit a headset just like the one he had seen Heath wearing on the way out to the bridge. 'It will help the spotters feed you targeting data.'

'It'll what?'

'There's a bunch of helicopters and airplanes in the sky right now,' said Igor in a manner that gave Dave to understand his question had been exceptionally stupid. 'They're fitted with all sorts of sensors, infrared, FLIR, ground-target tracking radar and a lot of other shit. Don't know whether they'll spot a demon in the dark, but anybody travelling with them will stand out like bright, cherry red action figures.'

Zach finished fitting the headset.

'It's a push-to-talk system,' he said. 'Choppers are going to sweep along the axes that your lawyer said he saw the Djinn heading out on.'

'It was the Grymm,' Dave corrected him, 'with some seer-scout Sliveen. UnderRealms special forces, if you like. But not the Djinn.'

'Whatevs, dude,' said Zach. 'You're going on a bug hunt. Let's give your rig a test.' The Chief showed Dave where to press a rubber button to activate his communications link.

'Any station this net, radio check, Trident Two-One,' Zach said.

'Trident Two-One,' a voice said. 'This is Ghostrider One-Eight. Solid copy. Out.'

Dave stood there, confused, lost, feeling a bit stupid. Just a few days ago he'd been miffed that he didn't have a headset. Now he was confused by it.

'So, you good to go?'

'Guess so,' he said. 'What are we waiting for now? Ah, what is my callsign?'

'Persuader.' Zach grinned.

'And what are we waiting for now?'

'Warm bodies,' said Igor.

Dave tore open another Snickers bar, his fifth, and chewed it up, swallowing it as quickly as he could without doing any magic tricks.

'Dude, really,' said Zach, 'you should be eating clean proteins and good fats, avocado and egg, instead of that garbage.'

'It's all I got,' said Dave, trying not to sound peevish. 'Unless you want to head back to the Cracker Barrel and grill me up a couple of T-bones with a blue cheese sauce, *chef.*'

Igor patted down the pockets on the front of his camouflage jacket and came up with a protein bar.

'Here, it's a little squashed. And warm. I might have sucked it, too.'

'It'll do.'

Dave took in all the food he could, trying to replace the energy reserves he'd burned off during the run up from the river. Zach was probably right. He'd have been fitter if he ate better–how many times had Annie nagged him about that?–but where the hell was he gonna get organic venison and quinoa salad on the edge of Omaha at this time of night? With daemonum on the loose as well. The front half of the Cracker Barrel was trashed but there were shelves full of Reese's Peanut Butter Cups, Tootsie Roll logs, bags of chocolate-covered cherries and an old-time ice cooler full of Sprite. He'd eaten four jars of fried apples and considered the salted ham still in the bag before deciding against it.

'Where's Boylan?' he asked around a mouthful of Pringles he'd also lifted when he got the Jim Beam earlier.

'Having a restorative nap,' Igor replied.

'And Heath?'

'On the net to National Command Authority,' Zach told him.

'When the fuck are we–'

'Got 'em!' It was Zach. 'Choppers picked up two groups. One heading due south across the fields and one running due west on the northern side of the freeway. They're about three miles apart, and getting further apart all the time.'

Dave's mouth felt dry, and not from all the cheap chocolate. He fumbled a water canteen from his hip and took a swig. It reminded him of the metal boy scout canteen his brother had when they were kids.

'Any idea which group is which?' he asked over his shoulder as he jogged the few yards over to the SEALs to retrieve Lucille. 'Sorry fellas. Got a date with my lady here.'

'Shoulda called her Excalibur, man,' said a wiry operator with a drooping moustache. 'She's not giving it up for anyone but the king.'

'That's right, she's not.' Dave said, before returning to Zach who was holding his hand up like a traffic cop. He had the appearance of someone who was listening, or trying to listen, to a conversation just out of earshot. Then Dave's own headset crackled into life and he didn't have to wait for the information to be relayed to him as he dropped into the same communications channel.

'This is Ghostrider One-Eight, I have eyes on dismounts,' the radio squawked in Dave's ear. In the background he could hear helicopter blades. 'Fourteen large dismounts plus three smaller dismounts, bearing southwest on the south of the interstate. One of the smaller dismounts is struggling.'

'What are dismounts?' Dave asked the radio net.

'Clear the net,' someone said, calm but firm.

'This is Ghostrider Two-One, I also have eyes on dismounts. Twenty in number, that is two zero confirmed, sixteen large, three small plus one who is very small. Bearing due west of your position.'

Someone struggling, he thought. He wondered if it was Emmeline. Compton was probably passed out with terror.

So. Fourteen orcs and three captives for one SEAL team to rescue, and sixteen orcs with four captives for the other team. But which group had Emmeline?

He heard Heath's voice calling his name and saw the dark, injured figure emerging from a tent pitched on the grass verge between the motel and the interstate. The SEALs, except for Igor and Zach who stayed with him, had broken up and headed at a fast trot down the road to a couple of helicopters which were using the I-80 as a makeshift landing pad. The rotors were already turning and the men embarked quickly and in good order, reminding Dave for a moment of the utterly different scenes on the Longreach when his terrified rig monkeys were scrambling to get away from the Hunn. These guys were heading toward them, and eager to get there.

'Dave,' Heath called out again, hobbling quickly toward him on a crutch he'd scrounged from somewhere. 'You're on the northern group. Go now.'

'That's Emmeline?'

'Just go,' Heath insisted.

But Dave stood his ground.

'Which one is Emmeline's group, can you tell?'

Heath gave him a cold and level stare. He was locked into that military frame of mind Dave was beginning to think of as their 'machine mode'.

'You know how triage works, Dave?'

Again, a flare of anger, almost ungovernable.

'Of course I fucking know how triage works. Highest priority first. I'm the safety boss of an exploration rig where...'

He stopped. Heath was still staring at him.

'You're on Compton. You go north of the highway. We don't have time for debate.'

Dave had Lucille in one hand, gripping her just under the solid steel head, as he took another long drink of cool water from his canteen. The helicopters, a couple of Blackhawks and two Apache gunships, had spooled up their engines to the point of takeoff.

'That's right,' said Dave. 'We don't.'

The half-empty canteen hit the tarmac with a muffled thud, spilling its contents over the asphalt with a glugging noise. Dave Hooper was gone. Headed southwest after Emmeline.

He covered at least five miles in the first burst of speed, by his reckoning, most of the distance to a small town south of the city which lit up in his night vision like a county fair. In his travels he tipped a cow, leaped an electric fence and blasted through a chicken coop before vaulting a windbreak nearly twenty feet high. He dropped out of warp, landing on both feet with no more difficulty than one might exert while playing hopscotch. He keyed his mike.

'Hi,' he said. 'This is Dave Hooper. I'm chasing the critters that took the professor and a couple of other hostages south of the I-80, heading for the Platte River. I've gained about five miles on them, but I need you to lead me in now.'

'Persuader, this is Ghostrider One-Eight,' a voice came back to him through the headset. 'Retask your effort to the northern objective, over.'

'No, sorry, change of plan. You get your commandos to go after the group north of the I-80. I'm almost on top of these other assholes, so I'm going to deal with them and then go help the others.'

'Negative, Persuader. You are ordered to one-eighty to the exfiltrating dismounts to the north...'

'Yeah, your boss don't sign my pay cheque, so you can fuck off. I'm here now, I'm ready to kick ass, and every fucking second you delay that happy moment you put Professor Ashbury and the other hostages that much closer to the cauldron. An actual fucking cauldron. Did you know that? They chop people up and they put them into big fucking cauldrons that they call blood pots. That's what's going to happen to nice Professor Ashbury and the waitresses from the Cracker Barrel. They're going into the blood pot and it will be your fault. Not mine. Because I'm here to rescue them. Now tell me where the fuck they are.'

'Hooper!'

It was Heath.

'Sorry, Cap, but you got more than enough badass Navy SEALs with big fucking guns to go get that asshole Compton. So go get him, I'm going after Emmeline.'

'Dave, you have no idea what you're doing. We need to get Compton first. Ashbury will have to wait. There're two birds in the air already headed for her. Out.'

'Then turn them around and send them after Compton, because I'm not wasting time chasing that man-sized chunk of dick cheese. I'll go get Ashbury and whoever is with her, then if you need help I'll be all over that other shit like the Flash. *After* I get Emmeline... Er, over and out. I guess.'

Heath's voice was thick with rage when he came back on the comm net.

'Mister, you are endangering more lives than you can

imagine. What the hell do you think you are doing making judgment calls about stuff you know nothing about? Out.'

'What I'm doing,' said Dave, 'is looking for the orcs who are about to throw Emmeline into a fucking casserole dish. When I find them, I'm going to kill them all. Then I'll warp over and help you kill whatever is left when Zach and Igor and their buddies have finished getting all Tom Clancy on the war band *north* of the interstate. So please don't try to stop me. You're just wasting time.'

To emphasise the point, he accelerated at about three-quarters of his top speed, or at least the speed he'd reached before, assuming there was a theoretical limit to how quickly he could travel through time and space.

'Whoa!'

The voice he heard sounded like the guy he'd been arguing with in the helicopter, doubtlessly blinking at his instruments as Dave suddenly winked out of existence in one spot and re-materialised about a mile closer to the river a second or so later.

'This is Ghostrider One-Eight. What the hell just happened?'

Yep, same guy. Dave pressed the push-to-talk button with his middle finger while he scanned the countryside around him. He appeared to be standing in the middle of a freshly reaped field. Some kind of grain crop, recently harvested. This far away from electric light his night vision had really powered up and his surroundings appeared to him as though he'd taken a stroll with dusk coming on.

'Sorry for the gratuitous demo of why you won't be stopping me,' he said to Heath, the helicopter crew, and anybody who was listening, 'but you won't be. So best you just get on after Compton and guide me on to the other... dismounts. Er, out.'

'Motherf...'

If that was Heath he got himself under control before the word could escape him. Dave heard him bark out a string of incomprehensible jargon which sounded as though he was reassigning choppers and SEALs on the fly. He heard the words 'retask' and 'one-eighty' as before, but they weren't directed at him this time.

'Hooper, you there, still. Out?'

'Yep. Just waitin'.'

'Ghostrider One-Eight, can you guide Persuader in on the target. Remember, he's a civilian. June Bug out.'

Dave heard the crackle of a connection being severed before Ghostrider One-Eight came back on.

'All righty, Persuader. Can I orient you toward the river? Out.'

'I think I know where it is... umm, over?' This military radio bullshit was confusing as hell.

'This is One-Eight, Persuader. Just talk like you are on the phone. Don't worry about the other stuff. You were moving toward it before. Head in the same direction but bear, ah, move as though you're heading for ten o'clock on the dial. Not twelve. Make sense?'

'Thanks, Ghostrider. I think so. Lemme try something.'

He ran at warp for a few seconds. Stopped, and repeated.

'Is that the direction you want me?' he asked.

'A little ways back toward ten o'clock, but yeah. You're probably 2000... a mile and half or so from the exfils. You keep on that heading you'll intercept them in...'

'Thanks.'

He accelerated and the world slipped around him as easily

as black silk. Threading his way around isolated farmsteads, leaping three-post fences, and thundering down a few short stretches of sealed road when he could, Dave Hooper caught up to the raiding party a couple of hundred yards north of a large homestead, brightly lit. There were indeed fourteen daemons in the small raiding party, and three captives. All women. A Grymm warrior had slung one of the women over its shoulder, where she bounced off the armour and mail in a lifeless fashion, like a brace of birds. The other two were also being carried, but under the great, thickened arms of two more Grymm. One of the women was struggling and punching at the beast. The other was screaming, but offering no further resistance. The punchy bitch was Emmeline, he was sure of it. Had to be. Four Sliveen loped along beside the party, acting as outriders. They all had bows unslung, arrows notched. None had yet seen him pop out of thin air behind them.

Lucille thrummed in his hands, but he ignored her needs for the moment, quickly bending to the freshly turned soil and gathering two flat, fist-sized river stones. One he slipped into a pocket, the other he held as though to skip it across the surface of the Platte River. Then he took off again, accelerating to within twenty yards of the raiders, where he took aim at the unprotected heads of the outriders bringing up the rear. He threw the first stone, reached into his pocket and sent the other one after it. Then he charged the glacially slow-moving tableau.

At first he thought he could hear the wind roaring in his ears, which hadn't been the case on the run up from the river; a deep, sonorous tearing sound which grew and grew until it pounded at his head with physical force. He was only ten yards, a few strides, from the rear of the pack when the first stone struck and he understood. The skull of the rangy, loping daemon at which he'd aimed exploded in an extravagant shower of foul organic gruel. The next stone wasn't nearly as well aimed and struck the scout daemon in the small of the back. The creature's upper torso blew apart as though hit with a small missile and Dave understood that what he'd been hearing was a sonic boom as the rocks ripped through the atmosphere at something greater than the speed of sound. They took the Sliveen scouts unaware and obliterated them. Dave felt the blowback shower him with spots of ichor and offal.

He didn't slow down. Lucille was singing now, a mad high aria of chaos and slaughter. The human champion, the Dave, was upon them, performing a dark duet with her. The air screeched with the violent silvery arcs of the enchanted splitting maul while he cut at legs as thick as tree trunks, slicing through armour with great fantails of white and yellow sparks. Bone shattered with terrible crackling reports like the felling of old redwoods. Lucille's edged metal head cleaved through muscle and meat with sick wet chomps. Dark daemon blood geysered and boiled and misted in the air.

He split the skull of the Lieutenant Grymm carrying Emmeline. Lucille's axehead drilled deep down into the thing's chest and opened it up like a poison flower. Dave wrenched on the handle, freeing the steel with a deep sucking noise. The Grymm was already toppling, slowly, slowly, slowly, and would surely crush Ashbury beneath its great bulk. He jabbed at the elbow joint, lightning fast. The blow atomised the bones and caused the monster to lose its grip on her. Emmeline's face was contorted by terror and rage. One tiny fist was still clenched to beat at the Grymm's studded breast plate. Her knuckles were scraped bloody and raw. Dave stole her away, like intercepting a pass in college football. He took the time, so much time, to lay her gently on the soft soil a few yards away.

When he turned back he yelped and had to swerve to avoid a bolt that seemed to come at him with incredible speed, even in his accelerated state.

*Spaaang!*

He raised Lucille–or more correctly she flew up of her own accord–and bunted the missile aside. Seven of the daemons lay in their own entrails and organs. But two Sliveen yet lived and, as slow as they were to him, the bolts and arrows they sent his way left their bows and dart slingers like fastballs from a decent minor league pitcher. He felt Lucille grow lively in his grip and gave in to her, letting the weapon go where she would in ever more blurred arcs. His arms and shoulders ached and his hands felt as though they might cramp. He could feel himself grow hot with the inhuman rate at which his metabolism was burning energy, but there could be no slowing down. Not yet. He found more reserves and drew upon them, increasing his velocity as he charged at the threat, making straight for the nearest scout. As soon as he was within range he swung for the bleachers and the solid steel wedge smashed into a hammered metal breastplate like a small comet punching home. The Sliveen flew apart with a concussive roar. Dave could only follow the momentum of the blow, giving Lucille her head. It was almost like tales he'd heard of water diviners. The wooden grip went where it went, not as he chose. He was merely a channel.

Turning a full circle after destroying the third Sliveen he described a huge figure eight with the head of the sledgehammer, building power, letting it lift him off the ground. He sailed through clean air and brought the blunt steel fist down into the nasal cavity of the scout's long, insectile face. Just as he had done on the Longreach with Urgon. Something deep within him shifted and seemed to settle with an approving murmur.

But still more Grymm lived. He cut the legs out from beneath the two nearest to him, and their strange, drawn-out shrieks poured into the mad, caterwauling derangement of war shouts, death rattles, roars and, beneath it all, the screaming of two women.

Only two.

The third he ducked as the Grymm warrior which had been carrying her swung the woman's body like a soft club. Dave, still running in hyper-time, had plenty of opportunity to see her coming, to see the wounds she had already suffered. They had been eating her as they hurried across the fields. Probably tossing the poor kid between one another as each took a bite. He ducked under the slow, sweeping blow and drove Lucille up under the chin of the giant. Its head snapped back and a piece of broken fang flew out from the point of impact, turning with perverse beauty, like a jewel in the starlight. Dave flipped the maul around and drove the butt of the handle into the overlapping iron plates guarding the daemon's midsection. Monster and happy meal both flew backward.

He was turning to take on the remainder of the pack when something sandbagged him from the left and he was catapulted through the air.

'Oof,' he grunted as all the air was driven from his lungs and stars burst behind his eyelids. The world turned around and around, slowly, but not because he willed it. It was uncontrolled. It was vulnerability and danger and the end of things.

He hit the ground and rolled and rolled, dirt in his eyes and mouth. The long, dull, distant freight train roar of the world heard from the slipstream of hyper-time now became the all-too-real roar and clash of the remaining monsters coming at him with great swords and axes and mauls of their own. He tried to stand, but one knee gave way beneath him. Lucille lay a few feet away, wailing it seemed, somewhere in the back of his head. Crying for him. Dave had time to note that the other girl, the waitress they hadn't eaten yet, was crawling toward Emmeline. He tried to accelerate toward them to carry them away as he had before with Heath, but it was like turning a key on a dead car battery.

Nothing.

The Grymm war band came at him like a flying wedge, a solid mass of snarling fury and edged metal, nine or ten foot high, and three or four times that across. The leader raised a cleaver that looked as big as Dave...

...he disintegrated.

They all did, the whole tightly packed mob of armoured hide and monster flesh just flew apart as twin streams of painfully bright, hot human fire–tracer fire–poured into them, disassembling the last of the raiding party in a wet storm of flesh and bone. Stupefied, Dave could only shake his head as the helicopter roared over him and then he realised the voice in his head was not Lucille or Urgon or his own cries of horror but the oddly flat and alien tone of Ghostrider One-Eight.

'Come in, Persuader. Are you reading us? Come in, Persuader, are you reading us?'

Dave raised a shaky hand to his headset, which he'd completely forgotten about. It hung around his neck, bent out of shape. In the air above him Dave could see two of the

Blackhawks hovering above with a pair of the meaner-looking Apaches to either side.

'Persuader,' he said, almost choking on a mouthful of dirt. 'I mean, yeah, it's me, Dave. Thanks for that, Ghostrider. I... guess I owe you one.'

# 20

Dave woke up on a cot in a large green tent that smelled of old canvas, mould and disinfectant. His ribs hurt a little where he'd taken the body hit, but they didn't feel broken, or even bruised. When he raised a hand to prod himself gingerly, looking for damage, an IV needle and tube came with it. The needle was plunged into the back of his hand, delivering a clear fluid. He had no idea whether it was a saline solution, or some sort of nutrient mix, or painkillers or antibiotics. But he felt fine. Great, in fact. So the needle came out.

He watched, fascinated as the small wound healed itself.

'Man, that never gets old,' said Dave.

The medical tent was large. It had to be some sort of MASH, or whatever they called them now, because of all the bodies laid out, hooked up to drips just like his. He counted nine of them, including a Cracker Barrel waitress in the bed next to his, and Emmeline on the far side of her. He recognised the girl from the field... when? How long had he been out? She was the one who'd crawled over to Emmeline. The one who had lived. She was pretty badly banged up now, covered in dressings and hooked up to three drips. But she looked peaceful and Dave felt the warm inner glow of a job well done. He'd rescued a girl. An orderly who was dressing the wounded leg of a soldier or SEAL on the other side of the tent noticed him as he stood up.

'Hey! You shouldn't be up. Dr Limbaugh!'

Dave felt as though he'd been caught out at something, and almost climbed back into the cot. Then he saw Emmeline stir and lift herself up on both elbows, blinking at him as though clearing her head. He was glad she'd woken up before the other chick. She might be able to tell him what had happened after he blacked out. Then she scowled.

'You.'

She didn't sound pleased to see him. Or to be alive. Because, you know, he'd rescued her and everything.

'Er, yeah. Me. You okay, Prof?'

'Oh, I'm fine,' she said in a tone that let him know Professor Emmeline Ashbury was a good week's journey from being fine.

'So. What's happening?' Dave asked cautiously.

An army doctor, in camouflaged scrubs appeared at the tent flap, summoned by the orderly. This Limbaugh, presumably. Dave wondered if the man really needed the stethoscope or whether it was just to announce to everyone that he was the doctor.

'Mister Hooper. You took out your drip. It needs to go back in right now, sir. And to stay in until I say otherwise.'

'I'm fine, Doc,' said Dave. 'Seriously. Whatever you gave me. It worked. I'm good to go.'

He became aware of sounds outside the tent. Heavy vehicles, choppers in flight, the shouts of men and women issuing orders and acknowledging them. But he had no sense of impending doom or unravelling chaos. So things were cool then.

'Sit,' ordered the doctor.

He sighed, but he sat back on his cot which creaked under his weight. He wondered where Lucille was and realised with a start that she'd have to be back out in the field where he'd dropped her. Nobody else would have been able to pick her up. He smiled, even though part of him felt like he'd lost a child at the mall. He smiled even wider at that, but the grin died on his face when he saw the thunderous glare levelled on him by Emmeline. Dave took cover in submitting to Limbaugh's examination. The surgeon attended him, doing the things those guys always do: pulse, blood pressure, lights in the eye.

'Turn your head this way. Good. Now back. Good. Raise your left arm. Okay. Now your right. Good.'

He pressed in on Dave's ribs, frowning, and pressed in again, a little harder.

'No pain? No sensation of scraping when you breathe?'

'Nada.'

Limbaugh frowned again. 'Remarkable. You came in here with four broken ribs.'

'And thanks to your expert care I got over it, Doc.' Dave smiled. 'Can I go now?'

'No.'

The doctor stood up and moved a few feet away to consult with the orderly in hushed voices that Dave's Spidey senses had no trouble at all picking up. Limbaugh wanted more X-rays, an MRI and blood work in addition to what they already had, plus hourly monitoring of all the vitals and… Dave tuned out. That wouldn't be happening. He was ready to roll.

'So, you're really okay?' he asked Emmeline, who was still frowning at him, but at least she'd dialled down the furious scowl. She looked pretty badly banged up too, bruised down one side, with fresh white bandages wrapped tightly around one arm and a large dressing taped to the back of her head. Her eyes were blackened and bloodshot and she looked even paler than normal. Dave wasn't really asking if she was okay. He was wondering if *they* were okay.

Turned out they weren't.

'It doesn't even dent you, does it? You never get a bloody scratch.'

'Sorry.' He shrugged. 'Not my fault.'

'But it is your fault!' she hissed with such vehemence that Dave backed away a little and the two med staff broke off their discussion to turn and stare at them. He felt as though everyone in the tent was suddenly staring, although the other casualties were all deeply sedated.

'Piss off,' said Emmeline, pleasantly enough, to Limbaugh and his orderly. They walked away, taking their discussion out of free-fire zone.

Dave had recovered enough of his balance to be feeling a little put out now.

'Hey. Twisty McKnickers. You notice you're not dead? Not even a little bit? Perhaps a simple, thanks, Dave, for saving me from the blood pot?'

She eyed him like he was a toilet that needed cleaning. When she did speak, she didn't sound grateful. She sounded even angrier.

'Thanks, Dave. For saving me from the blood pot.'

'Well it was…'

'It was a fucking cock-up, is what it was.'

Dave felt something not unlike going over the top on a roller-coaster. His skin grew electric as the heat built up on his face. He was just about finished with this hero crap.

'Really? Saving your life was a cock-up was it? Would you like me to put you back on the next bus to Monsterville?'

'Don't be an idiot. You've already proved you can do that. It's time to move on.'

'The fuck you say.'

He was a few seconds away from just storming out of the tent before the red mist at the edges of his vision began to close in. He'd find Boylan, and catch the first ride out of town. They could make Vegas in time for dinner and a show. LA if they pushed it and he didn't have to stop to kill anything. But Emmeline, he could see, made an obvious effort to rein in her own anger. She sat up in her cot, leaned back against a tent pole and crossed her arms protectively. Or tried to. The bandage made it difficult and uncomfortable and Dave got the impression she held the awkward pose it forced on her only because she didn't want to look like she couldn't. Her face flushed with colour for the first time.

'How many men do you count in this tent, Hooper?'

'Seven,' he said, without checking. He knew the figure the same way he knew he had five fingers on each hand.

'Yes. Seven men. And three in the tent next door, and four in emergency surgery in Omaha, and five dead.'

His skin felt even warmer. And prickly.

'How's Compton?'

'Missing. There's four missing by the way. He's one of them.'

She fixed him with a stare that made him feel like he'd been mounted on the long pin of a butterfly collector.

'Your. Fault. Dave.'

'But I…'

He trailed off. The smell of the temporary ward was making him sick. Disinfectant. Blood. Faeces. Pus. The hot tingling just under his skin turned cold again and left him dizzy.

'They didn't get him? Igor and Zach, they're...'

'Alive. And in one piece. Igor put down half a dozen of the things with that ridiculous cannon of his. I understand Chief Allen killed some sort of monster with a knife.'

'Wow. That's cool. And Heath?'

'Not cool. Not happy.'

The look she gave him was complex. Somewhere between accusing, grateful, sympathetic and... guilty.

Before he could stop himself, he asked, because maybe it would lead him out of this mess.

'You feeling like shit because you're alive and they're not?'

He knew it was a dumb thing to say even as he was saying it. All the higher centres of his brain went into turbo-drive, trying to get him to shut his dumb mouth, to say something else, or even just to trail off mumbling. But when Dave Hooper was of a mind to run off at the mouth like a dumbass, he could take a gold medal at the dumbass Olympics.

'You fucker,' she said, without any hint of anger, which was worse. Her voice came out thin and broken. 'How fucking typical that a man with absolutely no insight into his own weakness should see so bloody deeply into someone else's. Of course I feel guilty. If you hadn't done exactly the wrong thing all of those men would be alive. Compton would be...'

At the mention of Compton's name Dave felt the red mist close in around his vision.

'Fuck Compton and the jackass he rode in on. You're worth two of him.'

'Oh,' she said, 'I'm sorry. Did the middle of my sentence interrupt the beginning of yours?' She shook her head then, looking utterly lost. 'You don't understand, Hooper. You've never understood. Just because Compton's an arsehole it doesn't mean he's a useless arsehole. Unlike me.'

'Oh come on, Em…'

'Don't. I'm not looking for a sympathy fuck. And I'm not saying I'm an arsehole. I know my blunt manner and funny accent don't always make you Americans comfortable.'

'But you've got your thing, your autism.'

'It's Asperger's, you tosser, and it's not an excuse. I'm at the very mild end of the spectrum. I'm blunt, and focused. And increasingly irrelevant to the concerns of this operation. I'm an exobiologist, Hooper. Not a professor of medieval monster studies. I write papers about extremophile bacteria on the moons of Saturn and around deep ocean flumes in the Pacific. It's what I was known for before Compton took me on and made sure all the really interesting research I'd ever do would never be read in public again.'

She had turned inward, and was talking less to Dave now than to herself. An unworthy part of him was glad to have escaped the spotlight of her attention and anger. Like Emmeline, he was dressed only in a hospital shift. He started to look around when her eyes were off him, searching discreetly for some clothes he could change into.

'We thought the Hunn and Fangr you killed were xeno-morphs. Aliens. That why I took the lead on the Longreach. And why Compton was such a surly git. He hates to play second fiddle, as you Americans say.'

'I never say that,' Dave muttered, and she focused back in on him again, as though she'd forgotten he was there. Some of the anger was back too, unfortunately.

'But it became quite obvious quite quickly that we

weren't dealing with space bugs. We were dealing with some Dark Ages civilisation that somehow crossed over into our own, possibly via some sort of dodgy passage or portal between separate quantum bubbles of the multiverse. And that, I'm afraid, is where Compton shines. Not in quantum theory. But in civilisational conflict. Don't you see? He's the ranking authority from OSTP on this matter. Heath is the muscle. Compton, quite rightly, is the brains. I'm surplus to requirements. And you're the fucking clown who just upended the manure cart and spilled everybody out. Killing a lot of my colleagues in the process.'

There was no escaping it. Something must have gone badly wrong with the SEAL teams Heath had sent after Compton. Maybe an ambush? Maybe it was just a bad idea for tiny, vulnerable human beings to mix it up with the Horde? But there was no escaping the discontent stirring behind Dave's own guilt.

Fuck Compton.

These pinheads might rate him as some sort of genius but to Dave he was just a puffed-up sphincter.

'Well,' he said, climbing to his feet. 'I apologise for saving your life. Perhaps when that girl in the cot next to you wakes up, you could pass on my regrets to her as well. I'm sure she'll understand why she counted for nothing.'

'When I get though writing letters to the next of kin of the SEALs who died,' she said coldly.

He turned away from her then and strode out of the tent with as much dignity as possible, holding the flaps of his hospital gown closed over his bare ass.

# 21

'Whoa. Dude. This upgrade was the money shot. These losers are toast.'

Lord Guyuk ur Grymm knew not what Thresh-Trev'r meant exactly, but the minor empath daemon seemed pleased with the results of the latest trepanning. A trepanning in the terminology of the Scolari Grymm. 'Awesome fucking noms' according to the testimony of Thresh-Trev'r. Three of the four captured human warriors–Guyuk still had to force himself not to think of them as calflings–had his acolyte consumed in this fashion; punching a hole through the thin bone of the creature's forehead, while simultaneously opening up the rear of the cranium with the thrust of a single claw to create a small vessel out of which it could suck the animal's thinking sweetmeats. The fourth human had been cut down when it somehow contrived to break free of its bonds and kill–actually kill!–its guard with a concealed blade.

Guyuk found himself as disturbed by this one small incident as by anything that had happened since that fool of a Hunn had blundered into the Above and had himself put down by the Dave. The human which had killed its Grymm attendant was no champion. The tiny thing had none of the

Dave's powers. The weapon with which it struck was in no way enchanted. It was a fine blade of tempered steel, if ludicrously small, but nonetheless, it was just a blade. It sang no hymn. It had no soul. And yet this mere *calfling*–he spat the word out of his mind–had struck at its captor, a superior being, and killed it with one hard strike to drive the point of the weapon in through the nasal cavity, burying it up to the hilt. All of the humans had been stripped after that, and thus they had arrived naked before him, the Diwan and Guyuk's marshals.

After some initial delay, while the Lieutenant of the Guard reported the atrocity committed by the now dead human male, Guyuk excused himself from the marshals and the Diwan, promising to tell them of the success or otherwise of this next trepanning experiment.

The holding pits of the Lord Commander's Keep were nearly full with captives taken around the far fringes of the battle between the human forces and the luckless and unbelievably stupid Djinn. The one pleasingly dark moment of this night was the way in which those urmin squirts had been so thoroughly humiliated and crippled. He very much looked forward to conveying every detail to Her Majesty. In the meantime though, Guyuk determined that these prisoners would not go into the blood pots like the last ones, not until they had been questioned by Scolari Inquisitors, with his personal Thresh in attendance. The Thresh had suggested this course, somewhat to the chagrin of the Inquisitor Scolari, but Guyuk had insisted on the procedure in the face of resistance from the Consilium. He had, however, agreed with the masters that it might be best to restrain the Thresh from gorging itself on all of the humans' cranial sweetmeats. There could be no doubt now the Thresh was able to consume the human thinkings along with the soft grey offal, just as the Scolari had conjectured. But the experience of extended exposure to the conjoined mind of Thresh-Trev'r has been enough to caution Guyuk against overenthusiastic experimentation in this regard. Best that they restrict their underling to ingesting the brains and associated thinkings of a few choice subjects, all the better to interpret the results.

'Oh man, that dude was like some premium shit. I mean, Guyuk, boss, don't get me wrong. Those Navy SEALs, they were snacktastic and I can give you chapter and motherfucking verse on exactly what happened to those Djinn bitches now, and why they gots their shit handed to them by a motherfucking butler. On a silver platter, man! Zing! You see what I did there? By a butler? Oh. Okay. But this guy, oh, *this* is my guy.'

It held up the lifeless carcass of the slain *ienamic*. The Thresh's forked tongue nipped in and out of fang tracks, as if seeking out every last morsel.

For such an apparently satisfying repast it was not much of a carcass. The other warriors at least would render fine lean meat when they reached the slabs up in the kitchens. The dead humans, of strikingly different hues–different clans, perhaps– were obviously well-bred animals and had been raised...

Guyuk had to stop himself. He was thinking of them as cattle again. They were not cattle. They were, these ones at least, warriors. The lighter skinned corpses even boasted some quite elegant tattoo work, and the lord commander found himself wondering if he should have apprentice Scolari copy the designs before they were lost under the cooks' knives. There might be great tales of these warriors' clans and sects inked into their skin. To know the way of their battle doctrine would be to strike the first real blow against them.

He stifled a growl at how close the Horde had come to disaster. If the Hunn had been given their way on this matter, they would now doubtless lie dead and smoking in some field Above. He blocked out the screams and cries of the other captive humans in the holding pits and refocused his attention on the Thresh.

'Tell me, Thresh. Why this one in particular? It seems a feeble specimen, and it showed itself to be possessed of far less *gurikh* than its companions.'

'Oh, man, you got that right,' Thresh-Compt'n chuckled.

That's how it thought of itself now. Or Compt'n ur Thresh. The once upon a time Thresh was still in there somewhere, but buried deep. And Thresh-Trev'r, that charming devil. Oh he was still with us. There was something about your first human brain. Busting your zombie cherry. It imprinted *deep* on a motherfucker. So Thresh-Trev'r weren't going nowhere, and Compt'n ur Thresh was cool with that. All the Threshies were cool with it.

Thresh-Trev'r was what he'd become when the dumbass Scolari had him eat that kid from New Orleans. And so it seemed Thresh-Trev'r was how he was fated to carry himself in the world. Still, better than spending an eon as Thresh-D'rryl the Doughnut Orc. But he knew this, he *understood* it at a molecular level, because no sooner had he sucked the goo out of the nobbled head of the supernerd they'd grabbed up at the Cracker Barrel, then he suddenly understood the shit out of everything! The dim, foggy sense that he sometimes had as Thresh-Trev'r, of not really following right on the hind-claws of events? That motherfucker was history.

*History, bitches.*

Compt'n ur Thresh was a grizzly bear for fucking history. Compt'n ur Thresh could tell those puckered asses in the Consilium to sit the fuck down, shut the fuck up and then lecture them on the whole damned history of human civilisation and exactly how and why the rise of that civilisation meant the entire fucking Horde was chopped liver. Yeah, that's right, and more. All of the clans, all of the realms, every royal house. Every motherfucking Sect. Deader than fucking Elvis if they chose to mix it up with these dawgs. Unless of course, they were willing to take a little advice from an expert in the field. To listen to the personal genius ninja of the motherfucking predator of the United States of Kickin' Ass.

To him.

To Compt'n ur Thresh.

'Whoa, sorry, Lord Vader. Lost my Zen master focus there. What were we talking about? Oh, yeah. The Profs here?'

He threw the inert remains of the dead man to the flagstone floor of the dungeon. It landed in a heap on top of the others. Old Guyuk was right. The Profs hadn't had much *gurikh* to speak of. No warrior spirit. Not like the wiry little SEAL who shivved that dopy Sliveen cocksucker on the way down from topside. Now that took some *cojones.*

Of course, they were gonna eat the SEAL's nuts now in a delicious broth, but at least they'd sing the motherfucker a tune to send him on his way. He'd earned that. Crazy brave, treacherous little fuck that he was.

The Profs though? Meh. Not so much. All that crying and blubbering and begging for his life. Offering to tell them all about this Dave asshole, whom Profs totally did not think of as no fucking champion. Lucky thing, that alone in all the

UnderRealms, Thresh-Trev'r had known what he was babbling about. Luckier still that the little weasel was smart enough to know that if Guyuk and his butt boys figured out Profs had such a low opinion of the Dave, then they might not need Mr T to help them understand the Dave and his mysterious mother-fucking ways. Quite the advanced calculus our man Trevor worked out for himself there.

Guyuk needed him to explain the threat of the Dave and his human Horde.

The Profs, lieutenant to the Dave, thought they had this dude all wrong. He was more of a threat to his own kind and probably should have been put down, or at least 'contained' somehow. Profs had a hard-on for containing shit. Threats, problems, secrets. Like the secret Compt'n ur Thresh now knew because he'd gobbled it up at the source.

The Dave was not responsible for the slaughter of Scaroth's remnant band at New Orleans. Profs was. And the Dave was not universally loved of his kind. There were many who feared him. Profs had even intrigued with the Agent Trinder, that they might contain the Dave together.

But that hadn't worked out for Profs or for this Trinder asshole, had it?

Nothing had worked out for poor old Profs because, as smart as he was–and damn but his tasty brains were just throbbing with the thinkies–he was one unlucky motherfucker who got his sorry ass grabbed up and then woefully fucking ignored by the Dave when it came to rescue time.

Man, the Profs had been shitty when Threshy told him that.

But mostly he'd been terrified. He'd screamed and blubbered and soiled himself. He'd tried to bargain and beg and offered to help Thresh-Trev'r, who Profs seemed to mistake for the leader of the Horde, probably because he could speak English.

'I can help you. I can negotiate. I can put you in contact with the top people,' he blubbered, and Thresh-Trev'r almost had trouble understanding him, his words were so thick with fear. But he had no trouble understanding the implications of Compton's mistake. This Compton, this lieutenant who shared the counsel of the most senior human war lords, thought Thresh was the leader of the Horde. Not Guyuk or that Diwan bitch or any of those dumb Grymm mopes.

Nope.

He just assumed that little ol' Threshy was the boss man.

And who was to say he was wrong?

Certainly not Compton.

Because when Thresh's mandible jaw shot out and punched through Compton's skull as easily as cracking open a new-laid urmin egg, he sucked out the contents and...

'Whoa. Dude. This upgrade was the money shot! These losers are toast.'

# 22

Igor was stepping into the medical tent as Dave was stomping out. They almost collided, but at the last minute Dave instinctively accelerated around the chief petty officer. He didn't think before doing it. The reaction was becoming instinctual. He'd thrown back the flap of the tent, carried through it on the surging wave of his anger, and found his way blocked by a big gay man mountain coming at him with almost as much speed. They each pulled up, facing the other, Igor with his back to the entrance now, and Dave facing it. He had a clear view of Emmeline glaring at him before the flap of canvas dropped down again.

'Hi,' he said, not sure what else was appropriate under the circumstances. Not even sure what the circumstances were anymore.

'I see you came through with your ass intact, again,' Igor grunted. 'Nice work if you can get it.'

'Hey, fuck you, buddy. You got a problem with what I did, you can tell me straight.'

Igor squared his shoulders. The temporary lighting the army had rigged up threw his expression into unforgiving relief, his face a flat combination of grey planes, deep lines drawn too long and an essence of something leaching out from beneath them. Contempt.

'I got a problem with what you did, asshole. I'm telling you straight. You got people killed.'

'I didn't get anybody killed, you fucking jerk. The orcs did that. And they'd have killed just as many, maybe more, if you'd got off your asses and gone after Emmeline and those two girls.'

He had that unpleasantly familiar sense of having said exactly the wrong thing, until he saw that it had brought the SEAL up short, and he was suddenly glad he'd said it. And so, of course, he took it too far. 'Emmeline said you killed five of them yourself.'

'Yeah, so what?'

'Well, what the fuck was everybody else doing then?'

And he knew, he knew in the same way he'd known every time he pushed it just that little bit too far with Annie or his bosses, or some drunk in a bar, or with Marty Grbac the time he'd ribbed him about spending so much of his time at revivalist shows, he knew he'd gone just that one step too far. He knew because Igor's fist cocked back and then described a short, vicious arc into his face to acquaint him with the truth of it. Dave found himself starting to accelerate, to dodge the blow, and to strike back with his own fists, or an elbow, or a head-butt. The way he'd learned fighting in bars when he pushed it just that little bit too far with some drunk who was an even bigger asshole than he.

But he caught himself before he did that. Before he killed the man standing in front of him for no good reason. Instead Dave Hooper took the hit. He was not unfamiliar with the sensation of another man's fist smashing into his face. He felt the blow land as a train wreck of sensations piling one on top of the other; the first dull impact of knuckles on flesh, the sharp biting pain as a ring Igor wore torn open the skin on the side of his nose, the brief, blinding white light and soaring pain as the cartilage in his nose collapsed, and the roaring agony exploding into and then out of his head in a violent red spasm.

Then, nothing. Or rather, nothing more. He didn't fall. He didn't stagger. The wound he'd been done was undone, almost as though a switch had been flicked somewhere and the last half-second had run in reverse, drawing out the force of the blow and the damage it had done like poison sucked from a snakebite. He was momentarily groggy, and then he shook it off.

Igor still stood in front of him, his fist cocked again. It was smeared with Dave's blood, so Hooper knew it wasn't some new form of time-warp trickery. He had been struck a blow in the face, and he'd shaken it off. His nose was blocked, and probably bleeding. He could feel something hot and wet running down into his mouth, seeping in between his lips, and he recognised the coppery taste of his own blood. But when he wiped it away, and wrinkled his nose, it merely throbbed with discomfort. He could already feel the cartilage and crushed tissue resuming their original form, like a rubber squeeze ball bouncing back into shape.

'Sorry,' he said, spitting a stream of blood onto the grass at their feet.

The SEAL stared at his fist as though it were not his own. The blood glistened bright black, like spilled ink. He shook it out, a man drying his hands after washing them.

'Go fuck yourself,' said Igor, before turning his back on Dave and disappearing inside the tent.

'Yeah? Well you hit like a girl!' he called after him.

Dave's nose had stopped bleeding, and wasn't even hurting much anymore, but he knew he must have looked like shit with blood smeared all over his face. He couldn't go back into the tent to clean himself up. Not after that confrontation. Instead, he checked the time, or started to. The watch he'd been wearing was gone. He looked around to see if he could spot Zach Allen anywhere nearby, and resolved not to make the same mistake with him as he had with Igor and, if he cared to admit it, with Emmeline. He would find the young chief petty officer, make his apologies, even if he didn't feel he should have to, and then go find Heath. Dave had no illusions that meeting up with the angry cripple would be the highlight of his night.

And it was still night. He could tell that much. The moon had moved into a different quarter of the sky, and he couldn't see any stars because of the light pollution from all of the army's spotlights and overhead rigs, but looking back toward the city it had the appearance of a metropolis at slumber, many hours from waking up.

Hard to believe people were in bed. You had to think that anybody who'd stayed was probably up, glued to the TV, watching the news coverage. The networks and cable channels would be gorging themselves on this. Even so, he thought as he searched around, he couldn't see any news vans or choppers like down in New Orleans. Maybe the military had learned something about media management down there.

Still looking for a set of clothes he could change into, Dave stepped down off the wooden pallet that served as a makeshift porch in front of the medical tent, remembering then that he was barefoot. He was walking on trampled grass and mud, avoiding the tyre ruts in some farmer's field not far from the Cracker

Barrel. In the hours he'd been out, the military appeared to have brought in great masses of men and war machines. He could hear the rumble and clank of tanks in the fields to the south, and frowned, worried that an Abrams or something might run over Lucille. He doubted she'd be damaged–it was just possible she'd trash the tank somehow–but she could be lost out there if the ground got churned up.

Jet aircraft flew high overhead, their engines a steady roll of thunder. Closer to the surface of the Earth, helicopters hammered and thumped through the sky in all directions. The lanes of the I-80 remained open, with enormous trucks and long lines of armoured cars and Humvees rumbling east and west, but mostly west, toward the Platte River. Tents stood everywhere, as well as prefab huts and even modified shipping containers that appeared to have been dropped into the field by heavy-lift choppers. They reminded him of the flight ops centre on the Longreach. Generator trailers joined the cacophony of noise, providing light and power to the growing military presence. Dave stepped gingerly on his bare feet, but they seemed to adjust to the discomfort as quickly as his nose had recovered from being punched flat by Igor. He was soon able to walk as freely as if he were wearing a favourite pair of old boots.

His ass was still hanging out in the breeze though. So there was that.

He walked through the dumbfounding chaos of the military with no sense of where he was heading, or even where he should go. After a few minutes of drifting this way and that, he struck upon the idea of walking over to the motel, when he might be able to find a suitcase with some clothes left behind in the scramble to evacuate. For sure the army or even the air force could probably rustle up some clothes for him, but he didn't much feel like asking and having to explain why he was wandering around half naked like an escaped mental patient. In this state he stumbled across Zach by accident rather than design. A small group, six men and two women, were standing in a circle, holding hands under a lone tree, their heads bowed in prayer. A soldier stood in the circle with them, much older than the rest, with an embroidered cross on his uniform. Dave could at least recognise a cross when he saw one. He felt like a bit of a dick, standing there undressed, looking on while they made their peace or their pleas or their confessions or whatever, and he thought about walking over to the Countryside to search for some new clothes while they finished up. But he didn't want to lose track of Zach Allen, so he stayed.

'Almighty God of Battle,' the chaplain continued. 'Be our strong right arm in this test of our faith...'

Dave tuned the man out. His brother had been into that sort of thing and all it got him was a flag-draped coffin.

The service dragged on, as they do, even though he got the impression the chaplain was moving things along at a fair clip, cutting corners and getting to the good bits as quickly as he could. Dave worried that there would be communion or some other elaborate ritual that would drag the process out even longer.

Maybe they were Protestants, he hoped. They were quicker, weren't they?

Dave was annoyed to find himself anxious, but whether that was from worrying about what he might say to Zach and what Zach would say to him, or because, you know, he was stood out here with his ass in the breeze, he couldn't say. He had just decided–*fuck it*–that he was gonna go get dressed, even if he had to warp into town and 'borrow' an outfit from an Eddie Bauer, or something, when the chaplain blessed the tiny congregation. They said their 'Amens', and the circle broke apart.

Zach was talking with a young woman in a flight suit. He smiled sadly and nodded as she patted him on the arm. It wasn't a scene Dave felt comfortable interrupting, but then again he didn't feel comfortable with much at that moment. Also, it really wouldn't help if she got a sniff of his super-powered man mojo and suddenly reached in under his hospital gown to give his dick a friendly squeeze. So he kept his distance. Zach was still talking to the woman when he noticed Dave standing on the verge of the grassed area, waiting for him. He didn't scowl like Emmeline or snarl like Igor, but he made no move to approach Dave or break off his conversation. He eventually parted ways with the woman, apparently agreeing to call her again in the future. At least that's what it looked like to Dave. They didn't pass each other notes, or bump phones or anything, but to his eye she looked like a woman who was satisfied she'd put the hook in. He wisely resisted the urge to say as much when Zach walked over.

'Captain will want to see you,' the SEAL said before Dave could speak.

'Figured as much,' said Dave. He noticed that the second woman from the service was standing a short distance away, staring at him, looking as though she wanted to come over and say something, but was fighting the urge. She had brushed past him a few moments earlier and he realised he was going to have to move away from her before she made a difficult scene even more so.

'Look, man, I'm sorry...' he started to say, taking a few steps toward the motel and away from his new biggest fan. Zach Allen did not follow him.

'I know you are, Dave. You're always sorry. And it's always too little, too late.'

That hurt way more than Igor's fist in his face. It was an old wound. Annie had said the same thing to him so many times he'd lost count. He'd heard those words, or variations on them, from his mother, his brother, and a long line of teachers, professors, sports coaches and friends. On every occasion Contrite Dave had tried to fix the situation by throwing more apologies in on top of the first one, stacking them up for a bonfire of the apologies. But it never worked, and eventually Resentful Dave turned up to tell them all what they could do with their goddamned guilt trips and their bullshit accusations.

'I know apologies are crap,' said Dave. 'I know they don't change anything...'

Zach smiled that same disconsolate smile again, and shook his head. 'Have to be made though, Dave. Apologies, confession, whatever you want to call it. But it's not me you should be talking to.'

'Heath?' Dave asked, withdrawing a few more steps as the woman in the flight suit took a couple of halting paces toward him. 'Zach, do you think we could talk somewhere? I mean somewhere else. Private like. It's just...'

'Dave, some people are angry with you. Some others, some of them friends of mine, don't have that luxury. They're dead. They'll never be angry again, or happy, or anything.'

Dave fought not to cringe as the softly spoken surfer dude served up his sermon.

'But it's not my place to judge these things, man. Those

two young ladies you brought back, the waitresses from the restaurant? I'm sure they're grateful for what you did. I'm sure their parents will cry actual tears of joy and thanksgiving because you saved their babies.'

'I could only save one,' he said. It sounded like a confession, and a poor one at that.

'One soul saved is a good thing, Dave.'

'That's what I told Igor,' he exclaimed, and before he could stop himself he added, 'before he tried to punch out my lights.'

'I'm sorry to hear you couldn't help both of them,' said Zach, ignoring the petulant outburst. 'But Dave?'

'Yeah?'

'You did the wrong thing.'

Dave Hooper didn't get angry, not the way he had with Emmeline, but he wasn't ready to shrug it off the way he had with Igor either. The air force woman had moved a few steps closer and the closer she got the more determined she seemed to come on.

'I didn't kill your friends,' he said, and hated himself for the miserable weakness of it.

'No,' said Zach. 'You didn't. The demons did that. And there's no saying who would have lived or died if you had done it differently. Just that some would have lived, and some would have died.'

'Yes, exactly,' said Dave. Finally, someone was seeing it his way. 'I heard you got a bunch of them. Killed like half a dozen or so?'

Zach shook his head, but confirmed the story.

'I got lucky with a couple of grenades. Didn't matter in the end. They got away somehow. Just sort of... disappeared. But Dave?'

'Yes?'

'None of that matters.'

The woman had stopped in her advance toward them. Dave could see the confusion and contending urges playing out on her face. Backing away from her, he had opened up a large gulf between Zach and himself. He stared across it at the young man he'd thought he could be friends with. He could think of nothing to say, except sorry, again, and he already knew that meant nothing.

'What matters, Dave, is that we were counting on you and you let us down. It's not the consequences, man. That's just war. There's always blood. There's always consequence. But if we can't count on each other, we got nothing.'

He opened his mouth to say something, to defend himself. But nothing came out, because he had nothing.

'Where's Heath?' he said at last.

Zach checked his watch. 'He'll be in D-Tac. The new one.' He jerked a thumb in the direction of the Countryside Suites. 'Just got back from feeding the media in town.'

'Okay,' said Dave. 'I guess I better go see him.'

'Yeah,' said Zach. 'Whatever, man.'

Dave reached for Zach but the SEAL turned and walked away without saying anything further.

The air force woman was gone.

## 23

It had been quite the walk from the field where the Army was gathering, down the side road until he could make his way across I-80 to the motel. Yes, he told himself. He could fold space and time and be there in a second or two but for once in his new existence he decided to take his sweet-ass time getting to what was promising to be an epic ass-chewing. Soldiers gawked and pointed, but they did nothing to stop him. His bare feet were cut and shredded a dozen times over, healing after each injury, giving him time to reflect if not repent. In the surge of emotions—anger, guilt, annoyance and exasperation—he searched for any sense that he might be even just a touch repentant.

Nope. Nothing.

There were two Captain Heaths in the office of the Countryside motel, which had been taken over by the military and turned into a make-do command post after their first one was destroyed. Dave briefly forgot his many discomforts—his slight embarrassment at not being dressed, his guilt over the men who had died, and his anger, which was considerable, that nobody but Zach seemed to acknowledge he'd actually done a good thing in rescuing Emmeline and the other girl.

Confronted by two Heaths, both of them glowering at him, Dave performed a double-take to make Daffy Duck proud, especially given his cartoonish outfit. And then he realised the real Heath was glaring at him, while a double on a big-ass TV screen was merely glaring at some reporter, sometime in the past. The other Heath was replaced by a talking head he didn't recognise and little pop-up windows running footage of the battle a few hours earlier. The vision looked like it was all sourced from the military: black and white gun cameras, the slightly fuzzy green video of night-vision systems, and computer graphics. Lots of really bright, cheery CGI of high-tech weaponry falling on vast, slow-moving squares of monsters that appeared to have been copied from the art assets for *Gears of War*.

'Motherfucker,' said Heath through tightly pressed lips, the first time Dave could remember really hearing him curse. 'And you still can't do what you're told. What the hell are you doing up and around? You're supposed to be on a drip. Did you walk over here like that?'

'Yeah, I got better.' Dave shrugged. 'Thought I'd best come find you. Ashbury told me what happened.'

Heath said nothing. None of the military personnel in the small overcrowded office spoke. Dave could feel his face growing hot and for maybe the three or four hundredth time since he'd stormed out of the tent, he was made painfully aware of how he was dressed.

'I'm, you know, sorry about Compton,' he said when he could stand the silence no longer. The sound was turned down on the television where Heath had reappeared, looking less stern and even smiling as he answered questions from forty or fifty journalists at a press conference in a hotel function room. The Sheraton Omaha, according to the logo on the lectern. Dave wished they'd left the volume up, and he felt his hand involuntarily twitch for the remote.

'Compton wasn't the least of it,' said Heath. His face seemed completely devoid of animation, as though the image of the man smiling and even joking on-screen was the real person, and this thin, stone-faced ogre in front of him an avatar awaiting some motive force to bring it fully to life.

'I know,' said Dave, struggling to keep the impatience out of his voice. Because that would be wrong, and inappropriate, he supposed. 'I spoke to the others.' He tried to reach for something to say, something that would set everything right, but all he could come up with was another, 'I'm sorry.' He didn't even sound especially convincing. The words trailed off into nothing.

'You sound more sorry for yourself,' said Captain Heath.

As difficult as he found the exchange, Dave had more difficulty reining in a galloping need to explain himself, to justify what he had done, even to push back against the allegation that he'd fucked everything up. But he knew better than to argue with Michael Heath. And so he stood in front of a room full of uniforms, feeling hot shame creeping over him and hating it, biting back the angry bile that wanted to spill out of his mouth because he shouldn't have been ashamed of doing the right thing, and a large part of him was still convinced that he had done exactly that.

And still, Heath just stared at him. Dave Hooper had never felt himself judged so harshly before, and that was saying something. He was not inexperienced with being judged and found wanting.

'So they... they took Compton?' he said, mostly to fill up

the dead airspace that was pressing down upon him. 'Is he still out there, you think? Because I could, you know, go and look for him or something.'

From the way the junior officers and enlisted men working at various screens and keyboards around the room stared fixedly at whatever was in front of them, this was almost as excruciating for them as it was for him.

Heath limped forward a few steps, and Dave saw they'd stuck his leg back on, or at least a workable replacement. The captain wasn't moving anywhere near as freely as he once had, but he'd ditched the crutches he'd been using earlier that night. He hobbled all the way across the room, right up to Hooper, right into his personal space. His eyes were bloodshot and yellow with exhaustion. The collar of the fresh shirt he'd put on for the press conference was dark with grime.

'Do you even care about how badly you screwed us?'

Not wanting to lie, Dave found himself unable to say anything at all. But even though his silence was an admission which pealed out like the ringing of a church bell, Heath would not let it go.

'Well? Mister? Did you just decide at the last moment to go and do your own thing, or were you going to fuck us in the ass all along?'

Dave felt a flicker of heat somewhere inside his head, and it didn't matter whether the flame was lit by remorse or resentment, what mattered was the bonfire of ill feeling which quickly mounted from a slow burn to a white-hot rage.

When he spoke, however, his voice was soft, almost chilling.

'I'm sorry,' he said, 'I don't think we've been properly introduced. I'm the guy who saved your ass on the bridge a couple of hours ago, after telling you not to go down there in the first–'

'Don't,' Heath ground out between clenched teeth, as though he had been struck a physical blow. They were close enough that Hooper could see his lips change colour as he pressed them together, and watch the muscles in his jawline flex as Heath bit down on whatever he had been about to say. For his part, Hooper felt as though he'd become detached from the confrontation, indeed from himself, and that he was floating above them a few feet away watching everything unravel. From that abstract vantage point it was easy to just not care about the stupid, hurtful and unthinking words that began to spill out of his own mouth.

'I don't know whether you noticed or not, but I don't wear a uniform. Hell, I'm not wearing anything at the moment, not even underpants. I don't have to be here. I don't have to do this. I don't have to take shit from you or anybody for doing the right fucking thing. And I did the right thing, Heath, even though you can't bring yourself to admit it. You were going to let those women die. I asked whether you decided at the last moment that their lives counted for nothing, but we both know you had been planning to fuck them in the ass all along.'

'It would be best if you kept your mouth shut now' said Heath.

The other men and women in the room, all of them military, were staring openly.

'Why? Is that an order? Because last time I checked I didn't have to take orders. The last time I took orders I was a teenager flipping burger patties at McDonald's. I've moved on since then. And I think I'll be moving on now.'

Heath jutted his jaw out at Dave, as though it could somehow shoot bullets at him. But when he spoke his tone, although thick with strain, was almost conciliatory.

'Dave,' he said.

'Hooper will do,' said Dave.

Heath's nostrils flared as he sucked in air and made an obvious effort to calm himself, much more of an effort than Dave was making.

'I understand,' he began, 'that you are here of your own accord.' Heath talked slowly, enunciating each word with the care of somebody who spoke perfect English, but only because they had studied it intently as a second language. 'I understand you have no obligations to us other than an expectation that you will do the right thing.'

'And I did it,' Dave said, feeling himself falling back into his own body from that strange floating place. Heath stepped back a pace. Dave noticed the strain around the corners of his eyes.

'I am trying to explain that I know you are a free agent,' Heath said. 'But I need you to understand that you do not have that freedom as a matter of course.'

'What'd I wake up in North Korea or something?'

'If Emmeline was here right now she'd tell you not to be stupid. You know that, don't you?'

'If she was here it's because I saved her, and yes, telling me not to be stupid is her natural state of being.'

A keyboard clacked somewhere behind Heath, and a phone rang. The suspended moment with everyone staring at them had passed.

'Trinder, the CIA, Fox News and all your new best friends, Dave, they all want a piece of you.'

'I understand that. It doesn't bother me.'

'Fine. But none of them, not on their own at least, can *take* a piece of you.'

Dave frowned. He wasn't sure what Heath was getting at.

'But the state can.'

'Nebraska?'

'No, Dave. The state. The government.'

'You're not making any sense.'

'Uncle Sam, Dave. Not just agents, or agencies, or departments or the military. The United States government, Dave. Not the one you vote for, the one that delivers your mail, or builds your roads, or takes the cream off your pay cheque. I mean more than that. I mean the vast, sentient entity that is the state. The state that reads your emails. The state that listens to your phone calls. The state that decides whether you live or die. Whether you disappear from history. That state that exists so far above the law it cannot break the law. It has detached itself from law, from morality, from what it is to be human. That state, Dave, which manifested the merest fraction of its power out on the Platte River this evening.' He held his thumb and forefinger up, pinched together to make the point. 'That state is watching you. It watches everyone, but it very particularly watches those it fears. And yes, it fears everyone, but some more than others.'

'That's bullshit, Heath. What's to fear about–'

'About a man they can't kill, or control, or even hurt without going nuclear? What do you think, Dave? Would you fear someone like that?'

He had no answer for that. No answer he felt like giving anyway.

'As long as they think you're with us, Dave, as long as

they think you're on board for the big win, they'll tolerate you. They'll even celebrate you, make a hero of you. It'll be all hookers and blow for good ol' Super Dave. But be not mistaken in this, my friend, the moment they fear they cannot control you, they will lay plans to destroy you utterly, because they fear you would destroy them.'

'I don't think I understand,' said Dave, even though he did, or was beginning to at least.

Heath leaned against the check-in counter, taking the weight off his leg stump.

'You know that I have had to fight to maintain control of you, Dave.'

'Yeah, I guess so,' he conceded. He'd even been amused by it back in Las Vegas.

'Well controlling you doesn't just mean keeping you topped up with Snickers bars and Gatorade. It doesn't mean pulling you out of strip clubs before you bring the house down, literally. Controlling you, Dave, means calming and soothing the fears of the state that you might go rogue. It means showing them, every day, that you are working to serve their ends, to further their interests. The day I cannot convince them of that is the day they begin to lay plans against you. Oh, Hell, they've already got the plans, they'll just take them out of the bottom drawer.'

But Dave was only half listening to him. He was distracted by the sight of his own face up on screen. Not the smiling heroic Dave of the media that came out of New Orleans, but the balding, tangle-headed Dave of his mugshot from a drunk-driving bust in Georgia about five years ago.

'Hey, turn it up,' he said and before anybody could stop her one of the young, uniformed women hurried to comply, bringing up the volume with a remote, beaming at him as though waiting for a reward.

'Turn it down,' said Heath, but without result. The woman stared at Dave with goo-goo eyes, while he stared at the TV with an increasingly thunderous expression.

'Can you confirm then, Captain Heath, the number of men who were killed?'

'I don't intend to give a running body count,' said TV Heath.

A babble of voices rose up attempting to question him, with one loud male winning out.

'But you can confirm that it was Mr Hooper whose actions led to the casualties?'

TV Heath shook his head, frowning.

'I can't confirm anything at this stage...'

'What the fuck.'

It wasn't a question, more of a snarl of outrage.

'You can't confirm that I didn't kill anybody?' Dave snapped, the hot rage which had been subsiding suddenly flaring up again. 'At this stage? At this stage? What, you think you might get around to telling everybody it was my fault somewhere down the track? Is that the plan, Heath?'

His mugshot was back, leering stupidly, drunkenly out at the viewers. Yeah, you could totally see that asshole getting a bunch of brave, clean-shaven commandos killed because he ran off after his rock-hard cock. That wasn't a thousand miles away from the truth of what'd happened just before his DUI arrest, in fact.

Heath was trying to say something, attempting to explain himself, but the red mist was down, and Dave could see nothing through the fog of his righteous fury. He turned away and stomped out of the room, almost knocking over a soldier who was coming in at the same time. He didn't recall much of the next few minutes apart from raging around the parking lot of the Countryside cursing Heath and Ashbury and Igor and Annie and Baron's and everybody who'd ever done him wrong or talked him down or made him out to be the asshole when all he was trying to do was the right thing.

It was in this state that Boylan found him. The lawyer was sporting a large sticking plaster over a wound on his forehead, but he'd found himself a fresh suit from somewhere, and seemed to have located a barber to judge by his new haircut and pink, freshly shaved jowls. He did not have much hair, but what he did have he'd spent a hundred bucks on, to Dave's eye.

'Dave,' he called out, 'Dave! At last. I have been looking for you all over. Come along, come along. We have work to do.'

A terrible weariness came over Dave as the hot zephyr of his anger guttered and died away.

'Oh man, X, not now. Really, not now.'

But Boylan would not be denied. 'Yes now, Dave. Yes, very definitely now. Come along, I've got the girl's family locked in for a live cross from their lounge room and a van with an outside broadcast unit for your piece to studio.'

He looked like the Energizer Bunny he was bouncing around so much.

'What? They want to ask me how I got a bunch of guys killed?'

His eyes narrowed as he pondered the hyperactive figure capering around in front of him. But before he could say anything, before he could lay the blame for what had happened on someone else, Boylan surprised him.

'No! Of course not. A tragedy, Dave. A terrible tragedy.

But unavoidable. You rescued the ones who needed rescuing. Professor Compton? He's not a civilian. He's a government operative, a trained operator, a top agent of a secret bureau. And the war band which took him carried him off with a squad of Navy SEALs, some of them still armed. If they couldn't look after themselves, who were you to do so? You were the man who rescued the pretty waitress from the Cracker Barrel, that's who! And who risked his life, in vain, it sadly, *sadly* transpires, for her pretty friend. Come along now, Dave. Let's get ahead of this. Those MSNBC fools have only just started in on this crusade. We'll crush them, Dave. Crush them like bugs. But we have to move now!'

So he moved.

# 24

The Chinese uncorked the first nuke shortly after Boylan and Hooper hitched a ride on another business jet, this time comped by Warren Buffett as a thank you for saving his home town and Darla Jean Murnane, the waitress from the Cracker Barrel, where he was wont to stop in for mac and meatloaf when he was done piling up money for the working day. The jet, like the last one, had a fighter escort, but not one organised by Compton, of course. Boylan claimed responsibility and credit for all the arrangements, and Dave was happy to leave him to it. The lawyer started using the inflight WiFi to mainline newsfeeds as soon as he'd strapped himself in. At first he just needed to stay on top of the story in Omaha, specifically the story he was trying to spike; the one in which Dave got a bunch of Navy SEALs killed by being an irresponsible jerk. That difficulty lasted all of twenty-five minutes, until the interview with Darla Jean Murnane's family was released into the wild. Their heartfelt blubbering thanks to Super Dave for rescuing their little girl, and Dave's aw-shucks t'weren't-nothin'-really response killed the spin that he was somehow to blame for the other rescue mission going wrong. The last gasp of oxygen rushed out of that story when footage surfaced of Dave's heroics on the bridge and in the field where he caught up with the Grymm war band.

It wasn't grainy, highly controlled military video. A camera crew freelancing for *Ghost Hunters* had avoided the media exclusion zone by the happy accident of already being inside it, filming a special on a haunted farmhouse when the barriers went up. By another happy accident the production company which owned the *Ghost Hunters* franchise was a sometime client of attorney-at-law Professor X Boylan Esquire. The farmhouse turned out not to be haunted at all, which was disappointing, but in a third, almost unbelievably fortunate accident, it was situated so as to give the crew ready access to the Platte River Bridge, the makeshift military base on the I-80, and by a stroke of luck which really did have nothing to do with the machinations of one X Boylan, Esq., the field in which Dave performed his rescue.

The freelancers, who were already being spoken of for Pulitzer nominations, produced a slick, professionally edited video package, with a hard rockin' background track by AC/DC ('Highway to Hell' as Dave carried Heath away from the Djinn in super slow motion, and 'Back in Black' as he kicked ass while rescuing Emmeline and Darla Jean). It ran wall-to-wall across all the major networks and cable news outlets after upload to YouTube, where it racked up seven and a half million views in less than an hour.

The *Ghost Hunters* crew only caught the tail end of his all-in brawl with the Grymm and Sliveen and he wasn't much more than a blur on the screen. But everywhere that blur went, monsters exploded, and by the time the captain had turned off the seatbelt sign, and the flight attendant (a dude, unfortunately) had served Dave his first brew, he was a superhero again.

'They love you, Dave,' Boylan cried out across the aisle, waving a half-empty champagne flute around for a top-up. He had two laptops open now, and an iPad, and he was watching another screen deployed from the cabin ceiling. 'Oh I love this bit,' he said as Dave appeared in a pop-up window on the big screen to tell the country that they could rest easy knowing the United States military was on the job.

'That doesn't really sound like something I'd say, X,' said Dave, who was starting to feel a little guilty about lighting out on Heath and the others. He was also feeling bad because he could sense himself being lifted up onto the shoulders of hundreds of millions of Americans and cheered out of the stadium for rescuing Emmeline and Carla May or Darla Jean or whatever her name was. But he hadn't been in time to save that other girl. If he'd gone even a minute or two earlier perhaps she could have had a happy story too.

'Pfft!'

Boylan had no time for such nonsense.

'You have to say things like that, Dave. It's part of the script. Remember, you're working from a script now. It might feel wrong, but it scans a hell of a lot better. And if our resident paranoid Captain Heath is even halfway right about keeping the powers that be on side, that's exactly the sort of anaesthetic they're going to want you feeding to the ignorant masses. Not that I'm against the ignorant masses, Dave. In a mass consumption economy, the ignorant masses are the very engine of a life well lived by me and thee, my friend. God bless them. God bless them one and all.'

He slopped some more champagne around.

Dave thanked the flight attendant as his dinner was delivered, although maybe it was an early breakfast now since the sun was already coming up. A carpetbagger steak with baked potatoes and steamed broccoli, a concession to Zach Allen and his dietary scolding.

'Holy crap would you look at this,' cried Boylan, newly excited by something he'd seen on one of his laptops. 'The Chinese have nuked a whole army of monsters that boiled up out of the earth near the Three Gorges. That's just marvellous.'

'Doesn't say what sect they were?' Dave asked around his first baked tater.

'Sect?'

'Sort of like a nation of monsters.'

'How would they know?' Boylan shrugged as he sipped at his refilled champagne glass. 'I don't think they bothered asking. They just decided to play atomic whack-a-mole. Told everybody about it too, which isn't like them at all.'

As Dave ate his breakfast-dinner and drank his breakfast-dinner beer, some extra heavy lager brewed by lesbian nuns or something, Boylan fed him titbits of news from around the world. Nobody was criticising the Chinese for dropping the bomb, in fact a couple of undeclared nuclear powers had declared they'd be doing the exact same damn thing if it came down to that. The United States Air Force had shot down another four dragons. The RAF had accounted for eight. And the North Korean regime was claiming a hundred 'fire-breathing criminal monster lizards' now lay scattered in smoking kebab chunks all over the People's Democratic Republic. But that claim remained unconfirmed.

In Russia, the armed forces had been mobilised and placed 'on the highest alert', but they were withdrawing from the country's massive borders and redeploying to population centres.

'And listen to this, Dave,' said Boylan, whose giddy, childlike glee grew giddier with every story that he read. 'Details are emerging of a pitched battle between humans and monsters in the town of Fester, down in Georgia, and it didn't go well for the monsters.'

'Buttecrack,' said Dave, finally grinning for the first time in hours.

'I'm sorry, Dave?'

'Beau-cray, sorry,' he said. 'Fester is the seat of Buttecrack County in Georgia. Knoxy told me about that, you know, the orcs coming up there. Except it wasn't a real story then.'

'Well it's a real story now, Dave, and the heroes are citing you and the defence of New Orleans as an inspiration to them.' He waved his champagne at the laptops, slopping more fizz over the rim. 'Oh, what does it matter? Even Apple will be comping us freebies by close of business, Dave. We're riding a wave here, my friend. A tsunami of opportunity.'

Boylan's energy seemed almost frenzied. Dave supposed it was a reaction to living through the massacre and aftermath at the restaurant. He couldn't blame the guy for getting high on life, although he couldn't share the feeling. He kept seeing images of that poor girl, the other waitress, whose name he couldn't even remember. Kept seeing her body tossed about like a rag doll.

He forced the visions from his mind, the way he was learning to tamp down on Urgon's memories that came seeping up behind his eyeballs when he didn't much feel like seeing them. Another couple of lesbian beers, another steak, a whole bowl of baked potatoes slathered in some sort of blue cheese sauce, and he found himself drifting off to sleep.

\* \* \*

Dave awoke on descent into Los Angeles and when they landed at a private area of LAX, he was refreshed and relaxed after a short nap and a second breakfast. A proper breakfast this time, with scrambled eggs and German bacon, and thick, glistening pork sausages and crispy hash browns and grilled mushrooms and coffee with cream. And to finish, he had a blueberry and banana muffin (his favourite kind), baked especially on the say-so of Mr Buffett, by Chef Donna of Sweet Magnolias, certainly the finest bakery in all of Omaha, and quite possibly the whole Midwest.

'Damn fine muffin, X,' said Dave, who was feeling less guilty with every passing minute, and every new report of his awesomeness and the surprising stupidity of the various Sects in presenting themselves for systematic destruction all over the world. They were proving to be like Dark Ages barbarians who drew themselves up into huge fighting squares to shake their spears and shields at the Imperial Death Star hanging low in the sky above them.

'The finest,' Boylan confirmed. 'I am nothing if not diligent in pursuit of your interests, Dave. And today your interests were best pursued, in my professional judgment as your attorney and advisor, by securing that muffin. But as your advisor, I must now advise you that the muffin, while excellent, is not the highlight of this day. I do not wish to disappoint in this, Dave, but rest assured I will always give you the hard news. And Dave, the joy you knew while eating that muffin will be as nothing compared to the girlish *squee* I feel compelled to utter upon telling you that we have lunch with Mr Brad Pitt and Mr Zack Snyder and a small team of contract lawyers who will not actually be eating with us, but will be passing around papers before the appetisers arrive, that we might conclude our business, that business being the option Mr Pitt has agreed to purchase on *Dave Hooper Saves the World*. A working title, but I like it. I like it a lot.'

Boylan dragged in a mouthful of air, having forgotten to breathe while speaking.

'Squee,' he added dryly.

And so lunch like champions they did, and the contracts were signed for *Dave Hooper Saves the World*, which was a working title, but Dave liked it almost as much as Boylan. Brad Pitt was kind of cool, and Zack Snyder was very funny, and promised to get signed copies of that *300* comic for Dave's boys. And Dave congratulated himself on having such a Super Dad moment as he swapped parenting tips with Brad Pitt, and then Bruce Willis stopped by the table and joked that he should totally play Dave, because Pitt was too scrawny and worn out from changing diapers. And later Boylan checked them into a very nice hotel, and Dave met Jennifer Aniston for a drink, as Dave had wanted, and she was very hot, as he had always thought, and she found him very funny and charming and even intriguing. She was thinking about not going home to learn her lines for some movie she was doing, and he didn't much care that she was totally drunk on his overproof pheromones because... *Jennifer Fucking Aniston!*

He did have a brief, sad moment when he wanted to call Marty and Vince and tell them he was having a drink with *Jennifer Fucking Aniston!* But then he remembered that Marty was dead, eaten like a big meat popsicle by Urgon. And Vince... well he wasn't quite sure where Vince was. He hadn't seen him or spoken to him since losing track of the other survivors at the marines' secret base where he'd found out he'd turned into a Marvel character.

But another pitcher of martinis with Jen—yeah, she was Jen now—and then all of a sudden he was shaking hands with Matt Damon and some guys from Google, or maybe Facebook, and Jay Z was backslapping him. Alex Rodriguez appeared from somewhere and a party kicked off, and he was doing lines, and tequila lay-backs, and everyone was cheering and he was aware in a distant way that this party went on forever, all over the world. He did some more lines, and people everywhere were celebrating this bizarre thing that had happened. Dark magic and monsters had come back into the world and the human race had totally kicked their fucking asses! So Dave dropped some acid, which was a pleasant buzz that he felt as a tactile colour, but only for a few minutes. And he knew, because people kept telling him all night long, that he was the reason for it all, for the big, warm hug the whole world was giving itself right then, or part of the reason for it, because he'd dropped some ecstasy, or something, and he'd shown people they could stand up for themselves. And by God they'd done it. In Omaha, and New Orleans, and Fester, and China, and England and somewhere in the Middle East according to the last news report he'd seen on a TV over some bar. But fuck, you know what that place was like—they'd killed the orcs and gone straight back to killing each other—and maybe something happened in Japan too. Or Korea. Might have been Korea.

But what the hell did it matter?

For a few days there *everyone* had been scared, even if they weren't saying so. Scared in a way people hadn't been since they hid in caves from things that growled and fed in the night. And then they weren't scared anymore and they crawled out of the cave with a burning stick and started to reshape the world, and Dave did a line, and he did another line, because the monsters were gone. And then Jennifer Aniston was gone too, but it didn't matter because he looked down and found Paris Hilton on his arm and then Paris Hilton was at his side and giggling and stroking his chest as he fumbled for room keys and discovered that he was actually a little drunk, which was awesome, and maybe even a little fucked up after doing a heap of lines and some pills, and then they spilled through the door and he ripped off his shirt and someone said, 'I'm afraid you're going to need another shirt.' And Paris went 'Huh?' and Agent Trinder smiled at him.

# 25

'The fuck?' said Dave, who couldn't understand why Trinder was standing there in his dark blue, big boy suit, but without the colourful tie this time, and why Boylan was standing next to him, beaming at Paris Hilton, who was still laughing but not as much as she had been in the elevator coming up to the room. He could smell hamburgers too. That was odd.

'Dave, I'm sorry to interrupt at this special moment between you and Ms Hilton but I never sleep, Dave, I never rest in the pursuit of your interests, and Agent Trinder has approached me with an offer we could totally refuse, and if you want to refuse it, Dave, consider it torn up and thrown to the winds, the four strong winds, Dave. But as your attorney and closest advisor I would advise you to consider his offer very carefully because it could save us a considerable amount of time and effort and, to be quite frank about it, chickenshit administrivia in fending off the outrageous demands of the Internal Revenue Service, and quite possibly the machinations of your good lady wife, or soon-to-be ex-wife and the execrable M. Pearson Vietch...'

'You're married?' Paris asked, nibbling his ear.

'Was.'

'That's cool.'

'Ms Hilton,' beamed Boylan, 'I did so love your work in *The Hottie and the Nottie.* Perhaps we could discuss a role for you in Dave's upcoming feature with Mr Pitt?'

He detached the hottie from Dave's arm and steered her gracefully toward the door, all the while discussing in surprising detail her performance in the eponymous movie. Dave was still too surprised and befuddled to do anything about it, and then Paris was gone and he was left with Boylan and Trinder and the very real impression his night had not taken a turn for the better.

'Mr Hooper,' said Trinder, nodding at him, as though seeing him for the first time across a crowded room at a party. A party like the one Dave had just left, say. A great party. He wanted to go back to it. 'I apologise if we got off on the wrong foot in Las Vegas.'

'Whatever,' said Dave, still foggy and struggling to catch up. 'Where's Paris?'

Boylan reappeared. 'I shall resist the obvious under-graduate quip, Dave. My wit is better spent in the service of your interests, and Agent Trinder has reached out to us on behalf of the federal government to seek an alignment of our interests, which is to say yours, because your interests are my interests and hence ours, Dave and–'

'Just get to it, X,' said Dave, suddenly feeling tired. He dragged himself over to a soft brown square he assumed was a lounge chair, suddenly aware he had no idea where he was, beyond being somewhere in LA in an expensive hotel full of people he'd only ever seen on magazine covers. He saw Lucille leaned up against a well-stocked bar, but only vaguely recalled recovering her from the field outside Omaha.

Man, he'd really hit it hard tonight.

Outside, the city lights reached toward the horizon. The view through the floor-to-ceiling windows seemed to stretch away forever. He squeezed his eyes shut and then opened them wide. His head spun a little and his stomach threatened to flip over and spill its contents everywhere.

'Mr Hooper,' said Trinder, taking the soft brown square opposite him and lighting up a cigarette, 'Professor Boylan is correct. There is much we could do to help each other, although much more I could do for you than I would ask in return.'

Dave frowned. He felt like a hungover undergrad trying to follow a complicated math problem at a morning lecture he really should be sleeping through. Trinder took a small hamburger from a platter sitting on a coffee table that seemed to have been fashioned out of a solid block of aluminium. The platter was full of tiny hamburgers and they smelled great. One mystery solved.

'Slider?'

'What?'

'Pork belly and prosciutto,' said Trinder, taking one for himself. 'Which is Italian bacon, I think.'

'Indeed it is. Tasty, tasty Italian bacon cut very thin,' Boylan confirmed. 'But to the business at hand, Dave. They're willing to wipe out your tax debt, all of it. And here is the cherry on top, Dave. Agent Trinder says the federal government is amenable to an arrangement allowing you to earn whatever you want for a twenty-four month period, tax free, as a consultant to the...' Boylan looked to Trinder to make sure he was getting it right, '...the Office of Special Clearances and Records?'

'You are correct, sir,' said Trinder, swallowing his tiny pork belly burger in one gulp, like a boa constructor with an unlucky gerbil.

Dave was still having trouble following the thread. Dave was having trouble remembering exactly how much he'd drunk and blown and dropped and...

'Sorry, what?' he said, 'They're gonna gimme a free pass if I work for this asshole?'

'Yes,' said Boylan. 'This asshole and the even more unpleasant, but very powerful assholes for whom he works. And since this work would be defined as combat, even if there was very little actually combat involved,' he hastened to add, 'you or a corporate entity legally constituted in the Cayman Islands to contract with you to provide services to the federal government, would attract the tax-free status afforded to all combat pay earned in combat zones as defined by the president who, in your case, would declare the entire world to be a combat zone for the duration of the current crisis, or twenty-four months, whichever lasts longer.'

'But... but...' Dave was struggling to follow any of this and wondered if he should go get Paris back. 'I just got clear of Heath and his bullshit and you want me to go back into harness again. Plus, you know, I'm still on the clock for Baron's and nobody's offered anything like this so far and...'

'Mr Hooper,' said Trinder. 'Let me bottom line it for you. We wipe out your debt to Uncle Sam. We give you a running start, two years, to earn what you can, however you want while we look the other way. I understand Professor Boylan has already come to an arrangement with your commercial creditors, but rest assured if he hadn't, we could have made them come to heel too. As for your family law issues, a word to the judge, whom we will appoint, and you will find any and all matters quickly resolved to your satisfaction.'

Dave's head was clearing, slowly, but it was clearing.

Sitting directly across from him, Trinder didn't look any prettier than he had in Vegas, but he didn't look nearly as much like a rabid dog either.

'Are you supposed to be smoking in here?' Dave asked.

'No,' Trinder replied, and took another drag on his unfiltered cigarette.

'Okay. All right then,' Dave grunted, playing for time to unscramble his thoughts. 'So what sort of things would you want me to do, and what sort of hours and conditions are we talking, because I gotta be honest, I just walked out on an unpaid gig with Heath and mostly what I got outta that was being told what I couldn't do and how much I fucked everything up.'

Trinder blew a thin stream of blue smoke at the ceiling.

'Let me be frank, Mr Hooper. OSCAR sees you as a fall-back option, to be called upon only under special circumstances. Everything has changed since Omaha. We're now confident we can take these things without breaking a sweat. Hell, New Zealand could probably take them. Are you familiar with military history, Mr Hooper? No, don't bother. I know you're not. I understand your antipathy to these things. But let me quote the Duke of Wellington to you, sir, on the arrant stupidity of the French at the Battle of Waterloo. "They came on in the same old way and we defeated them in the same old way." The Jabberwockies are the French of this war, Mr Hooper. They have come on in the same old way seven times in the hours since Omaha.'

'Seven?' Dave couldn't keep the surprise out of his voice. 'Jabber what now?'

'Yes. Seven regiments, all them deploying exactly as happened outside Omaha. Six of them destroyed in very much the same way, with overwhelming firepower.'

'I heard about China,' said Dave, trailing off.

'You heard about the regiment they nuked. Another was targeted and destroyed in Mongolia by us at the request of the Chinese...'

'But...'

'They would prefer we didn't brag.'

Trinder took another burger.

'These are good. You really should have one before they go cold. Keep your strength up.'

Dave took one of the sliders and popped it into his mouth. It was very good, so fresh it must have been delivered shortly before he arrived.

'You said seven?'

Trinder nodded.

'Yes, another regiment emerged in northwest Pakistan. It was engaged by a series of local forces in an uncoordinated fashion. Some Taliban, some Pakistani military, some local tribes, even a couple of Kabul's units we lifted in. It's a mess, but we don't much care about that.'

'Let me guess, you can see an angle where it works out for you?'

Trinder grinned, showing off his yellowed teeth again.

'Maybe if we got to Dave's part?' Boylan suggested.

The man in the dark suit nodded as if he was making a concession.

'All right. Mr Hooper, we need people to know we can handle this threat. Without you. You played your role and you played it well, but I'm sure you'd agree it would be better if the whole world wasn't relying on you to turn up and save them every time some hungry jabberwocky shows its face.'

'Guess not,' Dave said, leaning forward and taking another slider. His head was clearing as he ate.

'No, not at all,' said Trinder. 'You see, you're not normal, Mr Hooper. Why, I imagine if you jumped out that window behind you, you could fall all twenty storeys to the sidewalk and bounce back up like a nerf ball. Couldn't you?'

Dave shrugged.

'I'm not planning on trying.'

'Fair enough. But, sir, the less we see of you on the frontline, the better. The more you just put in the occasional appearance, calming everyone down, assuring them the government, their government, has everything under control, the better.'

'Fine by me,' said Dave, who was starting to think he didn't mind the idea of not being Heath's fireman, rushing here and there, and never on his own say-so. Hell, if Heath had his way, Dave would never have met Jen Aniston or come this close to having his way with Paris Hilton.

'But there are things you can still do for us,' said Trinder, interrupting his thoughts.

'Like what?' Dave asked cautiously.

'Oh, don't be like that, Mr Hooper. We're not about to put you in harness, as you describe it. Most of the time, sir, you'll be free to pursue your own interests.'

Trinder waved his hand at the world outside the hotel room, where the great glittering map of Los Angeles at night receded toward infinity. 'All this can be yours, sir. The whole world, if you want it. I'm sure Professor Boylan has plans and schemes...'

'Oh yes,' Boylan confirmed. 'Cunning plans, ingenious schemes. The world, Dave, it's a sweet, sweet plum for you, just waiting to be plucked.'

'And what do I have to do?' Dave asked, still suspicious. This wasn't the Trinder he'd met in Las Vegas; the arrogant bully and blundering oaf. But it was another version of the same man, he was certain. In fact, if he reminded Dave of anyone, or anything, it was the carpet-walking assholes back in Houston, the ones who'd been ready to throw him to the wolves when the Longreach went up.

'We don't need you to sell war bonds or anything like that, Mr Hooper. But from time to time there will be certain jobs that you can do for us that, to be honest, nobody else can handle.'

'I thought you said you could handle the orcs.'

'Oh yes, they're going to be no trouble at all, sir.'

'So what's your problem, Trinder? I'm guessing you already have one, or you wouldn't be here offering me pork sliders and the world.'

Trinder grinned again, but it was not an expression which sat well on his face.

'Yes, Mr Hooper. I do have a problem. In New York. Her name is Karen Warat.'

'What? Girlfriend?'

Again, Trinder moved his face into the shape of someone being friendly and engaging, but it wasn't convincing.

'No. And I can't tell you anything more about her until you have signed the papers Professor Boylan is holding.'

Boylan held up a sheaf of documents with his own guilty grin.

'Heath never got me to sign anything.'

'Remind me again what Captain Heath did do for you, Mr Hooper. Besides blackguarding you to the media, by omission, if not commission, after the Battle of Omaha.'

Dave felt as though he should defend the man, but when he thought about it, he couldn't actually think of anything Heath *had* done for him, whereas he'd been as busy as a one-legged man at an ass-kicking contest on Heath's behalf. Boylan offered him the sheets.

'I've read them, Dave, and I've struck some pars which were unconscionable, and added a few of my own which are also unconscionable, but favourable to your interests, specifically as regards your ownership of any intellectual property which might arise from you performing services as a consultant which, in my view, the federal government should have no call on. But they have accepted the amendments.'

'Sorry?' said Dave, trying to read and listen at the same time, and finding himself unable to make any sense of the impenetrable jargon of the documents he now held. They were worse than the ones the process server had laid on him in Vegas.

'Should there be a comic spun off your adventures as a consultant to the Office of Special Clearances and Records, or a video game, or some other property, rights are vested in you or whichever tax-exempt entity you assign such rights to, not to Washington, as your retainer or "employer" in the first instance.'

He used air quotes around employer.

'So, are they gonna be paying me? Do I have to tell Baron's?'

'Oh they'll be paying, Dave. They'll be paying handsomely,' said Boylan who shot Trinder a look, as if daring him to disagree. The other man seemed profoundly uninterested.

'Should I sign this?' Dave asked.

'You should, Dave, with all dispatch. I believe Agent Trinder is anxious to be about his business. You'll notice the documents are backdated to cover the period in which you consulted for Captain Heath and the Office of Science and Technology Policy. That's a generous concession, which allows us to include the deals we've already struck under the rubric of the tax concessions for your twenty-four month consultancy period.'

His body felt as though it had processed most of the chemicals he'd put into it and his head was now clear, but he still wasn't sure what Boylan was on about. What he did know, however, was that the funny little lawyer who reminded him of Larry from the Three Stooges was the one person who had been working for him from the get-go.

'And what if I say no?' he asked Trinder. 'You gonna audit me? Go after my family?'

Trinder shook his head.

'If you're not interested, sir, I'm sure you'll find Ms Hilton is still wandering around outside. I fear it will take her some time to negotiate a passage to the elevator and untangle the Gordian Knot of the up and down buttons. I will make my apologies for wasting your time, and say my goodbyes.'

'And I will get to work on your tax matter, Dave,' said Boylan. 'But I would much prefer not to. I have some other, very exciting–'

Dave waved the lawyer quiet with one hand. 'S'okay.'

He signed the papers. It took a while. There were four or five different documents and many copies of each.

'Excellent,' said Boylan when he was done. 'And with that, gentlemen, I will leave you to your business, for which Agent Trinder insists I am not cleared, and frankly, I do not care. I must be about *your* business, Dave. The infinitely more lucrative and interesting business than anything Agent Trinder might have for you. For us, because we are in this together. I shall join you in New York, when I have finalised the merchandising arrangements for the film and settled on a publisher and developer for your video game. Be aware that you have signed non-disclosure agreements, but these relate to specific aspects of our arrangement with Mr Trinder's agency, and will in no way affect your ability to do promotional and publicity work. I added that clause too. Good luck, Dave. And we shall meet again in the city that never sleeps. Two days hence. Agent Trinder, a pleasure, of sorts. I shall forward copies of the contracts to your office, unless you would prefer some sort of dead-drop arrangement, or a tricky exchange of similar-looking briefcases in a public park?'

Trinder indicated an emailed PDF would be fine.

Boylan excused himself, probably to return to his room and crawl into bed with more contracts.

'So, this is awkward,' said Dave, as the door closed behind the lawyer. 'I work for you now?'

'Only in the loosest sense, Mr Hooper. You work for the American people.'

'Awesome. They're a soft touch. So, this Karen chick?'

'Colonel Ekaterina Varatchevsky,' said Trinder. 'Of the Russian GRU. Also known as Karin.'

'The GR-what?'

'A spy, Mr Hooper. Karin Varatchevsky is a spy.'

'Fuck, really! You want me to go catch a spy?' He thought about it for a moment. 'That's cool, I guess, but couldn't you just do that yourself?'

'Yes and no,' said Trinder. 'Colonel Varatchevsky is special, Mr Hooper. She was special when she was just Karen Warat, her jacket, or cover identity. She was the best field manager *and* operator the Russians had in this country. We only became aware of her as we broke open another Russian spy ring, run by the FSB. Putin's CIA, if you like. They weren't nearly as professional as Colonel Varatchevsky's military intelligence network and some rather fortuitous intelligence leakage led us to Warat. It wasn't GRU incompetence which exposed her. It was her FSB colleagues' incompetence. And her bad luck,' he added.

Dave was interested now, not because it affected him, but because it was an interesting story. Russian spies in New York? Who knew that was still a thing?

'So what? You grabbed her up? You're tailing her? I'm sort of wondering where I come in?'

'You come in because Karen Warat is not only special in all the ways I just explained, Mr Hooper. She's special like you.'

Dave didn't understand at first. He picked up another little burger and ate it in two bites before speaking again.

'Like me? How? There nothing special about...'

He stopped.

'Yes, sir,' said Agent Trinder. 'You killed your monster, and she killed hers, right in the middle of the FBI raid that was supposed to take her down.'

'How?' asked Dave. He considered his own slaying of Urgon to have been pure dumbass luck.

'Pure dumb luck,' said Trinder. 'The thing emerged from a sewer grate and rampaged through the warehouse where Karen Warat, in character, was hosting an art exhibit.'

'A what?'

'Her cover, sir.'

'Okay,' said Dave. 'I understand.' But he didn't. 'What then?'

'The beast killed a number of her guests and was targeted by FBI and Clearance officers on site. They shot it to pieces, but

Ms Warat finished the job. She cut its head off.'

'Whoa! With what?'

'A 400-year-old Japanese katana. A samurai sword, Mr Hooper. That was the subject of her gallery exhibit. Military arcana of the ancient world.'

'Wow. Cool art.'

Dave was starting to get it now, even though it didn't make much sense. He felt twitchy and had to get up out of his big, soft cube chair and walk over to the windows. Looking out at the view let him feel less trapped.

'So, Karen what's-her-name kills this thing, and she turns into…'

'You, Mr Hooper. She's just like you.'

His heart was beating hard now. He breathed in and out to try to slow it down.

'Fuck,' he said softly.

Now he understood.

# 26

'I should be getting miles,' said Dave.

The jet was smaller and less luxurious than the last two rides, but it still got him across the continent in half a day.

'To get the miles you have to fly the miles,' said Trinder. 'And I'm sure you'd prefer to avoid coach.'

'You fly coach?'

'I am a humble civil servant, sir.'

'Bullshit.'

He still didn't like Trinder, and he surely didn't trust him, but he was finding him a lot easier to deal with than Heath. He was a helluva lot less judgmental for one thing. He didn't care about Dave flirting with the hostess. Didn't nag him about his nutrition choices. Didn't make him feel bad about any of his choices in fact.

Trinder insisted he fuel up and rest before they descended toward a secured strip at some military base about fifty or sixty miles north of Manhattan, but he didn't much care how Dave saw to that.

'I just want your tank topped up. Plenty of calories in bourbon,' he said, patting his own stomach where it rolled over his belt. 'If that works, good luck to you, sir. I am envious.'

Dave ate steadily: a couple of steaks, some baked potatoes with sour cream, couple of bowls of mac and cheese, but real gourmet shit, none of that Kraft crap for Super Dave, all washed down with three or four beers. He napped, and landed at the Air National Guard base feeling like he could flip cars.

Two dark-suited agents waited for them next to a black SUV, parked on the tarmac. He recognised them from Vegas. Comeau and the woman. She greeted Trinder and Dave in turn, holding a door open for them.

'Good afternoon, sir. Mr Hooper.'

Oh, yeah, he still had it.

And that was the last they heard from either agent, who both climbed in up front and drove them out of the base and into civilian traffic. The trip into Manhattan took an hour and a half, with the agents occasionally using a siren and flashers to manoeuvre through traffic that wasn't moving quickly enough for them. Trinder used the time to go over the briefing he'd given Dave in the plane. Pictures of Karen Warat–quite the blonde Russian babe-bushka. Plans and pictures of the Russian consulate where she was almost certainly holed up.

'She should have gone to a safe house, but I guess she was a little freaked out.'

Dave recalled his own encounter with Urgon on the Longreach.

'A little, you reckon? Did she pass out after killing it?'

'No,' said Trinder. 'Not even for a moment. But the… transformation was immediate. The agents on site described an opponent with unusual strength and speed. She put three of them down. Wiped off a jolt from a taser, just plucked out the prongs. And the… ah… the weapon she used to kill the demon?'

'Yes?' Dave asked, wondering where this was headed.

'It was a sword. She dropped it after taking the head off. One of our men tried to pick it up.'

'And he couldn't?'

'Oh no, he could. But his arm fell off. As though cut through.'

Dave looked at him without speaking for a few seconds.

'You didn't mention that before I signed on.'

'I've mentioned it now. Perhaps it won't affect you?'

'Perhaps?'

'She retrieved the sword. We don't need you to pick it up.'

Trinder showed him a pair of open palms, to prove he wasn't hiding anymore. 'We're in uncharted waters, Mr Hooper. You probably understand more about this woman and what she can do than we do.'

It was Trinder's turn to stare at him, waiting for an answer. But Dave found he didn't have one.

'Nope,' he said, after consulting Urgon. 'I got nothing.'

They were coming up on a bridge that would carry them across to the island.

'So this chick, she was like you guys, a trained killer, right?'

'Even more so. I am not a field operator, Mr Hooper.'

Trinder pursed his lips as if pondering something that had only just occurred to him.

'She would have had advanced combat training, judo, jujitsu, *krav maga* and the like. But she was also...' he frowned. 'She was not an amateur with a sword, Mr Hooper?'

Dave had been looking out of the window at the skyline of Manhattan. 'What?' he asked, turning his attention back to Trinder.

'Our work up on Colonel Varatchevsky indicates she was recruited to the GRU from an old Soviet-era Olympic program.

One that survived into the Putin administration and–'

Dave cut him off. 'I don't need the whole history lesson. Just get to the bit I'm not gonna like.'

'She was an Olympic fencer. Or a trainee at least. Talent-spotted at an early age and taken up into the training cohort for the games in Sydney. But she didn't make it. Her parents died and she disappeared from the program and from public view until we found her living under the name Warat in New York. She was a sleeper. Do you know what that means?'

'I watch TV,' Dave said, losing patience. 'And I don't care about that. What I do care about is going up against some woman who could've kicked my ass *before* she got bumped up to superhero status, *with* a magical sword, *that* she knows how to use.'

He found himself tightening his grip on Lucille, but she was strangely silent, seeming not to care about whatever fight he was speeding toward.

And they were speeding now. The mid-afternoon traffic was surprisingly light, but he already knew why. As soon as they'd left the airbase they'd passed long lines of cars queued up for gasoline.

'They rationing anything but gas here?' he asked, partly to avoid thinking about what Trinder was expecting of him and whether there might be any more surprises on the way to doing it.

'Not quite the same when you're not partying with the A-List, is it?' said Trinder with a nasty smirk.

'Fuck off.'

'For what it's worth, yes. The governor and the state house agreed on a package of emergency measures when it became obvious the transport system was going to seize up.

Food rationing mostly. They haven't had to manage the power grid yet and we're confident we can contain the threat to the interstate...'

'Whatever,' said Dave, who realised he'd had very little contact with the real world since this whole thing started. He wondered if Annie and the boys were okay and dismissed the thought almost as soon as he had it. Her old man had a root cellar full of preserves and emergency supplies. That was his way. He also realised he hadn't really thought of them much since New Orleans and wondered if Trinder would object to him calling his sons at least. But then Boylan wouldn't want him talking to Annie, so maybe he was better off just leaving it.

Dave let his gaze drift out the windows again. He didn't know New York as well as the oil towns he'd worked out of since graduating. Houston. Galveston. Even Riyadh. It was hard to tell, as they rolled down some riverside expressway, how the city was dealing with the emergency. Everything was open. There were long lines here and there. But that could have been for theatre or Yankees tickets he supposed. As Comeau, the driver, took them into the city proper he saw newspaper displays crying out the news of the day and the week. 'Monsters Crushed in Nebraska.' 'The Second Battle of Britain.' 'Take That, Mordor!'

He even thought he caught sight of a picture of himself sitting across from Jen Aniston in LA on some trash mag poster outside a Duane Reade drugstore. 'Jen's New Superman?' But the Surburban flashed past too quickly for him to be sure. It seemed way too soon after meeting her for anything to have made it into print.

Trinder said they were getting close when the northern end of Central Park appeared ahead through the traffic.

'We have an observation post in the same street as the Russians,' he explained. 'We'll head there now and you can prepare for the extraction.'

'So you want me to bring her out?' Dave asked.

'If at all possible,' said Trinder. 'If not, you are authorised to use deadly force.'

'Me? Against her?' Dave scoffed.

Trinder sighed.

'Mr Hooper. The beast you put down was at least two and a half times as large as the one Colonel Varatchevsky killed. And she was just mopping up. She evaded the FBI in the chaos of the moment, but she was obviously disoriented otherwise she would not have fled to her handlers at the consulate mere days after going dark. She is not that poor an agent. I have seen you operate, sir. At minimal power. I am confident you can take her. Just as confident as I am that nobody else can. You do what you did in Las Vegas, Mr Hooper. You speed in and out and nobody will be any the wiser. Take your lady friend with you, by all means, if that helps.' He nodded to where the hardwood shaft of the splitting maul stuck up between Dave's knees. 'And if the worst comes to the worst and you have to kill the Russian, you do it. You have been authorised to do so at the highest levels. We cannot have this woman loose on American soil.'

'Then let her go home,' said Dave, who wasn't at all sure he wanted to tangle with this bitch. Was there even a chance Trinder was hoping they'd cancel each other out?

'That is not an option,' Trinder replied in a voice that allowed no contradiction. 'She was going to be captured before all this happened. She will be captured or killed now. But if you are able to effect the capture, sir, the chances of a lot of other people being killed in the process, Russians and Americans and all of these innocent bystanders...' He waved out of the window at crowds on Fifth Avenue. 'I guarantee you the chances of them being killed will be immeasurably reduced.'

For a second Dave wondered what Heath would say under these circumstances. But he already knew. Heath would never have put him in this position.

He rubbed one calloused thumb over the butt of Lucille's handle. Nothing there. If she cared a jot for what he was supposed to do, she was keeping quiet about it.

The SUV mounted a driveway and descended into an underground lot. The bright afternoon light disappeared as if turned off at a switch. The door rumbled down behind them and the SUV came to a stop next to a late-model sedan. The agents who'd driven them hopped out quickly and opened the doors for Trinder and Dave. He stretched the kinks out of his back as he hopped out. Another agent, a conservatively dressed man, appeared and passed a folder of documents to Trinder.

'No change, sir.'

Trinder nodded and started walking toward an old elevator, leaving Dave to follow him.

Dave Hooper fetched Lucille and hastened after them. They rode the elevator up three floors and emerged into a simple hallway. Polished parquetry floors. Closed doors, frosted glass, everything secured by swipe-card readers. Feeling surplus to requirements, Dave waited to gain admittance. He was disappointed to discover the office on the far side of the locked door was just an office. It could have been processing insurance claims or managing exploration certificates for Baron's.

'This way,' said Trinder, leading him between the desks and into a conference room. Floor plans of the consulate lay unfolded on the table. Photographs of what Dave assumed were the building's interior hung from pin boards around the walls. Trinder motioned for him to sit in front of a wide-screen TV. He turned it on with a remote.

'We've used architects' software to render a faithful recreation of the internals of the building,' Trinder explained. 'You have three hours before they finish business for the day. Best familiarise yourself with the layout. We surmise Colonel Varatchevsky will be somewhere on the top floor. The windows up there are covered over and much stronger active electronic countermeasures are employed against our surveillance. And yes, in case you were wondering and before you ask, they do know we're here and they do know we have them under constant observation. It's just the game.'

Dave took up what looked like an Xbox controller–no, it was an Xbox controller– and pushed the stick forward. His point of view on-screen moved through the foyer of the Russian building.

'But grabbing one of their agents right out from under them, that's not part of the game is it.'

It was a statement, not a question.

'No, sir, it is not. And we would not attempt such a thing if it weren't a matter of paramount importance.'

'And if I wasn't here.'

'That goes without saying.'

Trinder pulled up a chair next to Dave.

'Look. I understand this is a lot to take in. But you've coped with a lot more the last week. And what we need you to do here, it's directly connected to what happened on your rig, in New Orleans and at Omaha. If it weren't for the Horde, Colonel Varatchevsky would now be in custody, charged with espionage. Maybe with treason.'

'Treason? She's Russian.'

He shrugged.

'She has American citizenship. I told you. She was a sleeper. But she has run back to the Rodina now, and no matter what happens with the creatures who created her, she cannot be allowed to escape this country. Not given what she has become. Somebody with her training, her experience, and now these... abilities. It is not feasible to allow her back into the wild. She was always a weapon, Hooper. Now she is an infinitely more dangerous one. She cannot be allowed to escape. Do you understand this? Think of what you can do now. Think of that power in the hands of a hostile government, and make no mistake, Putin's Russia is intractably hostile to this country.'

'You sound like Bush,' said Dave. 'When he talked my brother into getting killed.'

Trinder examined him carefully. Nodding.

'I probably do, sir. Your brother was killed in Iraq, was he not?'

Dave bristled. 'He was.'

'This woman,' said Trinder. 'She's dangerous. But in a different way. Not just because of what she's become, but because of what she was before.'

'*Dar ienamic*,' said Dave in the Olde Tongue.

'Say what?'

'Don't worry.' He settled himself in front of the screen. 'Don't worry, Trinder. I'll go get your lady spy for you. Hell, I might be able to charm her into giving it up. I do that now.'

'So I noticed. Agent Madigan appeared to have quite an attack of vapours around you.'

The chick in the Suburban? She'd hidden it well.

'But just so we're clear, Trinder. I'm saying yes now.

Doesn't mean I'll always say so. Don't come to me with a laundry list of shit jobs you need done, or shit *people* you need done. I'm not your hired killer, or your step-n-fetch-it bitch. If you got a monster problem, yeah, okay, I'll be your very own ghostbuster. Otherwise, you better send Nikita or 007.'

'Fair enough,' said Trinder.

# 27

The Diwan dar Sliveen ur Grymm joined them in Guyuk's private chambers. She expected to find the Marshals Select in attendance but Lord Commander Guyuk had already dismissed them to their duties. Only Guyuk and his little Thresh were present. Or Threshrend now, she supposed, to pay the creature its due. After all who was she to question the judgment of the lord commander in elevating the daemon inferiorae to his new exalted status.

'Yo bitch! Threshy's been embiggened!'

Who indeed?

'Threshrend, please, some respect for the Diwan.'

The tiny empath grinned so widely she could see the fresh meat still trapped in its fang tracks.

'I'm on it, boss. Respect to the Diwan. She be a sexy biatch and I am all over that like a cheap suit. Er, made of skin. A cheap suit made of human skin,' he said, and bowed to her. The Diwan dar Sliveen regarded the creature with some curiosity, examining it the way she might a particularly difficult rune cast or one of the more arcane Seer Stone readings from the older scrolls. She had from the Masters Scolari not merely an explanation of the process by which the Thresh had consumed the cranial sweetmeats and thinkings of the captured calflings, but the latest thinkings of the Consilium itself as regards their understanding of the processes and magicks involved. She could sense some of the empath's power emanating from the creature which now referred to itself as Compt'n ur Threshrend, but the rites of the Threshrendum and the Diwanae were not entirely sympathetic disciplines. She could not read it. She did wonder if it could read her.

'Indulge the creature in its eccentricities, my Lord. It fascinates me. These are interesting times and the Sanctum Diwanae would learn as much as we might of man and his thinkings.'

'I thank you for your indulgence, your Worship,' said Guyuk.

'I think she likes me,' said Compt'n in an exaggerated whisper. 'You think she'd ever date a Threshrend? She's kind of hot in a Cate Blanchett sexy vampire way.'

Lord Guyuk shook his great armoured head and rolled his yellow, slitted eyes toward the rough-hewn stone of the chamber roof.

'He has been like this since he ate the human Scolari,' Guyuk explained. 'Much less... diffident.'

'So the cattle have their own Scolari?' the Diwan asked. The Masters of the Scolari Grymm had not thought to mention as much.

'Not many with my mad thinking skills,' boasted the Threshrend while it scooped freshly peeled urmin eggs and fried insectivore from bowls that Guyuk's personal attendants had laid out for his guests.

'Threshrend!' Guyuk barked. 'Attend to your masters and restrain the worst of your base calfling urges lest I crush them from you with my very claws.'

Startled, the Threshrend jumped and went rigid with the congenital terror that flickered still in some remnant of itself beneath all the layers of human infection.

'Yes, my Lord,' it said, and for just that one moment the Diwan could see the small, frightened daemon inferiorae at the centre of this bizarre psychic mutant. And then it was gone again. And Compt'n ur Threshrend was back.

'My bad, sorry. Guess we should play through the tutorial and get on with the missions, right?'

The Diwan looked to Lord Guyuk. The lord commander sat atop an old and favoured rock, its surface worn smooth and contoured to his hind quarters.

'That would be excellent, Threshrend. We must not delay the Diwan from her stations.'

'What would you have of me, my Lord Commander?' she asked.

'A family-sized bag of Sliveen McNuggets,' the Threshrend answered out of turn.

'What?'

Her tone was cold. The creature, or amalgam of creatures she supposed, was indeed fascinating. But the Diwan dar Sliveen ur Grymm was used to a reflexive respect bordering on natural-born terror, and this… this thing seemed incapable of paying her the respect she was due.

'Threshrend!'

'Sorry!'

Guyuk levered himself up from his rock and shuffled over to the granite slab, which offered a fine spread of delicacies. Besides the urmin eggs and crunchy insectivore skins which the Threshrend seemed intent on eating all by itself there were trenchers of slow-roasted Drakon tail, long strings of blood pudding, Black Shuck pies, Chupacabra on skewers, and what looked like a plate of jellied worms but which on closer inspection turned out to be hundreds of the soft little digits that humans had instead of claws. They had been pre-chewed and part-digested by the lord commander's own master of the blood pots, then regurgitated fresh onto the huge iron plate stamped with the crest of his former regiment.

'Finger food,' said Comtp'n ur Threshrend when he saw her looking at the unique treat. 'It's awesome. You should try some.'

The Diwan demurred, but Guyuk picked at the light refreshments.

'Worship,' he said, 'we have need of your finest. And not just a band, but a full talon of them.'

'I see,' she said quietly.

'No,' quipped the Threshrend. 'We'll all see, once you've eaten their braaaaainz.'

The Diwan ignored the tiny empath daemon which now appeared to be shaking with laughter. It was, she had decided, not far from the grey lands of madness. The minds it now contained, the alien reasoning through which it must by necessity filter its own thinkings, had disordered the thing, pushed it toward insanity. And yet did not the scrolls speak of the wisdom of seers which manifested in seemingly mad and tortured visions?

Yes. Yes they did.

'And to what ends would a full talon of my finest be put to the sacrifice, my Lord?'

She half expected the Threshrend to answer but it was too busy stuffing an entire string of blood pudding into its maw.

'Compt'n ur Threshrend and I have deliberated at some length, Worship,' Lord Guyuk explained. 'When Thresh took the thinkings of the captured human warriors we were gifted with some insight into the horrifying capabilities these creatures have developed during our banishment from the Above.'

'The Masters Scolari caution their magicks are indeed strong,' she conceded.

Guyuk grunted dismissively. Not at her, but at the warnings of the Scolari.

'Pah! The masters cannot bring themselves to admit there are no magicks. No human magicks at least. They have not changed that much. What they calls magicks men know as their learnings, no more arcane than the curriculae of the Gnarrl. They are no arcanists, Worship. They are merely engineers. But if it aids comprehension to think of their power as magicks, then do so. Threshrend here,' Lord Guyuk waved a claw at the little daemon who waved back with a length of fire-grilled Drakon tail, 'was much better able to explain exactly what befell Scaroth and the Queen's Vengeance in the village of New Orleans after he had taken up the thinkings of the captured human warriors.'

Hard to believe, thought the Diwan, controlling her disgust as half-chewed chunks of Drakon meat and cartilage flew everywhere.

Lord Guyuk, who seemed to have reconciled himself to the creature's baffling manners, pressed on, as though the floor of his chamber was not being buried in scraps of food.

'The human Horde is not to be trifled with, Worship. We have seen as much more than once now. Indeed your finest have assisted us to that understanding. The other sects remain wilfully ignorant of the great and terrible changes come upon the Above, and this, I believe, affords us the chance, if seized, to defeat both humankind and our traditional *ienamicae*.'

'Defeat humankind, Lord Commander?'

The Diwan could not keep the scepticism from her voice.

'You speak of them as though they were true *ienamic*, not food.'

'You ever seen a regiment get owned by a fucking cheeseburger?' said Compt'n ur Threshrend, pausing in his gluttony. 'Oh, yes, you have. Remember when those Djinn motherfuckers got smacked down by a bunch of fucking calflings.'

'Threshrend,' growled Guyuk. 'You overstep yourself.'

'Yep, sorry. Shutting up.'

'Your plan, Lord Commander?' said the Diwan.

'My plan really.'

'Threshrend!'

Lord Guyuk picked up the tiny empath and carried him to a corner of the receiving chamber. As he passed along the banquet table he also lifted up a whole roasted leg of man meat, depositing both in one corner.

'Sit and eat. Do not speak again.'

Compt'n ur Threshrend went 'oof', once as he landed on his tail bone, and again when Guyuk jabbed him in the guts with the heavy end of the broiled leg. He was happy enough to sit and feed himself as the higher-ups discussed their plans. Or his plans, really. Probably better this way. For all of the clarity and insight which had come on him when he finally got some decent brains into him, he couldn't shake the influence of that first dumbass he'd scarfed up.

Trevor the doughnut-eating fiend.

It seemed it didn't matter how many fucking head-melons from how many professors and black ops ninjas he cracked open and sucked down, he was stuck with Trevor. Fucking mind like Einstein, he had now. If Einstein had been a badass navy SEAL. But every time he opened his jaws he came off like Beavis or fucking Butthead. Whichever was dumber.

Compt'n ur Threshrend unhinged his lower jaw and jammed half the fucking leg in there, just to stop himself running off at the mouth.

'The Threshrend, speaking as my Pro-Consul and Adept of War, Scolari Compt'n, advises that even the combined forces of the Grande Horde arrayed in Dread Order would not be enough to best even the modest forces of a middling human sect,' Guyuk told the Diwan.

Credit to the bitch, she didn't get all snippy like those Grymm motherfuckers before. Didn't hardly say or do nothing. She just stared at Guyuk all frosty and shit, waiting on the explanation.

'This is not to say the human Horde is invulnerable however. As an Adept of War, the one called Compt'n was himself responsible for adapting the tactics of the greatest human war sect when they were beset and laid low in battle by lesser clans hardly worthy of the name.'

*You got that right,* Compt'n ur Threshrend snarled to himself.

The Diwan looked at him again, as he stripped the last of the soft thigh meat from the upper bones of the roasted leg. Compt'n could feel the bitch pressing at his mind, trying to feel out the contours of his thinkings, but she was a seer, not an empath, and he easily held off her attempts to read him– wondering again whether he might have her thinkings as he'd taken those of the calflings.

Guyuk ripped off a small piece of blood pudding and gnawed at it while he thought.

'The Threshrend, again speaking with the knowledge of the adept he consumed, advises that wherever the Horde or any of its clans might mass for battle, they will be destroyed, just as the Djinn were. And just as other clans have been at our connivance this last turning.'

That got the Diwan's attention. She tried to play it cool, but Threshy could tell ol' Guyuk had really goosed her with that one.

'I have not seen this, my Lord.'

'I did not ask it of you, Worship. Again, it was a suggestion of Compt'n ur Threshrend and one I wished to test before involving you or my Marshals Select. All of the sects now know of the breach in the capstone between the realms. Some of them pushed through of their own volition. Others did the same, encouraged through the effort of my own spies and provocateurs long emplaced within their war councils.'

'And what of the *Sectum Ienamicae*, my Lord. How stand their forces in the Above?'

The Threshrend, having finished eating, and feeling kind of stuffed, belched enormously and threw aside the last of the leg roast.

'They don't stand at all,' he said. 'They got knocked on their asses.'

'All of them?' she asked Guyuk, ignoring Compt'n.

'The Djinn, Morphum and Skarr'ash all lost entire regiments. The First Legion of the Gorgon, the Second of the Toth, annihilated. Smaller sects and clans lost smaller formations. The Churel did best of all, but again Threshrend predicted it would be so. The Churel emerged into their traditional feeding grounds, a mountainous region where it is all but impossible to mass great forces. Even so, while not destroyed, they were repelled by those human clans which now control the area.'

'Tribes,' Compt'n ur Threshrend corrected. 'Not even clans. Just motherfucking tribes.'

Again the Sliveen Seer did not protest the news, or try to deny it as the Marshals Grymm had done at first. She took a moment to digest the information before asking another question.

'And what of daemonum minorae and roninum?'

'They also spill through into the Above,' said Guyuk, 'but not in any organised fashion, of course. The filthy Tümorum have already spread throughout the rift thanks to the Djinn. And of course, *dar Drakon* too.'

'Burning light! And what of them?'

'Toast,' said Compt'n with an evil grin. Although, when your mouth is three feet of fang track, it's hard not to look like a scary motherfucker when all you're really doing is smiling.

The Diwan's facade seemed to slip and she lowered herself down on Guyuk's favourite rock, her petite backside taking up only a quarter of the groove worn into the dark basalt over the centuries by his butt cheeks.

'It vexes me still that the calflings can bring down *dar Drakon.*' she said.

'From such distances with such speed and surprise that the great beasts have no warning,' Guyuk said, almost sadly.

'And the calflings do all this with... engineering? Like mere Gnarrl mechanics?'

'Indeed, Worship.'

She seemed to lose herself in her own thoughts for a

moment and when she finally returned it was Compt'n ur Threshrend to whom she spoke.

'And what say you, Pro-Consul and Adept of War? How are we to contend with this foe? How are any of the Horde?'

Threshy was so full of hot meat and smug satisfaction it was all he could do to lever himself up from the floor where Guyuk had deposited him.

'No problemo,' he grunted, almost groaned really. 'I got a plan to beat these motherfuckers like a drum. And to put every other sect under the fucking yoke while we do it. Wanna know how?'

'Yes, Adept,' she said quietly. 'I would.'

'Adept of War, eh?' said Compt'n ur Threshrend. 'A bit of respect from the maximum hottie, after all? I like it. Sounds cool. So, let me tell you a story. About how the most powerful of all the human sects kept getting their asses handed to them, over and over. By a bunch of busted-ass motherfuckers who made the dumbest Hunn look like Sun fucking Tzu.'

'And who is this Sun Fuck'ng Tzu?' asked the Diwan dar Sliveen ur Grymm.

'Oh, him? He was a badass. Just like me. And he knew the last thing you want to do with a heavyweight is get into a stand-up punching competition. No. What you wanna do with a heavyweight is sweep his fucking legs out from under him. And when he goes down and he's wondering what the fuck happened? You stomp his brains out.'

Compt'n ur Threshrend did a stompy little dance, just to demonstrate.

'That's what we gonna do,' he promised. 'No more standing round in a fucking kill box like idiots. Fuck honour and tradition. No, we're gonna get Tet on these motherfuckers.

We gonna bring the jihad and the motherfucking intifada. We gonna hit 'em where they think they strongest. We gonna show them just how weak they are. We gonna eat their fucking cities from the inside. Man gonna learn to respect the monster again.'

# 28

At 5.59 pm Dave Hooper winked out of existence.

He had been standing in the underground garage where the agents had delivered them to the building on E91st Street, holding Lucille, dressed in black coveralls, feeling like a bit of a dick. The OSCAR people had insisted on the outfit. They'd insisted on him carrying a pistol too, but he dropped that to the ground as soon as he could. As soon as he warped.

Dave was not comfortable with guns. He didn't like them. Didn't understand them. Unlike his brother Andy, he had no real experience with them. Better to just leave them out of the picture. This Karen Warat-Varatchevsky chick, he was sure, would have hundreds, maybe thousands of hours practice with all sorts of guns. He didn't imagine he'd be able to match her in a shoot-out. He did keep the long-bladed knife strapped to his leg. As an occasional fisherman and camper he was more familiar and comfortable with a good workman's blade. He didn't imagine for a second he'd be able to cut another human being with it, though. Truth be told, he'd have been more comfortable with something like a Leatherman multitool. He could see it being more useful in a tight fix.

Lucille remained quiet.

In the other pockets of his coveralls Dave carried energy bars and gels and a couple of sets of flex cuffs. He'd eaten some more protein bars while he'd played with the virtual tour of the Russian consulate, and a packet of M&Ms because the protein bars didn't taste that great. Trinder was still wishing him good luck as Dave hit the accelerator into warp speed.

The more he used the ability, the more he learned about it. For one thing, it had nothing to do with his own subjective speed. He didn't need to run or sprint or even jog away from the OSCAR agents. He just needed to step into the *slipstream* as he now thought of it. He could stroll up E91st, but he would pass by the pedestrians and traffic, all but frozen in the moment of his acceleration, like a barely perceptible blur at the edge of their vision. He did wonder if they would notice the wind of his passage, but had begun to doubt it. Maybe he should ask, one day.

The gun he'd dropped to the floor back in the garage was still falling slowly, slowly, slowly through the air as he mounted the front steps of the consulate and slipped around a couple of visitors who were exiting moments before the front doors closed for the day. His pulse quickened and he had to swallow against a dry mouth, but that was just nerves. He put them aside.

The entrance to the grand old building, he was pleased to see, was exactly as he had experienced it in the walk-through on-screen. But then, if OSCAR couldn't get that right, he was in trouble, wasn't he. One security guard was caught mid-stride as he crossed the foyer, his eyes locked on a door which stood open. Trinder had told him to expect this. They had an asset in the consulate they were willing to burn to give Dave this small leg-up. Had the door not been open, he could have smashed his way through with Lucille, but that would have been the end of any hope he had of carrying off this caper without being noticed. Dave slipped past the open door, winked at the pretty young woman who was holding it open–Trinder's burned asset, he supposed–and walked through into the secured area where the daily business of the consulate's dealings with the city outside took place. It was still busy, with clerical workers and diplomatic staff tidying their desks, filing away the day's papers, catching up on emails, making last-minute phone calls and so on, the familiar shutdown routines of any office.

Dave took a moment to breathe deeply and concentrate on the slipstream. Without speeding up, without hurrying across the office at a run, he found he was able to 'tap the gas' and increase his warp speed from–What? Three to four? Warp four to five? He didn't know, but he could tell he'd done it. The stasis in which everyone around him was trapped seemed to deepen and become more profound. The background hum of the building and the city beyond it noticeably slowed and deepened. He rolled his shoulders to loosen up and hefted Lucille into a comfortable two-handed grip. She remained quiescent. Uninterested.

Something was bothering him. He looked around and his eye passed over the girl at the door. The door the security guard in the entry hall had been headed toward. Was she really gonna get burned for letting him in? He didn't like the idea, or the casual way Trinder had mentioned it. Pressing the warp button again he carefully picked her up and carried her out of the building to the far side of the street. It'd put the zap on her head when she came to, but she'd at least have a chance of getting away.

With his conscience settled he hurried back inside, running up the steps this time, even though nothing had changed. Unable to use the elevators Dave called up his mental map of the ground floor and followed his memory into a corridor which led to the rear of the building where he found a rather grand-looking stairwell. It was guarded by two uniformed men wearing sidearms, but they were as deeply glazed as everyone else. He stopped at the foot of the stairs and listened intently for any sound of movement above him. Neither he nor Trinder had any idea whether Varatchevsky would be caught up in the warp effect, or whether she could travel through the slipstream like Dave. The OSCAR and FBI agents who'd attempted to take her during the aborted raid described her escaping them at 'inhuman speed' but that didn't mean she was slipstreaming. After all, they'd been able to see her, even if she was just a blur. When Dave put the pedal to the metal, everyone who'd seen it said it was like he simply disappeared. Maybe zipping away like the Roadrunner was the extent of her ability? Maybe, like him at first, she had been unaware of what she could do. He had no idea. She could be frozen in aspic in a room upstairs. She could be waiting for him on the next landing with a magical sword or, even worse, a submachine gun.

Dave stopped climbing, frowning again. Would a gun even work in the slipstream? Again, no fucking idea. Those snipers in Omaha had been able to fire on the Djinn, and the Djinn's archers had fired back, but he hadn't gone to full warp then. He hadn't even really understood it. Still didn't. A gun was a mechanical device just like an elevator, so maybe he should assume it wouldn't work in full warp. Then again, it was a relatively small piece of handheld machinery. Maybe that would make a difference? Maybe it could get dragged into the slipstream.

The only way to know was to find out. He started up the stairs again. They creaked underfoot and his heart jumped, before he smiled nervously at himself. It wasn't like he had to hide from the two guards, or the other spies who doubtless worked in this building. When he stopped and thought about it, as he did now on the turn of the stairwell, there were only two possible ways this could turn out. Either she was already frozen and he could just throw her over his shoulder and carry her out like he had the other girl. Or she was not, but everybody around her was, and in that case she damn well knew he was coming. Or something was. She'd had just as long as Dave to get used to their changed circumstances, and even though Trinder was certain she'd been hiding in this building, probably until the Russians figured out what to do, she would not have been completely cut off. Hell, she was probably better informed than most about what was going on because she'd have had access to the information resources of the whole Russian government and her own agency. After all she was, as Trinder said, a very senior operator. She'd only run afoul of American counterintelligence because somebody else had fucked up.

Dave paused, his brow furrowed as he tried to think this through. If she knew he was coming, and she had picked up most if not all of the same powers as him, he was in the shit. Unlike him, she *was* a trained killer. She wouldn't hesitate to pull a trigger or put a blade in his throat, and if it got down to trading blows he might find he had no advantage at all. Trinder said she had close combat training. Years of practice and years in the field. What did Dave have? A couple of messy bar fights under his belt, none of them worth bragging about. He swallowed nervously. Took a deep breath. Let it go. And pushed out his Spidey senses. He tried to feel her out within the walls of the building.

Nothing.

No. Of course, there wouldn't be. She wasn't normal. She was totally not normal in the way that he was totally not normal anymore, but she was different in other ways too. Well before the Longreach and Urgon, she probably could have slipstreamed him into a shallow grave before he knew he was dead.

Dave Hooper's testicles tried to crawl up into his body.

Somehow he didn't think he'd be charming Colonel Varatchevsky into bed. He called up a memory of her face. Not the severe-looking headshot from her passport–her *American* passport–or the grainy black and white image Trinder insisted the CIA had accidentally captured of her brushing past a known spy handler at an art show in Berlin a few years ago. He tried to remember her in the happier snaps the FBI had seized from her apartment and searched out via the greatest spy service on the planet: Google. She was anonymously pretty in the way of all fit, healthy blonde women. Her features had none of the hard angularity Dave thought a defining characteristic of women in big cities. They were soft and rounded without being doughy, unlike a lot of suburban women of her age. In his memory she looked like someone who could have traded on her looks, but had grown past that some unknown time ago. Her eyes were bright and round. Her smile warm. It was hard to think of her as being the sort of danger to him or anyone that Trinder had described.

He made a decision.

'*Karen*,' he called out, using the American pronunciation of her name, the name by which she'd been known most of her adult life. He stepped onto the second floor of the consulate. It reminded him of an upscale hotel, some place that specialised in wedding receptions. The corridors were painted off white and bright chandeliers twinkled from the high plaster ceilings. Striking floral arrangements stood in two jars halfway down the hallway. They seemed to be standing too far away from the wall. As if someone had started to move them, but then walked away with the job undone.

'Karen Warat?' he cried out again. 'My name is Dave Hooper. I'll guess you know who I am. They sent me in here to get you. But if you can hear me, perhaps we could just talk ab–'

He felt Lucille come alive in his hands just before he took the full force of the blow from his right. It came out of a darkened room. He hadn't even noticed it, his eyes drawn to the bright splash of colour where those flower vases were placed so strangely away from the wall. He moved without knowing he'd done so. Or Lucille did. It would be fairer to give her the credit for saving his ass. Or his skull. He wasn't aware of the blade flashing down toward his head until it was far, far too late to turn that awareness into anything useful. Split seconds, long minutes, many, many hours too late. But Lucille, who had remained dormant the whole time he'd been in New York, who hadn't so much as hummed a single note since leaving behind the slaughter in Nebraska, awoke like a small nuke going off in his hands.

Everything was filled with pure white light and the real world seemed to fall away from beneath the soles of his feet, just like a plane hitting an air pocket and dropping thousands of feet in a couple of heartbeats. The splitting maul flew up from the casual position in which he'd been carrying her, as though walking out into the back garden to do a bit of yard work on a slow Sunday afternoon. She flew high and fast, up to the right, toward the glimmer of sharpened steel whistling through the still, suspended air to bite deeply into his neck. Dave resisted Lucille's sudden movement, staggering in the opposite direction, losing his balance and overcompensating for the momentum.

He cried out, feeling all the muscles tear down his right side as he was wrenched this way and that by the violent discontinuity of his own motion. He immediately felt the unpleasant warmth of his flesh repairing itself at an even faster than abnormal rate. At the same moment steel crashed on steel and he squeezed his eyes shut against a shower of hot white and blue sparks that fountained off the maul head and katana blade. Dave was struck another great blow, this time at the base of his rib cage, and he yelled out in pain as he felt ribs shatter and other, softer things tear and shred.

No follow-up attack was possible however, because by then he was flying through space, propelled bodily across the corridor to crash into a wall. Into it, and through it in a dull roar that filled his head before the insane pain of more breaking bones and tearing flesh exploded through him. Dave had the unusual sensation of seeing his attacker–*the woman*–receding from him at great speed, as though he'd been snatched away from her. But he hadn't. She'd just kicked him through a fucking wall!

Everything was bright and hot and then it was dark and hot and, for a half a second that seemed to last longer than every year he'd spent alive, he could see her advancing on him, murder in her eyes, an improbably long sword in one hand. She raised the sword in a practised two-handed grip, shrieking a war cry.

She was dressed like a motorcycle courier, all black leathers, and for a second his mind seized up and he wondered if maybe she was a motorcycle courier and he'd made a terrible mistake, cut her off in traffic, grazed her ride...

'Kiiiiaaaaiiiii.'

Then she was airborne too, but not like he had been. She was leaping and flying and descending on him like a dark angel from the seventh level of the Inferno. And he was reeling and dizzy and losing consciousness, as his body seemed to bake inside his own skin, repairing the terrible damage she'd already done him. And then Lucille was flying again, raised in his hands, but not of his will, and he felt himself pulled forward, and his arms braced against the contact as the heavy steel head jabbed forward and up, into the woman's solar plexus. He heard the air rush out of her body and perhaps the sound of one or two of her ribs breaking just as his had a moment earlier. Without knowing to do it, Dave went with the flow of her energy, leaning back and thrusting up with the maul to throw her over his shoulders as though he were an engineer shovelling coal into an old steam train engine. Her low cry of pain turned into a higher pitched yelp of alarm and surprise as she picked up speed, flying over the top of him and into the room behind them.

He felt Lucille move again and this time he went with her, rolling backward over his shoulder, grimacing as he waited for the pain to surge through his body when the movement ground broken bones and bleeding flesh together. He felt nothing beyond a staggering dizziness and feverish heat. Dave heard the crash as the Russian spy's body hit something.

A heavy oaken desk that looked like a naval museum piece. It splintered under the impact and he felt Lucille pull him forward, felt her raise herself on high for a killing bow, the edged metal of the axe head turned toward Karen Warat for the down stroke.

'Nuh-no,' he grunted, forcing the trajectory of the steel head to waver and veer away from her skull at the last moment. It crashed into the antique table, which exploded under the force of the blow, throwing long wooden shards out in all directions.

Too late. She'd moved anyway. Rolling out from under the line Lucille had tried to describe and away from the uncontrolled, wobbling descent Dave had forced upon the magic weapon by trying to save the woman.

The room suddenly spun around him, and he found himself looking, dumbly, at his own boots as they swept up where his head had been. The ceiling of the office was now beneath him, as though he could walk across the plaster roses embedded up there, while the rich red carpet, now thoroughly ruined, rushed up to meet his head.

'Ughnh.'

He crashed into the floor, vaguely aware she'd somehow swept his legs out from underneath him and now he was looking up at her.

'Stop!' he tried to cry out, feeling weak and stupid for doing so.

But she didn't stop. She raised the sword again and it whistled down at him, aimed to cut him in two. Again, Lucille was there to check the stroke, the steel head jabbing upward and bunting the blade away while Dave felt the base of the maul's handle dig sharply and painfully into his side, knocking him in the opposite direction. It was just enough to move him out of the way of the blade's tip, which dug into the wooden floor.

He felt himself dragged up, as though somebody was pulling him out of a pool or into a boat away from the jaws of a shark. But there was nobody. Only him and Warat and Lucille.

And her sword, of course. He wouldn't want to forget that, because she'd wrenched it from the floorboards and was carving up the air in front of him again. The 400-year-old steel fang bit into air, cleaving it with a hissing whisper that seemed almost to sing in the same note as Lucille. He backed away from it, unsure of his footing, no idea where he was heading, just desperate to get away from the keening song of edged metal.

The woman wasn't even looking at him. She was staring through him as though he wasn't there, or if he was, as though he were simply a door through which she must pass. Dave held the splitting maul in a sort of improvised guard position in front of him. At random times it darted forward and struck the sword from a path he had no hope of anticipating, and no chance of turning with any design for his own safety.

He tried to talk to her, to beg her to stop, but he was panting so hard, and concentrating so furiously on not getting cut, or tripping over the obstacles that littered the floor, that it was impossible. Plus, of course, the woman was a homicidal maniac. Metal clashed and clanged and sparks flew and he felt the impact of every blow run up his arms like electric shocks. He had backed halfway across the office, a large airy space with indirect glimpses up to Central Park, when he bumped into someone and nearly lost balance.

It was a man. Frozen in the world outside the slipstream

where he was fighting for his life against a pretty blonde woman who was doing a better job of trying to kill him than any member of the Horde had yet managed.

He doubled down on his speed, pushing the warp drive out as far as he dared, but she simply came along with him. Lucille continued to jab and parry and occasionally thrust aside slashes and strokes meant to cut him down or hack off one limb or another. The din of it was deafening. Occasionally he even leaped forward, surprising himself, and without a doubt the crazy Russian bitch, with a counter-attack of sorts. In that fashion they had destroyed most of the fine antique furnishings when he bumped into the under-secretary or over-attache or whoever it was he'd frozen on that side of the room. Lucille dragged him off balance and to the left, forcing him down onto one knee. He went with the motion, turning it into a roll to escape the threshing machine of Warat's katana, but nothing stopped her, including her countryman.

Dave gasped and then gagged as the poor bastard flew apart in gross, gory chunks and extravagant blood sprays as the old Japanese sword carved right through him without slowing down. It was like watching a man being fed to a daemonic Cuisinart.

Dave found himself on his feet again, standing unsteadily next to an old wooden globe, one of those massive free-standing numbers you only ever saw in museums or libraries. Lucille swung in his hands, looped around and scooped up the globe, shovelling it into the air where it flew into the sharp steel cloud that floated around Karen Warat. It came apart with a bang, a whole series of them, and he was suddenly dragged forward again by Lucille, who was charging into the gap she had just created by destroying the piece of furniture.

Now it was Dave who advanced, Dave who was shielded by a blurring orbit of heavy metal. Warat gave up ground, falling back in a much more controlled fashion than he had managed, but she did fall back, retreating all the way across the ground she had made up on him before disengaging by jumping backward through the hole he'd made in the wall. He was momentarily stunned by the vision, as though he'd hit rewind on a video player. But Lucille drew him on, never slowing. Indeed she seemed to grow heavier and more massive as they approached the breach in the wall and then punched through it like a wrecking ball. Plaster and wood chips exploded in white clouds all around them and Dave squinted and crouched into the storm of debris. He expected to be ambushed again but saw Warat disappearing down the stairs.

He leaped after her, not thinking. Just following Lucille. She seemed to hold him aloft as he dropped down the stairwell. He landed with a terrible splintering of floorboards beneath his boots. Another convulsive leap and he cleared the last flight of steps landing with another thudding crunch of shattered beams in the hallway leading back to the main office. He charged after Warat, only to find himself sandbagged from the left as she appeared from nowhere and crashed into his flank, where he was protected, yet again, by Lucille suddenly tearing herself around and into a guard position. Dave hit another wall and punched through it, feeling bones dissolve and skin tear, microseconds before the same dull heat of hyper-accelerated healing repaired the damage. He grunted and bit his tongue, tasting hot coppery blood in his mouth, just before a white-hot hand grenade exploded in his chest and he flew up and back again, this time hitting a window which disintegrated around him with a crash of glass and the searing pain of his skin being sliced open.

More heat. More light. More pain as he crunched to earth, this time hitting hard pavement. She had kicked him out of the consulate. Literally kicked him to the kerb. She came at him in a rush, the sword high over her head, in a posture he recognised from old samurai movies. Dave didn't think or act. He didn't do anything. He felt his grip tighten around the lower end of the hardwood shaft. Lucille blurred out like the sweep of a clock hand, and Dave felt the dull metal head slam into the woman's thigh just as she landed ready to strike home the last, lethal blow. Instead he felt, he actually *felt*, her thigh bones disintegrate under the hammer blow. She screamed and flew sideways, hitting the solid brick wall of the building like a bag of wet shit. The sword clattered out of her hands and before Dave even knew he was up on his feet, he'd scampered over and knocked it away with Lucille, mindful of the story Trinder had told him about the FBI guy who lost an arm trying to pick the thing up.

His eyes grew wide as he watched Warat's broken leg straighten and presumably mend itself. That's what it must look like to people when he pulled that sort of shit. But her face remained ashen and she did not climb to her feet or attempt to restart the battle again. She stared at him coldly, wheezing and panting for breath, and he kept his distance, wary of getting too close to a woman who probably knew a dozen different ways to snap his neck.

The street, where the day had darkened toward dusk, remained in stasis. That was interesting then. Time still passed even when nobody moved through it. From the lengthening shadows and deepening twilight it felt close to sundown. Dave carefully reached into one of his pockets and fetched out an energy gel tube. He tossed it to her.

'That faith-healing trick, it tires a body worse than getting kicked through a wall,' he said. 'I've done both today. Dave Hooper,' he added as he she warily bit the cap off the gel tube and sucked greedily at the contents.

He slowly withdrew a protein bar for himself, but didn't take his eyes off her while he ate it. It was crushed into a chocolatey pulp.

He held a hand up, then carefully put Lucille down, and held up the other, as if to signal his surrender.

'I don't fancy going another nine rounds with you, lady. You got my number. If it's all right with you, I'd like to talk about what's been happening. To us, to the rest of the world.'

'You fought well,' she said, still breathless, but recovering. He was taken aback at her broad American accent, perhaps a little more New England than New York, but then he remembered she was a deep cover agent. She'd been here most of her adult life.

'No,' he admitted. 'Lucille fought well. I was just the donkey she rode into battle.'

Karen Warat frowned.

'Lucille?'

'My friend here,' he explained, holding up the splitting maul again. 'Mind of her own. Like yours, I suppose?' he said, nodding to the sword.

He could tell from the look in her eye she knew exactly what he meant.

'You give it a name, yet? That's what seems to power them on. Naming them.'

She looked down the street to where the sword lay on the pavement.

'It had a name already. *Ushi to yasashi to.*'

'Okay?'

'Sorrowful and unbearable,' she explained.

'Catchy.'

'It is from a poem. "I feel the life is, sorrowful and unbearable, though, I can't flee away, since I am not a bird." I didn't name the blade, but I knew the name. It is my job to know.'

Dave sighed in exhaustion and nodded.

'Look. Let's not get off on the wrong foot.'

She smiled at that. A small smile, but an honest one.

'Little late for that, cowboy.'

'Okay. Zing. But let's try again anyway. I know who you are. I know what you are.'

'Back at you. Although I thought you stuck to monster killing, not politics.'

He dropped to one knee, grateful for the pads he wore there. He opened another gel sack and ate it before replying.

'Yeah. I don't much care for politics. I got a feeling that sort of shit might be redundant now. Might even get us all killed.'

She watched him carefully, but said nothing.

'They sent me in to get you, Karen. Is that what you prefer. Karen, not Karin or Ekaterina? I was supposed to bring you out, or bring your body out.'

'Karen,' she answered. 'I'm Karen, in here.' She touched a blooded finger to the side of her head. 'Not such a great first day on the job for you then, Super Dave?'

The way she said that, it didn't sound like she thought him very super at all.

'Not so much, no. But maybe we can turn it around.'

Karen Warat pushed herself into a slightly more

comfortable sitting position and leaned against the walls of the consulate.

'How do you figure that?' she asked.

'Well, I figure if you and I don't kill each other, maybe we could help each other out. Maybe kill a few things desperately need killing. Like the daemon that you put down.'

'A Threshrend daemon,' she said.

'And who told you that?' asked Dave.

'It did. After I killed it.'

It was his turn to nod.

'I thought I was the only one,' he said, as much to himself as to her.

'So did I, for a day or two. Until I saw you in the news out of New Orleans. That was when I knew I had to exfiltrate. Get home.'

It felt weird, listening to that American voice coming out of that pretty American face, talking about getting out of the US to go home. To Russia.

'What are you going to do, Karen? I think we both know I can't stop you.'

'I'm going to kill more Threshrend. And Morphum, and Krevish and Djinn and whatever needs killing I suppose.'

'In Russia.'

'That is my motherland. I am vowed to defend her.'

'Well, I'm supposed to put a bag on you, but I think we can both see that's not going to happen. And you've already figured out I'm not good enough to do that anyway.'

She shrugged noncommittally.

'But do you think you and I could talk for a bit, before you go?'

'About what?'

'All of it. I know some stuff. I killed a Hunn. You must know different stuff. Don't suppose your Threshrend had any idea what the fuck you turned into. What we are?'

She shook her head.

'No.'

'Any idea if there's any more of us?'

'I think there might be twelve,' she said.

He was surprised enough by the answer to make a face which made her laugh.

'Why?'

'Because there are twelve realms. You knew that right? Maybe it's as simple as there being one of us for each realm?'

Dave blinked at her. Stunned.

'I never thought of that. And Urgon sure as shit wouldn't. He's kind of a dumb lug. Like me. So the thresher you killed. Where was it from? Which realm? Or sect or whatever?'

Dave found himself frowning, trying to interrogate Urgon's understanding of UnderRealms geopolitics, but he'd been right. The BattleMaster of the Fourth Legion was kind of a dumbass who only ever thought of rivals to the Horde, all the sects from the other realms, the same way he thought about everything. Crush, kill, destroy.

'Qwm Sect,' she answered simply.

'I'm Dave ur Horde,' he smiled wanly. 'Pleased to meet you, orc-sister.'

'I think we're supposed to be blood enemies, not allies.'

'*Dar ienamic*?'

'Yeah, that's it.'

Dave nodded, mostly to himself, trying to find the energy to take control of this clusterfuck.

'So what do you say we get our bosses to work out some

sort of detente while we get a few things straight.'

The smile disappeared from her eyes.

'Your bosses want me dead.'

'Yeah, well, they're not gonna be real happy with me either. Come on. Worth a try. You can always just warp out if it doesn't take.'

'Warp out? You mean, like this?' She gestured around them, taking in the frozen city.

'Yeah.' He knitted his brows. 'I've never held it as long as this.'

'Nor I,' she agreed.

'So you can warp on your own?'

'Not like this. This is you.'

'Huh. I don't get it. I thought you did this. Look, we got stuff to talk about, Karen, but we're going to need to chill some folk the fuck out first.'

She grimaced.

'I will need to explain why the third secretary is in so many pieces now.'

'And I need to prepare Trinder for disappointment. At least he's still in one piece. Can we agree to meet in an hour? And if shit gets out of hand, we go to warp and catch up and talk to each other without starting a war this time?'

She eyed him as though weighing up the potential downsides.

'An hour,' she agreed.

But an hour later, the city was already at war.

# ACKNOWLEDGEMENTS

Who to thank first? *Dr Who*, I think. It drove me nuts as a kid that guns seemed to have no effect at all on monsters. Like, why did Brigadier Lethbridge-Stewart and UNIT even bother? The Dave Hooper series is an attempt, in part, to rectify that.

I'd also like to thank the producers of *Reign of Fire*, who annoyed me greatly with movie posters promising all sorts of dragon vs helicopter gunship awesomeness. And failed to deliver.

Less flippantly I have to thank my ur Champion publishers Cate Paterson, Tricia Narwani, Haylee Nash, Deonie Fiford and the incomparable Alex Lloyd who all took up sword and shield with me on this long, strange quest. To their efforts add the sage advice of BattleMarshal S.M. ur Stirling, who helped me out of a difficult tactical conundrum.

To my wizardly agent, Russ ur Galen dar SGG, I offer tribute from the highest blood pot.

And for my armsman, SF Murphy, acknowledgement of his skill with blades and fire staff. His *gurikh* is second to none.

Finally, for my nestlings, Jane, Anna and Thomas... You are my Realm.

# ABOUT THE AUTHOR

John Birmingham is the author of the cult classic *He Died With a Falafel in His Hand*; the award-winning history *Leviathan*; the Axis of Time series: *Weapons of Choice, Designated Targets* and *Final Impact,* and the *Stalin's Hammer: Rome* ebook; and the Disappearance trilogy: *Without Warning, After America* and *Angels of Vengeance.*

Between writing books he contributes to a wide range of newspapers and magazines on topics as diverse as the future of media and national security. Before becoming a writer he began his working life as a research officer with the Defence Department's Office of Special Clearances and Records.

You can find John at his blog, http://cheeseburgergothic. com and on Twitter @johnbirmingham. You can also buy his books at johnbirmingham.net.

Want to save the world? Join the conversation on Twitter at #TheDave.

# DAVE VS. THE MONSTERS

## ASCENDANCE

### BY JOHN BIRMINGHAM

As a hardworking monster-slayer, Dave Hooper tries not to bring his work home with him. But nowadays it's hard to keep them separate. Email, cellphones, empath daemons, they never let a guy rest.

The Horde has been raising hell and leveling cities from New York to Los Angeles, keeping Dave and his fellow monster-killer, Russian spy Karin Varatschevsky, very busy. But when the legions of hell invade the small seaside town his boys call home, Dave has to make a call. Save the world? Or save his family?

Not as easy a choice as you'd think, since Dave's ex-wife expects to be saved too. And there's no convincing her that the supersexy Russian spy isn't his girlfriend. She's just his sidekick—and an assassin.

### AVAILABLE JUNE 2015

# DAVE VS. THE MONSTERS

## EMERGENCE

### BY JOHN BIRMINGHAM

When an oil rig off the Gulf of Mexico digs too deep, a torrent of nightmares is unleashed—the creatures of legend, always thought to be figments of our imagination, are now a very real threat to the survival of humankind.

Safety worker Dave Hooper has the hangover from hell, and the last thing he needs is an explosion on his rig. But this is no accident, and despite the news reports, terrorists aren't to blame for the carnage. The rig is swarming with monsters.

As he fights to save his co-workers from the ravenous demon horde while holding down last night's tequila, Dave is suddenly transformed from a foul-mouthed, overweight, booze-soaked slacker into something else entirely. An honest-to-goddamn monster slayer.

# WITHOUT WARNING

## BY JOHN BIRMINGHAM

March 14, 2003. In Kuwait, American forces are locked and loaded for the invasion of Iraq. In Paris, a covert agent is close to cracking a terrorist cell. And just north of the equator, a sailboat manned by a drug runner and a pirate is witness to the unspeakable.

In one instant, all around the world, everything will change. A wave of inexplicable energy slams into the continental United States. America as we know it vanishes. As certain corners of the globe erupt in celebration, others descend into chaos, and a new, soul-shattering reality is born.

# AFTER AMERICA

## BY JOHN BIRMINGHAM

On March 14, 2003, the world changed forever. A wave of energy
slammed into North America and devastated the continent.
The U.S. military, poised to invade Baghdad, was left without a
commander in chief. Global order spiralled into chaos.

Now, while a skeleton U.S. government tries to reconstruct the
nation, swarms of pirates and foreign militias plunder the lawless
wasteland of the East Coast, where even the president is fair prey.
With New York clutched in the grip of thousands of heavily armed
predators, is an all-out attack on the city the only way to save it?

# ANGELS OF VENGEANCE

## BY JOHN BIRMINGHAM

When an inexplicable wave of energy slammed into North America, millions died. Around the globe, wars erupted, borders vanished and a new reality was born.

From shattered streets to gleaming new cities, three women are fighting wars of their own—for survival, justice and revenge. In South America, a special agent trails a ruthless terrorist, in Texas, a teenager vows to avenge a brutal murder and in Australia, a smuggler is hunted by unknown assassins. As a conflicted U.S. president struggles to make momentous decisions in the face of rebellion, the final battle for America and the new world begins.

For more fantastic fiction, author events, exclusive excerpts, competitions, limited editions and more:

**VISIT OUR WEBSITE**
titanbooks.com

**LIKE US ON FACEBOOK**
facebook.com/titanbooks

**FOLLOW US ON TWITTER**
@TitanBooks

**EMAIL US**
readerfeedback@titanemail.com